HARLEY

In the Company of Snipers

Book 4

Irish Winters

WINDY DAYS
PRESS

COPYRIGHT

HARLEY; In the Company of Snipers, 4

Edited by Cas Peace http://www.caspeace.com

Cover design and author photo by Kelli Ann Morgan,
http://www.inspirecreativeservices.com

Interior book design by Bob Houston eBook Formatting

ISBN Paperback: 978-1-942895-09-1
ISBN eBook: 978-1-942895-10-7
Library of Congress Control Number: 2014946996

Irish Winter's author website is
http://www.irishwinters.com or irishwinters.blogspot.com

In the Company of Snipers

You can find Irish Winters on Facebook: https://www.facebook.com/author.irishwinters

On Twitter: https://twitter.com/irishwinters1

For news on upcoming releases, sign up for Irish Winters' Newsletter at IrishWinters.com.

For more information about all my books, visit IrishWinters.com.

IN THE COMPANY OF SNIPERS

This series revolves around ex-Marine scout sniper, Alex Stewart, and his covert surveillance company, The TEAM, home-based out of Alexandria, Virginia. An obsessive patriot and workaholic, he created the company to give ex-military snipers like him a chance at returning to civilian life with a decent job.

This is not a serial with each book ending at a cliffhanger. I wouldn't do that to you. *In the Company of Snipers* is a collection of passionate love stories involving women and men who are tough enough to take on the world alone. Each is a stand-alone read, where in the course of an active TEAM operation, one agent comes face to face with his or her demons. The men and women I write about are all patriots and warriors, dealing with what they've lived through or the mistakes they've made

Spoiler alert: Every novel contains adult scenes including sexual situations (some explicit), language, and violence. I don't write sweet romance, so be forewarned.

At the end of each story, it's my hope that you, along with my heroes, will come to realize...

Love changes everything.

Prologue

"Remember, the idea is to grab her. Don't punch her. Don't hurt her, and for the love of Mike, don't let her scream. You gotta clamp her mouth shut or you're gonna get caught. Got it?"

Raymond nodded at the old woman, his gaze fixed on the hamburger in her grimy hands. No pickles, ketchup, or mustard. Just the way he liked 'em. He felt like a big, old lap dog, drooling and panting with the fast food so close to his nose like it was.

"And then what? What's next? Tell me. Oh, hell, never mind. You're dumber than dirt. You can't do it."

"I kin do it," he muttered, rubbing his extra large tennis shoes together beneath the extra small table.

Her reflection glared back at him in the window. "Then do it. Tell me the plan. All of it."

His nostrils flared. This particular no-kidding hamburger was a rarity and had been made just for him. Its aroma teased his taste buds with promised deliciousness. He'd do anything to get it into his mouth—if he could only remember.

"Hey. Dummy." She snapped the back of her grimy index finger right between his eyes, jolting him out of his daydream. "What's the plan?"

Raymond gulped, determined to get it right and the hamburger inside his mouth. "Ah, the first thing is, ah, I gotta be real quiet so's I don't disturb nobody. And then, and then, I gots to be real quiet when I grabs her, so's I don't hurt her cuz you don't want me to squish her. That's real important cuz you said so. And then I gots to run faster than fast, so's I don't get us all caught. And then... And then..." He scratched the top of his head, scraping together enough courage to look her in the eye. "I dunno. I forgot."

"You forgot? All you gotta do after that is throw her bony ass in the truck!" She smacked the side of his head, but it didn't hurt much. "You don't get nothing 'til you remember the whole thing, or it ain't gonna work. None of it."

"But I almost got it, huh?" He shuffled his feet again. Them kids in the next booth were staring, so Raymond ducked his head into his shoulders and tried real hard not to make a peep. Big guys got laughed at when they cried.

"Stop kicking!" The toe of her boot made hard contact with his shin. "For the love of Mike, keep your big feet off me."

"Sorry." His lower lip stuck out as his eyes dropped. Raymond wanted to please his new friend, but she was always angry. The bag of greasy food was off the table and he couldn't see the hamburger either.

"Get it right, or I'm gonna find someone smarter, and you won't get nuthin'."

Embarrassment crept up his neck. His feet itched to move, but Raymond concentrated on making them hold still like that one time when he was little. The neighborhood kids called it freeze-tag. He held perfectly still like a statue. They said they'd come back and play with him if he didn't move a muscle, so Raymond made his whole body freeze, and he almost didn't even breathe either. He was good at that game, but they didn't come back. Some bigger, meaner kids came instead. They laughed and punched him and said he was a big, stupid dummy. And he cried. Those big kids were kinda right. He wasn't very smart in his head.

"Stop staring like you got someplace to be." His mean friend smacked his head again. "Pay attention. Do what you're told."

He sucked in a deep breath and tried one more time, watching her mean eyes so he could tell if he was on the right track. His brain hurt he was trying so hard. "Okay, so's I be real quiet, and then I grabs her. And then I be real careful, so's she don't scream or nothing, and then... and then..."

The old woman cocked her head as if she were going to get mad again. Then it came to him the way one of those light bulbs flashed over Bugs Bunny's head. Or wait. Maybe it was Mickey Mouse's head. Or wait....

"Ray-y-y-mond."

"Oh yeah! I runs for the truck and then I gets another hamburger."

"Finally." His new best friend blew out a nasty breath, rolled her mean eyes, and tossed the hamburger across the table at him.

The second that greasy grilled pattie touched his tongue, mouth-watering rapture rippled all the way to his toes. He closed his eyes and chewed and chewed, afraid to swallow. A fresh hamburger was a mighty rare thing for a kid on the streets, especially a big kid like him. He wanted it to last forever, but eventually, he had to swallow. Bit by salivating bit slid over his tongue and down into his cavernous stomach.

The old woman stared at him with those mean, black eyes. He almost remembered why she scared him, but no. Not going to happen. 'Sides, she had fries in that bag. He could smell 'em.

"Now listen." Her voice turned kinda sweet but kinda conniving too. "You get the fries when you can tell me the whole plan without stopping one single time."

His eyes glazed over at the expectation of his very own bag of greasy potatoes. It was super-large. His bestest dream come true—ever. "Mmm-mmm."

She hit him again.

One

Ambushed!

"Rick! Can you hear me?" US Army Corporal Harley Mortimer bellowed, his voice lost in the grinding noise of battle. "Kent? Snakes? Anyone?"

Rick didn't answer. No one did. Only the roar of the fire came back to him. Acrid fumes poured off his overturned and now obliterated Humvee. Smelled like the whole damned Iraqi oilfield was burning again. He rolled for cover.

The chopper overhead sounded odd for a Blackhawk. Maybe a Cobra? Combat Rescue? Already? No way. He knew better. They'd be here eventually, but not this soon. Had to be one of Saddam's. Even that conclusion felt hollow. USAF owned the sky. Every one in the world knew that. Saddam's Air Force was rubble.

Enemy bullets zinged too close, kicking up plugs of dirt and razor sharp bits of stone that perforated his face and arms. Blood filled his ear where his earpiece should have been. The link with his men must have blown clear when the Humvee exploded. Panic climbed up his throat. Blood gushed down the back of his neck. *Damn, I'm cut off and injured too.*

Could things get any worse? He slapped his palms to his chest pockets and thighs. Sure enough, they could. He didn't even have an empty holster where a pistol might have been.

No tactical vest, no headgear. No knife. Nothing. *I'm screwed.*

Time to leave. American soldiers alone had better keep moving or face certain capture. Not going to happen. Pumped full of fight or flight, he crept around the front of the MRAP, the Mine Resistant Armored Personnel Vehicle that accompanied his Humvee on this foray into hell. Yeah, right. It didn't look very mine resistant now, not spewing its guts the way it was. Looked worse than his ride, both piles of steaming crap.

Fumes and smoke seared his eyeballs, making it impossible to see. What kind of an IED could have caused this much damage? Scrubbing both hands over his face, he muttered a quick Hail Mary. And then he saw them. All six of them. His men. His friends. Kent. Snakes. Carlton. Robbie. Rick. Garth. Their bodies in pieces and bleeding chunks. He faltered. *Who to run to first? Should I run at all?*

One second he was debating how to rescue body parts; the next he was kneeling at Corporal Rick Cross's side, his body stabbed through with a huge shard of metal. So much blood. Harley ripped the dead man's belt off. Every soldier knows how to wrap a tourniquet. Adrenaline pushed his shaking hands.

"I got you, man. You're gonna be fine. Promise." His mouth would not shut up until his ruthless brain engaged and squashed the hope rolling off his tongue.

There's nothing to tie off.

He backed away, choking at the eerie sensation of déjà vue creeping up the back of his throat. This was not happening. It wasn't real. Couldn't be. Rick wasn't dead—

again. Was he? A long lost memory invaded what sure felt like reality.

I am here, aren't I? Sure smells like Iraq. Sounds like Iraq. But didn't I already—leave?

Panic sucked the air from his lungs. Like a stupid frog on a hot plate, he jumped to Specialist Robbie Smith next. Blood gurgled from the fist-sized wound in his friend's neck. Suddenly, Harley was with Corporal Carlton Jenner, still and lifeless on the ground, his body twisted in an impossible-to-live-through position. Without walking or running to get there, Harley crouched over Sergeant Kent Roosevelt, and then Kent's arm, which until then had been in a black-red pool of coagulated blood a yard away.

He didn't remember taking a step. Logic failed when he needed it most. He scrubbed the smoke and dust out of his stinging eyes. Dazed. Afraid. Scared he'd lost his ever-loving mind.

Abruptly, Kent's unattached hand jumped from the oil-covered ground and clutched Harley's sleeve, tugging him back to his men. "Save us," Kent snarled with the grotesque lip twitching of the dead.

"What the hell?" Harley crab-scrambled backward, inhaling disbelief instead of air. The dismembered limb fell, four fingers tapping the dusty ground as if waiting for an answer. He shook his head to clear his vision. *No way! I'm seeing things for sure.*

"You gotta do something." Bloody words gurgled from the dead man's mouth. Harley lunged back, but Kent persisted with mercurial eyeballs instead of the once deep brown. His stare brimmed with unsaid accusation. *You lived, you bastard. I died, but you got to live.*

Just as quickly, Carlton sprang to a ninety-degree angle, his hips twisted in the opposite direction to his shoulders. He cocked his head sideways and taunted. "You gotta save us, man. You got to."

Harley groaned at the frightening quandary of seeing is believing. Kent and Carlton were obviously dead with a capital D, but they were talking?

Rick joined the ghostly moan. Robbie sputtered. Captail Snakes Flynn growled. Then Corporal Garth Schnidt. Their voices rose in an eerie chorus of condemnation, while six pairs of unseeing eyes stared him down for help. For rescue. For anything. "You gotta save us this time. All," they chanted. "All. All. All."

"But you guys are... dead." Harley was sure of his words not his eyes. "I can't save you. You already... died."

Are you sure? He shook the demon of doubt away. It was lying to him. It had to be. Misgivings prevailed. *Why are you talking to them if they're dead?*

"I don't know," he answered himself.

"Don't leave us behind again," the six-man chorus whined over the hissing fire. Even the twisted carcass of the Humvee groaned in haunting accompaniment. A tire exploded. Hard rubber ripped past his head, leaving stifling fumes and heat in its wake.

He watched the horror show, unable to save the men he loved any more than he could save himself. His dead buddies waited, their tongues flicking over their lips from the same thirst in his mouth. But just in case.... He crawled back to assist.

A veil of fumes descended upon the stage, encompassing wounded and would-be rescuer alike. His windpipe constricted. Harley choked until he could choke no more, spitting to clear his throat. Air would not come. When unconsciousness threatened, he bowed his forehead to the dirt and wished to wake the hell up—or die with his men. Like he should have.

As quickly as it came, the haze lifted. He could breathe, but his friends were gone. Not even limbs remained. No puddled blood. No tapping dismembered fingers. Nothing.

It dawned on him then. The Iraqi's fought dirty. Sadaam was a bastard. They'd used nerve gas on him. Either that or his men really spoke to him. No. Nerve gas explained everything. It had to be.

Thunder shook the ground. Shrapnel and bullets pinged too close and personal, pushing him to act. So that's the way it was, under fire and his men had been forced to leave him behind. He was alone. Instinct kicked in. Training took over.

Move it, soldier. Move it. Move it. Move it!

He steeled his jaw, stiffened his spine and secured his belt around his own bleeding leg, padding it with a rag from the dirty ground. The chemicals in the smoke provided an acid eyewash that would not quit. He could barely see to stagger away. His feet would not follow. No matter. He carved a drunkard's path into the desert and away from hell. One more step. Then another. Time and distance. All he needed now. Three things were sure. He wouldn't be taken alive. He'd live to fight another day. And he'd catch up with his men.

Keep moving.

Confusion and guilt ruled the day. It sure looked like his men were dead back there. He was sure they'd begged for help. But then they were gone. That meant they were alive, that they walked away. Didn't it? Parts felt real. Parts did not.

Like that detached hand. How could those fingers tap like they were attached to Kent when they weren't?

Harley collapsed against a wall. Scrubbing the pain away, he tried desperately to remember or forget. The puzzle remained. Hadn't he seen this same damned movie before?

Shreds of bizarre nonsense swirled inside his tired skull.

"Nine o'clock team meeting, don't be—"

"Your favorite peppered shrimp—"

"Mark's baby girl... JayJay... looks like—"

"Judy."

The last word, that name tugged at his weary mind for further scrutiny. It meant something. He could tell. It was a pleasant name. Like the piercing beam of a lighthouse cast high above the pitch-black storm in his head, it called to him. 'Look at me. Remember me.'

Harley sucked in another breath of desert air, his soul whipped and beaten by the war.

Who the hell is Judy?

"We've got casualties. Move it everyone!" Judy O'Brien called over the noisier than usual emergency room racket. Three ambulances were unloading at the door with two more en route. They were about to get busy.

"What happened?" She turned to Emergency Medic Tech Dash Willis, one of her most faithful buddies in the EMS business, Emergency Medical Service. His name fit his work ethic. If he wasn't dashing off to save the world on his job, he was on his way to coach a local sports program for underprivileged children. The man was a no-kidding godsend. Strong as an ox and Hollywood handsome, he looked grim this morning, his face darkened with soot and sweat. Whatever had happened on the interstate must have been bad.

"Diesel rig pulling doubles clipped a car, jackknifed and rolled. We've got hell on steroids out there." The two-way radio on his collar barked another demand. "I gotta run. You got this?"

"How many?" she asked before he made it too far down the hall and out the door. As nurse in charge of the entire floor, it was up to her to call heaven and hell for support, but only if needed. She needed facts, not blurbs of panic.

Dash met her with the same relentless dedication she hoped she reflected. "The rig rolled, Judy. It's early Saturday morning rush hour. I honest to God do not know how many. We've got buses, commuters and tourists. Hell, we've got bystanders in the wrong place at the wrong time. Plan on thirty-five for now. We'll divert to other hospitals, but you'll need everyone. Call everyone."

"Done." Her two-way radio was in use before he hit the exit.

Since 9-11 every hospital in the Washington D.C. area belonged to a high-tech emergency notification system called Alert D.C. She made two calls, one to her shift scheduler, the other to notify the Alert switchboard. They needed to send an automated text notification to all text capable devices, and they need to do it pronto. Avoid the interstate. D.C. proper was in full-blown disaster mode.

Two nurses pulled the patient gurney from her capable hands as she assumed the role of emergency room dictator. Until the crisis passed, she would rule the floor with precision and every last bit of her extensive and very capable medical skills. She'd give orders, her people would comply, and by God, no one would die without her say so.

Despite her ironclad will, Judy's heart fluttered across time and space to the man she loved. Her live-in boyfriend and beyond-debonair hunk of walking testosterone was on his way to work this morning. He usually avoided the interstate. He hated hectic traffic. It reminded him of rats in a maze. Harley would never get caught in this disaster.

"Git off! What do you think you're doing in here?"

"I scared," Raymond wailed, full-blown panic adding an intense feeling of suffocation to the too tiny quarters of her tent. He'd never moved so fast. In one second flat, he'd plowed over the old woman and tucked his butt and feet into the tent behind him.

"I don't care if you're scared or dead. It's the middle of the night. Git outta my tent." With a grunt, she heaved him back outside. As fast as she pushed him out, he burrowed back in.

"But I seen a bear."

"There ain't no bears 'round here. Git in the truck."

"But I don't wanna be out there all by myself. It's dark."

"Git out or... or... I'm not bringing any more burgers back for you!"

He gulped, his heart thumping throughout his whole body. No more hamburgers was a really bad thing, but a bear might be worse. It looked scary waddling around their camp, and it was sniffing. What if it was hungry? What if…? An enormous shiver wiggled down his spine. What if it wanted to eat him?

"I scared." His voice might have lowered a decibel, but his backside hadn't moved an inch.

"You been messing with her, haven't you? Is that what this is all about? You been looking under the tarp?"

"Uh uh." He squirmed, glancing at the blacker than black patch of ground in front of the tent. Under the tarp was the hole. He'd digged it all by himself, but now it creeped him out. Someone was in it. Her. He folded his body into a tighter wedge. No way was he messing with her. Nope. Too creepy.

"Dumb ass. I ain't wasting my money on you no more." The old woman wormed her way around him, but he wasn't moving. His feet were still mostly outside the tent. They might get eaten. As quickly as she vacated her sleeping space, he moved them inside. Let her get eaten. He was staying where it was safe.

She grunted and groaned all the way to her feet. Maybe she was trying to scare the bear? A momentary flash of security comforted him. It didn't last.

"I. Said. Move!" She punctuated each word with a smack of the long hard thing in her hand.

He raised his arms to shield his face. "Ouch! Stop it. Quit hitting me!"

More blows answered. She struck the top of his head until he had no choice. Ducking out of the tent and away from her, he scrambled into the dark. She kept hitting. He kept crawling. The truck might be safer after all. At last out of her reach, he backed away before she could come after him again.

"What'd ya hit me with?"

"This." The beam of a flashlight lit up her wrinkly face. In one split second, she transformed her already scary looking features into a harsh black and white mask of terror.

"You is scary!" he wailed. "And you hurted me. I is bleeding. Wanna see?" He kept an eye on the hole in the ground while he showed the old woman his blood-smeared palms.

"I'll give you something to cry about." She snarled like a demon in the distorted light. "Now stay away from her, or you know what will happen, don't you?"

Raymond ceased bellowing. He hated hard questions and this one was not only hard but unexpected. Every muscle on his face wrinkled deep in thought while his brain searched for the answer. *Hmm. What could happen possibly happen if he didn't stay away from—?*

"No more burgers!" Scrubbing her face with both hands, she spit she was so mad.

"Oh, yeah." No hamburgers might be worse than seeing the bear. Maybe worse than the creepy hole. He sniffed back his tears along with some of his fright. "But I really seen a bear."

One last glare from those scary black eyes of hers and he bowed his head. Raymond made his way back to the truck. One thing had gotten through. There were bigger things at stake than a bear. He paused with his hand on the door handle. "If I bees real quiet, can I have a hamburger tomorrow? Just one? Huh?"

The flashlight beam flicked off. All he could hear was her snorting and cursing from inside the security of her tent.

"Biggest idiot I ever did see. Dumber than Nicky. What the hell was I thinking?"

Raymond climbed into the truck, shut the door, and resigned himself to spending the rest of the scary night alone. He didn't know who Nicky was, but he must have been awfully dumb too. Raymond felt an instant connection. Maybe the old woman hit that poor Nicky person too.

Streaks of pink light filtered through the trees. It wouldn't be dark for much longer, but it was still plenty scary. He pulled his arms out of the sleeves of his flannel shirt. It kinda kept him warm with his arms tucked against his body. Sometimes.

Squeezing his arms together, he tried to cover the sound his heart kept making. The old woman was mad enough already; he didn't want her to hear all the thumping in his chest. It kept pounding. He kept breathing. At last it slowed, but the moment he looked outside, it kicked up again. The forest was still full of shadows. Maybe more bears. He didn't like it. Not one bit.

On the streets, a guy could find comfort under a streetlight or a flashing neon sign. There weren't any lights out here, not even the moon. The sun seemed to be taking an extra long time to rise. A sneaky suspicion crept into the truck with him. Shivers danced over his shoulders. Big shivers that made his stomach clench so hard he was afraid he was gonna be sick.

Did that lady in the hole sic the bear after him? Was she mad on account of what the old woman did to her? Or worse. What if she was dead but really alive like one of them zombie people like he saw one time on the television set at the Rescue Mission? What if she was gonna climb outta the hole and eat his brains?

Thump, thump, thump went his heart.

Raymond pulled his knees to his chest, squeezed his forehead to his kneecaps and waited. The cool breath of morning air tiptoed over the exposed skin on the back of his neck exactly like cold, dead zombie fingers. He ducked his head farther into his shoulders; sure the moment he looked up he'd see a half-rotted face at the window, its lips vacuum-sealed to the glass and trying to suck his brains out.

A tear squeezed out of his tender, swollen eye. "But I is really a scared."

Two

"Have you seen Alex yet?" Ember asked at the Situation Room door.

"No. Harley hasn't come in yet either." Mother looked up from her stack of handouts for the morning's briefing. "You think they stopped for coffee?"

She eyed Ember, calculating her next move. Mother wanted a raise. The question was how to get from point A, the salary she had now, to point B, the increase she needed in order to buy another car. A consolidated effort would work best if she were to broach this sticky subject with Alex, her boss, on behalf of herself and Ember. He'd shoot her down otherwise.

Her contrary boss made Mother smile. In truth, Alex Stewart, owner of the covert surveillance company known on the East Coast as The TEAM, was a poor businessman, more worried about his team than his balance sheets. That combination didn't usually work, but it seemed to for him. He was also a tough mix of rapid-fire machine gun and gentleman rolled into one. Mean and nasty when provoked, he could be just as kind and thoughtful the next minute. It was all in the way a person handled him, something Mother was still trying to figure out.

Ember flipped up the laptop cover and retrieved the morning's briefing. A truer, smarter technical assistant was never created, nor one who dressed more eclectically. The shorter-than-short eggplant-colored leather skirt gracing her hips today was met by thigh-high boots, and nothing but the whitest vanilla skin in between. The cream-colored sweater layered over her *girls* should have been enough to subdue them, but Ember could make a black plastic garbage bag look sexy.

Most guys would call a girl with her measurements 'stacked,' but not the men on The TEAM. They knew better. Over-endowed and two hundred percent feminine, she was a solid fit in the mostly male workforce. The guys respected her, probably because she also handled firearms certification. They didn't mess with the gal who could ground them to desk duty if they shot their mouths off.

Her crowning masterpiece, though, was the honey blond topknot high on her head with wispy tendrils dangling down her neck and into her face. It wasn't dyed gothic black anymore, the color she had submerged in after the tragic loss of Junior Agent Todd Chandler. Like everyone else on The TEAM, she'd nearly returned to normal. Of course, she might show up with green hair tomorrow, but today, Ember was a Marilyn Monroe look-alike in all her glory.

"Alex always brings a cup from home," she said. "Kelsey takes good care of him. You know that."

"True." Mother craftily changed subjects by outright asking, "How much do you take home every month?"

"Excuse me?"

"Go on. Spill. We both need a raise. We're due. Give me a starting point, so I'll know how to negotiate." Mother could tell by the smirk on Ember's face she did not intend to divulge personal info. "Well?"

"Alex pays me enough." Ember chuckled evasively. "Why do you really want to know?"

"The new Escalades are out."

"Already?"

"By the time I get my raise, they will be."

A smile lit Ember's face and the discussion over. "I can't believe Alex signed another contract with the FBI, not the way he cusses them."

"This one's different." Mother filed the salary argument for another day. Ember's reluctance to join in the fray did not make getting a raise easy, but it would come one way or the other. "The Bureau needs all the help they can get."

"Senator Conway left a wife and three little ones behind." Ember scrolled through slide after slide. "He didn't deserve to die like that."

Mother caught the pensive tone. Alex had just signed a contract stemming from the current, front-page news story. Once again, a sniper had struck the nation's capital. He'd already killed Senator Jeff Conway and Representative Cheryl Winston, both as they strolled with reporters and onlookers among the grand monuments D.C. was famous for. Winston went down on the steps of the Jefferson Memorial, Conway as he crossed the Arlington Memorial Bridge. Both hits were clean, almost identical headshots.

The FBI was frustrated. They were present during both assassinations. No one was yet in custody. They had no leads. The Bureau looked bad.

Ember scrolled through a few more slides, reading quietly as she went. "Wow. They know what weapon he's using yet?"

"FBI suspects a sniper rifle. They want him dead or alive," Mother muttered. "The press is eating them for breakfast, lunch, and dinner."

"Not like that's hard."

"Did you see Channel 16 last night? They had an—"

"Sit Room. Now!" Senior Agent Murphy Finnegan slammed the door open, startling Mother. He grabbed the TV remote. Instantly, the big screen flickered to life. Mother took her place at the conference table while the room filled with the rest of the agents not on assignment.

"Oh, God." Ember gasped.

Mother froze. It couldn't be.

"Coming to you live from Alexandria, this is Crosland Webster with Channel 16 News reporting on a possible abduction. Mrs. Kelsey Stewart disappeared shortly after eight p.m. last night. Curiously, her husband, Mr. Alexander Stewart, did not notify authorities until early this morning."

Kelsey? Kidnapped?

The camera panned to the police cruiser and back to the Stewarts' humble brick home as two uniformed officers escorted a cuffed Alex out his front door and down the walk. Dressed in black running pants and a gray USMC T-shirt, he looked grim.

"Mr. Stewart!" The reporter thrust his microphone into Alex's face. "Why didn't you contact the police sooner? People are wondering what could have been more important than your wife? Do you have an explanation? What did you do to her? Did you kill her?"

Stoically, Alex ducked his head and climbed into the back seat of the police car without responding, but Mother caught the way he rolled his neck. The audacious reporter should be thankful Alex was restrained.

"As you can see." Webster's left brow arched with drama. "The police have a suspect in custody. Stay tuned for further developments. Remember. You heard it first and you heard it right on Virginia's Fastest to the Scene News Channel."

"Dumb ass," Murphy growled. "Alex isn't a suspect. He's the victim."

Words failed Mother as the reporter rattled on. Crosland Webster seemed unusually focused on Alex's successful business of pay-for-hire mercenaries and his prior career as a scout sniper in the United States Marine Corps, both volatile talents according to the reporter. He cut to an exposé splashed across the airwaves that embellished the tragic deaths of Alex's first wife and only child. With Sara and Abby Stewart's innocent faces on the screen, the man had the audacity to speculate, "Is it possible these were not accidental deaths after all?"

"How'd Webster throw this crap together so fast?" Junior Agent Connor Maher asked. "What's he got, a smear campaign staff waiting for tragedy to strike?"

Mother bristled along with Connor. "It's Channel 16. What'd you expect? Their claim to fame is their punch line. Fastest to the scene doesn't mean it has to be true, just sensational."

"Alex wasn't even in the States when Sara and Abby were killed. He was deployed overseas," Senior Agent Roy Hudson declared.

A record of the only senatorial investigation Alex had ever been involved in was now presented as definitive proof that all was not well in the Stewarts' household. "After all,"

Mr. Webster played to the camera, his face transformed into a stern mask of superiority, "why would the United States Senate need to investigate an honest citizen?"

Mother's Irish flickered to life. Her fists curled. Webster was impugning her family. One more word out of his lying mouth and she'd march down there and knock him on his ass.

"Yellow journalism at its best," Roy said. "Turn this guy off, Murph. He's making me sick."

Before Murphy could comply, Crosland Webster diverted to his anchor in Florida. A blond-haired woman stood at her open front door facing another reporter.

"Hell." Murphy paused. "Not her."

"What can you tell us about your ex-husband, Mrs. Wilshire?" the woman reporter asked, her microphone stuck in the surprised Mrs. Wilshire's face.

"Alex?" she asked, still blinking the sleep out of her eyes. "Alex Stewart? Why, umm, he's okay. He's—"

"But wasn't he out of the country most of the short time you were married? Didn't he travel a lot? Was he a mean alcoholic? Did he ever hit you?"

"Not Alex." The blond shook her head. "Like I said, he's o—"

"Did you know he's been charged with the murder of his third wife?"

Mrs. Wilshire stared at the camera, her mouth opened in surprise. "Alex got married? Again?"

Ember leaned into Mother. "Ex-husband? Alex was divorced? Did you know that?"

Mother shrugged. Her manicured fingernails were cutting into her palms. Divorced and secretive or not, Crosland Webster was the one out of line, not Alex. "Alex hasn't been charged with anything. I'm going to Alexandria," she declared, "and Mr. Webster ain't gonna like it when I get there."

No one responded, everyone too focused on the nightmare unraveling on screen. Mr. Webster had done his homework, and while not accurate, he'd done it fast. Another face flashed overhead—Brady McCormack, the son of Alex's friend and long time business associate, Jed McCormack, billionaire and steadfast Department of Defense advocate. Webster was on a roll. His camera followed him up to the door Kelsey had painted deep red for Christmas only last year. A spring wreath of silk cherry blossoms and twined laurel set the backdrop for yet another lie.

"Maybe it's time the public demanded justice." Webster posed. "Should the United States Marine Corps reopen their investigation into how Brady McCormack, son of billionaire Jed McCormack, was reduced to a quadriplegic under then USMC Sergeant Stewart's flawed leadership? Our lines are open. We'd love to hear from you, our dedicated listeners."

Mother shoved her chair away from the table, her mind made up. She was on her way to set Webster straight, once and for all. Let him film that.

"What an ass," Junior Agent Mark Houston rasped. "Everyone with a brain knows Alex saved Brady's life."

"Jed sure does," Roy agreed. "Hold on, Mother. I'm going with you. You might need a witness."

She'd barely stood when the door burst open. In walked a very focused Alex Stewart. Murphy snapped the television off. Alex acknowledged his second in command as well as his self-proclaimed gal Friday with a curt nod before he strode to his usual position at the front of the room.

He looked awful, his face haggard and gray from the sleepless night. Dressed in his gray business suit now, there was only one reason he was there. Without Kelsey, he had no place else to go. The TEAM was his family. Channel 16's finest might be out to create a media frenzy, but Mother knew better. No man loved his wife the way Alex loved Kelsey.

"Boss." She didn't know what she wanted to say other than, "I'm so sorry."

He spared another quick nod and turned to Murphy. "We assigned the FBI contract to Roy and Connor, correct?"

"What are you doing here, son?" Murphy gripped his younger boss's shoulder. "You need to be talking to your lawyer or the police, not worrying about what's going on here. I got it covered."

"The police have nothing. They know it and I know it." Alex rolled his shoulder in the way that told Mother he was carrying the weight of the world. "But I'm still required to show for questioning."

She couldn't believe her ears. "Questioning? Boss, you're not guilty."

Instead of answering, he stared at his team. "I don't have a lot of time. You've seen the news. What else can I tell you? Ask."

"What really happened?" Murphy spoke for everyone. "We've heard the news report. Now we want the real story."

Alex sat at the head of the oblong conference table. "Kelsey and I went for a late run with the dogs last night. We don't see each other enough. You know how it is. When I'm home early, we take the boys for a walk or we run together. There was an old blue Ford pickup parked in Spencer's driveway across the street when we got back. No big deal.

They've got a teenage grandson staying with them. I didn't think twice."

He raked a hand through his short-cropped dark hair. "Kelsey went inside while I kenneled the dogs and refreshed their water. When I went in, she was in the kitchen working on some kind of clay recipe for her kindergarten class. The dogs started yapping. I went to the door and told 'em to shut it. They quit, but started in again while I was in the shower. I couldn't figure why Kelsey let them carry on like they did. When I got outside..." He gripped his chin, rubbing his jaw as he struggled to speak. "She was gone. The back gate was open. I turned the boys loose, but they lost her at the front walk."

"Where was the truck?" Murphy asked.

"Gone." Alex raked his hand over his head again, his jaw clenched tight and his voice strained. "I've been up all night, Murph. I've called everyone, even her sister in Oregon. I've gone to every gas station within driving distance asking if anyone saw the truck, if it filled up or drove by. Anything. I can't... find her."

Mother's heart plummeted. Whisper and Smoke were the best tracking dogs on the east coast, and Alex by far the absolute best covert operator in the world. If they couldn't locate Kelsey— She shook the hopeless thought out of her head. This can't be happening.

Alex glanced at his watch, composed and all business again. "Roy. Connor. This op will be tough. Don't let the Bureau run you around. You have a problem, take it to Murphy. Understood?"

"Sure, Boss," Roy answered, "but wouldn't you rather we help find Kelsey? Seems to me that's a helluva lot more important."

"We'd rather be helping you." Junior Agent Connor Maher spoke up.

"No." Alex's voice tightened. "Stay focused. Do what we do best. Find and neutralize the sniper. That's your only job right now." He was almost out the door before he turned back to his team. "Where's Harley?"

"Not in yet, Boss," Mother promptly offered. "He probably stopped for coffee. You know how he is."

Alex looked like he might say something else, but then he was gone.

Murphy stepped to the front of the room. "The way I see it, only two agents are assigned to the D.C. sniper op. That's all the FBI requested, and that's all they're going to get."

Senior Agent David Tao pointed across the table to Junior Agent Rory Dennison. "Rory and I will check traffic cameras. Maybe we'll spot the Ford, or someone who's seen it."

Mark nodded at Junior Agent Zack Lennox. "Zack and I will canvass the neighborhood. Fresh eyes might catch something the police missed."

"Me and Ember were already checking satellite feeds on the sniper business," Mother said. "We'll pull more data from other systems. We'll find her."

Murphy raised his hands for silence. "I don't have to tell you the first forty-eight hours are the most critical. Alex can't be out searching for Kelsey, but he'll be back. Let's have something to tell him."

Three

"Move your fat head."

"Huh?" Raymond awoke to the old woman pushing him out of her way to make room for her wide backside. She was half in the truck, her keys jangling in her hand, and shoving him out of her way.

"Move!"

"Kin I come?" He unfolded his cramped legs while he opened the door and dropped both feet to the ground.

"No. Get out." She rammed the key into the ignition. Her jaw worked as if she'd been chewing.

His nose twitched. "You gots a hamburger?" he asked softly, still rubbing the sleep out of his swollen eye.

"You can't remember anything, can you dummy?" Her face didn't look scary in the morning light, but her disposition was as ugly as ever. "What'd I tell you last night?"

He scratched his itchy head. "Umm, I think maybe you—"

"I'm done feeding you." Her jowls wiggled under her chin. "Shut the door. I got places to go."

"But I is hungry."

"Shut the door, Raymond!" she barked, but before he could she turned to him and stabbed him with those mean eyes.

He gulped, scared what she was going to do to him next.

"Stay away from that hole," she commanded. "You hear me?"

Raymond bobbed his head as fast as he could.

"I'll hurt you if you don't, boy." Those eyes kept digging into his. There wasn't a doubt in his mind. She meant what she said.

"'Kay," he whispered. His stomach gurgled. When she revved the engine, he stepped farther back hoping she'd notice he was being a good boy. She didn't. Worry escalated into panic. Didn't she remember that he saw a bear?

"Don't go!" His heart thumped like crazy in his throat. "I be good. I won't even look at the hole. I promise."

With his shirtsleeves flapping at his side and his belly exposed, he reached for the door handle. The truck wheels rolled, fishtailing over the damp forest grass. The handle, wet with morning dew, slipped from his grasp. Even the truck seemed mad at him, spewing black fumes as it disappeared around a stand of pines.

Raymond stood there for a long time, watching and listening. She might be playing one of her sneaky games. He never knew what to expect. Sometimes, the old woman walked into camp instead of driving. Sometimes, she'd reappear out of nowhere. She said she never met a man she could trust, and that included him. It didn't make sense, but then, he didn't understand a lot of things she said. Still—she might come back. She might bring a hamburger. It could happen.

The sunrise spilled through the dark forest around him, its branches full of extra noisy birds and shadows. Raymond lowered to the ground, crossed his ankles and dropped to his butt. He tried not to shiver, but sitting so close to the scary woods didn't help. Besides, the birds were talking and squawking about him. They kept calling him 'dummy' like everyone else in the city did. He ducked his neck into his shoulders as an extra big one floated right over his head. At the very last minute, it pulled up. *Whew. That was close. He almost pecked my eyes out.*

His gaze drifted to the hole. He used to like it, but it was scarier than the woods. A tarp stretched over it, held in place with rocks along the edge. Didn't matter. Raymond knew better. A sheet of thin blue plastic couldn't stop a hungry zombie from getting out. 'Sides, the old woman told him to stay away and that's what he was gonna do.

"Ouch." He fingered his sore eye very carefully, but then he remembered. He didn't need to be quiet. "Ouch," he declared loudly to the trees and those mean birds that were calling him—

"Hello. Is anyone out there?"

He scrambled to his feet. The zombie lady was talking.

"Hello?" she called again. "Can you help me?"

She was talking to him. Ewww. Raymond backed away. He wasn't supposed to go over to the hole, but should he talk to her? But he'd never seen anyone talk to a zombie before. Usually they just shot 'em in the head with a big gun. Goosebumps lifted up the back of his neck and into his scalp. Last night was bad enough.

She'd scared the heebie-jeebies out of him when he'd grabbed her. The old woman said it would be easy, but it wasn't. Uh huh. Not at all. The zombie lady was a lot like one of them cute baby kitties living with their mama behind the diner. During the incredibly long half-second that he had hold of one of them one day, the darn thing turned into a baby buzz saw that liked ta took his whole hand off. Same with her. She didn't quit kicking and scratching 'til the old woman whopped her one with the shovel.

Fortunately, the pretty gal who was now a zombie kinda mewed like one of them baby kitties when he put her in the back of the truck. He was pretty sure she was alive. Then. But what if she'd been dead all along? More shivers rattled over his shoulders and wiggled down his spine. Ewww! Zombie! Right here!

"Please help me."

He stopped moving. Shouldn't she be all growly and gurgling cuz maybe half of her chin was missing, and she was hungry to munch on his brains? And they didn't get sad like real people, did they? He tiptoed to the edge. The old woman was gone. She'd never know. Leaning back as far as he could, he lifted one corner of the tarp very, very carefully—just to make sure.

ARGH! There she was! Right at his end of the hole. She looked straight up at him. Her eyes got wide. She stepped back. He kinda screamed like a little girl and dropped the tarp. In one fraction of a split second, he was behind the tent shaking in his tennis shoes. The worst thing on the whole planet had just happened. Now she knew what he looked like.

"Don't leave. Please come back."

"Nah ah." He mumbled past the terror stuck in his throat. "You is scary and I ain't supposed to look at you."

"I'm sorry. I won't do it again. I promise."

That was kinda funny. The zombie was talking like a regular person. And she had a face. A whole face. Like him. *Hmm.*

His heart stopped pounding. Curiosity got the best of him. Raymond circled around the tent to the edge of the hole. With just the very tips of his index finger and thumb, he lifted the corner of the tarp again, extra careful so he could see the zombie.

Once again, she came into view. The zombie looked awful little in the nice big hole he digged. She was looking at him again even though she said she wouldn't, but she didn't look mean or nothing. Whew. She was just a regular person only smaller. A lot smaller. He didn't remember zombies looking so little.

He had to say something. She'd seen him. "Umm, hi."

"Hi," she said very quietly, squinting up at him. Her jaw was still intact, always a good sign when a guy's alone in the forest. "My name is Kelsey. What's yours?"

"Umm, Raymond. Ah, yep. Everyone calls me Raymond cuz, umm, that's my name."

"Hello, Raymond."

Wow. She didn't call him dummy or stupid or big ox. "You want a hamburger or something?"

"Yes, please."

"Well, sorry, but, umm, I kinda ate all of them last night, and so I don't have one right now." Heat flamed his face. Was she gonna laugh at him for being stupid?

"That's okay. It was nice of you to ask anyway." Her voice sounded like sad music instead of mean and nasty croaking. She hadn't moved an inch, only rocked back and forth like he'd been doing. His body automatically followed suit.

"The next time I get me some hamburgers, I is gonna share with you. Would that be okay if I shared my hamburgers with you? And maybe my fries too?"

"Yes, that would be very kind."

Wow. Not only did she say he was nice, he was very kind too. No one ever told him that before. It was like getting two compliments in a row.

"I sorry." He scratched his big square head. "But is you a scared of something?"

"Yes." She blinked harder.

"Did you see a bear too?" He settled himself to the ground so he could see her better.

"No. I'm scared because you took me away from my home, and I don't know where I am. So why did you kidnap me and put me in this hole?"

He answered as quickly as the reasons came to him. "I... I... Umm, she made me do it, ya know. She did it, and she is very mean to me if I don't do what she wants, and so I had to do it right, cuz then she might give me a hamburger only now...." Guilt shuddered over his shoulders. He wasn't supposed to be looking at the hole. Oh, oh.

"Who is she?"

"She's the old woman, and you is the pretty woman on account of there is two of you, and so she is the old woman, only I thought maybe you turned into a zombie only you isn't." He took a deep breath, his guilt forgotten in the need for Kelsey's approval. "I'm kinda smart for a big dummy."

The pretty lady who was really not a zombie had her hands on her hips, but she didn't holler at him or say nothing mean, so Raymond kept sharing. "I don't like being called dummy and stupid and big freak, so I'm gonna keep calling you Kelsey." He rocked faster, pleased with himself. Talking with her made him feel warm all over.

"That's a great idea."

Wow. He almost didn't have enough fingers to count how many nice things she'd said.

"Are you the man who grabbed me last night?"

"Ah, huh, but I didn't hurt you, and I wouldn't never hurt no one. Not ever cuz I don't like it when people hurt me so's I don't hurt no one."

"But you did. See?" She pointed to the bloody bump on the side of her head. It was real easy to see with her hair pulled back in one of them ponytail things, but still. He didn't do it.

"Nah ah. Did not. The old woman hit you. Not me. She mean."

"What old woman?"

"That one." Raymond pointed to where the blue truck had left a trail through the grass. "She went to git me a hamburger and maybe some fries. She's coming back."

"What's her name?"

Hmm. He'd been calling her the old woman for so long, her name eluded him. Embarrassment crept up his neck. "I dunno."

"Is there anyone else here besides you and her?"

"Nah ah. There's just me and you and her and she might bring me another hamburger if I'm real good only now...." He paused. "I been bad. She told me not to be looking at the hole."

"It's okay, Raymond," Kelsey said. "I won't tell anyone that we've been talking."

Despite the swollen eyeball, his face crunched into a big smile. Kelsey was fast becoming his best friend.

"How long have you been living out here?"

He lifted one hand and began counting his fingers. "One. Two. Umm, three. Hmm." This was where it got tricky. He peered at her from beneath his bushy brows for any indication he might be getting the next number right. "F-f-f-o-ou-ive."

Kelsey studied him for a long minute. "You've been here a very long time. This hole is deep."

He smacked his lips together. "Yep. Sometimes I can't dig so much cuz I git tired, but I digged it extra deep anyway. Just for you."

"Where are we?"

Raymond looked around the campsite. "In a bunch of trees, and you is in the hole I digged for you. Does you like it?"

"But exactly where is that? Are we in a park? The old woman's backyard? Where is this bunch of trees?"

Wow. She asked a lot of questions. He scratched his scruffy chin, trying to recall the first one. "Umm, no, we ain't in a park or nothing. It's kinda like the trees down by the river only there ain't no river. Only lots and lots of trees. And there is a tent and a ladder and...."

She took a step toward him. His nose twitched. He didn't remember the hole smelling like flowers. Her hand stretched like she might want to touch him. Raymond peered closer, everything forgotten but Kelsey.

"Do you remember how we got out here in the trees?"

"Ah huh. I know. I know" He rocked harder, filled with the need to get another question right. This one was easy.

"How Raymond?" she asked sweetly, her fingertips on the back of his hand.

A little splash of something that felt like warm sunshine rippled from the pads of her fingers straight through him. No pointy fingernail stabbed him. No poking. No mean pinching. Just the soft sensation that an angel had reached down from heaven to touch him. He closed his eyes. His heart did a funny flip-flop that didn't even hurt this time. *Wow.*

"Do you remember?"

He blinked. "Huh?"

"How did we get here?"

"In a truck," he declared proudly. "In a big, blue truck. You and me got to ride in the back, and it was noisy and blue only it ain't here right now on account a it's gone. I got it right, huh?"

The barest hint of a smile tugged the corners of her mouth. "Very good, Raymond. You remembered. Did you see any road signs while we were riding together?"

He beamed. Kelsey made him feel smart. "No, cuz it was dark and windy, and she was driving real fast and I was a scared you was dead, so is you still gonna be sad?"

She stepped away, her brown eyes filled with tears. "Can you take me home?"

"Nope."

Kelsey turned her back to him. Br-r-r. The magic moment ended. One thing he knew for sure. He was as lost as she was. The need to make amends surfaced. Raymond had never been confronted by a crying woman before. Scared, maybe. Angry, plenty of times. But as sad as this one? Never.

"Ah, Kelsey?"

"What?" She sniffed, but she didn't turn around.

"I is really happy you is not a zombie, but if you was, I would let you eat a little piece of my brains if you was hungry."

His apology fell flat. Her head bowed into her hands. Kelsey's shoulders trembled.

"I gotta go," he murmured. Very carefully, he covered the hole and secured the rocks until it looked the same as before. Raymond walked away. His stomach gurgled like always. It was time for the old woman to return. Maybe when she did, she'd bring him a nice bag of hot hamburgers. Fries would be nice. A soda, too.

Four

Damn. How'd I get back here?

Harley woke with a raging headache. The sun hadn't moved at all. Black smoke still billowed overhead. Whatever was on fire, it had to be close. The stench of it seared his nostrils. In panic, he searched his shoulders and thighs. *Where's my rifle? My gear?*

He had nothing. Worse, the path he'd taken didn't make sense. How could he have walked so far only to end up back where it all started? For that matter, had he walked at all? It sure didn't look like it.

Pieces of a nightmare flashed to life. Humvee hit an IED. Buddies blown away. Only he survived? No way. It had to be a dream. Couldn't be real. So where was everyone if they weren't dead? And where'd the blood on his hands come from?

God no. Please, let it be me, not my guys.

He checked for a bullet hole. Nothing seemed evident on his arms and chest. If it wasn't his blood, maybe the dream was real then. Maybe his friends were dead.

Gulping against the possibility, he raked both hands over his head, his heart hammering. It didn't take long to ease up on his skull. The moment his fingers came into contact with the grit-filled and tender flap of scalp, panic subsided. He brushed the dirt away from the bloody hole. *Good. It's me. I'm bleeding. Not them.*

The crazy pounding in his chest slowed while he self-diagnosed. No wonder he couldn't think with a softball-sized bump on the back of his head. Life got more complicated when he tried to stand and couldn't. His leg was numb. Loosening the belt, he readjusted the ragged bandage he vaguely remembered applying. Relief flooded his lungs, the blood fully explained by the gash on his leg and the divot on his head.

He froze, his mind overcome by a strobe light kind of a movie in his tired brain. The image of a gun safe flashed, quickly followed by a bolt-action tactical rifle. Leupold scope. Two pistols. Boxes of ammo. Brass shells. Reloading equipment. A sleek leather sofa with cashmere-scented candles aglow on the glass coffee table. A black dog with a jagged patch of white on her chest. A woman's soft lips on his neck. American-style food cooking. Somewhere....

His nose twitched to take in the pleasant aroma, but the rancid stink of burning diesel set him straight. No, it was just imagination. He was U.S. Army. No candles. No girls. Not yet.

Groaning at the wicked trick of his mind, he pushed the nonsense away. A man relied on cold, hard facts to strategize, not daydreams. But that dog, a feisty Labrador bitch -what was her name? The elusive memory faded as others bombarded him. The Military Police Brigade at Fort Hood, Texas. He'd wanted to be a Ranger. Ended up a military working dog handler. Affection. It was all about affection for the dog... The children... And her....

Explosions in the distance brought his mind back to zero. Shielding his face with his hand, Harley stared at the fire in the distance. Funny. It didn't seem so near anymore, maybe two klicks away. Looked like the Army was holding a major meeting. They'd even brought a shiny red fire engine, its siren screaming as much as the pain in Harley's head. He would've taken a step in their direction if the engine hadn't looked odd, along with the caravan of camels lumbering toward the smoking wreck.

He blinked, not believing his eyes again. The mirage had turned into enemy soldiers, not camels. It wasn't the U.S. Army come to help at all.

Harley turned his back on the puzzling disaster behind him to face the dilemma before him. The time for dreams and stupid questions was done. He needed to get out of sight and he needed weapons. That hidden arsenal was in the city might be the safest bet.

He was dizzy and thirsty, but alive. The best part was that all of his buddies were alive too. They were out there in the desert. He'd catch up with them if it was the last thing he did.

"Honey, I'm home."

Judy set the two grocery bags on the kitchen counter as she kicked off her comfortable work shoes. She was exhausted, weary to the bone. After an excruciatingly difficult graveyard shift, she'd ended up staying six hours into the next shift to assist with the victims from the rollover disaster. Walking through her apartment door never felt so good.

She planned on a few minutes under a hot shower, but not until she had her hands on the handsome man she loved with all her heart. Maybe he could join her? She hoped. His workload had been fairly quiet lately. For the first time since she'd known him, he'd agreed to take the afternoon off just to attend a concert at the Kennedy Center. Tonight was the night. She had a titanium ring in her purse. If he was too shy to ask, by heck, she wasn't. Harley Mortimer was going to get the surprise of his life—a marriage proposal.

She'd promised to fix his favorite dish, peppered shrimp Alfredo with heavy cream. That ought to set the stage. After all, the way to this man's heart was definitely through his stomach. Yes, it was terribly unhealthy, but he never put on an ounce of extra weight. Harley was one of those people who burned their extra calories as soon as they ate them. And tonight, she intended to indulge.

"Harley," she called. Opening the refrigerator, she put the fresh cream on the top shelf next to the bottle of white wine. Thinking about that lanky male body of his brought a smile to her lips. He wasn't the big bruiser like his buddy, Mark Houston, but he was just right for her. She'd always wanted to marry a man who was taller. Harley fit the bill by three inches over her five-foot, eleven-inch frame.

All he had to do was look down at her with those teasing hazel eyes, and her heart skipped a beat. How he did that she did not know. He just did, turning her into a silly girl who'd moved across country to be with him. Sometimes, it seemed a mistake, but the moment he cranked up the sexy Mortimer charm, all was right with her world. She'd do it again. In a heartbeat.

He thought he was a funny guy, but she saw through the self-deprecating humor. More boy than man, he was simply a recovering addict who'd evolved from the chaos of self-medication to the healthier addiction of running. He worked hard, trained for the next marathon, and spoiled her rotten. Yet beneath it all, he suffered too. Night sweats and bad dreams still haunted. Judy didn't know which hurt him worse; the things he'd survived or what he'd put his body through while trying to forget. She only knew she loved him.

If she had her way, he'd find a less dangerous job, but Alex Stewart was his hero. That was the only fly in the Mortimer ointment. Alex could get Harley to jump in a moment's notice and ask, "How high?" Her influence did not strike the same cadence, not yet anyway. The man had some kind of mind control over Harley. It was always, *'The boss this and the boss that.'* He didn't seem able to complete a sentence without bringing Alex into it.

The overseas operations in Afghanistan had to stop too. Harley and Mark were out of the country for weeks at a time. How did Mark's wife, Libby, put up with it, especially now that they had a newborn baby? And the danger? Fear clutched Judy's heart every time Harley kissed her goodbye.

Glancing at her china cabinet, she pushed Alex out of her mind and selected a pair of crystal candleholders with scarlet tapers. Tonight was the night. After she and Harley indulged in the perfect evening, maybe they'd find something else they could indulge in. Somewhere between the peppered shrimp Alfredo and dessert in bed, she'd tell him when he was going to get married. He'd smile his sexier than heck smile, probably drawl his usual, "Whatever you say, darling," and their future together would be planned and perfect.

"Harley," she called, wandering out of the kitchen and straightening things as she went.

The odd floor plan of his bachelor's pad had always puzzled her. It felt like a racetrack as the small entryway dumped visitors nearly into the kitchen at the right. From there, a person could walk around the breakfast bar into the living room, and in a few steps, end up back in the entry hall.

The living room led to a small hallway complete with a closet and two bedrooms with the bathroom in between. The bathroom was another puzzling feature. While kitchen was more the size of a kitchenette, the bathroom sported a king-sized shower with three showerheads and a built in tiled-bench. Not that she minded.

Headed toward that very spacious bathroom with Harley definitely in mind, the sight of his open and empty gun safe startled her. Both pistols were missing. The locked station for his sniper rifle stood empty.

Alarmed, she checked the hall closet. The door was shut, but when she pulled it open, the inside light had been left on. Olive-drab ammo boxes lay scattered on the floor. Empty. Her first thought was she'd been robbed, but no. She'd used her key. He had to have been here and locked the door behind him when he left. By the looks of it, he'd been in a hurry.

Judy checked farther. His gear bag was gone, which stood to reason. He'd need some way to carry all the ammo. She dialed his cell phone, her toes tapping at the odd scene before her. He had some explaining to do. Harley might leave his socks and shoes in the living room, but he was meticulous when it came to his gear.

His voicemail answered promptly. "You want me? You got me. Leave a number."

Anxiety crept into the hallway with her. She did the only thing she could think to do. Judy called his buddy.

"Good morning. Mark Houston."

"Hi, Mark. This is Judy. How are you doing?" She tried to sound calm.

"Judy? What's wrong?"

"I'm sorry to interrupt you at work, and if you're busy, I'll understand, but—"

"What's going on? Is it Harley?" As usual, Mark got right to the point.

She blurted her question. "Have you seen him today? Do you know where he is?"

"We were hoping he was with you."

"He isn't. I've been at the hospital all morning. We'd planned to take the afternoon off together. I thought he'd be home by the time I got here only he's not. It looks like he's taken his guns and—"

"What guns?"

"The ones he keeps in the safe, his sniper rifle and both pistols, the SIG and his Glock."

"Is the ammo gone too?"

"Yes. Everything. It looks like he left in a hurry."

"Are you sure you weren't robbed? Look around. Is anything else missing?"

She paused. It certainly looked like a robbery. "No. I used my key to get in, and nothing else is missing. He isn't answering his cell either." Her heart stalled. She could feel it. Something was very wrong.

"He didn't show for a mandatory briefing this morning. We've had some trouble here at the office."

"What trouble?"

"Haven't you seen? Turn on your TV. Kelsey was abducted last night."

Judy gasped. "No, not Kelsey! I'm sorry. I was busy with the victims from the tanker rollover on the freeway. Did you see that?"

"We've been following both stories, but mostly we're watching for updates on Kelsey. Alex is still down at the police station. Seems like all hell broke loose today."

"Where could Harley be if he's not at work? He's got most of his gear."

"The last time you saw him was this morning, right?"

"No, last night before I left for work. I work graves. He mentioned he had a meeting, but he planned to ask for the rest of the day off. We were supposed to go to a concert tonight."

"Listen, I'll have Mother track his GPS. Maybe she can pinpoint his location. It's probably nothing. Call you right back."

"Thanks, Mark." Judy hung up and checked the rest of the apartment to make sure she'd spoken the truth. Nothing else was out of place. When she pulled the safe door open wider, the handle was sticky. She jumped as the ringing phone startled her. Dark red stained her fingers and the palm of her hand. Blood. Her very practical heart stuttered. Harley was bleeding.

"Judy, Zack and I are on our way over. Ring us up. We'll be there in twenty." Mark's calm and very much in command tone did not ease her anxiety. She used the same voice when she had to deliver bad news to loved ones at the emergency room.

"Harley's injured," she blurted out. "There's blood on the safe. He had to have been here in the last couple minutes. It's still sticky. What aren't you telling me?"

"Stay put. We're in transit. Don't—"

The doorbell rang. At the same time, someone pounded on her door.

"Oh, for heaven's sake, what now? I've got company. Wait a minute, Mark." She was only half-listening because the doorbell rang again. The pushy person on the other side of the door was getting on her last nerve. "I'm coming," she called.

"Judy!" Mark's voice shouted through the phone.

"Hold on. Someone's at my door."

"Don't answer it," he ordered.

Too late. Two men dressed in black business suits, white shirts, and with very official FBI badges in their hands stood in the hall. One had his pistol drawn, the barrel pointed at her. The other instantly placed his foot inside the door, his palm pushing it open wider. He took a menacing step into her home and lifted the cell phone out of her hand.

"We'd like to speak with Harley Mortimer. Is he here?"

Five

"So I've been reading up on Conway and Winston to see if they have anything in common," Connor offered as he and Roy walked the National Mall. Stretching from the Washington Monument all the way to the United States Capitol building, it was a huge public gathering place for protesters, tourists, citizens, and now—one sniper.

Roy eyed his junior agent with interest. Connor was wet behind the ears, but smart and good with computers, a definite plus for a covert operator. They'd left their office after the unexpected Saturday meeting with Alex. Both were casually dressed; the only thing in common their matching black polo shirts with the gold insignia of The TEAM on their chests. They could have been any two of the thousands of visitors enjoying the spring morning. Their ex-military life showed in their ramrod straight posture, as well as their bearing. It made Roy proud; his love of country only bested by his love for the men and women he served with.

"And what did you learn while you were doing all your studying?"

"Well, for one thing, neither of them did any military time," Connor stated.

"Shouldn't matter. The military must always bow to the civilian in our republic," Roy said knowingly. "Founding Fathers planned it that way."

"True, but that's not my point. Not only did they not serve in the military, they're also two of the most vocal politicians against the military. They're the extreme left of the extreme left. They don't want to approve any defense funding, not even for the guys who are already deployed. They want everyone brought home, and they don't care where they are, even the troops on friendly soil. Can you believe that?"

"They sound like a couple of isolationists. It takes all kinds."

"But why send a man to war if you're not going to support him once he gets there?"

"Don't let it get to you. Nasty politics happen in every war."

A sharp popping sound jerked Roy's head toward the sparse crowd gathered at the World War II Memorial.

"Gunshot," Connor declared, already running toward the scene.

Backfire, Roy hoped as he sprinted the distance.

The ambulance had barely pulled away when they arrived. Police, Secret Service, and FBI swarmed the area and had already cordoned off the crime scene. Roy hailed one of the FBI agents he recognized, and shortly, he and Connor were allowed within the police line. According to the officer at the scene, this shooting was identical to the others. Senator Covington had been killed with one round to the forehead.

Roy scowled. "You need to be finding out if Covington was another one of those extreme left politicians like the others. Then we might have something to work with."

Connor's fingers were already tapping on his cell phone. Roy could read the answer in his eyes.

"Okay. We've got possible motive. What else do these three politicians have in common? And where'd the shot come from?" He eyed the range of buildings to the north. Any of them would make a perfect sniper hide, but they were too far away and trees stood between them and the Memorial. All those trees would hinder a clean shot.

Even now an army of law enforcement, FBI, and Secret Service swarmed the street and the buildings. Metro police blocked Constitution Avenue. Another ambulance sounded in the distance. There was no sign of a covert concealment among the trees. No sniper hide. Nothing.

"We're missing something."

"You're telling me. There's too much security and law enforcement on the scene," Connor observed. "Any one of them could be the sniper. They're all carrying ARs."

"Good point." Roy activated his earpiece and contacted Mother to double-check traffic cameras and any other video surveillance along Constitution. Anything that moved before, during, and after the shooting he wanted to see it.

"Found something." Connor crouched by the sidewalk snaking through the tree-lined path north of the memorial. With the end of a pencil, he lifted a cylinder out of the trampled mud.

The sniper had not policed his brass.

"Like I've told you, we'd barely gotten in from walking the dogs. It was ten after eight. I know because I checked my watch." Alex was tired of the same questions over and over again, first by the police officers and now Detective Hemmings.

"What year was the Ford?"

"Maybe a sixty-five. Full of rust. The back left tire was low."

"And that's all you know? That someone in an old truck might have taken your wife?"

"What I said is the truck was the only thing out of the ordinary. Have you got anyone at all looking for her?"

Detective Hemmings ignored the sarcastic question. "What we've got is a warrant to check your home."

"And?"

"Besides a mighty fine gun safe which we couldn't get into, we found three sets of fingerprints—yours, your wife's, and some fella's named Harley Mortimer. You know him?"

"Yes. He's a good friend and employee. He's always at our place." Alex sighed heavily. "Everything I've told you is easy enough to double-check if you'd call—"

"We did call your office, if that's what you're gonna say next. Your secretary gave us some real interesting news."

"What?"

"Seems like your *good friend* didn't make it to work today, or did you already know that too?" Hemmings leaned forward with a know-it-all look on his smug face. "You want to explain one more time why your employee's fingerprints are all over your home?"

"Harley didn't come in?" Alex rubbed both temples in an attempt to ease the fracturing headache pounding behind his eyes.

"Seems mighty funny that your friend goes missing the same day as your wife. Makes me wonder."

Alex caught the implication. "Harley has a girlfriend. Judy O'Brien. Check with her if you want to know where he is."

"I'll just bet he does."

"Listen, I know my wife, and—"

"And the husband is always the last to know. I get it, but let me tell you something, buddy, I've seen this kinda thing happen a thousand times before, and—"

"I'm not your buddy!" Alex hit the table with both fists, startling the detective enough that he jumped.

"Get used to it," Hemmings shot back at him. "She's a cute little thing. You work long hours. Figure it out. Once they leave, they never—"

"You arrogant—"

"You told me yourself. You're a busy man. Well, maybe she got sick of waiting for you to show up. Maybe, she went looking for something on the side like—"

"No!" Alex slammed his fist down again. This time it was he who leaned across the table. He wasn't handcuffed or shackled, and he'd had enough. "You need to be real careful what comes out of your mouth next."

Hemmings blinked, straightened his tie and screeched his chair away from the table. "I'll be back."

Alex glared at the glass window across from him, not caring who was on the other side. He'd only stayed to give the police their due, but he was done playing nice.

Within minutes Hemmings returned. "You're free to go, but let me make something perfectly clear. There's nothing suspicious about your wife's disappearance. There's no evidence. It looks like she ran away with your friend. This is a domestic issue. Nothing more. And you can't prove otherwise. Call us when she turns up. I'll bet she's in Tahiti soaking up the sun with your buddy. They're laughing at you and drinking margaritas while they do it. You should've called the airlines. Not us."

Alex jerked the interrogation door open and walked away, choking on words that would only create more trouble. He'd wasted enough time. First call he made was to Mother on his way out the main precinct doors. "Any news?" he barked, his temper loaded and ready to fire.

"Umm, Boss, on—?"

"My wife!"

"David and Rory returned from your place. They didn't come up with anything unusual, but Mark got a call from Judy. He and Zack are on their way to her apartment right now. Ember and I are gathering everything we can get our hands on. We've pulled images from DPS, the Defense Support Program, and GOES, the Geostationary Operations Environ—"

"Stop!" His last inkling of patience was gone in an instant with her incessant techno babble. When she ceased jabbering, he knew he was being an ass. Redirecting what was left of his unvented anger, Alex softened his voice to deal with the woman he truly understood was working her guts out for him. "Has anyone found a clue? Anything?"

"No," she answered meekly. "We're still looking, Boss. Honest. We won't quit."

He stopped walking, his heart dashed to pieces in the middle of the Alexandria police station's parking lot. *Tell me something I don't know. Tell me where on this sonofabitchin planet my wife is!*

"I'll be in shortly. Thanks." He hung up, not knowing how to staunch the gaping hole in his heart. Kelsey was everything—his reason for breathing, working and living all rolled into one. Not knowing where she was ate up every last shred of patience, and he never had much to begin with. An old mantra kicked in, reminding him how useless he was. *You should have been there.*

Walking quickly to his truck, Alex remote unlocked it. His dogs, Whisper and Smoke, would be hungry, so he detoured home, not able to think if he'd fed them or not. When he pulled to the curb and hurried to his front door, Alice Spencer, the neighbor lady, intercepted him.

"Alex." She stopped with one foot on the bottom step to his three-step porch, her fingers on the rail as if she didn't dare come any closer.

"Anything I can do for you?" He spared her a quick glance. All he knew about Alice was she lived across the street with her husband, Rand, who'd had a stroke several years ago. Her grandson lived with her to help manage her husband's needs. Alice was friendly enough when he'd run into her on the street, and she minded her business.

Kelsey was the friendly one who made pies at Christmas if only because someone might have extra family come to visit. He, on the other hand, was the neighborhood's endangered species, rarely spotted and only when migrating between office and home. After his wife and daughter's funeral, he'd barricaded himself behind closed doors and pulled drapes, hell-bent on self-destruction and his mind made up to keep the world at bay. He'd done a good job.

"I think the better question is what can I do for you? We're so sorry about Kelsey." Alice did look sincere.

"Thanks." He unlocked his door as he answered, not intending to be rude, but not going to feed the gossip mill either. "But no. I'm fine."

"No, you're not," she snapped and took another step closer, the sympathy in her eyes mixed with a touch of defiance. He didn't remember the gray tinting her dark hair. "Stop acting like I don't live right across the street from you, Alex Stewart, like I don't know what's going on over here. I saw what the police and that stupid reporter did to you."

He swallowed hard. Her words sounded like they came from the stern but loving woman who'd raised him, only Grandma Stewart would have used his entire Christian name if she were still alive. Alexander Bradley Stewart. He could almost hear her. Tender and tough, it was the last thing he needed.

"I'm not some stranger, Alex. For heaven's sake, let me help."

"Okay. Did you see anything unusual last night?" he asked hoarsely. "Anyone prowling around my place?"

"No, and the police asked me about the truck in my driveway," she answered. "I wish I knew who it belonged to, but I don't. Some of your neighbors are organizing a search. I can't leave Rand, or I'd be out there with them, but I can help in other ways. My grandson, Jimmy, can take care of your dogs while you're busy. This is an awful thing you're going through."

"I might need help with the dogs if you're serious. Jimmy is it?"

"You're darn right I'm serious." Alice visibly relaxed, her smile sad and caring at the same time. She looked so sincere. "I'll send him over."

"I'd appreciate that." Alex opened his door to signal the end of the conversation, but Alice had a different idea. Her hand on his arm brought him about-face.

"Don't do it again," she scolded, her eyes welled with tears. "Not like last time. Please don't shut us out, Alex. You have to know by now how much we care about you and Kelsey."

"Yes ma'am," he said, struggling to maintain his invisible force field.

"Good." She nodded like she'd solved something. "I'm bringing dinner over so plan on it. Every night. You've got to keep your strength up. I'll leave it here on your front step. Go ahead and keep the dishes. I'll make sure they're disposable." She gave him no chance to argue, just turned on her heel and marched across the street. Her kindness touched him. Alice must have been watching for him to come home. She'd just showed up—like the good neighbor he'd never been.

Stepping into his home, the silence stopped him cold. There was no lunch waiting in the microwave and no radio down the hall in Kelsey's office. Just chaos. Evidence of the police search warrant was everywhere, from the books pulled off his bookshelf to the couch cushions left on the floor. Kitchen cupboards were open, the silverware drawer too. Even the carefully folded contents of the linen closet in the hall were left in disarray.

Kelsey's cologne hung in the air, a reminder she'd slipped through his hands the same as that atomized mist. For the first time in their married life, he did not know where she was. A familiar paralysis crept into his heart, its mantra bitterly accusing. *I should have been there.*

Refusing to succumb to the hopelessness of the day, he reached for his cell phone and speed-dialed Murphy.

"Covert Teamwork, Murphy Finnegan speak—"

"What's this about Harley not showing for work?"

"How'd you know?"

"The police. What's going on? Where is he?"

"All we know right now is what Judy told Mark. Said she can't raise him on his cell. There's blood on his gun safe at their apartment. His weapons are gone. Ammo too. Hang on. Mother's got something."

Alex stilled as Murphy spoke with Mother in the background. In seconds, he was back on the line. "Guess Mark already had her checking Harley's GPS. Looks like he's on the freeway. Ah, never mind. Hold on. Sorry." Murphy covered the phone with his hand. All Alex could hear was muffled conversation before Murphy came back with a quick, "Let me call you back. Give me a couple minutes." He hung up.

Alex sat with a thump on his sofa. First Kelsey? Now Harley? Hemmings' snide comment replayed in his head. *Maybe, she went looking for a little something on the side.*

But Alex knew better. He'd mentally gone over every case he'd ever worked, every black op, surveillance and mission. There were many in the world who might want to strike out at him, and maybe that's what this was all about. Abducting her would certainly destroy him. The nightmare had to be his fault. He was the one with enemies. Not Kelsey.

His phone rang.

"Speak."

"Got his GPS, only it's not good news. Seems he was involved with the oil tanker disaster on the interstate this morning. I know you probably didn't see it, but it was all over the news. Five people died. Dozens were injured. Eastbound traffic's been shut down. They've got one lane open now, but it was a helluva fire."

"Murph?" His breath caught. *Is there no good news in the world today?*

"I already checked with the Highway Patrol. He was there. His Jeep burned, but none of the injured matched his description. Mother's double-checking hospitals to be sure."

"And?"

Again the muffled conversation on Murphy's end of the line before he came back with, "He's not at any of the local hospitals and Ember checked the morgue. No one there we know either."

"What about the blood in his apartment? Is Judy sure it's—"

"It was still sticky, Alex. Judy would know. He's been home since the accident. No doubt about it."

Alex shoved a hand through his hair, his nerves wound beyond the breaking point. "Then where is he?"

Six

"Thirty-aught-six? Not military issue?" Murphy asked about the brass cartridge Connor had found. For now, it was the only evidence in a notorious case that was quickly leading to martial law. Citizens were urged to stay indoors as much as possible until the sniper was caught. But citizens were not the problem. They knew how to listen. Congressmen and women obviously did not.

"It would do the job," Roy countered. Everywhere he looked in the office, television sets were tuned to news channels for any break in the three operations The TEAM was suddenly engulfed in.

Murphy pushed back from the table, his arms folded across his chest in his prove-it-to-me posture. "So answer me this. How could a man in a crowd get a rifle shot off without being noticed?"

"Just because these bozos thought they were untouchable, didn't mean John Q Public wanted to be out there with them. And just because we found an empty shell does not necessarily mean it's the murder weapon. Covington should have listened to the FBI."

"He told the press he was not going to be bullied by some two-bit thug."

"Well, how'd that work for him? A two-bit thug with a gun is still deadly."

Murphy shook his head in disgust. "I checked with Metro PD. A few witnesses do remember hearing noises that sounded like cars backfiring at the first two murders too."

"But, guys. The shooter had to have been pretty close to the targets. None of these victims had their heads blown off. All three entries show very little tear." Connor slid the three photos from the morgue across the table to Roy, referencing the terminal ballistics damage caused when a round the caliber of a thirty-aught-six passed through the human body. "I gotta give it to him. This guy's got guts."

Roy studied the photos. Each showed a whitened face with a hole centered in their forehead. Understandably, the exit was larger, but none showed the devastation of a long distance hit. It was the simple physics of kinetic energy, velocity, and the trajectory decay of a bullet en route. Less distance equaled greater accuracy equaled definite death, but it also equaled less physical trauma, not that it mattered to the victims. Dead was still dead.

"Maybe he's using a ghillie suit," Connor offered.

"No way," Roy said. "You and I would have seen him. I'm more inclined to think he was passing himself off as one of our boys in blue. Maybe even FBI."

"I'm surprised he's not using a fancier gun though," Murphy said.

"Hell, Murph, you and me used whatever we could get our hands on in Vietnam," Roy explained. "We didn't have it easy like kids these days with all their fancy designer rifles. Even Hathcock used a heavy-barreled Winchester and thirty-aught-six rounds."

"When he wasn't using a fifty-cal," Connor added.

"You're right." Murphy scowled. "I'll have Mother and Ember check military records for malcontents and dishonorable discharges, anyone with a grudge. Who knows? Maybe it's one of our boys."

"I'd bet on it." Roy's mind back in the days when he'd owned a weapon like the assassin appeared to be using. It had been one of those coming of age things, the rifle given to him by his dad on the best three-day fall weekend ever. His father and a few neighbor men rounded up their sons and a few of the less fortunate boys whose fathers didn't hunt, and off they went. It was a simple thing. They'd gotten hunter safety training up close and personal in the forests of Virginia. Three of the boys bagged their first deer. Not Roy. All he got was his very own rifle – and closer to his old man. Best weekend ever.

"I hate to give our current jackass with a gun any credit, but Connor's right. This guy's good. He's got ice water in his veins."

"Or she's good," Connor corrected. "Could be a woman out there pulling the trigger. Just saying."

"Oh yeah?" Roy smirked. "You know any female snipers do you, you with your co-ed boot camp training?"

"Sure do. Isabella Ramos. She was an MP before she deployed. Check this out." Connor wrangled his wallet out of his tight back pocket and pulled a silver Iraqi dinar from the inner folds of it. A neat hole pierced the three date trees on the face of the coin. He tossed it to Murphy.

"She did that?" Murphy examined the coin, his brow spiked. "What distance?"

"Far enough I couldn't see it anymore," Connor explained. "A couple of us guys were blowing off practice rounds one day. Up she comes and tells us to watch and learn. Then she trots out past our targets and sticks two coins into an old dead tree stump. We thought she was toying with us. Didn't say another word. She came back, dropped to her belly in the sand, and pop, pop. Nailed both coins, one shot each. I'm telling you, she's got the eyes of an eagle."

"Oldest trick in the book." Murphy chuckled. "Bet they already had holes in 'em."

Connor rolled his eyes. "You think we'd fall for that? No way. My buddy, Jamie, ran all the way out there to make sure. She's the real deal."

"Man, I'd like to meet a cute gal who can shoot," Roy agreed as Murphy passed the dinar for inspection.

"Maybe I ought to interview your girlfriend, see if Alex needs—"

"She's not my girlfriend." Connor cut the banter short. He snagged the coin out of Roy's fingers and tucked it back inside his wallet. "But let me tell you something in case you ever do interview her, which is highly unlikely. Don't mess around with Izza. She's tough as nails and she means every word that comes out of her mouth. If she says she's gonna bust you one upside your hard head, get ready for a slap down. And don't bad mouth female snipers either. She's cute all right, like a baby rattlesnake is cute."

"Sounds like you been bit by this particular baby," Roy teased. It wasn't often this particular junior agent let a cute gal get away from him. Connor was single and looking. There had to be more to the story.

"Let's just say Izza won't be friending me on Facebook real soon," Connor muttered. The warm glow spreading over the younger man's clean-shaven cheeks confirmed Roy's suspicions.

Murphy turned the television volume up. Again, the media circus centered on frivolous details that had nothing to do with the actual investigation. Harley's face flashed to the screen as Crosland Webster revisited more of the Stewarts' personal lives.

"Man, I do not like Channel 16 reporters." He turned the volume down.

"Yeah, Murph. What's this guy got against Alex anyway?" Roy nodded toward the TV screen. "He and Webster have a history I don't know about?"

"I guess," Murphy said. "Damned punk thinks he's got the right to drag a man's name through the mud just because he carries a press card."

"And who's Mrs. Wilshire?" Roy leaned over his crossed arms on the table. That little nugget of information seemed to have blindsided everyone but Murphy. "I didn't know the boss was divorced before he married Kelsey. Thought he'd only been married twice."

"There's a lot you guys don't know about Alex." That Murphy didn't make eye contact when he answered told Roy the discussion was closed.

It almost felt good watching Whisper and Smoke roar around the backyard like a couple of happy dogs. Almost. The good feeling didn't last. Everything, even the purpling wisteria twined in the arbor over and around the swing he was sitting on, reminded Alex that Kelsey wasn't where she belonged. He'd failed her.

His backyard used to be nothing more than a patch of dried, dead grass with a bare dirt path from the back door to the dog kennel. She'd come into their lives and changed everything.

Those were her tulips, daffodils, and crocus in blossom against the foundation of the house, not his. Her French lilac stood heavy with buds in the corner and the pink Snow Fountain cherry at the backside of the kennel was her idea too. He could envision her at either tree with her face in the blossoms, drawing in a deep breath and smiling. She couldn't seem to surround herself with enough flowers, maybe because of all she'd suffered. Hell, he didn't know a single plant's name until she came along.

Alex stiffened his legs to stop the gentle sway of the swing. Every molecule in his body ached to know where she was. Helplessness engulfed him. He didn't have one solitary lead, no ransom call, no threats, nothing. He'd pay anything. Everything!

God, I miss her!

The last twenty-four hours had overwhelmingly stomped the life out of him. And if that wasn't enough, he had an endangered and missing agent on top of an already dangerous operation with his idiot friends, the FBI. The weight of his business world pressed down on him. Maybe Roy was right. Maybe every agent ought to be called back home to search for Kelsey.

Lost in deliberation, he almost didn't see his black Shepherd. Whisper seemed to materialize out of nowhere, all of a sudden planted at Alex's feet, his black-brown eyes fixed squarely on his unhappy master. The silver dog, Smoke, had settled beneath the swing content to be the more obedient dog. Whisper whined softly, content to be the one who didn't believe he was a dog.

"You miss her too, don't you?" Alex ruffled the big fellow's head.

Whisper growled in his funny dog-speak that made Kelsey declare he could talk. The big oaf sounded like it. Funny thing, Alex could not recall Whisper talking until Kelsey. If he had to pinpoint the day Whisper found his voice, it would be the moment when Alex thought his dog had found a corpse on his cabin porch. Instead, he'd found both Alex and the crazy mutt's reason to live. Neither of them had missed a day of total loyalty, devotion, and love since. Whisper hadn't quit talking either.

He thumped a paw on Alex's knee, offering one soft pig-like grunt.

"Whatcha want?"

Whisper persisted with growly dog-speak. He grasped his master's forearm in his mouth. His growl became more anxious as he tugged Alex out of the swing.

"I give. What do you want?" With his arm clamped in the dog's mouth, Alex was pulled to his back door. He was about to distract the comical brute with a ball or dog bone, when he saw the edge of a manila envelope stuck inside the locked screen door. Brushing Whisper aside, he unlocked the door and tore the eight-by-eleven sized envelope open.

Three Polaroid photos slipped into his hand. His breath caught. Kelsey. In the first, she resembled a crumpled ragdoll in the back of a blue pickup bed, the same one he'd seen parked across from his house. Still dressed in the tank top and bicycle shorts she had on last night, black bruises circled her biceps. Blood dripped across her forehead and cheek. White as a sheet with her mouth half-open, she looked dead.

"Oh, hell." His heart sank in his chest as he focused on the next image. Laid out in the bottom of what looked like a freshly dug grave, her arms had been folded across her chest in the pose of a corpse. "What have they done to you?"

The third picture was the most revealing. A huge monster of a man stood with Kelsey, her arms flung wide with his hands gripped across her chest. The man made no effort to hold her carefully. She was just something the ugly fool had posed with.

Alex stared at the man's face with total hatred in his heart. Who was he? The monster didn't look familiar. Why had he stolen Kelsey? This ugly brute hurt her! She was bleeding. Anguish stabbed Alex. Years of experience and discipline flew out the window. The frustration of knowing nothing rolled over him in pulsing, angry waves.

He forced a deep breath. His own words came back to him. How many times had he asked it of his team? *Think!* Scrutinizing the third picture, he compartmentalized his rampaging emotion and opted for self-control. It was a wider shot taken last night, possibly in the beam of a vehicle's headlights. There were trees and bushes in the background. The man stood in front of a small tent for two.

There was obviously something wrong with him. Freakishly large, his head seemed out of proportion with the rest of his body. Elongated and rectangular, the man's forehead jutted over the rest of his face, almost Frankenstein-ish in shape and size. One shaggy eyebrow stretched over both eyes, adding to the ledge effect of his forehead.

His size made Kelsey look smaller than she was. Despite his baseball mitt-sized hands, he did not appear to be groping her. As Alex analyzed with more logic and less rage, he realized the man might be mentally, possibly emotionally compromised.

The guy smiled directly into the camera. He looked proud and happy. All of his crooked teeth showed. It was an ugly smile, but the innocence behind it was apparent. Alex had seen this look before on adults with Downs Syndrome before. There was no way the man could have orchestrated the abduction. He might have been the brawn, but he was surely not the brain. That meant at least two people were involved, the compromised individual in front of the camera and the mastermind in the shadows.

For the first time, hope fluttered. With the genius of his techies to help unravel the photos, Alex had a way forward. There was work to be done. He was in possession of evidence in an active police investigation. There might be fingerprints. Should he call Detective Hemmings? Should he wait for the police to show? Depend on others?

Hell no. Sonofabitches haven't helped so far.

Energized and swearing a blue streak, Alex retrieved his fingerprint kit from his truck and carefully dusted the back doors, the gate, and everything in sight including the porch swing. Thinking like a detective instead of an emotional husband, he placed the envelope and photos in a plastic evidence bag. Hope created energy. He could find her.

Before he headed back to his office, he tossed Whisper and Smoke an extra treat on their way back into their kennel. Even that simple act reminded him of the woman missing from his life. He'd never used to buy dogs treats. Of course,

Smoke snarfed his before it hit the ground. He was a dog, after all. But Whisper dropped his treat, and barked one short grumbled dog word.

Alex's heart sank and hope went with it. What was he thinking? Even on a normal day, Whisper wouldn't eat until he caught sight of Kelsey. That dog biscuit would lie on the ground until Smoke helped himself to it, and Whisper would let him. His black Shepherd was pining away.

Alex dropped to one knee and gathered the big fluffy armful of dog hair into his arms. His eyes brimmed with tears while Whisper whined and licked his face. All the evidence in the world did not change the fact. Kelsey was gone. Whisper knew it. God, Alex knew it.

Reality sucked the hope out of him. Hell, he didn't know if he was holding proof of life or proof of death in those evidence bags. He'd gotten excited for nothing. Maybe all that was left of her was the flowers and his dogs. He buried his face in Whisper's mane thankful to be hanging onto something Kelsey loved.

Whisper laid his head over his master's shoulder. The dog pushed into Alex, nearly knocking him backward on his butt. Normally, that was just the way of dogs, but today it felt like something more. He adjusted his knee to counterbalance the dog's hug.

A soft growly whine rumbled out of Whisper's chest.

Alex could have sworn he just heard, 'Hurry!'

"Look at me," he whispered. "I'm talking to you like you're human. She'd be so proud of us, boy."

Seven

Raymond couldn't resist. He was hungry and alone and bored. His stomach gurgled like when he was back in the city. And his face hurt. It hurt a lot. The old woman had been gone a long time. The sun was sinking lower in the afternoon sky and it was gonna get dark again soon. He was sure of that. He'd be out here in the scary forest without a truck to sleep in.

When he couldn't take it any longer, he ambled back over to the blue tarp and plopped himself at the edge. Lifting the cover, he was surprised to see the pretty woman doing push-ups. She scrambled to her feet the moment light filled the pit.

It looked like she'd been doing some digging too. There were little holes in the soft part of the earthen wall, plus her hands were dirty and her nails were black. A smudge of dirt lined the side of her nose, and her face was red. Most people on the street got that same look when they saw him right before they'd walk in the opposite direction. He started to lower the tarp.

"Don't go. Please stay." Her voice was a little cheerier despite being out of breath. "I was hoping you'd come back, Raymond."

"Oh. Okay." He flung the cover aside and settled to the ground with his legs dangling over the edge.

"What's my name?"

He froze. Was she trying to trick him?

"It's all right if you forgot. I forget things all the time. Might forget my head some day if it wasn't screwed on."

Ha. What a funny picture! "Nobody's head is screwed on."

"You're quite smart, aren't you? Look at this nice hole. You did a good job." She looked around her deep, dark pit.

His chest swelled with pride. "Ah huh, I did. I made the corners extra square and pointy, ya know, because, ah... because..." He stopped talking. Why was it important to keep the corners pointy?

"Because if you didn't, you wouldn't get to eat, would you?"

"Wow. Does you know everything?" He had to ask. It seemed like she could see straight through him.

"No. Some days I don't think I know anything at all. How about if you call me Kelsey?"

"Oh, yeah. You is Kelsey. I remember now. I not so dumb."

"I need a favor," she announced.

He'd do anything to keep her talking. "What do ya want, huh Kelsey?"

"I need to use the bathroom."

"You what?" The smile dropped off his face like a ton of bricks off a ten-story building. He didn't know nothing 'bout how a woman used the bathroom. How was he gonna help her do that? His skin got all sweaty thinking about it, and his face felt hot. Raymond shook his head at the impossibility of such a thing. "I never... ah, no, I never..."

"It's okay." She had the prettiest smile. "I just want you to help me out of this hole. Hurry. I need to find a tree."

Oh. Hmm. Just like he did first thing every morning. Okay then. He could help her find a tree, but he'd learned one lesson very early in life. Never help anyone unless they help you back. "Whatcha gonna do for me?"

"I don't know. What do you want me to do?"

"I hafta think about it." He scrunched his entire face so Kelsey would know how hard he was thinking.

"Think about it while I go to the bathroom. Help me up. Hurry."

"'Kay. I'll git the ladder." In a minute, he'd thumped it down into the pit. "Only be careful it don't pinch your hand, cuz it mashed me a good one. Wanna see my blood blister?"

When she scrambled up the ladder, Raymond stepped back. A flush of embarrassment warmed his entire body. Wow. She was a fairy princess in navy blue shorts, her big brown eyes all trusting and kind. Maybe he should run away before she could speak another word. Maybe the earth should swallow him whole. A tear welled up.

She took a step toward him, looking at his dirty hands. "Let me see it."

"See what?" He took another step back, afraid she meant the tear.

"Your thumb. I want to see the blood blister. I bet it really hurt, didn't it?" She closed the distance between them, and he forgot he was embarrassed because by then he could barely breathe. This pretty girl was actually coming close to him. On purpose.

Kelsey took his hand, and he was amazed. He could scarcely feel her fingers on his dirty hand, but when she looked at his face, her expression changed. The sun was up now. She'd stepped into his shadow. Her eyes widened. His heart pitched. She was gonna run for sure.

"Oh, Raymond. Honey." She reached for his cheek instead of screaming. "You poor thing. You're hurt. What happened?"

"She hit me," he bawled, feeling sorry for himself but very surprised too.

Kelsey didn't run away. Instead, she stroked his sore cheek. "Let's get you cleaned up. Is there any water around?"

He pointed to a plastic bag near the entrance to the tent. "She keeps bottles of water over there only don't take the last one cuz she'll be really mad if you do."

Kelsey grabbed a bottle of water and some napkins from the bag. Dousing the napkins, she returned to him. "Sit down so I can reach you better. This might sting. Can you be extra brave for me?"

He plopped to the ground at her feet and tensed his shoulders into the bravest muscles he could, squeezing his eyes shut too. He was ready. He could take it cuz he was really big. She poured a little water over his eyes and wiped the crusted blood away. Ha! He started rocking again. Didn't hurt at all. He was the bravest man ever.

Folding the damp napkin, she cleaned under his eyelid, then smoothed over his forehead and down his cheek. His stupid noisy heart nearly stopped beating because she leaned in so close, and she didn't even punch him. Not once. Her hair smelled kinda like flowers. He opened his one good eye to look at her.

"You have the prettiest baby blue eyes." She winked at him and ran the cool cloth over his cheek one more time. "At least one is blue. The other is kind of black and blue."

Something about her hand cupping his cheek made him want to wiggle. Her breath on his cheek sent a shiver through him as she gently wiped his face.

"Hmm. Some of these cuts are deep. If we were in town, I'd take you to a doctor for couple stitches."

"What's a couple stitches?" He wished she'd never stop talking.

"Stitches are the same as the threads that hold our clothes together. Doctors stitch cuts to help them heal faster and keep them clean."

He chuckled at her good joke. "Stitches in a person. Ha."

She took a step back. "There. That will hold you for a while."

Raymond couldn't wait to ask his very important question any longer. "Did you know I saw a bear last night?"

"You did?" Her brows lifted in delicate arches over sparkly eyes.

"Uh, huh. It was black and white." He spread both arms wide. "And it was this big."

"Was that what all the noise was about?"

"Ah huh." Raymond nodded emphatically. "Cuz I did see a bear. I really, really did."

"Did you say it was black and white? Maybe this big?" She held her hands a foot apart.

He couldn't resist the smile on her lips, so he confessed, "Ah huh, and it looked at me. Don't tell no one but it really did. I seen its eyes. It was looking right at me."

"Did it have a bushy tail with white stripes?" she whispered back.

"Did you see it too?" His bushy eyebrows lowered. She knew exactly what the bear looked like. *Wow.*

"Raymond, you saw an animal more dangerous than a bear. You saw a skunk. Everything in the forest is afraid of skunks."

"Really? Wow." He was convinced. She was very smart.

Alex took the long way back to his office, scrutinizing his neighborhood for any sign of the Ford pickup. It was a futile search at best and only made him more aggravated by the time he parked in The TEAM's parking garage. What made him think he could find her that easily? Mark and Zack had barely returned from Judy's apartment, spun up and angry themselves.

"The FBI just arrested Judy," Mark blurted out before Alex shut his truck door. "They took her in cuffs to D.C. Wouldn't let us talk to her."

"They what?"

"They claim Harley is the sniper and she's his accomplice," Zack answered.

"What's their proof?"

Mark shook his head. "They weren't saying. Just shoved her in the back of their van and took off."

Alex rolled his shoulder like that would possibly alleviate one iota of stress. This day just kept getting better and better.

"How'd it go at the police department?" Mark asked.

"They're no help, but I found three photographs of Kelsey stuck in my back door. Got some fingerprints too."

"They leave a ransom note?" Zack asked.

"Just Polaroids." Alex pulled his briefcase out of the back seat.

"What the hell do they want?" Mark asked.

Alex couldn't answer. He'd already jumped to all the worst case scenarios. If she looked dead in this first batch, what would she look like in the next? And the ones after that? His mind provided answer after ugly answer. There were so many things worse than death.

"What do you need, Boss?" Mark asked quietly. "Zack and I have already decided on a search grid. We'll find Harley while Mother and Ember run the prints. Then we'll find Kelsey."

"He's hurt." Alex cringed at the useless information he'd offered two of his best.

"Understood," Mark reassured him. "I'm not sure why he thought he needed to go home for his weapons, but we'll approach him with caution. I'm just worried he's holed up somewhere and bleeding to death."

"Yes, but there's more." Alex rolled his shoulder again, not wanting to break his friend's confidence.

Mark cocked his head not understanding. "We'll find him before the FBI, but I'd like to use your dogs. Whisper and Smoke can track him easy."

Alex took a deep breath and spilled. "Harley ever tell you how he got hurt in Iraq?"

"Sure. An IED took out his Humvee. He suffered a traumatic brain injury, a TBI. Spent three months in a coma."

"That's right. He survived an IED, but he still gets confused. Told Kelsey once I was in Baghdad during the first Gulf War. Told her that's where Jed's son got hurt. It wasn't.

No Marines were in Baghdad back then. I sure wasn't. Neither was Brady McCormack. All that happened later."

None of this information was earth shattering. Mark and Zack stood waiting.

"He wasn't alone that day," Alex said. "He doesn't know everyone in his squad was killed."

Mark let out a small breath. "But it's all in the after action report."

"You're right. I've read it, but Harley has not."

"So you're telling us he doesn't remember any of it?" Mark asked.

"I'm telling you he doesn't remember his men. None of them. He knows he was injured in an IED, but that's all. For some reason, his brain buried everything else. His doctors thought it would be better if he remembered it on his own."

"He might be thinking he's back in Iraq," Zack said. "That's why he went for his weapons."

"Makes sense," Mark agreed. "Or one of his operations."

"Hell, that could take him anywhere from South America to Afghanistan," Alex said. "We won't know until you two catch up with him. Just be careful. Don't hurt him."

"Maybe we're way off base," Zack muttered. "He was into drugs. What if he's looking to score?"

Alex stopped the downward spiral they seemed to be on. "Listen. The important thing is you find him before the FBI does. Get my dogs. Check the derelict buildings on the other side of the freeway from his apartment. Think like the soldiers you once were. When you find him, be whoever he needs you to be. If he thinks he's under hostile fire, back him up. If he's looking for cover, make it happen. Understand?"

"And if he's looking for drugs?" Zack asked.

"Hell, I don't know." Alex raked a hand over his head. "Play along with whatever he thinks is going on. Improvise. Call in a sitrep every hour on the hour."

Mark and Zack headed back to their vehicle.

"And guys," Alex called to them.

"Yes, Boss?" they answered in unison, both with one foot in their SUV.

"For God's sake, be safe."

"A skunk looks really cute, but it's very dangerous," Kelsey emphasized as dramatically as she could without smiling too much. Poor Raymond. He looked so baffled.

She'd never seen anyone so big. When he'd lifted the tarp, her first inclination had been to scream. Raymond could literally block the sun, but the moment he opened his mouth, her panic subsided. The poor guy had the mental capacity of a five or six-year-old. Maybe.

Whoever'd beaten him last night used something with a rounded edge. Half-moon shaped cuts and bruises mottled his cheek and forehead. His right eye was puffy and purple. He was nothing more than a kid, a really big kid in dirty sweatpants and a tent-like flannel shirt.

"Wow. Do you think it will eat me?" He scuffed his big feet together. "And I get a scared of the dark especially when I sees dangerous bears, umm, I mean skunks, and the old woman won't even let me sleep in her tent."

"You're safer in the truck. When a skunk gets scared, he sprays his very own poisonous gas."

"Why's he gotta go and do something like that?"

"That's how skunks protect themselves. He was smaller than you, wasn't he?"

"Ah, huh."

"He probably thought you were going to eat him. Did you ever think of that?"

Raymond stopped scuffing. "But I ain't a animal, and I would never hurt nothing, not even a very dangerous skunk with poisonous gas cuz I don't be mean to no one."

"I believe you. You're not the one I need to worry about either." Kelsey glanced around at the thought of the real monster in the woods. "Let's see your blood blister. Does it hurt?"

His magnificent unibrow furrowed into a deep V. "No, not so much. I guess."

"That's a good sign." It didn't take much to befriend this lost and very talkative child. "Blisters need a couple days to reabsorb the blood. You'll be fine."

"Huh?" Despite the layer of grime, a crimson flush painted his cheeks. Raymond was embarrassed and easily distracted, his soft blue eyes dazed but definitely smiling.

"How about you point me to a big tree? Then we'll talk some more."

He waved toward a set of tire tracks in the tall grass. "There's some really good trees over there. See 'em?"

"I do. Thanks. I'll be right back. Don't go anywhere." She waved and followed the tire tracks. Out of his sight, she pulled the napkins from her pocket and quickly took care of business.

"Is you coming back?" he called through the brush.

"Be right there." She didn't want to lie, but Kelsey was ready to run, her heart pounding at the prospect of escape. There was no going back. Her love for Alex pulled her away. Now was her chance. She'd find a road and someone to help. They'd call the authorities. She'd be home by dark, and Raymond would be someone else's problem.

"Ah, Kelsey?" The tremulous question drifted through the trees. "Is you out there?"

That innocent voice pricked her conscience. Raymond had no business being left alone in the wild outdoors. Had he been left to die too? It seemed logical. There weren't many bottles of water left in that bag. He'd be dead in a week.

"I owe Alex, not this stranger," she argued with herself.

"Kel—sey. Oh, Kel—sey." His words grew quieter and more tentative as he circled the camp. The poor guy didn't have a sense of direction much less a memory. He'd already forgotten which way she'd gone. "I can't see you no more. Is you lost?"

"I want to go home." Anger flared that she could not persuade her heart to follow her feet.

The truth whispered. *He's not strong and brave like Alex.*

"But he's not my problem. Alex is."

The instant she heard the words spoken out loud, she knew better. Alex would never leave a man behind. Neither could she. Reluctantly, she faced back toward the despicable hole in the ground and Raymond. Darn, he was a giant of a— kid. That realization made her choice both easier and more difficult. How on earth could she rescue someone so big yet so helpless?

She blew out a deep breath, bowing her head to follow her heart.

"I'm coming home, Alex," she whispered to the trees, "and I'm bringing a friend."

Eight

Damned Iraqi Republican Guard seemed intent on destroying everything and anything that got in their way. Harley stumbled against the rubbish blocking the narrow passageway. In a few feet, he'd be under cover enough to avoid the steady onslaught of enemy fire.

It had been a stroke of sheer, dumb luck finding ammo and weapons in the last abandoned home. He'd gone in quickly, always a good thing when a man's breaking and entering. And yet, it seemed he'd known exactly where to look. He shrugged the spooky feeling of déjà vue away. Sometimes a guy's just lucky. That's all.

Grimacing from the pain in his leg, he ducked into a doorway and out of sight. His eyes took a moment to adjust to the darkness of what looked like a concrete barn minus windows. Big enough to be a warehouse, the smell emanating from the depths was more stink than storage. Animals lived here, human and the four-legged kind. Wood smoke drifted along in the draft with those other smells.

He kept to the shadows, weary of packing the gear he'd stolen. Hope urged him forward, but he was no fool. Dark did not equate to safety. He paused. An orange glimmer from deep within enticed. Campfire? Kent and the guys maybe? Gambling with his life was never Harley's forte, yet he had to do something. Pass or play? He took a few halting steps forward, his senses on high alert.

Rounding the first corner, a rusted barrel came into view. Orange flames flickered from its mouth casting shadows on the walls. Cautiously, he peered into the larger area, almost the size of a banquet hall, only empty and full of debris. No one else was around, but people had stayed here. He could tell. There were too many cardboard boxes and grocery carts against the walls. And someone had started the fire.

"Kent?" he whispered quietly, in case his guys were hiding, maybe thinking he was an enemy soldier. When no one answered, he called a little louder. "Snakes? Rick? Anyone out there?"

Only the quiet crackle from the barrel answered. Good enough. He selected a corner and hunkered down behind a stack of old wooden boxes, hoping to catch a few ZZZs. Lowering his butt to the concrete, he pulled the pack off his shoulder and secured it behind him to serve as a pillow. His rifle on the ground beside him provided immediate protection if hostiles showed.

The relief of not marching or carrying a hundred plus pounds of gear felt good. One nagging reality persisted. The person who had built the fire would return. Still, Harley needed to rest for a minute. Maybe two. He stretched his legs and relaxed. Okay. Maybe five.

He'd have fallen straight to sleep, but the horror movie kept running through his exhausted mind in vivid Technicolor. Bright stabbing lights jolted him with images of bloodied bodies and vacant eyes; a baby girl in pink pajamas crying that she wanted her daddy. The next moment, a black dog with friendly eyes barked as if it expected a treat. All oddly familiar, all nagging for him to remember them.

One of those shopping carts rolled toward him, its wheels creaking as it approached. The cart stopped a few feet short of his boots. The crazy thing was…

Wait a minute. A shopping cart? Here in Iraq?

"What?" he asked out loud, like it might talk to him. Seeing the cart was just plain weird. It didn't move again. Probably just, umm, gravity or maybe the wind. That's why it rolled. He'd sat downhill. Yeah. There was a logical reason for everything. It wasn't really looking at him either.

Easing his spine into the makeshift pillow, he rubbed the knotted tension out of his neck. A soldier needs solid facts to plan decent strategy. He seemed to be working with sand. Thinking took considerable effort. The throbbing in his skull escalated to squeezing.

Smoke swirled his way, bringing with it the smell of brimstone and the awful stench of body odor and burning flesh. In the midst of it, a lady in flowing white stepped through the conflict. Green eyes blazed with a wonderfully warm light that radiated peace and comfort into his tortured brain. The veil of her auburn hair flowed in the breeze behind her. Whoever she was, just seeing her brought instant relief.

"Harley," she whispered enticingly. Even her words floated. "I'm here."

She reached for him. He held his hand out for her to take. Their fingertips met. With a sigh, he relaxed, breathing in the perfume of her hair where she now lay tucked under his chin. He could not recall pulling her into his arms, but no matter. She was there now.

"I've been looking everywhere for you," she breathed.

Just as he relinquished the weariness of the awful day—she evaporated. Harley scrambled back to his feet, jolted awake by the smell of death and his loud breathing. There was no cozy flame in a barrel, only billowing smoke that suffocated. There was no woman either. He was holding an armful of air. Hyper-vigilance replaced the peaceful feeling.

And then he saw them—two enemy soldiers, cocky, young, and cruel as sin. Something or someone struggled on the ground at their feet. It whined. *A man? A child? A dog?*

Harley looked again, blinking to see better. It was a dog. A black dog. A white lightning bolt slashed her chest. Best EOD dog in Army K-9 forces. The only female in his life. His dog.

"No!" He exploded across the battlefield. "Don't hurt her!"

Evil eyes slanted in his direction, but their muzzles pointed at his dog. It took three shots to put her down, each a vicious gouge out of his heart. She yelped. He ran so fast that he fell, his rifle sliding out of reach in his haste. Scrambling on all fours, he pushed off the ground, intent on reaching her in time.

Don't die! I'm coming. Wait for me!

The apparition faded. He skidded to a halt, his heart stuck in his throat and the fear so real he could taste it. But no Iraqi guard stood over his dog. There was no dog. There was only concrete walls and empty space where the murder of his K-9 companion had taken place. Thunder vibrated through his chest. The walls closed in as the pain in his heart fell out.

Harley sank to his knees, his head in his hands. But it looked so real. Felt so real. Her final whimper still hung in the air. He could hear her.

God, not my dog too!

For the second time since she'd been arrested, Judy sat at the interrogation table at FBI headquarters in Washington D. C. When they had first detained her, she'd thought how hard could this be? Once she answered their questions, they'd see how mistaken they had been. She and Harley were innocent, so she gladly surrendered her computer and anything else the FBI agents demanded. Only when one of them pulled a federal search warrant out of his inner suit pocket did she realize she was sunk.

Within minutes, her home was in shambles. In the end, the FBI removed everything computer related. They even boxed up Harley's music cassettes and CDs, like there was anything suspicious with a collection of old cowboy music. Of course, they'd taken what little was left in his gun safe. Like storm troopers, they advised they'd return for the safe. They needed a hand truck for that.

But they had also taken the ring she'd planned to give Harley. Her very orderly plan for a marriage proposal had been upended, and her romantic plans dashed. Worse, the FBI suspected her of conspiring with Harley in two successful assassination attempts. How stupid were they?

It was early afternoon when the door flew open and in walked the same expressionless agent who'd arrested her. He slid a black folder to the table and took the seat opposite. With meticulous care, he arranged several photos in a perfect line in front of him.

Judy watched him run the field. Middle-aged with slicked back gray hair, he looked the type who thought he could intimidate her. He wanted her to fall all over herself and confess just because he was FBI. The idiot wanted her to—what was the word? *Squeal?* That's why he hadn't spoken yet. Well, two could play that game.

She crossed her arms and leaned back into her chair. Just to irritate him, she closed her eyes and willed the world of the federal government away. It was either that or break down, something she refused to do in front of this guy. Besides, Harley was her man. She had his back no matter what this federal agent wanted.

Silence. The agent had finished placing the game pieces in order. Great. He was probably staring at her now and waiting. Well, let him wait. She certainly was. Biting her lip, the frustration of her predicament built into a tsunami of rage. How could this man be so dumb as to think she'd even consider helping him?

"Miss O'Brien," Mr. Nameless began smoothly. "We already have enough evidence to put your boyfriend away. You might as well look at it."

Her hackles rose as the game began again. If they had evidence, it was contrived. Nonetheless, she leaned forward and did as requested. The seven pictures showed a figure, possibly a man in a baseball cap with a rifle. All the photos were dark and grainy. The subject in them was not in downtown D.C. and nowhere near the monuments.

It could have been anyone, but it was definitely not Harley. He hated wearing anything on his head, said he already had hat-hair, he didn't need to make it worse. She suspected the real reason was the injury he'd sustained in

Iraq. He disliked anything restrictive on his head, but she was not about to share that personal info-bite either.

"You call this evidence?"

"These were taken near West Point three weeks ago."

"Don't you have to tell me who I'm speaking with first?" she countered. "What's your name?"

"All you need to know is I can put you away for life."

"Let me get this right. You want me to cooperate, yet you don't have to introduce yourself? Aren't you supposed to show me your badge or credentials?"

Mr. Nameless pulled a leather wallet from the inside pocket of his suit and slapped it on the table, like that was any help. Before she could read anything more than the words *Federal Bureau of Investigation*, he palmed it and back it went undercover. "Satisfied?"

Judy glared. Satisfied was not the word that came to her mind. Prick, maybe. Asshole definitely. Satisfied? Never.

"We know your boyfriend's been to Afghanistan several times during the past year. Did you accompany him on those trips?"

"You tell me. Don't you guys have surveillance cameras at every airport in the country?"

He stiffened. "What was he doing over there?"

"His job. Why do you care?"

"And that would be?"

"His business. You know he works for Alex Stewart. Why aren't you asking him these questions? You hire him to do your dirty work often enough."

"Oh, don't worry," Mr. Nameless purred. "We will."

"Then let me go," she demanded.

Instead of answering, he pushed another photo at her. "Maybe you recognize the man with your boyfriend?"

Judy glanced at a similar shot of dark, grainy and stupid. The second suspect wore a covering over his head, possibly a turban. Maybe a shemagh. "Who is he?"

"That's what we want you to tell us."

She shrugged. "How would I know? Kaddafi? Arafat? Prince Abubu?"

Agent Nameless scowled. "Who introduced you to your boyfriend? When and where did that occur?"

Her stubborn streak kicked into over-drive. What did Mark and Libby Houston's wedding have to do with anything? "I give. You tell me."

"Why did you suddenly decide to move to the east coast?"

"I hate snow."

"Who did you meet up with in Florida last winter?"

Enough already!

"Why don't you get my lawyer like I asked you to before?" she snapped. "Why should I tell you anything?"

Agent Nameless jumped to his feet. "Because you're a terrorist."

"I'm a United States citizen." She jumped up, as well. "I know my rights. I don't have to say anything to you without counsel. Call my lawyer!"

"You don't get it, do you? You're not entitled to attorney client privileges."

She pushed her chair back, headed home regardless of what he thought. That's when she noticed. A groan filled her. There was no doorknob.

Nodding to her chair, his top lip curled in a sneer. "Feel like talking now?"

She sat.

Agent Nameless smiled as if they were suddenly best friends. "I guess what I don't understand is what a college educated dame like you sees in a grunt like Mortimer. He's U.S. Army trash and you're Fifth Ave. Tell me about that."

Judy folded her arms and offered an icy stare. Did this G-man think he'd stepped out of a 1950s black and white gangster movie or what? He'd just used juvenile jargon from the stone ages. This jerk had no clue.

"I'm not saying another word without my attorney."

Agent Nameless reached across the table and placed a hand on her wrist. His eyes flickered from her eyes to her chest. "You have no idea how much I'm looking forward to another chat."

Judy jerked away from his creepy touch.

He winked. Gathering his pictures, he nodded at the two-way window behind him. The door opened, and out he went. It sealed shut with a gentle hiss leaving Judy staring at the jerk behind the glass. Or jerkette.

Fighting fatigue, she laid her head on her folded arms and closed her eyes. Harley's actions over the last few hours raised a wealth of questions she had no answers for, but there was a good reason. The only thing that mattered was that he was hurt. Everything else could wait.

His goofy smile came to mind. The man was a born flirt. Agent Nameless ought to take lessons. Harley knew how to make people feel at ease. He had that inherent talent of demeaning himself while at the same time drawing people out.

She sighed at the memory of their last kiss. He'd been in the shower, soaking wet and his face lathered to shave. Hazel eyes lit up when she peeked in for a quick goodbye kiss. They'd instantly shifted to dark and hazy. The sight of him naked always got her heart pumping. He might not think he was much to look at, but she knew better. So what if he wasn't six-pack sculpted and body-builder perfect? Running kept him trimmed and toned like a jungle cat. He stood there ready to pounce, his body lithe and agile. And firm. And hard.

For a split second, Judy had wavered. The sight of him dripping wet and aroused was more temptation than she'd anticipated. The steamy bathroom was no help. Primal attraction crackled between them. She licked her lips, her body ready and willing to submit. Harley held out his wet hand in invitation. Despite the call from the hospital, which she should have responded to instead of him, she'd thought of joining him right then and there.

"You going or coming, darlin'?" he'd asked, a sexy smirk tweaking his lips, his innuendo unmistakable. He was irresistible with water clinging to his eyebrows and dripping off his face. The dusting of hair on his chest funneled water down his belly to all her favorite parts below. The brat. How could he tempt her like that when she had to be on the ER floor in less than twenty minutes? And dressed. And dry?

"Join me," he coaxed, the deep rumble vibrating through his fingertips to light a fire in her belly. "The water's almost as hot as you are. Come on in."

"I can't," she whispered even as she leaned forward. Her feet might have been firmly planted on dry ground, but her playful side was already stripped bare and pounding out a happy dance in the shower.

"Sure you can." He reached a gentle hand for the back of her neck, and took a step forward, his head lowered for one of his panty dropping, hello darlin' kisses.

The whiniest whimper climbed up her throat when common sense re-engaged. Judy's hand connected sure and firm with the middle of his chest. "No," she said, her impetuous heart at war with her very practical head. "I'll be late. I have to go to work."

Instead of what would have no doubt been a glorious scrubbing at his very capable hands, she'd settled for a shaving cream kiss before pulling away.

"Damn," he growled playfully, his eyes cast down to his very impressive, umm, reason for her to stay. "What am I supposed to do now?"

"Hold that pose." She'd winked, and like the fool she was, scurried away and left him standing there wanting her. Needing her.

A sob sneaked up. Judy wanted that other kiss now, the one where he'd pull her under the spray, clothes and all. She knew it was an act, but there would have been nothing so erotic as hearing that sexy drawl while he peeled her out of her soaking wet scrubs. The clothes would have ended up on the tiled shower bench while she would have gotten what she really wanted. Him. The delightful tease. The charming romantic. The forever playful companion. That guy.

She bit another nail to the pink and painful quick. *Where are you, Harley? Why did you come home? Why didn't you stay?*

Nine

"Raymond," Kelsey said when she drew close.

He nearly jumped out of his skin, and of course, he was facing the wrong direction. A crimson blush swelled over his cheeks. "I wasn't looking, umm, honest."

"I know. I trust you. Did you think I'd left?"

"I thought you runned away."

"I was going to, but I decided not to. Do you know why?"

His shoulders scrunched together like a shy little boy's. "Umm, why?"

"Because I need your help."

"You do?"

"Yes, I do." Kelsey played to his need for positive reinforcement. "I'm going home, and you're coming with me."

The shaggy unibrow lifted. "Me?"

"Yes, Raymond. You. Would you like that?"

He scratched the side of his grubby face. "But what if she comes back, and I not here, and you is not in the hole, and, umm, what about that? She gonna be awful mad. 'Sides, I made it for you."

"And you did a real good job." She opted for praise instead of confrontation. It was a good-sized hole with fairly straight walls. By the time her head had finally cleared enough that she could get to her feet, it was morning.

Raymond was prowling and her chance to maybe dig some footholds and escape had passed. But there was no way she'd voluntarily climb back in there. It wasn't just a hole. It was a grave. "It's deep. I'll bet it took you a long time to dig."

"Ah huh. It took me a real long time cuz I gets tired, but it's okay cuz I gets hamburgers too." Raymond was rocking again. "If you don't get back in it, umm, the old woman is gonna hit me really, really hard. Same as she hit you."

Kelsey rubbed the tender knot on the side of her head. "What did she hit me with anyway?"

"This." Raymond lumbered over to the tent and retrieved a shovel. "You was wiggling, and she gave you a smack, and then you was very, very quiet. You didn't even wake up when she told you to smile."

"She told me to smile?" This story got more bizarre all the time.

"Uh huh. For your pitchers."

"You mean pictures? She took pictures of me?"

"Yeah. Pitchers. You know. With a camera. She wanted to remember you when you was asleep, only I kinda had to hold you, cuz you didn't stand up very good. Umm, them pitchers."

Kelsey didn't say anything, so he kept explaining.

"She made me put you down in the hole like I been telling you, so I had to be careful I didn't step on you, or she was gonna thump me again. I was real careful. Honest, I really, really was. And I didn't step on you not one single time, and she said I was a good boy."

"Did she take other photos?"

He scratched his head. "Ah huh, and I had to hold the light extra careful cuz she needed the perfect ones for the perfect person, and so," He drew in a deep breath "I holded the light extra good, and it was very hot."

Whoever this old woman was, she was one twisted person. Kelsey's heart thudded to a dead stop. It couldn't be. Not that twisted person. Not—her.

"Do you remember your friend's name yet?"

"She ain't my friend," he answered. "I don't care if I never eat another hamburger in my whole life cuz I don't wanna be her friend no more. Never. Never, ever." His last word came out with a stomp of his big foot. For a minute, he looked fierce and scary. At least he tried.

"She's been mean to you for a long time, hasn't she?" Kelsey's kind question took the false bravado away.

"Ah, huh, but sometimes she gives me hamburgers and calls me good boy." Raymond's eyes lit up. "Ethel. Her name is Ethel. That's a funny name, huh?"

The world spun. Kelsey turned away. *Oh hell. Oh damn. Oh damn it to hell. God, no.*

"What's a matter?" Raymond peered down at her. "Is you gonna fall over or something?"

"No. Yes. Maybe." Kelsey crouched, her head bowed to her knees and her fingers stabbed into the ground for balance. In the universe of evil, Ethel Durrant tipped the scale when she'd convinced her weak-minded son, Nick, to kill his baby boys. On that heartbreaking morning, Nick destroyed everything near and dear to Kelsey and all because of his twisted excuse for a mother.

How had Ethel found her? It had been three years since she'd seen that old witch's ugly whiskered face. The last day of eternity would be one day too soon to see it again. It made sense though. A hole in the ground—a grave— matched Ethel's brand of cruelty.

"Are you sure, Raymond? Is her full name Ethel Durrant?" *Please be wrong. Please.*

He crouched beside Kelsey, his head nearly down to the ground as he peered up at her face. "I dunno. She's wrinkly and short and a hundred years old."

"Does she drink beer and whiskey all day?" *Please say no.*

"Ah, huh, and she spits at me when she's talking too. She gots whiskers. I'm a scared of her."

"No." Kelsey groaned. He'd just described Ethel Durrant to a T.

"Yes, I is. I is really a scared of her," he declared. "She mean. You want me to sit down with you?"

"No, I'm fine. I just got dizzy for a minute." She sucked in a deep breath, more positive than ever. Raymond could stay or leave, but she was out of there.

"It's okay. I gotta rest when I git dizzy too cuz if I don't, I fall down a lot." He grasped her elbow to support her.

"I'm leaving. Are you coming with me?"

"'Kay." He was excited until Kelsey pushed off the ground and began untying the tent flaps. "Don't do that. She gets awful mad."

"It's all right. We'll be out of here by the time she gets back, remember?"

"Oh, yeah." He chuckled. "I forgot."

Urgency quickened her step. Now more than ever, she wanted to run.

Kelsey cringed when she bumped the red gas can just inside the door of the tent. The five gallon can was full.

Terror shuddered up her spine at all the ways Ethel might use fuel. None had to do with transportation. A rumpled sleeping bag covered most of the floor. The only other thing inside was a small backpack. The confined space smelled of body odor and booze.

"Hurry," Raymond whispered.

Kelsey hurried, shaken now to her core. In the backpack, she found another couple bottles of water, two cartons of granola bars, the flashlight, a long-stemmed lighter, and an old fashioned Polaroid camera. A manila envelope tucked inside an interior pocket caught her eye.

"Ple-e-e-ease. You gots to hurry. She gonna hit me again."

"I'm almost done. Found some food," she said to quiet him down.

"Oh? Food? Is it a hamburger?"

"Not exactly, but it will put something in your stomach." She slid her fingers under the flap of the envelope.

"Is it fries? You is my bestest friend ever, Kelsey."

She hurried faster now, her fingers trembling when several photos fell out. All were of her.

Oh, my gosh. I look like I'm dead. Why on earth—?

Her heart stuttered. That's why the camera. These images were meant to hurt Alex.

"You gotta get outta there," Raymond urged again. "Please?"

"Almost done." Kelsey stuffed the pictures into the bag. Icy tendrils of anxiety crept up her backbone. Quickly, she rolled the sleeping bag. They'd need some way to keep warm through the night. Opting for the pillowcase to carry the tarp she also intended to take, she parted the tent flaps and pushed everything out ahead of her. "Here. Take this stuff. We'll need it."

For once he did not nag. She scrambled to her feet and blew out a deep breath of relief. "Come on, Raymond. Carry the sleeping bag. I'll take the tarp and the backpack. Let's go."

Ten

Judy groaned inwardly. *Alex to my rescue? How ironic.*

He shadowed the arrogant FBI agent when Mr. Nameless finally returned to the interrogation room. Another man, almost a head taller than Alex, but with silver hair followed.

"How are you holding up?" Alex asked the moment he cleared the door.

"I still don't know why I'm being detained. They won't let me call my lawyer. All they keep asking is stupid questions I've already answered, and... and..." Her words came out in a rush. "Where's Harley? Have you found him yet?"

"No. We're still looking, but you won't need a lawyer anymore. The Bureau is releasing you into my custody." Alex turned to introduce the stately man beside him. "I'd like you to meet a good friend of mine, Jed McCormack. He made your release possible. Jed, Judy O'Brien, Harley's girl."

Mr. McCormack extended a warm hand and pulled her to her feet. "You're coming with us, young lady. The FBI has asked enough questions for now, isn't that right, Agent Holman?"

The man who'd refused to introduce himself nodded without making eye contact. Holman tossed the envelope with her personal belongings to the table. "You're free to go, Miss O'Brien, but do not leave the city. We may require your participation in the rest of the investigation. We will be in touch."

After that less than satisfactory and totally pre-recorded sounding statement, Judy latched onto the envelope. All Holman had returned was her keys, cell phone, and what felt like her hospital ID badge.

She stood, her knees shaky with relief. As soon as she faced her accuser, her compliance evaporated. "That's all you've got to say to me? Just like that, I'm free to go? You barge into my home, slander me and my boyfriend, and I'm free to go? You trash my life, and that's all you have to say for yourself?"

He nodded toward the door as if she'd better hurry. Alex reached for her elbow to escort her into the hall, but she was angry now.

"Oh, no, wait a minute." She twisted away from him, intent on a few more words with the smug Agent Holman. "You aren't getting off that easy. I want my computer equipment back. I want all of Harley's things. Most of all, I want the ring you guys stole and—"

"We need to go," Alex urged in her ear.

Judy elbowed him. She was in the middle of the worst day of her life, and the ring was going home with her, no two ways about it. "What gives the FBI the right to—?"

"Judy!" Alex jerked her into his side. "We need to go. Now."

One look into his fierce, blue eyes and she relented. Maybe now was not the time to rip into the man who'd trampled her rights as an American citizen. Alex tugged her out the door and down the narrow maze of hallways, finally exiting out the side door with his buddy, Jed McCormack, close behind. She had no choice but to speed walk to keep up. Alex barely gave her time. It wasn't until she reached the final step that he released her.

"Don't think for one minute it was easy getting you out of there. Get in the car." His eyes flashed as he glanced at the nondescript federal building behind them. "Please," he added.

Feeling a little meeker, she followed him to the street. At least he'd chosen one of his business cars instead of his monster pickup truck. A girl couldn't climb up into the front seat of that thing without some guy manhandling her butt to boost her up. She smoothed her scrubs and fastened her seatbelt, still out of breath from the forced march and angry with Alex. He'd just treated her as if she were one of his minions. He had his nerve.

"They sure pull the terrorism card out of their butt, ah, excuse me, ma'am. I mean out of their hat, don't they, Alex?" Jed McCormack remarked as he climbed into the back.

"Yes, they do. Thanks for taking time out of your busy schedule to help me get this done." Alex looked sharply at Judy. "That's why we couldn't let you argue with them. You're absolutely right. They're wrong, but they'd have no trouble putting you in a cell if they thought you were in any way involved in the three assassinations."

"Three?"

"Yes. Senator Covington was murdered this morning."

Judy sank back in the passenger seat, blinking tears and turning to mush in front of Alex no less. Facing the side window, she brushed her emotions away and hoped neither man noticed. The strong hand on her shoulder told her otherwise.

"You didn't know?"

"The FBI thinks Harley is the one killing them," she whispered.

"They're stupid." Alex pulled away from the curb.

Silently, she agreed.

He dropped a cloth handkerchief onto her lap. Downtown D.C. flew by as he pointed his vehicle south across the Potomac. Tourist river cruises sailed beneath them, but all she could see were Harley's smiling, hazel eyes. Only she didn't have a clue where he was and neither did his boss. She composed herself and faced the last man on earth she'd expected to come to her rescue.

"Thanks, Alex. I'm sorry I acted like that. I've never felt so...."

"Helpless?"

"More like violated. They're such... such...."

"Assholes?" Alex hit the nail right on the head.

"Don't worry about it, young lady." Jed McCormack spoke up from the back seat. "You had every right to ask those questions. The FBI owes you and Harley an apology. Don't hold your breath waiting for one though."

It took a few more minutes of driving through busy traffic, but shortly Alex pulled to the curb in front of a prestigious office building on the outskirts of Rosslyn. Graced by a semicircle of tall, spindly pines, it was a peaceful, elegant entry to a huge business plaza. Streaming water flowed from the top of a monolithic red granite rock standing on end in the center of a bed of red gravel. The name *McCormack, Inc.* etched in gold lettering on the rock gleamed for all to see.

"Close enough for you, Jed?" Alex stretched his arm over the seat as he shook hands with his friend. "Thanks again.

You're one of the few I could ask for help fighting the Bureau."

"That's what I'm here for." Jed unfolded his long legs and stepped onto the curb. He rapped on Judy's window. When she rolled the glass down, he reached in and shook her hand. "It's a privilege helping a lady in need, Miss O'Brien. Call me anytime."

Judy nodded. "Thank you, Mr. McCormack."

"Harley is a good man. When all this is said and done, you and he need to come over for dinner." Jed peered into the car at Alex with a stern eye. "You and Kelsey too."

Alex nodded, but Jed didn't step away. His voice was uncommonly firm as he pointed past Judy to Alex. "Have faith in that little wife of yours. She'd tell you and I'm telling you. Have faith, Alex."

"Yeah. Right. Thanks again." Alex pulled slowly into traffic, leaving his good friend and trusted advisor at the curb. He drove in silence until Judy spoke up.

"Have you heard anything on Kelsey yet?"

"No."

The temperature in the vehicle chilled. It was clear he did not want to talk. She changed the subject. "I didn't think anyone used cloth handkerchiefs anymore."

"Always carry one."

"Why?" The old fashioned item was the perfect distraction for this crazy day.

"Guess I never know when I'll run into a woman in tears." His voice cracked while he maneuvered through the hectic traffic.

"We're a fine pair," she said softly. "I'm sorry for the way I acted. Agent Holman made me so mad."

"The FBI has the same affect on me. Where do you want me to take you? Your apartment or my office?"

"Home. I want to go home. How are you holding up?"

"I'm good."

"Come on, Alex, you can't be good. You've got a—"

"I said I'm good. Drop it."

Judy hugged herself as the temperature in the car dropped to frigid. The barrier Alex had erected crackled like an electric fence between them. He drove in silence. When the vehicle stopped at her apartment, she opened the door intent on a hasty escape. No such luck. He'd already hurried around the car as if he hadn't just a moment ago snapped her head off. Alex opened her door and extended his hand to assist.

"Thanks," she said woodenly, not knowing what to expect. One minute he was the perfect gentleman, but the next openly hostile. Without a word, he escorted her to her fourth floor apartment door. It wasn't until they stood in front of it that she saw the tape stretched in a huge X across the frame. *Police crime scene. Do not enter.*

Her strength wavered. The FBI had been back. And that was the last straw.

"Damn it!" She beat the sealed door with both fists. "What do they expect me to do now? Sleep in the hallway?"

"I should have expected this." Alex looked the door up and down. His lack of a more hostile reaction spiked her fury. Removing crime scene tape was illegal, but she wanted to do something. He, on the other hand, stood and stared as if he didn't have a clue. At last, he gripped her elbow and steered her back down the hall to the elevator.

"Where are we going?" she snapped when they were once more in the car.

"To a hotel. You can keep in touch with me at the office, and... and..." Words failed him again. He sat staring into space with his hands clutching the steering wheel.

Judy turned to really look at Alex. Instead of evenly combed, his hair looked every bit as disheveled as Harley's. He hadn't shaved. Pronounced cords in his neck betrayed the inner torment only she could understand. "You're worn out, Alex. You need to rest."

"I don't see that happening for either of us. Do you?" Impatiently, he started the car and pulled away from the curb. "Let's just go."

She tried again. "No. I mean… I guess what I'm trying to say is... Harley needs you." Her throat squeezed shut while her eyes overflowed, not the way she wanted him to see her. "I need you. Please."

He jerked the car back to the curb and shoved the gearshift into park. Angry did not begin to describe the lean man beside her. He didn't so much as glance her way. His breath came in short, hard huffs against the fist clenched to his lips.

"Are you all right?" She clutched his arm, concerned he might be having a heart attack.

"What do you think? The police believe Kelsey and Harley ran off together; that her abduction is a hoax. The press is broadcasting lies that I killed her. And now the sonofabitchin FBI thinks Harley's the sniper. What the hell else can possibly go wrong?"

Traffic buzzed by, an oddly normal sound in the middle of such a chaotic day.

"We're in this alone," she whispered. "What do we do? Tell me."

"What the hell else? We find 'em."

Diamond blue eyes stabbed her with their intensity. And Judy fell apart. Talking with this man was excruciatingly like playing with a rabid dog—one minute sociable, the next biting her head off. She pulled away from Alex, too full of her own despair to deal with his.

"I'm sorry." Now it was his hand on her shoulder. His voice softened. "Judy. Please. I'm sorry."

"No." She shrugged him off, fighting a complete emotional breakdown. "Leave me alone. I can't take much more today, and I don't like you to begin with."

She should have known he wouldn't listen. The know-it-all's hand tightened on her shoulder until he'd turned her around to face him. For that single moment, he was no longer Alex Stewart, powerhouse CEO and man in charge of the world. He was just a devastated husband doing the best he could on an enormously bad day. The hard diamonds had softened to sad sapphires.

Her resolve crumbled.

"I don't know where he is."

"Don't give up," he said, biting his lip hard. "Mark and Zack will find him. They've got my dogs to help. I know they will."

She voiced her worst fears. "But what if he's... dying? What if I never see him again?"

"Think, Judy. He wouldn't have come home for his weapons if he was dying, would he?"

She gulped, every nerve raw from the horrible day and this fierce, angry man at her side. The worst part was she knew exactly how Alex felt. Every bit of her wanted to lash out too. The tsunami of rage and fear building inside her was more than she could hold back and the FBI's confinement made it worse. They'd wasted precious time Harley might not have.

"Think," Alex said softly. "Some logical thought process is going on inside that hard head of his. Harley's on the move. He was coherent enough to know where he kept his gear and to come looking for it."

She had to agree. Harley might be bleeding, but he was not dying. Not yet. "He even locked the apartment when he left. But the FBI is hunting him. What if—"

"Then we get to him first. It's as simple as that."

She nodded, wanting so much to believe the theory. If only she could offer the same encouragement. Judy inhaled a deep breath instead of speaking patronizing words. Alex knew better. Finding Kelsey was a whole different problem. "What can I do to help you?"

"Let me take you to a hotel. I'll get you a room so you can get some rest. Then come into the office. You can hang out with us until we find him."

Her breath hitched. He sounded so positive they'd find Harley, but did not mention one word about his missing wife.

"I'm sorry I said I didn't like—"

"Never say you're sorry." He leaned back into his seat, the weariness of the day etched on his face. "I don't like myself most days either."

Harley ran for cover. He hadn't seen a single military chopper until now, but these black birds had to be Iraqi. Had to. They skimmed too low over the ground with shemagh-wearing gunners leaning out the open sides looking for something to shoot. Maybe him. No longer sure what to trust, he stuck to the narrow corridors linking the impoverished villages. That would keep him undetectable. He hoped.

But he was in desperate need of rest and water. A bandage for his leg wouldn't hurt either. The fire burning deep inside it forced him to limp slower. Dread at being discovered by insurgents rankled in his gut. They could be anywhere. Capture meant torture and death. It wasn't going to happen, not to him.

Finally, he stopped in the dark corner of an ancient passageway that smelled of fish, an odd smell for the middle of the Iraqi desert. Fish? Really? His stomach gurgled in protest over his forced abstinence. It was hard to know the last time he'd eaten. Time was as abstract as catching up with his men. Shadows swirled in his head, either mirage or dreams. Nightmares maybe.

With a groan, he muscled the gear bag off his shoulder and dropped it against the wall of what he hoped would be a safer place to stop for the night. Gently setting his rifle flat to the ground, he crouched and let his good leg buckle while he straightened his bad leg in front of him. At last on his butt, he leaned against his bag. The hard lumps of ammo and magazines brought comfort to a soldier's weary mind. It might not seem like much to civilians, but what did they know? Luxury was in the eye of the beholder, and a bag full of ammo nearby was the only way to catch any shuteye in the field.

He kept the rifle loaded and alongside his injured leg. It would be hidden from sight if he managed to doze off, but still readily available. The SIG, on the other hand, stayed secure in the holster on his thigh. One never knew who or what was around the next corner. He'd been primed for warfare all day, and he wasn't going to stop now. Some XO's wise words drifted through his mind. *At all times, be prepared in all things, and you'll never get surprised—or dead.*

Grimly, he searched his pack for one of those chewy dry protein bars Judy liked to pack for him. She called them a treat, but—

Not again! Harley stopped cold. His mind had played another trick on him, but this time, he'd caught himself. He didn't know any Judy, did he? Besides, there was no such thing as a protein bar in his pack. He'd checked the last time his mind tricked him. *Damn, it's getting old.*

His mind wandered aimlessly. He let it go where it wanted. Thinking about the dream woman soothed him to his core. Slumping deeper into his pillow, his tired arms relaxed and went limp at his sides. The ground swelled up to cradle him. Tension lifted with every steady breath, and sleep became more essential than food.

The rifle at his side eased out of his grip. Gunfire erupted in some far off Iraqi neighborhood. While his ears registered the noise, he didn't respond. Sleep deprivation demanded total compliance. His hard head came to rest on his outstretched arm with a soft thud. That was the problem with holding still too long after the stress of battle. Once a soldier stopped moving, he simply fell... asleep.

Eleven

"How you doing, sonny?"

Startled, Harley snapped awake, his SIG already out of its holster and in his hand, blinking hard to see where that voice had come from. The hair lifted off the back of his neck. "Who's out there? Show yourself."

"'S just me." Someone moved at the edge of the dark, a shadow he could not distinguish for enemy or foe, male or female. Hell, it might be another figment of his imagination the way his day was going.

A struck match instantly blinded him, but his vision adjusted quickly. Two bright eyes glittered from a grizzled face that seemed wrapped in a black and white rag, possibly a shemagh. Yeah, that's what it was, one of those scarves the Iraqis wore to cover their heads and necks. Nervous tension skittered up his spine like spider legs. This person didn't sound Iraqi.

When he or she scuffled closer, Harley stiffened, not wanting to shoot until he had no choice, but damn it. Nobody should approach a soldier with a loaded gun. It just wasn't done.

"Put your gun down. I ain't gonna hurt you."

Harley blinked hard, not sure what or who he was looking at. "What's your name?"

"Miriam."

Harley shook his head. Miriam sounded like a woman's name, but she sure looked like a man with a five o'clock shadow. The long skirt covering her legs all the way to her boots might identify her gender. Maybe not. The boots looked new, but everything else seemed shabby and old. Several sweaters were layered over a hooded sweatshirt. Dirty gloves with the fingertips missing concealed most of her hands. She licked the lips of her open mouth, round and around.

"Miriam who?"

"Miriam Santorini. This is my piece of the tunnel. You shouldn't be here."

Harley glanced around. "State your business."

"State yours. You're the one with the gun. You a cop?"

"No, I'm not a cop." Why would this guy, umm, gal think a soldier in cammies and battle gear was a cop? Harley reached for his helmet only... Oh yeah. He'd lost it. Confusion stabbed his mind as much as pain stabbed his leg. He double-checked his rifle. Still there. Good enough.

"You're sick." Her voice gentled, adding another dimension Harley did not expect. What was a woman doing in the middle of a war zone?

He offered the least amount of information. "Corporal Mortimer, Army, Fourth Infantry Division...."

It was hard to think with a memory that felt like a slippery slide. He shook it off. The only words that came back to him were *Fourth Infantry Division*. Even they seemed incomplete. He repeated it silently; sure he knew the name of his own company. Something about a battalion and combat team shifted through his brain. It belonged in the Army designation. Somewhere.

"What are you doing here?" *And what the hell am I doing here?*

Miriam faded in and out of the shadows. Something about the guy, umm, gal was fishy. She moved in closer, brushing his rifle aside, and he let her. Him. Whatever.

"I'm the oldest person in this part of the tunnel. You know where you are, sonny?"

"No." He grunted, licking his dry lips. "Baghdad? Tikrit?"

"You're sicker than I thought." She smoothed gloved hands over his face, and he didn't care if she touched him or not. As long as she spoke English, he allowed a small measure of familiarity. "What'd you do? Get in a knife fight or something? Your leg's a mess and your head's bloody."

"Not knifed. Iraqi guards shot me. Killed some of my squad." *I think.* He blinked the sweat out of his eyes. It was getting harder to focus or breathe. "Killed my dog too." *I think.*

"Don't look like no bullet hole to me." She tugged at the makeshift tourniquet on his leg until it unraveled. "Looks more like someone took a shiv to ya."

"No. Iraqi soldiers. I seen 'em. I need to get to my base. It's where... It's...." He couldn't remember where he was going. "You got a radio? A phone? A shopping cart?" Cringing, he focused inward at the illogical question he'd just blurted. *A shopping cart? Really? Am I losing my ever-loving mind?*

"I got water." She pulled a plastic bottle out of thin air. Without asking if he wanted it, she unscrewed the cap and pressed it to his lips.

He clutched the bottle and sucked it dry. Best drink in the world is the first one after a day in the scorching desert. It soothed all the way down his throat and into his empty stomach. Nothing tasted better.

"You want more?" She tossed the empty plastic aside, still squatting on her haunches in front of him. "I can get it for you."

He nodded.

Once again she moved in, her hand to his forehead. "You're burning up. You need a doctor. Can you walk?"

"Nah," he murmured, his energy fading fast. "Need to rest awhile. Then I'll leave. What tunnel is this, anyway?"

"Don't matter." She moved alongside, her grubby gloves skimming up his arm and down to his wrist. "Where'd you get your watch? Looks expensive."

He lifted his arm to see what she was jabbering about. By hell, she was right. A real nice gold watch hung on his wrist. "You want it?" That seemed fair. After all, she had given him water. He unfastened the timepiece and handed it over.

The oddest expression slithered across Miriam's face. It wasn't so much delight as enlightenment. Greedily, she snatched the watch from his fingertips. A lighter flickered to life in her other hand. She turned the watch over, her eyes bright in the flame, licking her lips like she might taste the timepiece. It disappeared into the folds of her skirt.

"Sure you can't walk?" She scrambled to her feet.

"Don't think so," he muttered, but she was determined he try.

Miriam linked her arm through his, pulling him to his feet. The woman was stronger and bonier than she looked. "Come on. Try. Get up. I'll help you."

"No," he argued. "Let me be."

"You got to move," she insisted, leaning over him with her nose stuck in his face. "You can't stay this close to the exit. There's dangerous folks out and about. They'll kill you just for looking at 'em."

Prickles of caution poked at the back of his mind, but she had given him water. How bad could a defenseless old woman be? Harley struggled to his feet, trying hard not to lean too heavily on Miriam for support. When he grabbed his gear bag, she clutched his forearm tighter. Suddenly, she was leaning on him. "That yours? What's in it?"

"Stuff." His leg throbbed more with every step. It didn't matter if he put weight on it or not, the damned thing hurt. "How far are we going?"

"Not far," she crooned. "Just taking you some place nice and safe."

Judy had no intention of resting in her plush hotel room. Unexpended frustration had built to a dangerous level of nervous energy. After Alex left, she contacted her credit union to explain her lack of funds. They sent a clerk to the hotel with a replacement debit card, mostly because she told them they would. The department store down the block provided the few articles of clothing she'd need until she could get back into her home. Onto the debit card went a pair of sturdy walking boots and a shoulder handbag, not that she had much to put in it.

The fact that the FBI maintained possession of the ring she'd intended to give Harley rankled her last nerve. They held her future in their devious hands, and with Harley missing, maybe her life. Who did they think they were to trample her rights? And Agent Holman was it? When she was done with him, the last thing he'd be was a *whole man.*

Setting her mental rant against the Bureau aside, she hailed a cab. It was late Saturday evening. She'd deal with the FBI later. Right now she needed to hook up with Mark and Zack. Once inside the cab, she directed him to take her back toward the area of her apartment while she placed a call to Mark's cell phone.

He sounded out of breath when he answered. "Hey, Judy. I heard Alex got you out of jail. Good. What's up?"

"Give me your exact location. I'm ready to help."

"I'd rather you not do that."

"Tell me where you are, Mark." She kept her tone crisp and irritated. He needed to know she meant business. "Let's not make this more difficult than it already is."

"No. I'd rather not. You need to—"

"Listen. I'm not asking, I'm telling. Either I search for Harley with you, or I'm going out alone. It's all the same to me."

The cab driver turned around at her stark authoritative tone.

"You are not, I repeat, you are not to come down here," Mark shot back at her. "This is no place for a woman. The last thing I need is—"

Of all the sexist things for him to say! She hit the end call button on her cell phone, fed up with the whole damned world of men who thought they knew better and needed to protect her. Rampant anxiety far outweighed her last shred of patience. Sitting in the cab didn't help. She'd waited all day to do something while the FBI played their games. Enough was enough! Mentally cursing every male on the planet but Harley, the last thing she needed was an incoming call. It was Mark. Who else?

"What?"

"Let me explain what's going on out here." His voice was calmer, but she sensed the steel in his words. "We've witnessed a stabbing that has nothing to do with Harley. The police are rounding up the instigators, but Zack and me have been kinda busy. I'm sorry. I should have explained things more accurately when you—"

"Where are you?"

"In the abandoned rail house off Figaro Avenue. We've got Alex's dogs tracking Harley's scent. They led us here, so we are on his trail, but we witnessed the stabbing not two minutes after we arrived on scene. Two thugs ambushed an older man. I'm not telling you to go home, Judy, but I'd really appreciate not having to worry about you down here."

"You need to understand something too, Mark. I've handled homeless and vagrant people for years. I'm as capable out there with you and Zack as I am in the emergency room."

"This is not a nice, sterile emergency room," Mark growled back at her, firm and reasonable as he made his point. "But if you're determined, then come prepared. Bring a flak jacket and steel-toed boots. There are needles and blades all over the ground, not to mention a few drunks and dopers who look more dead than alive. Police are combing through the building searching for the—"

"Why, Mark? Why'd the dogs lead you to that particular building?"

His previous words finally registered, but her question was met with silence. He had his hand over the mouthpiece to his phone. Every word was muffled. At last, he came back to the line, shouting over sirens and a heavy engine in the background. "Listen—"

The connection went dead. Judy stared at the call-ended message on her phone's screen, undecided if he'd hung up on her to get rid of her, or if he'd truly been disconnected.

As an RN, she'd seen it all: stabbings, axe wounds, chain saw injuries, suicides, drug overdoses, living nightmares, you name it. But tonight it was Harley. She wanted to be the one who found him. She needed her hands on him.

Her phone rang again.

"Judy." It was Mark breathing heavily in her ear.

"What?" she bit out, unable to be civil with the fear ratcheting up her throat.

"You do understand he's going to need medical help when we find him, don't you?"

"Of course I do."

"Where would you prefer we take him?"

"Washington Central."

"Washington? Great. I needed to be sure."

"Are you sure there's nothing I can do?" She backed off her demand to join the search. Mark did sound like he and Zack had their hands full.

"We found his jacket, Judy. That's what the dogs located, but... he wasn't there. We searched the place until the police showed up. Then someone started a fire... and now the fire department's here. It's a free for all. The dogs... are on his scent again. Me and Zack are trying to keep up."

"Are you running?" Judy finally realized what was going on.

"Yeah, but... I'm not... doing it very... well." It sounded like he'd stopped.

She wanted to cry. Hindering Mark and Zack's efforts was not what she'd intended. "I should never have called. It's just that—"

"No, you're fine. Take it easy." He gasped for air. "You're worried... like the rest of us. It's okay. You can... always call me. I'm following two of the best noses in the country right now, and… I've got to keep up. These dogs are really something. This is all a game to them. He's another big dog as far as they're concerned."

"He does turn into a kid when he's around them." Her voice cracked. Mark Houston had just reduced her from rude and demanding to the frightened woman she really was. He was as bad as Alex, turning the tables on her before she knew what happened.

"Don't worry. We're going to find him. We've already found his jacket. He's close. Stay by your phone. I'll be calling." Mark's last words to her were rushed and abrupt. "Gotta go."

The phone went dead. She sat staring at it, scared and angry. This was not how she lived her life, protected and safe in the background. No, she was a frontlines kind of a nurse. She wanted to be with Mark and Zack when they found Harley, to hold him and doctor him and tell him she loved him. And now she might not get the chance.

A sob ambushed her. She covered her mouth, ashamed at her weakness. Nurses don't cry. They're the strong ones who hold everyone else's hands when the world is falling apart. They're the dynamos in the medical profession, able to read doctors' minds, anticipate worst case scenarios, and ensure proper medical procedure gets followed. Only now, her world had turned upside down, and her heart was breaking.

The cabbie's kind eyes met hers in the rearview mirror.

Judy stifled her emotions. "Change of plans. Take me back to Alexandria."

Twelve

Mother stood at her boss's door debating how to break more bad news. She'd exhausted all leads. The facial recognition program had returned zero matches. Not a single security tape showed even the hint of the blue Ford which only meant the driver had kept to side roads and residential areas when he made his way out of town. Ember was still running the fingerprints, but the way everything was going, that seemed doubtful too. Whoever kidnapped Kelsey, they were good.

About the only hope the TEAM had left was the picture Mother had released to the news and police of the man holding Kelsey. She'd cropped the photo so Kelsey's portion didn't show. The world did not need to see her in that condition—just him. The freak.

Mother lifted her hand to rap on the door, but paused. Telling her boss she'd failed was hard. Alex was a loaded spring. It wouldn't take much to push him over the edge.

Steeling her nerve, she pressed her ear to the door in case he was on a call. She'd never let it stop her before, but today was different. There was no sense walking into a frag zone if she could avoid it. Hmm. She heard nothing. Opting for the gentler approach, she turned the knob instead of knocking and peered past the door.

The second her eyes settled on him, she calmed. Bad news could wait. Her over the top, very domineering boss was stretched out in his chair, his long legs in front of him and his head tipped back on the neck rest. Sound asleep. Poor Alex. Both eyes were definitely shut. He didn't even snore he was so beat. The quiet, steady breaths confirmed he was running on empty and out like a light.

His suit jacket draped the hook of his corner coat rack, but it sure looked wrinkled. She looked again. Why was he dressed so professionally on a Saturday? This man needed to learn how to relax in the worst way.

As quietly as possible, she shut his door and tiptoed back to her and Ember's shared workspace. "Found anything yet?"

"I hope you didn't tell him we'd have it by tonight," Ember warned as she glanced at Mother. "The program is still running. It takes awhile to match fingerprints."

"I didn't tell him anything. Poor guy's sleeping," Mother whispered as if she could possibly disturb her boss at this distance. "You should see him."

"Aww. Really? I feel so bad for him. Judy too."

Mother did not reply. Ember still grieved for Todd. She was another one standing too near the edge.

"We're running out of time." Mother glanced at the digital clock on the wall. The TEAM was on the diminishing hope side of those vital forty-eight hours.

"We've done all we can."

"How did the terrain matching program go?"

"It's still working, but I have to be honest. There wasn't enough detail in any of those photos to match terrain with."

"Then turn it off," Mother advised. "I knew it was a long shot."

"Have you heard from Roy and Connor?"

"They called in an hour ago. Guess they've taken a boatload of photos from one end of the mall to the other hoping something will show up. Oh yeah, and they climbed the Washington Monument too." Mother brushed a curl of white hair out of her eyes. "Know what? I'm tired of staring at these screens and not seeing anything. You'd think with all the satellites in orbit one of them would have snapped a frame of something helpful."

"It's been an awful day," Ember agreed. "Where's David?"

"I'm sure he's following some kind of lead. He'll call in when he needs to."

"Are you giving up on us, ladies?" Junior Agent Rory Dennison asked from his post inside Mother's workspace. He and Junior Agent Eric Reynolds had volunteered to assist. Both were hard at work scrutinizing whatever Mother told them to analyze. Rory was dissecting satellite imagery at one side of the desk while Eric handled traffic cam footage on the other.

Rory swiveled around. He blinked hard, squeezing his face into a grimace and shaking his head. With wavy short, black hair, the guy was a killer in the good looks department. "Sorry. The eyestrain is murder after hours of staring at these monitors. You're both a couple of fuzz balls."

Ember offered a weak chuckle. "Gee thanks. You sure know how to make a girl feel special."

He leaned back in his chair, still stretching the kinks out of his neck and his arms over his head. "You know what I meant."

"I do."

Mother caught the wistful note in her assistant's voice, but she also caught the tenderness in Rory's deep blue eyes. Was he sweet on Ember? The second he caught her watching, he turned back to his monitor. She filed that interesting observation away for another day when she had more time to analyze this hunk from the Nebraska cornfields. All she knew was he'd served in the USMC the same as his father and grandfather before him. Hmm. A little Motherly research might be in order. Later.

"Well, I'm not giving up," she declared to divert his attention. "Wish I knew where else to look though. Maybe we should join Mark and Zack. At least they're getting closer to finding Harley."

"No." Rory turned in his chair, shaking his head adamantly, his eyes once more on Ember. "You gals do not want to be in that part of town. Alex needs you here, not worrying if you're safe or not. He's got enough on his mind."

Mother played indifferent, but Rory's statement had been directed at Ember. Was he worried about her assistant? It sure looked like it.

Eric yawned, his eyes still glued on his assigned array of traffic cams and security footage. "Anyone want to call in for pizza or something? It's almost dinnertime. I'm hungry."

Mother glanced at Ember. "I haven't eaten all day. Have you?"

"No one has. I'll bet Alex hasn't eaten since last night either. Let's order out."

"Pizza it is." Mother picked up her phone and hit her trusty speed dial. "I'll order sandwiches and drinks too. Anything else?"

"Garlic breadsticks would be good," Eric requested. "Dipping sauce. Extra marinara."

"I'm good." Rory had his hand in his back pocket reaching for his wallet. "Whatever you ladies decide is fine with me. Just tell me how much I owe."

"Oh, no. You're not buying." Mother shook her head at his attempt to pay. "Dinner at the office goes on the expense account. Your money's no good here."

Ember's computer program beeped interrupting the dinner order. It was her fingerprint query submitted through the local police department into AFIS, the Automated Fingerprint Identification System.

Eric leaned back in his chair to peer at data displayed on Ember's screen. "Remind me. Do we know an Ethel Durrant?"

Mother dropped the phone. "Are you kidding?"

"Why would I be kidding?" He straightened in his seat.

Ember bolted upright. "Wow. Really? Ethel Durrant?"

"What's going on?" Rory asked. "Who's she?"

Mother gulped, her eyes glued to Ember's. Did the world just drop out from under The TEAM? It sure felt like it. She couldn't swallow with her heart hammering a thunderous beat in her throat. Not Ethel Durrant. It couldn't be.

"You're scaring me, and I'm a Marine. I don't scare easy," Rory said. "Spit it out."

Mother gulped. "Ethel Durrant. Should I wake Alex? Should I tell him?" Her eyes flitted to Rory and Eric. They looked lost. Only Ember knew what she was talking about. "What should I do?"

Ember pointed to Alex's office. "Go wake him up. You've got to tell him."

"Tell him what?" Rory demanded.

Alex's door bumped open as a very exhausted man headed straight for Mother's workstation. Her gaze hit the floor. This might be the tipping point she'd been working her darnedest to avoid. How on earth could she form these next words? Worse—how could that demented woman be the one behind Kelsey's disappearance?

In the end, Mother had no decision to make. He'd overheard.

"Tell me what?"

She whirled around in her chair, her throat so dry she couldn't speak.

Tired blue eyes blinked at her, waiting for her genius to provide the way forward, a way she desperately wanted to give him. God, she loved him in her nosy, busybody way. How could she hurt him? Her hands shook. *I can't, but I have to. If I don't...*

"Tell me what?" He raised an impatient brow. She knew that look. He would not wait much longer.

"The fingerprints on your back door," she blurted before Ember or the guys could beat her to the punch. This kind of news should only come from her.

"Yes?" He was wide awake now and strumming his long, elegant fingers on the counter. "Whose are they?"

She couldn't stall any longer. "Ethel Durrant's. She's been at your house, Boss. I'm sorry."

Her heart stalled when his upper lip lifted in a sneer.

"Are you absolutely sure?"

She could only nod. "Don't worry. I made sure that big guy's face went out to all the news agencies. They should have—"

"You did what?" he roared. "Who the hell told you to do that?"

Never one to ask permission, Mother cringed. "No one. It seemed like the best thing to do. People need to be looking for him."

"People need to mind their own damn business until Kelsey's home!" Bowing his head, Alex shut his eyes as he composed himself. "My fault. My error. I should've told you to hold that information back. I didn't want... I don't want...." Feral rage seemed to build deep inside him. With a growl, he turned on his heel and stalked back into his office.

Rory waited until Alex's door slammed shut. "Will one of you spit it out? Who's Ethel Durrant?"

"Kelsey was married before Alex found her," Ember whispered, her eyes on the door across the hall. "Her name used to be Durrant. Ethel is her psycho ex-mother-in-law. Nick Durrant murdered Kelsey's boys and—"

"And he almost killed Alex and her while he was at it," Mother finished the ugly story. "It was awful. I've never seen Alex so, so—"

CRASH!

Rory leapt to his feet and bolted across the hall. "Call Murphy," he called over his shoulder. "Tell him to get his butt back here. Now!"

Sonofabitch! Now he knows we're looking for him!

Pushed beyond the limit of his endurance, Alex lost control. The first thing he laid his hands on flew toward the window. The office chair shattered the plate glass and tumbled two stories to the street below.

Every muscle, every nerve, and every cell in his body ached like he'd never hurt before. He missed Kelsey and now his lack of forethought had put her in danger. The possibility that more harm might come to her because of Mother's initiative literally sucked the light out of the sun and the breath out of him. All he had left was—*sonofabitchin nothing!*

Some stupid ass knocked on his door. When he turned to bellow his invitation for that fool to go to hell, Rory Dennison was already inside and closing the door behind him. He acknowledged Alex with a curt nod and, "Boss."

"Back off," Alex ordered before his junior agent had a chance to say anything more. Embarrassed and still livid, he didn't need mollycoddling, and he wouldn't accept advice. No. He needed something to hit. Ethel Durrant's ugly face came to mind.

The bitch! The cold-blooded, drunkard pig of a murdering coward! Give me one minute alone with her!

Rory planted his feet.

Alex couldn't stand to look at him. He bowed his head as rage swept through him, a wildfire he'd let get the best of him once again. Damn it to hell. There had to be a better way to cope with the thousand pound hole in his soul. He could barely breathe with her missing. Why did he think he could manage his stupid business? How dumb was he?

Shuddering with that grim possibility, he faced a man he could actually hurt. Rory stood poised with his arms at his side, fists clenched and his eyes dark. Alex wanted to hit him. He thumbed his chin, his fist curled and ready to strike.

Damned smart-assed punk thinks he can take me on because he's been in one war?

Rory stood tall and straight, equal as far as weight and skill were concerned. Both Marines, all this kid had going for him was his youth.

"What's next, Boss?" He nodded to the small conference table. "Another chair? Your desk? Your call. I'll help you toss whatever you want. Been a helluva day. Might do us both some good."

"Shut the hell up." Alex breathed hard, his edge gone.

"Mother's ordering dinner." Rory kept on talking as if nothing extraordinarily asinine had just taken place. "Pizza and sandwiches. You in?"

"Get out of my office."

Rory took a step toward him, his voice gentle and true. "No, Boss. Not until I'm sure you're not flying out that window next."

Alex looked away. God, he wanted to, but no. That day was passed. He'd thought of ending his life in the dark days following Sara and Abby's funeral, but Kelsey had shown him a better way. It was just so difficult to walk it without her. The pain of not knowing was bad enough, but knowing Ethel Durrant had her? Hell. Pure living hell.

Still, she was out there somewhere. Jed was right. Alex had to have faith in that little brown-eyed gal who'd come to him so beat up and damaged. Of all things, his finding her had saved her life—and his.

"I'm not that stupid," he ground out, knowing damned well he was exactly that stupid.

"No, but the universe is sure kicking the shit out of you right now," Rory said softly. "I might be thinking it if I were in your shoes."

Alex slanted a quick glance to his junior agent. He'd not expected Rory to sound so wise or so old. Maybe he did have something going for him besides youth.

"I've been there." Rory's words hit Alex's heart the same moment Rory's hand reached his forearm. "Trust me, Boss. I know what you're going through. Sometimes all you can do is hunker down and head into the wind, even when it's a sonofabitchin' hurricane."

Alex lowered his gaze, uncomfortable he didn't know Rory's background well enough to know what the guy was talking about. His steady hand offered support, not coercion. Not guidance. Not restraint. Just presence.

"You good now?"

Alex didn't answer. He didn't need to. The fire was gone. The need to kill with it.

"Okay then." Rory removed his hand. "Let me know next time you need furniture moved. Many hands make light work. I'll yell when the food's here. Will there be anything else?"

All Alex could offer was another quick nod and, "Plywood."

"I've got an extra sheet of CDX in my garage. That do the job?" Rory sized up the shattered window like he did this kind of repair work every day. Like he'd not just witnessed his boss being an incredibly stupid ass. "How about I sweep up before I run home to get it? I can be back in under an hour."

"I've got this." Alex had been taking care of his own messes for years. That's why the broom and vacuum stood in the back of his office closet. He never knew when his anger would get the best of him.

Without a single patronizing comment, Rory pivoted on his heel and exited, closing the door behind him.

Alex sank into his chair, weary to his soul. A breeze swirled in through the broken window, filling his office with all the smells she loved. He groaned, his eyes squeezed tight against the hole in his heart. "What do you want from me? How much do you have to take?"

The fragrance of spring and new birth drifting into the room unleashed the memories he'd tried to stifle all day long—the feel of her hands on him, the smell of her shampoo in his nose, and the light in her eyes. Everything he might never know again.

Sighing in resignation, he lowered his forehead to his steepled fingers. Tonight, he would break the oath he had made when Sara and Abby died. If only because Kelsey believed he would too. She made it easy. She showed the way.

"God." He bowed his head in humility instead of anger. "Just... Please, God. Damn it. Not her too."

Thirteen

"Where is we going?" Raymond asked when the camp was no longer in sight.

"Home," Kelsey answered. It sounded easy, but Ethel had a vehicle and means. Kelsey had Raymond.

He looked around the forest. "'S getting dark."

She caught the worried tone. "Don't worry. We'll stop soon. I'll build a fire."

With his usual, "Ah huh," they resumed walking. Kelsey would have preferred a quicker pace, but as big as Raymond was, he was also clumsy. Besides, she was worried. A more dangerous animal than bears and skunks roamed the forest. There was a time Kelsey had hoped she and her ex-mother-in-law might become friends, but then, she'd thought Nick could change too. She was wrong on both counts—wrong, naïve, and just plain stupid.

Life had taught her a hard lesson. Not all people were gentle like she'd been raised to be. Some were predators— cruel, calculating, and without conscience. They preyed on silly bookworm types who believed in common courtesy, obeying traffic laws, and random acts of kindness.

Once upon a time, Kelsey had been that bookworm, outmatched and outwitted when it came to the likes of the Durrants. Raised by strict parents, she and her older sister, Louise, led a sheltered life. The parochial schools they'd attended offered academics and preparation for college, but no social skills to maneuver the twenty-first century. As trusting as she was, she never stood a chance.

Well, no more. Kelsey was plenty educated now. Alex had taught her how to shoot and defend herself. If only she had her gun, but they didn't carry while they walked their dogs. Who needed a gun when two of the most lethal weapons in the Stewart household trotted obediently at their sides? Whisper and Smoke. She missed her four-legged boys almost as much as Alex.

Suddenly, Raymond stumbled, every breath labored. He plopped to the ground, panting like a big dog, his tongue hanging out and his face clearly flushed.

She crouched beside him. "Are you okay?"

He planted both palms to the ground and sucked in great draughts of air, his belly expanding with every huff. "Ah huh. I gotta breathe, so I can keep on going cuz... I'm a big guy, and big guys gotta rest more... than most people.... Ya know?"

"Shh. Stop talking." She pressed two fingers to the pulse in his neck. It raced like he'd just run through the forest instead of their very leisurely stroll.

"Walking... makes me woozy." Raymond couldn't shut up to save his life. "Please... don't be a scared of me. I ain't not... gonna hurt you, so... you don't hafta be a scared. I just out of breath."

"Shush. I'm not afraid of you. You're my friend." Kelsey looked around, contemplating what she'd need to do. They'd barely walked a mile.

"I is your friend?"

"Of course." She rolled her eyes at his verbosity. "You've had friends before, haven't you?"

He shook his head no even as he answered in the affirmative. "Yep. I kinda... had a friend once. He was named Stinky Fred, and he was old and wrinkly, like my other shoes before..." He sucked in a deep breath in order to continue, "I found some new, old shoes. I kinda stayed with him for awhile, only... he didn't need anybody as dumb as me cuz... I guess I'm a big dumb person, ya know." Raymond took another deep breath. "And 'sides, he was kinda stinky, and so... I don't have a friend named... Stinky Fred no more." By the time he finished his lengthy explanation, Raymond was barely able to breathe.

She pushed him flat to his back. "No more talking. Rest. Take slow breaths. You'll feel better in no time." She hoped.

He gazed in childlike wonder at the towering red oaks overhead. "Wow. The trees is really tall."

She looked up without answering. The trees were tall all right, but more worrisome, the last light of day announced their first night of sleeping in the great outdoors. Neither of them had eaten all day. The snack bars wouldn't make one meal for Raymond, much less last until they got to safety. She sat in silence until his breathing leveled out. When at last he seemed himself again, she pushed off the ground. "Stay here. I'll be right back."

"Where is you going?"

"To gather firewood. Don't worry. I'm not going very far." She headed into the shrubbery.

In a second, he crashed through the brush behind her. He held up a branch as thick as his forearm. "Like this?"

"Perfect." Before long she'd built a tidy little fire. He'd collected more branches than they needed, but that was okay.

A bonfire would chase the gloom away. It might also draw Ethel in, but Kelsey had a plan. Two could play that game.

She spread the tarp and unrolled the sleeping bag on top of it. The bag smelled of body odor, but it was better than nothing. Kelsey blocked the mental picture of sleeping beside Raymond, who had his own particular fragrance. The bag wasn't large enough for two, so she decided he could have it. It would be a long, cold night.

Dropping beside the crackling fire, she opened the backpack and handed him a bottle of water and a couple granola bars. His ration was gone in one swallow so she gave him another bar.

"Is you okay?" he asked.

"Sure. Why do you ask?"

"Cuz you is bleeding, and you looks kinda like a scary zombie only you gots all your face and your chin."

She wiped the trickle of blood off her cheek, amused he'd thought she looked like the living dead. The poor guy did have a vivid imagination. "It's just a head wound. They tend to bleed. Don't worry."

"I not worried," he declared, his poor excuse for a meal completely gone and his fingers licked clean. "I is with you, and you is taking me home. We is gonna be okay."

Kelsey looked away. She sure had him fooled.

When he finally fell asleep, Raymond snored like a banshee, not that Kelsey would have slept if he hadn't. They were too exposed. She did not intend to be target practice, not one more time.

One of the good things about being married to a country boy from Virginia who'd served in the Corps was that Alex knew how to make do. Simple things like three fist-sized stones, patches of the torn pillowcase, and the cotton cord from the tarp were easily transformed into a small bolo. It took awhile to locate a sharp enough stone to saw through the rope, but Kelsey was determined. She had all night.

Listening to the dark forest around her, she couldn't have slept if she tried. But it was peaceful. She had no sensation of being watched, and she'd heard nothing but the normal sounds of nighttime. Settling for a compact weapon instead of a cannon, she labored on. Her victim days were behind her. The bolo she crafted was crude at best. It would not stand against a gun, but it was better than nothing.

A study tree branch became a good enough walking stick that, with a little more thought, turned into a spear. She sharpened the end with her primitive knife. Kelsey practiced throwing until she knew it would never work. Determined, she started over and found a stronger and straighter branch. This one served her purpose much better.

Finally satisfied she'd done all she could, Kelsey looked up to Raymond's curious stare from the sleeping bag. He looked like the product of two fairy tale giants, still full of innocence and wonder despite his magnificent size. His eyes were thick with sleep.

"I was dreaming," he told her.

That made her smile. What could he possibly have to dream of? "You were? What about?"

A goofy grin eclipsed his gnarly face. "Hamburgers."

Of course.

With her hands behind her head, she leaned back onto the tarp. Finally ready to sleep, Kelsey relaxed. Stars in the velvet black sky twinkled through the leafy trees overhead.

Raymond started to snore again. Morning would come soon enough.

Miriam was as good as her word. They'd passed through an entire village of makeshift cardboard habitations. Harley had to trust her; she had the only light, kind of like a guardian angel, leading him farther into who knew where.

Abandoned shopping carts lined some of the walls. One of the things rolled along behind them for awhile. He kept an eye on it. What was up with the shopping carts in this godforsaken country? They didn't belong here. Why were they after him? Thank goodness it couldn't follow for long. Too much garbage on the floor.

Stepping quietly through the next doorway, they entered a larger room, the ceiling overhead once lined with windows. The pale spring moon cast an eerie glow through the skeletal bones of broken window frames. Shadows moved in the dark. He could hear them. Some whispered. Others shuffled. It was slow going.

"I need to rest." His bad leg screamed to cease and desist.

"Just a hair farther," she coaxed, her arm linked through his, pulling him along.

The gear bag weighed more with each step, but onward they went. When the moonlight faded, she flicked on a lighter. She seemed to pull the oddest things out of her skirt. Within seconds, gaunt faces were illuminated in ghastly shadows, startling him they were so close. They weren't alone. More refugees ducked from the stark bright light of her fire starter. Others scurried away.

"Get back," she hissed.

"Only passing through," he reassured them in case they thought he was a soldier in the Iraqi Republican Guard, not like it mattered. He couldn't speak Farsi, Iraqi, or whatever these folks' native tongue might've been. Most of them looked like the transients he'd seen back home on the streets. Funny how the poor kinda looked alike the whole world over.

At last, the pain got the best of him. "No more. I gotta stop. Let me go."

She stopped moving, but she did not release his arm until he shrugged out of her grasp. Damn. Miriam had gotten awful clinging the deeper into the tunnel they'd gone. Harley aimed for the nearest wall. Without releasing his bag from his shoulder, he leveraged himself against the wall and used it to get him to his butt. The throbbing in his leg had turned to jackhammering. No more. He'd reached the end of his road until he got a few minutes rest.

Miriam stood in front of him, the lighter shining on her face. He wondered why he ever thought she was trying to help. Maybe it was the way the light flickered, but she'd gotten ugly real fast. The old bat looked annoyed, her top lip curled back, her crooked teeth exposed.

"We gotta keep moving. This ain't the right place," she complained.

"It is for me." He positioned his bad leg forward to take the weight off. It pulsed like some animal lay beneath the skin, writhing for relief. "You wouldn't happen to have any more water, would you?"

She looked around, her lighter casting only the faintest shadows into what appeared to be a cavernous tunnel. "Why? You still thirsty?"

He didn't know how to answer. Thirsty was nowhere close to how he felt. Dying, maybe.

"Stay here," she announced, taking the skimpy light with her.

He leaned his head backward onto his pack and closed his eyes. Like he had an option? Staying here was not the problem. His strength was gone and every muscle pounded in painful symphony with the growing fire in his leg. Worse, there was no way his squad could find him in this dismal cave. Harley sank against his bag, determined to keep it safe behind him. The rifle went alongside his thigh again, still in reach and handy.

He tapped his fingers on the handle of his SIG. Cocking his head to the side he strained to hear what lay in the dark. "Who's out there? Show yourself."

When they remained quiet, he decided first things first. As long as he knew where his rifle was, he was solid. Harley made himself as comfortable as possible, his wounded leg calm now that he was off of it. But he recognized his dilemma. What lost man would not? He didn't know where he was. How could his men find him?

"Miriam," he called softly into the shadows, wishing he had a lighter too. Anything. The fear pounding in his chest would not let him relax. Neither would his ears. Something was out there in the dark, slithering closer without footsteps or shuffles. He cocked his head to hear. Fingering the pistol out of his thigh holster, he raised it alongside his cheek.

Another noise caught his attention. This was definitely shuffling. No—sniffing.

Something big and furry crashed into him, whining and wiggling as it stepped all over his injured leg with sharp stiletto toes.

"Ouch! Damn it Whisper. Off," came out of Harley's mouth, and he hadn't a clue why.

The beast that stepped all over him sat solidly on his lap, pushing its full weight into him like it needed to hold him in place. Harley hugged the animal because it seemed to be hugging him. Another face lapped a washcloth-sized tongue over his cheek, and he had no idea why he was suddenly enveloped by a strange and wonderful animal with two heads.

A faint light glowed from across the way. Miriam was headed back. The beast on his lap reverberated with a deep throaty growl.

She called to him. "Whatcha got there? A dog?"

The animal braced its big feet over Harley's legs. The two heads evolved into two distinct dogs when her light drew closer. One dog was pitch black, the other silver with a black saddle. Both faced her with fangs bared and hackles raised.

"They just kinda showed up," Harley explained, his energy for the day about gone.

The closer she got, the more the black dog growled. He crouched low, his neck extended forward and the claws of his hind feet digging into Harley's thigh. He ruffled a tired hand through the creature's fluffy mane to calm him. There was something awfully familiar about the fellow.

"It's okay, boy. She's my friend."

As usual, a fluttering picture show flickered through Harley's worn out brain. He tried to keep up with the images, but they went so fast. A stern, stiff man with the prettiest dark-haired woman at his side beckoned, only to be replaced by smoking debris of bombed-out villages and houses. Children ran for cover while others shot at him. Fiery death fell from the sky. AKs pop, pop, popped! The sky rained thunder and hellfire while the desert wind scoured the life out of everything and blew sand in his eyes and nose. Oily black smoke filled his lungs.

When Harley choked, the black dog pushed its butt into his chest, growling fiercely. Protectively. Clinging to the beast's mane brought a sense of peace. A dog like this meant safety. Harley might not be with his men, but he wasn't alone either. He was going to make it.

Miriam stopped short. "I brought you some more water, but you gotta make that thing go away so's I can give it to you."

The beast braced for attack, but Harley stilled its anger with one word. "Down." Again, he seemed to know how to talk to dogs all of a sudden. *What the hell?*

When the dog settled firmly on Harley's lap, Miriam approached. The only thing that made sense was it might be a military working dog sent to locate him. Vague images of other dogs jostled through his mind for attention: Jock, Belgian Malinois and best buddy to Corporal Hernandez; Diesel, German Shepherd and another best buddy of another friend whose name Harley could not recall at the moment. A black lab named....

He squeezed his eyes to make his stupid brain work better. Why couldn't he remember that black dog's name? He'd worked with these kinds of animals before. They tracked. They served. They found. Maybe they'd been sent to find him? Maybe Rick and Kent had sent them? He needed to remember.

Another word surfaced out of the spidery darkness in his head. "Rescue," he muttered.

Both dogs bolted as if they knew what he was talking about. Before they could get too far away, he added, "Bring help," to the wish.

"Wow," he breathed as their running bodies melted into the dark. "Look at 'em go."

"Good boy." Miriam knelt, the lighter in her hand uncomfortably bright.

"They were good boys, weren't they?" He lifted his arm to shield his eyes from that piercing glare. There was hope for Miriam after all if she liked dogs.

"Oh no," she crooned, her arm tight around his shoulder as she plunged the thinnest sliver of a blade into the center of his chest. "I meant you."

Fourteen

Judy could not have been more surprised. Energy filled the air when the elevator doors opened, not at all what she'd expected for a Saturday night at The TEAM's headquarters. These people should have gone home hours ago. Instead, they looked busy. Murphy and a tall, dark-haired agent were angling a sheet of plywood through Alex's office door. Senior Agent David Tao sat at his desk, his phone to his ear. His eyebrows lifted in surprised recognition when he saw Judy.

Mother had a phone in each ear, chatting about satellite scans into one and what sounded like computer programmer language into the other. Roy Hudson signaled to her from across the work bay as he ducked into the Situation Room.

"Come get something to eat." Ember waved Judy over to her desk in the center of the work area. "What kind of pizza do you like?"

At the other side of her counter, Eric Reynolds leaned away from his big screen monitor. "Hey, Judy. I think Connor's expecting you in the Sit Room."

"Connor? Me? Why?"

"Mark called. He thought you were on your way, that you'd need something to keep you busy for awhile."

"He did, huh?" Leave it to these annoying men Harley worked with. They were all sexist and all thought they knew better than she did. "Thanks, Eric. I'll go see what Connor wants."

"Wait." Ember shoved a plate of pizza in her direction. "I know you might not feel like eating right now, but you've got to keep your strength up."

Judy shook her head. Food was the last thing on her mind.

Ember scowled, the plate with two slices still extended. "Please? It's important. You'll go crazy if you don't eat right. You'll be like me."

Judy caught Ember's drift. She meant her deep dark depression after her boyfriend had been killed during a recent operation. Harley had worried night and day about Ember's state of mind until Judy was concerned for his. She accepted the plate only to set it down before Ember crashed into her.

"Trust me," she whispered, her arms around Judy's neck as she pulled her in for a tight hug. "I know Mark and Zack. They won't quit until they find him. Just wait. You'll see."

Judy could only nod, her heart too full to speak. Poor Ember. She lived alone with her cat. At the moment when her solitary life might have changed for the good, Todd Chandler was ripped away by the senseless act of a gangbanger's cowardice. And she was such a sweetheart. This kind woman in her leather mini-skirt and thigh-high boots deserved so much more.

Ember let go of her as quickly as she'd grabbed hold and handed the plate to Judy again, her eyes shining. How did she just do that? How did she know exactly the right words to dilute Judy's impatience with the world? She turned and bumped into Connor's gentle smile, like that helped.

"There's root beer and milk in the fridge to go along with that pizza," he said. "Or I can get you a cup of coffee if you'd like."

She gulped, her emotions raw. Any minute now, the wall would come crashing down and she'd dissolve into one of those hysterical women who over-reacted instead of using their common sense when times got tough. People needed to stop being kind to her. It was more than she could handle.

"No. I'm fine," she answered, humbled enough to meet his eyes.

"You sure?" He cocked his head like he'd willingly jump to do her bidding. "Cuz I aim to please."

"Thank you, Connor."

"Don't even think twice. It's been a long day." He smiled, and she felt ashamed. Connor was one of those lovable, puppy dog types—blond, blue-eyed and handsome as heck. Honestly. Where did Alex find these guys? If they weren't Chippendale worthy, they were just plain nice guys.

He cupped her elbow and took her plate out of her hand. "Come with me. I know what would help." Connor steered her toward the Sit Room, and she was glad to go. The whole TEAM did not need to see her fall apart. With his palm flattened to the door, he pushed it open.

"Hey, Judy." Roy looked up from the conference table, a smile on his dark handsome face. "I was hoping you'd join us."

She swallowed past the lump in her throat. "What do you need?"

Connor pulled out a chair and placed the pizza in front of her. "Be right back."

"Your sharp eyes," Roy answered. A handful of photos were spread like a deck of playing cards in his fingers. "Would you mind helping me and Connor analyze a few pictures while you're here?"

Judy nodded, thankful for the diversion. Roy's idea of a few pictures was really hundreds of photos, some black and white, some color, littered across the table like a scrapbook party gone wild. Connor returned with the sound of clinking glasses. He'd brought three frosty root beers and two more plates of pizza. The brat.

"Here's the plan." He set the feast down. "We eat. We drink. Then we get back to work."

"'Bout time. I'm hungry." Roy took a heaping plate.

Judy had to give it to Connor. He knew exactly how to get around her. She had no choice but to eat because they were. Before she knew it, her pizza was gone. The root beer was refreshing, and she did feel a little better. But the table was a disorganized mess. Pushing her chair back, she collected the empty paper plates, bottles and napkins and deposited them in the trash. It wouldn't do to risk a spill. She walked around the table, scanning the wealth of photographic evidence. "What are we looking at?"

"Three crime scenes. You did know Senator Covington was shot today, didn't you?" Connor asked.

Judy nodded. "Yes. Alex told me. Wouldn't this task be easier done by computer?"

"Sure, but sometimes folks see things differently when they're looking at a physical picture instead of a digital one."

"But digital photos are smarter."

Connor agreed in his usual non-combative way. "I know, but my eyeballs aren't. I can look at a digital picture all day long and still miss things. If you'd rather not, that's okay. At least sit and talk with us."

Judy jerked her gaze away, not sure why she picked at Connor other than he was not the man her heart yearned for. She selected several photos, willing her mind to focus on this new task instead of Harley.

Each picture showed a different portion of the Mall, but the table lacked organization. She couldn't work like this. Selecting a few more images, Judy lined them up according to the location of the monuments. The WWII Memorial snapshots went due north, Lincoln Monument to the far left, with Jefferson in a straight line below the WWII. A picture map of sorts evolved, photo by photo. By the time she'd circled the table, Roy and Connor caught on to her methodology and started filling in the map with more snapshots.

"So what's up with the plywood?" Judy asked, the image in her hand possibly taken south of the red stone Smithsonian Castle. She placed it right of the photos taken from the Washington Monument.

Connor grunted. "In case you haven't noticed, the boss has a nasty temper. He gets a mite spun up sometimes."

"His chair don't fly so good either," Roy added with a charming smile. "That man threw it clear out the window. He's lucky there wasn't a bunch of folks on the sidewalk. Channel 16 would have a field day if he'd hit anyone."

"He did what?" Judy choked.

"Yeah. Never a dull moment around here," Connor replied in his best deadpan voice.

"Finding those Polaroids of Kelsey didn't help—" Roy said.

"Polaroids? Pictures?"

He looked up. "You didn't know about those? Oh, yeah. The boss found three photos stuffed under his back door this morning. They were intended to make him feel like crap, and they pretty much did. He dusted for fingerprints. It turns out Kelsey's ex-mother-in-law kidnapped her."

"And whoosh, his chair went flying," Connor continued calmly. "Rory's helping him cover the broken window. I think Murphy's in there too."

"He didn't tell me he'd found any pictures." Alex had been so uptight. Now Judy knew why. "Why did Kelsey's ex-mother-in-law kidnap her?"

Roy shot her a disbelieving look. "You don't know that story either?"

"I guess I don't." Obviously she was the only one in the dark about a lot of things. "So fill me in. What's going on?"

Roy pursed his lips, his dark eyes devoid of light or humor. "Ethel Durrant damned near killed Kelsey and Alex a couple summers ago. Her son, Nick, and his friends did the dirty work, but she was the shrew behind the scenes."

Judy dropped into the nearest chair in surprise.

"I'm surprised Harley hasn't told you. He's the one who rescued them both that night. Sniped Kelsey's ex and got her to the hospital in time. Alex too."

"He never mentioned any of this." Judy shook her head, disconcerted at her lack of information. Harley should have said something. "Wait. Did you say hospital?"

"I did. Alex and Kelsey were in rough shape by the time he found them. It's a miracle either of 'em survived."

"And Ethel Durrant?"

Roy set his handful of photos down. "Durrant got away. She's one of them small-minded people who's so bitter she can't tell up from down. She's a drunk, but she's manipulative as hell too. It was her who kept nagging at Nick to teach Kelsey a lesson when they were married. Well, the bastard finally did. Drowned his own two baby boys and almost killed her. That's when Alex found her half-dead at his cabin. Durrant went after them both a year later. By the time Harley got there, Alex was dying and Kelsey about beat to death."

Judy couldn't believe what she was hearing. "How old were her boys?"

"Two and four," Connor answered somberly. "She's such a nice person. You just never know what people have been through."

"You need to understand what's going on inside Alex's head, Miss Judy," Roy murmured. "He's hard as steel sometimes, but a damned good man. His problem is he can't predict the future, so he blames himself when things go wrong. No matter what, it's always his fault, even when Sara and Abby died a few years back. Hell, I guess it's been more six or seven years by now. Anyway, Alex wasn't in the country, but he figured he could've saved them if he had been."

"So he blames himself. Harley does the same thing," she whispered.

"The boss is an intense guy to begin with," Roy said, "but once you factor in that all the women in his life have died or nearly died, you'll get the picture. It chaps his hide something fierce that Todd got killed the way he did. Ember was right there when it happened. I don't know what hurt Alex worse, losing Todd the way we did or knowing what it did to Ember."

"So Alex is protective of her," Judy said softly.

"And you," Connor added.

"Me?"

Roy nodded. "Hell, yeah. No one knows better than Alex what he's asking your men to do every time they go undercover. He doesn't take any mission lightly. If anything goes wrong, he's usually right smack in the middle of things, busting balls and knocking heads."

"The thing is," Connor explained, "us guys coming back from the sandbox don't necessarily fit into society anymore. Alex found a way to keep some of us gainfully employed. Speaking for myself, if I wasn't working for him, I'd be stuck in some other high security job that might be more dangerous. He pays us good and, honestly, I don't know anyone I'd rather work for."

"Harley loves his job," Judy agreed. "And he thinks the world of Alex."

"Hell, we all do." Roy pointed a stern finger at Judy. "You should be proud of that man of yours. Harley's got a gift from God. It was a record long shot he took that morning to put Durrant down, but he saved Kelsey's life. That's something to be proud of."

"So Alex and Kelsey stayed together and got married?" Judy focused on the photos in her trembling fingers, her head spinning at her obvious understatement.

"I imagine they still had their share of troubles, but mostly, yeah, that's what happened," Roy finished.

No wonder Harley seemed drawn to Kelsey. He had no problem hugging and kissing her on the cheek whenever they'd gone out to dinner with the Stewarts. She was such a petite and beautiful woman. It was difficult for Judy not to be jealous. They looked like they were in love. In fact, they acted almost intimate with each other. He always called her 'Kelsey Girl,' a sweet endearment that seemed inappropriate, especially when he'd leave Judy standing there with the gruff and taciturn Alex.

Maybe Roy's story explained their feelings for each other. Maybe not. If nothing else, it gave her another insight she'd not expected. No wonder Alex was a control freak.

She should have recognized the symptoms sooner. Hers were the same, only her need to control evolved out of her brother's encounter with a chainsaw and one hard-as-nails English walnut that had once stood in her parent's backyard. The effect of the kickback from the buzzing saw caused horrific trauma to Joshie's thigh, more so to his thirteen-year-old sister who just happened to be watching.

That was the day Judy determined to be a nurse. Joshie got a fast as lightning trip to the emergency room, while Judy got the lesson of her life. No one would die while she was around. Joshie didn't, a seemingly good omen that her decision was more destiny than choice.

The irony that she and Alex had so much in common also explained why he irked her. They were the same—both arrogant because they held other peoples' lives in their hands, both bossy, and, damn it anyway, they both had to be right. Every single time. Lives depended on it.

"Know what the morale of the story is?" Roy asked slyly, interrupting Judy's inner examination of conscience.

She looked up into teasing brown eyes.

"Don't make the boss mad. Might be you who goes flying next time." He winked at Connor.

Judy relaxed. Alex was an angry man all right, but he had good reason. She stood back to look at what they'd accomplished, her fingers tapping her chin as she scanned the neatly organized mess. "What have we come up with?"

"A collage?" Connor quipped.

Roy joined them at the side of the table, for a moment quiet as he studied their handiwork. "You do a good job, Miss Judy. Thank you."

"Hardly. It's easier to work when things are orderly. That's all."

"Which explains why you and Harley are a good match," Connor remarked. "Opposites attract."

She relaxed. Talking with these men eased her mind. They weren't so much sexist as protective. Connor took a step back. Before she knew it, he'd climbed onto a chair for a bird's eye view. He pointed to the far left. "Pull that shot of the catering truck behind the Lincoln Memorial, Roy."

"This one?" Roy followed Connor's direction and lifted the photo out of the maze.

Judy spotted another shot of a similar truck near the Roosevelt walkway. She pointed to the truck's customer window. "What's this for?"

Connor jumped off the chair and peered over her shoulder. "I don't know. Looks like a rolled up canvas or something sticking out of the window."

"What? Stuck between two closed windows that latch upwards? I could understand if it were above the windows. It might be an awning, but rolled up and sticking out the way it is? I don't think so."

Before they were done, they had sixteen photos of the same truck from different angles and locations. Nothing looked out of place except for the rolled up canvas. In three of the pictures, it was bent and folded, but in the rest, it was neatly rolled and straight as an arrow. Obviously someone was caring for the mobile food truck—if that's all it was.

"Damn, Connor. How'd we miss that?" Roy asked.

"Because it's nothing out of the ordinary. That's why we needed an extra pair of sharp eyes," Connor replied. "Are you thinking what I'm thinking?"

"That it would make a perfect cover for a long barrel?"

"Exactly…"

"But I don't recall seeing a truck in the vicinity the day Senator Covington was killed."

"Which means it's mobile. It would make a good sniper's hide."

"You might be right. That could explain how he got so close."

"And why no one heard anything," Connor finished. "No one would've paid attention to this truck. They're all over the streets by the Mall. See here?" He offered a picture of three police officers standing at the window of an identical truck. All had a bottle of water in their hands.

Fifteen

She… stabbed me.

Harley sat stunned while Miriam jerked the pack from behind him. "You ain't gonna need this anymore. Now let's see what you got that's so important you tried to hide it."

"You… stabbed… me," he rasped, the shock of his precarious situation now loud and clear. Blood poured down the middle his favorite black shirt, the one with the gold badge high on his chest. He blinked. Hadn't he just been wearing cammies? The darkness shimmered around him. He couldn't see the blood but he could feel its wet, warm fingers trickling down his stomach. Shock and fear set in. His lungs closed down, making inhalation nearly impossible.

I should pull it out. He fingered the handle, but the slightest touch sent razor sharp tremors straight through him to his back, suffocating him with their intensity. *Maybe not.*

Dumbfounded, he could only watch Miriam empty his gear bag to the ground, rummaging through full magazines and ammo, his only pair of NVGs, the KA-BAR Alex had given him last Christmas. His crazy dream kept getting better and better. *Alex? Who the hell is Alex?*

The two-headed dog friend returned with a vengeance and growling like a freight train. It charged straight for him, its claws digging into the ground. Miriam fled, it came so fast and urgently to his side. The strange dog was his friend; he got that now, but Harley was done. He slumped to the wall behind him, skewered and dying. *So this is how it ends. Here, without my squad. Alone. Just a two-headed dog... and me.*

The creature whined and circled, licking his face with both tongues like it knew him or something. Another light brighter than Miriam's lit the inside of the cave. Two dark shadows loomed behind the brightness. Her friends? Great. Harley groaned and prepared to die. No doubt Miriam had brought reinforcements to chase the dogs away and finish him off.

"He's over there," a man's voice echoed. Didn't sound like Miriam.

"Rick?" Harley peered into the blinding beam. "Kent? That you?"

"Corporal Mortimer?"

"Yeah," he breathed. "Over here. It's... me."

The dog planted its butt on top of Harley's boots while the men with the bright light drew closer. "We found him," one of the guys spoke into his shoulder.

"Zack! Knife!" The other guy eased Harley flat to his back. "My God! You seeing this, Lennox?"

Harley squinted around the light, trying to figure out who was talking. Two men knelt beside him, and they weren't little guys either. They looked more like bouncers. Maybe MPs? The one with the shaved head, the one called Zack, snapped orders into a two-way radio for a medical helicopter and a trauma team. What the hell? Everyone knows they don't have that kind of stuff in Iraq. They got Army Medivacs. Combat Medics. Battalion Aid Stations. What'd these jokers think, that they were home in the States or something? Were they slime-ball contractors? He didn't much care. They were Americans.

"Good boy, Smoke. Good boy, Whisper." The dark-haired man cradled Harley's head in one of his big hands, and it felt almost strange, the guy was so gentle. He pressed his other hand against Harley's neck, but he wasn't choking him. Dark eyes seemed on the verge of—tears? "Hang on, man, we've got you now. We'll take care of you."

"I've gotta... get back... to camp." Harley struggled to sit, but he was weak. The most he could do was grab the guy's arm to get his attention. "Listen to me, why don't ya?"

"I'm listening, Harley. I'm here. What's going on?" The man leaned his ear closer, and the nightmare began again. An explosion lit the night sky, sending screaming death all around, only these guys didn't seem to see it. Were they stupid or what?

"Run!" Harley bellowed. "My damn ride's on fire! They're shooting at us! Get—"

"No." The man held Harley immobile. "Your men are blowing an Iraqi ammo dump. That's all. Settle down."

"They are?" Harley strained to see around the big guy. That would certainly explain the smoke and noise. His men were the best at blowing munitions, especially the Iraqi kind. The ground ceased vibrating beneath him. "Oh. Okay. That's good. Only—" The strobe light movie reel of everything he'd lost flickered in his head. "It can't be true. My men are gone. Kent. Snakes. All of 'em. Base camp... gotta get to... base camp."

"We've got your men, Harley. Everyone's been looking for you. You're the only one still lost."

"Really?" It seemed too good to be true.

"Yeah, man." The guy's eyes glistened with tears and stars.

"Who... are you?" Harley reached up to feel the stranger's face, afraid he might not be real after all. "You keep calling me... Harley. Do I know you?"

"It's me." A tear trickled down the guy's cheek "I'm Mark. I'm here. Me and Zack are taking you home."

Whoever this Mark guy was, he pulled Harley against him like a friend. The shoulder bump jostled the knife in his chest, but his arms around Harley felt so blessedly good that he endured it. Adrenaline scorched through him, sending his limbs flailing, but Mark held him still. Nothing better in the world than being found dead or alive by an American soldier. Harley couldn't help it. Tears came unbidden and he let them. Hell. Brothers don't care when a soldier cries.

"You're going to be fine. We're taking you home," Mark muttered hoarsely.

The other guy, Zack, loosened the belt on Harley's leg. The makeshift bandage of someone else's shirt fell to the ground. Zack pulled a blow out kit, the first-aid supplies all soldiers carried in case they got shot, out of one of his cargo pants pockets. He seemed to know what he was doing when he splashed some kind of antiseptic wash over the wound and wrapped it with elastic tape. Something about these two guys felt so—right.

"Whatever you do," Zack told Mark, "don't pull the blade out. Help is on its way. I'm calling Alex next."

"Alex?" Harley rasped, not sure he'd heard right. That name meant something. "He my CO?"

"Tell him we're transporting to Washington Central." Mark eased Harley onto his back and covered him with his jacket. Harley breathed in the scent of American aftershave and sweat from the leather jacket, an oddly reassuring odor when a man's dying. "No, Harley. He's your boss. Hang on."

The two-headed dog sat so close by that Mark had to keep telling it to back off. Harley's brain cleared. The anxious animal morphed into two dogs again. What a relief. The black dog kept whining and bumping his nose into Harley's cheek and snuffling dog-kisses across his mouth. *You're so dumb, Mortimer. There's no such thing as two-headed dogs.*

"Whisper, off," Mark ordered, but Harley didn't mind the dog. Touching it felt kinda good. Kinda familiar.

"His name's... Whisper?" He reached for the beast. The crazy animal almost sat on his head. "That's... a good name. I had a dog once." *I think.*

God, he fought for strength to focus, but Harley was losing ground fast. These guys seemed familiar, but they weren't dressed in cammies. Couldn't be soldiers. Certainly not U.S. Army. Not unless they were black ops. He needed answers.

"You guys... Green Beret? You John Wayne? Delta Force?"

Mark's hands smoothed up Harley's bicep and clutched him tight. "Not exactly. Hang on, Harley. Just hang tight."

Good enough. Maybe even the best American answer ever, but just that fast, the world fell out from under him again. Out of control panic flared.

"Where... where am I? Who are you? Oh, hell. IED... all of 'em... they're gone!"

"No," Mark cried. "You're safe. The battle's done. Stop fighting, man."

Harley gasped. He looked straight into Mark's eyes. Calm seemed to flow out of this man. The choking sensation ceased. Harley sucked in a deep lungful of the stale damp air. He reached a bloody finger up to touch the guy's cheek, half afraid the dream might pop like a bubble.

"Mark? That you, man? What... you doing here? Where are we?" A flood of memories roared back at the contact. The man did not vanish. He was real.

"We've been looking everywhere for you." Mark choked on his answer. "You're safe, buddy, and your men are safe too. Help is on its way. Stop fighting the war, do you hear me?"

Harley relaxed. As long as his buddies were accounted for, it didn't matter what happened to him. Only Kent, Rick, and that little girl in pink kitten pajamas mattered. Not him. Never him. He hadn't mattered in years.

Sirens screamed from very far away, an odd sound in the middle of a warzone. Mark never once let Harley go, but he didn't seem too happy with the other guy. "Call 'em again, Lennox! Call 'em, dammit. Get 'em here. Now!"

"They just pulled up." Zack pushed off the ground and headed toward the flashing blue lights in the distance. "I'll show them where we are."

"Who knifed you?" Mark asked, his fingers real gentle on Harley's cheek.

"An angel," Harley whispered. "I saw an angel, but then she... she kinda stabbed me." He stared into his friend's worried eyes. "Why you crying, man? Why'm I so... damned cold?"

Mark started to rock back and forth, but the gentle motion hurt. Harley groaned and closed his eyes. He wept. Being found by a brother American soldier hurt so damned good. This kind of pain he could handle.

"Lennox. Get the medics over here," Mark cried. "I'm losing him!"

No, you're not. I'm just ready to stop fighting. I'm ready to die....

"We're here," Zack announced as more lights drove the world of shadows away.

Harley opened a bleary eye just as Miriam dashed from her hiding place.

"It's-s-s-s mine! It's-s-s-s-s-s all mine!" The broken bottle in her clawlike fingers flashed once. Quick as death itself, she slashed Mark's forearm as he hunched over Harley, shielding him from her attack. Like a snake, she rushed in for another stab and feint, but she was not quick enough for the hammer of Zack's fist.

"Back off, bitch!" His voice boomed and she halted in her tracks, struck down as he connected full force with the side of her demented face. "It ain't yours now!"

Harley's scary angel-friend fell in slow motion. Zack's flashlight caught the rush of blood that spilled from Mark's arm. It looked so—red.

"Damn! She got you good," Zack murmured.

The nightmare would not quit. All at once, three medics hovered overhead, and Harley lost track of reality. Was anything real? Did anything matter anymore? Was he really found or worse—was he crazy?

"Press as hard as you can," one medic ordered Zack. "Hurt him if you have to."

"I am!" Zack yelled back, and it looked like he was wrestling with Mark, only Mark would not keep still. Zack's hands were the same bright red as Mark's arm.

The landscape shifted. Harley lost his view when he was lifted onto something firm and stiff. Gentle hands wrapped a warm blanket around his legs, and he knew he was dying. This was it. The end of his road. He closed his eyes, finally at peace. Mission accomplished. His men were safe.

"How is he, man?" Mark called out, his fingers still clutching Harley's sleeve from his own prone position.

"You gotta let him go, man," Zack replied.

"No!" Mark's bellow echoed in the hollow room.

Harley peeled one eyelid open to see what the ruckus was about. This was a different nightmare than the one he'd been stuck in. He watched the contest between the two giant men. Mark kept trying to hold onto him, but Zack was wrestling Mark to the ground. Whatever was going on, it sounded damned tragic.

"Get off me, Lennox! He can't be dead."

Once more, Zack muscled Mark to his back. "That's not what I meant. Believe me. He ain't dead, but you gotta let him go so they can move the gurney. You're holding on too tight."

Harley reached for the guy who seemed more brother than soldier. "'S okay, Mark. You can let me... go."

Mark's dark eyes stabbed through Harley's fog like very gentle daggers. Slowly, he released Harley's sleeve. "You good?" he asked weakly.

Harley managed a nod. *I am now.*

A man can only do so much. The world passed by as the medics carried him out of Miriam's deadly tunnel. His battle was done. The knife hurt with every step. Harley winced and endured one more time. He'd given all, and yet, he wished for absolution. Closing his eyes, he prayed one final prayer. *Forgive me, Mom. I know I've been a lousy son, but I love you. Always did. Dad too, even when we fought. Kent. Buddy. Please don't hate me too much. I'm sure sorry I lived. Maybe now....*

The image of the woman with auburn hair intruded. Where was she? Would she forever look for him even though he was dead or was she just another dream like all the rest? Nothing made sense, and yet—it did.

A thousand bright lights landed on him, chasing thoughts of her out of his head. Funny. It looked like the middle of the Ringling Brother's Circus instead of the Iraqi desert. Police officers stood along the route to the ambulance holding crowds back. A couple hands reached through the uniformed barricade to touch his arms or boots. Some folks even looked like American reporters. They had cameras and more bright lights. What could they be doing here? He wasn't famous. Sure not important. Just a man doing his job. Just a plain, old soldier...

He turned his face. Soldiers never talk to the press. Any fool knows that.

Sixteen

"They found him! Mark and Zack got Harley!" Mother burst into the Sit Room with the news flash, and Judy was off her seat and out the door. She grabbed her purse, but could not run fast enough to the elevator, her heart filled with an urgent need to fly.

Alex already stood waiting for her. "I'm driving. You coming?"

Of all the dumb questions. She didn't answer, just joined him on the too long ride down to the parking garage, her foot tapping all the way. "How is he?"

Alex took a moment too long in answering.

"He's hurt, isn't he?" She raked a hand through her hair, angry that she was not where Harley was at this precise moment in time. She should have anticipated this and been waiting for him at the hospital. She should have been in position. Ahh! She should've stayed home last night and joined him in the shower. Maybe none of this would have happened!

"He's been stabbed, but the paramedics have him stabilized."

"Stabbed?" Her heart sank. "Where?"

Again Alex hesitated as he remote unlocked the closest vehicle.

"Spit it out, Alex. Stop trying to be a nice guy. You're not good at it."

"In the chest," he said bluntly while he opened her door. "He's also got a deep laceration on his leg. According to Zack, he was out of his head when they located him. The knife is still in place."

Some of her panic diminished with this new information. Most people's first reaction was to pull the knife out of stabbing victims. They thought they were helping when it was actually the worst thing they could do. Thank God Mark and Zack were not most people. "Do they know who knifed him?"

"Some old transient woman." Alex eased the car through the rolling security gate. "Police have her in custody. She attacked Mark too."

Judy gulped. "Can't you drive faster?"

"Yes, ma'am." He pressed his foot to the accelerator the second he cleared the garage. The man drove like a speed demon, but it still took forever. Suddenly, Alexandria was a long ways from D.C. and traffic too slow. Every red light induced more jitters until she wanted to scream.

At last, the hospital came into sight. Judy leaned forward in her seat and pointed to where he needed to go. "Go around back to the employees lot," she ordered.

Alex obeyed, coasting past the ER entrance where several FBI sedans were already parked alongside vans from the press. A reporter stood talking into his cameraman's lens. "We've got company. Looks like capturing the wrong guy is big news."

"I'll show them." Judy pulled her employee ID out of her purse and handed it to Alex. "Here. Use this."

"Got it." He stopped at the parking lot gate and slid the card through the security reader.

Judy had to look twice. He'd turned into that calm under pressure kind of person while she was pinging off the walls in full-blown battle mode; her lips dry and her feet ready to run. She climbed out of the vehicle before he had a chance to open her door. "Follow me."

"On your six," he answered not two steps behind her.

She took him into one of the unmarked doors only medical personnel used. Hospitals had many behind the scenes hallways and off-limit examination rooms. Judy counted on her staff to have her back, that they'd have Harley safely stashed away. She ducked into the staff's locker room and grabbed two pairs of surgical scrubs, one for her and the other for Alex. No one needed to know a suspected wife-killer and the monument sniper's girlfriend were in the hospital. She intended to keep it that way.

"Tonight you are Dr. Stewart." She handed him a surgical mask to match his disguise. "Put this on. Act like you're important."

She caught the glint in his blue eyes as he adjusted the mask over his nose. Yeah. That ought to be an easy task. Alex already had arrogance down to a fine art.

Together they passed more reporters and the grim agents from the FBI on their way to the ER. Judy took Alex past the admittance desk and entered through another secure door down the hall. Immediately, they were in the quarantined section where things like suspected Ebola virus or bubonic patients were kept secluded and the rest of the world safe.

Heather, one of her best nurses, looked up from the chart in her hand. "We've been waiting for you. He's in 2A. Raj is with him."

"Thanks, Heather." Judy turned into the first corridor and entered cubicle 2A. She could have kissed Raj. He had Harley and Mark in separate examination rooms with two teams working their usual miracles. Not even the FBI could get back here.

Her heart still dropped when she parted the curtains. It's one thing to see a body prepped for surgery, but when that body belongs to the man you love and a knife protrudes from the middle of his chest.... She couldn't get her hands on Harley fast enough.

He looked so broken. A nasal cannula provided oxygen while his chest labored with the blade. The back of his skull had been shaved where a jagged laceration lay cleaned and ready for suture. Another nurse attended to the diagonal slash across his lower leg, already orange with an iodine wash. Overall, Judy'd seen worse, but her knees weakened anyway. She leaned into the edge of his exam table and took gentle hold of his bicep. Instant calm filled her.

"Stats on both men are good," Raj informed her. "Doctor Statler is prepped for emergency surgery. He'll remove the knife once he's got the latest diagnostics, but I'm here to tell you, Judy. Your man is one lucky guy. It does not appear the blade hit anything major."

"Not even his lungs?" Alex asked.

"No, sir," Raj replied. "Not his thoracic artery either. It's a good thing his assailant used a fillet knife. Anything wider and he'd be critical."

Judy glanced at Alex. She'd forgotten he was in the room.

"There is minor bleeding though." Raj handed her a stethoscope. "Statler won't know for sure until he's got him upstairs in surgery, but my guess is there'd be a lot more blood if he'd punctured a lung. Here. Take a listen for yourself."

With shaky fingers, she inserted the eartips and rested the chestpiece of the stethoscope near the knife wound in Harley's sternum. Adjusting the diaphragm, she focused on any high frequency sounds emanating from his chest cavity, any wheezing or crackling, anything that would indicate his lungs were compromised. Unexpected tears sprang to her eyes. Raj was right. Everything sounded good, but removing the blade would be the real test.

She lifted her eyes to Alex. He winked, and that simple act of friendship was very nearly her undoing. Here he was offering encouragement when she had nothing to give him in return.

"How'd he score on the coma scale?" She referenced the test emergency responders administered to victims in order to assess the severity of brain injuries. Focusing on the purely medical side of her patient helped get her emotions under control.

"He was coherent and responsive when the EMTs brought him in. I scheduled a CT scan after Statler finishes, but Judy," Raj placed a hand to her forearm to get her attention. "Harley didn't recognize me. Didn't have a clue who Heather was either. He thinks he's in Iraq."

"He survived an IED blast over there," Alex offered. "All of his men were killed."

Judy turned on Alex, the short fuse to her temper instantly lit. It seemed she stumbled over another secret every time she turned around. "Are you sure? He's never told me that."

"He doesn't know. He was in a coma for months. His doctors refused to tell him he'd lost his squad because it meant nothing to him. He doesn't remember them."

The implication of what lay ahead for Harley floored her. The man she loved with her whole heart still had to face one of his worst battles—the truth.

"Would that be Rick, Kent, Garth, Robbie and some guy named Snakes?" Raj asked. "Because he sure remembers them now. That's who he was asking for when they brought him in. Them and the Knicks."

"The Knicks?" Judy asked. "The NBA basketball team?"

Raj shrugged. "I guess."

"You know what? That's going to have to wait for another day," Judy muttered. She just plain did not have time for one more secret. "Alex, go see Mark. He needs you."

Obediently, Alex stepped away.

"Can you give me a minute?" she asked Raj.

"You bet. Let me know when."

The moment he left, Judy laid her hand on Harley's shoulder. "I'm here," she whispered again, her lips against his cheek and her tough nurse persona falling apart. The day crashed around her. "I'm here, and you are going to be fine, and I don't care what's happened in the past, do you hear me? You're going to marry me. We're going to live happily ever after. I'll help you through everything. We can do it, just...." She pressed her lips against his whiskered jaw, biting back the worst that could still happen. "Please stay. Don't leave me. God, I love you."

If he heard, he gave no sign. She composed herself, but Raj saw right through her when he peered around the curtain. She wasn't head nurse right now. Judy gulped, not used to being a patient's distraught companion. It reminded her too much of that other time when she was just a helpless bystander in the ER.

"Hey," Raj said kindly. "Don't take it so hard. We've seen lots worse. He'll be fine."

"I know. It's just that...." Words failed because they plain got stuck in her throat. Tears she'd been denying fell like raindrops onto Harley's bare arm. She wiped them away, but they kept coming.

"It's different when it's someone we love, huh?" Raj asked tenderly.

She bit her lip. It wasn't just her man on the table. Connor was right. Opposites did attract. Harley brought spontaneity and joy into her severely controlled life. She might be the person who brought structure and practicality to his, but he put the moon and stars in her sky every single night. In his teasing, self-deprecating way, he always made her smile.

"How is Mark Houston?" She changed the subject.

"He's lost a lot of blood, but he'll be okay. His wife's with him if you want to visit with her while I run Harley up to surgery."

"They'll close his other lacerations there?" Judy could not make move her fingers from Harley's arm.

"You know they will. He'll be fine. You'll see. We're looking out for the both of you. Catch your breath. Go visit with your friends."

She nodded, swallowing past the lump in her throat. Yes, she respected Dr. Statler and she loved Raj. A girl from the Midwest could not ask for better friends and co-workers. If all went well, Harley should be in recovery within the hour. Her training resurfaced as she brushed her tears away. "Okay. You're right."

"Just so you're prepared, the FBI's in the building," Raj warned. "When he's out of recovery, he'll be in their custody."

"Damn it. Do you believe they think I'm his accomplice?"

Raj raised a dark eyebrow. "You?"

"Right. I'm really an undercover sniper when I'm not busting my ass in the ER. Didn't you get the memo?"

"Sure had me fooled." He loosened the wheel brake on Harley's bed. "Don't worry. I'll call the minute he's out of surgery. You'll get him first."

Raj roll Harley into the private corridor leading to the elevator up to the surgical floor. The FBI had a fight on their hands if they thought they were going to run roughshod over Judy. This was her kingdom, not theirs.

Seventeen

"Harley," she whispered. "You're in the hospital. Everything is going to be fine."

Judy watched Harley's vitals like a hawk. It was early Sunday morning. The sun had yet to show, but the FBI still prowled the halls. For now, she had him all to herself.

Once out of surgery, his oxygen saturation was excellent and his blood pressure had fallen back into the normal range. The knife barely nicked his lung. He'd feel some discomfort from the stitches more than anything else. His leg had been treated, his head too. Dr. Statler only used a general anesthetic due to Harley's obvious head injury. He did not want to take the chance of causing another coma.

Harley huffed through his nostrils, a sign he might be close to waking up. Relief had replaced worry with bone-deep exhaustion. If he were at home, she'd be in that bed with him. Since they were alone, she took the liberty of giving him a sponge bath.

With a plastic basin of warm water, antiseptic soap and a washcloth, she began at his head, smoothing the damp cloth over his short, sandy-colored hair. The simple service of a sponge bath for a patient turned into anointing as she proceeded to cry all over his forehead. He breathed in short, shallow breaths while she kissed each feature—the top of his head, his eyebrows, the straight line of his perfect nose. That he'd never broken it struck her as odd considering all the things he'd lived through, but no. He had a handsome nose, which flared when she lifted the cannula to wipe the rest of his face.

"I love you." She placed a soft kiss on those too serious looking lips. They pinched together for a second as if he'd felt her love pouring into him. Another kiss and she lingered, drawing the life she thought she'd lost back into her soul. Her tongue traced his bottom lip, tasting him as automatically as loving him.

A pang of guilt sneaked up on her. Poor Alex. He wasn't breathing Kelsey's breath this morning. He wasn't kissing her lips. Judy wiped that thought away along with the tear that went with it. She could only handle one disaster at a time. Harley was hers. Alex would have to deal with his.

The scruff of a two-day beard graced Harley's cheeks and chin, not his usual look, but handsome. She washed gently around his ears, and down his neck to his collarbone. Touching his skin brought instant calm. He was alive and for the most part in good condition. Many of the accident victims from the pile-up on the freeway fared much worse.

Any moment now he would flutter those thick eyelashes open, peer up at her, and everything would be okay. He'd wink and pour on his usual Texas twang. She'd climb in bed with him and together, they'd work through whatever problem came up.

Easing the damp cloth just inside the round collar of his hospital gown, she pledged a more thorough scrubbing when he was awake. A recovery room was not the proper place for the kind of attention she had in mind. This man needed to be loved, and this woman needed to do the loving.

Judy contented herself with washing his arms and hands next with deliberate strokes. He did not have heavily muscled arms like his friend, Mark. Harley ran marathons, and, as a dedicated runner, he was athletically lithe and lean.

Judy settled for one more swipe down his elbow to his wrist before she placed his limp arm beneath the blanket. His groan brought her attention back to his face. Those eyelashes fluttered. She smiled as his nose scrunched beneath the plastic cannula. He brushed his fingers over his brows. His blood pressure spiked on the monitor. His eyes blinked open. Harley was awake.

He gasped, rolling from side to side as a full-blown panic attack hit. She wasn't quick enough. One minute he was flat to his back on the bed. The next he'd tossed the blankets aside and leaped over the bedrail, taking his heart monitor and IV lines to the floor with him.

"No, Harley. Stop—"

"Incoming!" He pulled her down with him, jerking the sensors and lines off his chest. "Get down, dumb ass!"

She joined him, but he couldn't work his body beneath the hospital bed like he seemed determined to do. He cowered next to it instead, wheezing from the too quick exertion he'd put his injured body through.

"You're in the hospital." She knelt next to him with her hand firmly on his elbow. "Let's get you back into—"

"Back off!" He scraped her fingers off his arm along with the IV line. "You seen my guys? You seen the CO?"

"Harley, it's me. Don't you—"

"No!" He roared, pushing her back to her butt. "Don't you get it? I gotta find 'em, and you gotta keep down."

His intensity scorched her. Judy had never seen him as angry or as focused—or such a stranger. He didn't seem to know her.

Raj's face appeared at the door window. He turned on his heel and backed off.

"Who are we looking for?" Judy played along, hoping Raj hadn't decided she could handle Harley on her own, that he'd gone to find Alex.

"My men. There's six of 'em. No, five. No, wait." Harley raised his fingers, becoming angrier as he counted off the names she'd only recently heard. "Rick. Kent. Carlton. Snakes. Robbie, and...." Starting over with his thumb extended, he shook his head, his breath coming in short hard bursts. "Rick. Kent. Carlton. Garth...." Another growl rumbled from deep in his gut, and Judy was scared. Who was this guy? The gentle man she knew was gone.

"Who are they? Do you know?"

She gulped, trying to be all he needed her to be. "Umm, Rick. Snakes. Carlton. Robbie. Kent. Garth."

"Oh yeah. I think you might be right. But... But...." A shadow replaced the momentary calm. His face turned into a savage mask. "It don't matter how many! We save 'em all. Never quit. Never fail. Never! You got that?"

"Yes, sir," she acquiesced as quickly as she could. He needed to know she was on his side. Right now, he didn't act like he knew any such thing.

"Who the hell are you, soldier?" Disgusted hazel eyes blinked over her without recognition.

She blurted the first thing that came to her mind. "Private O'Brien, sir."

"Guess you'll do." The door cracked open and he ducked, his hand clamped on the top of her head, pushing her to the floor with him. "Get down!"

"Corporal Mortimer!"

Judy peeked over the edge of the mattress, thankful for the intervention. Poor Mark was white as a ghost, supported by wide-eyed Libby at his side. "Atten-shun!"

Harley gasped, his Adam's apple bobbing like he couldn't swallow. "What the f—?"

"On your feet, soldier!" Mark stiffened and marched into the room. "I gave you an order."

"But...." Harley groaned, the fight gone out of him. He climbed to his feet. "But how... How'd you get here, sir? How'd you find me?"

"You're in a hospital." Mark kept his voice hard and firm. "Get back into bed before I give you fifty."

Judy shot Mark a quick glance of appreciation when Harley obeyed. She didn't know what fifty meant, but apparently Harley did. It worked.

Shaking and drenched with sweat, he climbed into the bed and collapsed on his pillow, his eyes riveted to Mark. Judy checked Harley's bandages and pulled the blanket over his bare legs, her own hands shaking plenty. She wanted to comfort him, but he didn't seem to know her. She held back.

Mark sat at the end of the bed, breathing heavily and Libby still at his side. Her blue eyes darted about the messy room. "Raj sent us. What was he doing out of bed?" she whispered.

Judy could only roll her eyes. Good question. Adrenaline and PTSD? Yeah, not a good combination.

"How you feeling?" Mark grasped Harley's arm right up to his elbow. His voice softened. "We've been worried about you."

Harley looked away, blinking hard. He looked so confused, and Judy's heart went out to him. "I don't know, sir."

"It's me. Mark Houston. Remember?"

Harley squeezed his eyes tight, his handsome face contorted with a barrage of conflicting emotions—anger, relief, fear, panic.

She busied herself reattaching his monitor feeds and bandaging the hole he'd left when he jerked out his IV line. Nervous energy pulsed off of him. For a man still recuperating from surgery, he was in no shape to have jumped out of bed like he had. His heart rate had skyrocketed. Mark's attempt to calm him wasn't helping.

"Do I know you?" He tilted his head sideways not meeting Mark head-on.

"You were best man at my wedding," Mark answered warmly.

No recognition lit Harley's eyes. Only suspicion. Frustration.

"Hey, buddy." Libby took his other hand as she sat opposite Mark. "You'll remember me. I know you will. You always tell me I'm unforgettable."

But Harley only stared at the curly-haired blond holding fast to him, looking like he might pull his hands away from these strangers until he figured things out.

Libby lifted his hand to her cheek. "Come on, Harley. You can't have forgotten me."

"No, I…" A guilty look replaced the anger. He blew out a deep sigh, swallowing hard. "It's just that… Wait. Libby? Is your name Libby?"

"There you go. I knew you'd never forget."

He dropped Mark's grip and grabbed her into a hug. "You're… Libby. Course I remember you, darlin'."

Judy blinked the tears out of her eyes when Libby pressed her hand gently to the back of his neck, holding him close. That was her place. Not Libby's.

"And you… You married that jarhead, didn't you?" he muttered hoarsely. "He's... Mark. My buddy, Mark Houston, isn't he?"

"That's right," Mark said.

"Hey. Sure, man. I know... you."

Judy caught Harley's emphasis on his last word. He knew Mark and Libby. Where did that leave her? The embrace he held Libby in looked like it came from a lost boy who'd finally recognized a familiar face in the crowd.

"Libby," he whispered. "I been looking for you. I think."

"It's okay. You found me. Mark and Judy too." Her arms were still around his neck and his face in her hair. "You're home now, Harley, where you belong."

Judy's heart pinched. He should be hugging her.

When he finally released Libby, Harley leaned heavily back into his pillow still clinging to her hand. He didn't seem able or willing to let go. "And you kids have a tiny little gal of your own now, don't you? You named her, umm... Let me think. You named her... Damn. I can't remember."

"You call her a bug." Libby filled in the blank space for him.

He swallowed hard. Anger flashed across his face again, but disappeared as quickly. "You named her JayJay only I call her ladybug because... she's so danged cute. Right?"

"That's right," Mark said.

Relief shuddered off Harley. Once again a soft smile lit his troubled face. "That's right. Oh, yeah. You named her after Mark's mother, didn't you? You could have called her Harley, you know. That's one of those kinds of names that fits all."

"That's a very good idea." Libby's eyes brimmed full. "We are definitely naming our next baby after you."

Judy bit her lip, standing on the outside of this friendly conversation like she didn't belong. All her plans screeched to a halt.

Harley's face relaxed again with Libby's hand still snug in his. "JayJay and Harley. That'd be way cool. Maybe I could come visit you kids after I get out of here."

The yearning in his voice shook Judy to her core. He wanted to belong somewhere, but he had yet to look her way. She was nothing more than invisible staff.

Tears filled Harley's eyes. "Look at you, Mark. Married to the woman you love. A family. I'd like to be happy like you someday."

Judy had to turn away. Every memory restored was another sucker punch she'd not expected. This was no happy reunion. Maybe for Libby and Mark. Not for her.

"It will happen sooner than you think," Mark said.

"Excuse me, nurse, but can I get something to drink?" Harley asked. "I'm awful dry."

Libby gasped. "Harley, this is—"

"No. It's okay," Judy interrupted, more determined than ever and a knot in her throat. "I'd be happy to refill your water bottle." To prove the facade, she lifted the bottle off his nightstand and filled it from the pitcher, fighting the stifling cramp in her chest. "Is there anything else?"

"Thank you, ma'am. No. I'm just tired."

She turned to Mark and Libby, her fingers clenched at her side. "Mr. Mortimer needs his rest. You too, Mr. Houston."

Mark shook his head sadly. "Call me if you need anything, Judy. You've got my cell." He waved to Harley at the door. "We'll be up to visit later."

"Sure thing." Harley offered a tired wave as Mark shut the recovery room door. Raj's dark eyes appeared in the window, but Judy shook her head. She needed more time with her man. He didn't even know who she was. The FBI couldn't have him. Not yet.

"Judy, huh?" he said softly. "I knew a Judy once. She had brownish-red hair, kinda long like yours, only—"

Hazel browns skated over the last one standing in his room. Judy held her breath. For a minute, he seemed frozen. He blinked. The flutter of information overload came too fast and too raw to handle. Harley squeezed his eyes shut, the next words out of his mouth laced with pain and guilt. "I. Left. Them."

She watched helplessly as the strong, self-assured man she loved shattered into unrecognizable pieces. Gone was the debonair gentle hero who'd caught her eye from the first second she'd seen him. This poor soul was desperately sad and ripping her heart out.

"There was so much smoke and.... They were dead. I checked them. I know what I saw. Honest. I'd never have left them if they weren't already dead." He covered his face with clenched fists, his voice filled with self-loathing. "But I did."

She sat at the edge of his bed. He was remembering. Still full of anesthetic and of all things, reliving what had happened years ago. It had to stop. He needed to heal first. Remember later. Even her. She could wait.

"Let's get you settled." She tucked the blanket around his feet and legs.

"You sure I don't know you from somewhere, darlin'?" he asked tiredly. "I might forget a lot of things, but I'd never forget a pretty filly like you."

The resurgence of his drawl didn't bring the relief she expected. Instead, it reminded her of the pain still ahead for this sweet man. Harley'd left his home in upstate New York after his parents forbade him to enlist in the Army out of high school. After they kicked him out, he earned his drawl along with his cowboy boots at Fort Hood, Texas. With his parents' unyielding decision, he'd changed from a naive city boy into a man who thought he had to save the world.

"You know what?" she asked as brightly as she could. "May I give you a back rub? It might help you relax."

"Sure. Why not?" He rolled to his side.

Judy lowered the railing to reach him easier and offered him an extra pillow to support his bandaged chest. "Does this position bother your knife wound?"

"My what?" He peered over his shoulder at her, his hand on his sternum. "That why I got this hard bandage on my chest?"

"You were stabbed. How about your leg? Any pain or discomfort there?"

"Nah. Go on. Work your magic." He collapsed face first into the pillow.

She untied the back of his hospital gown, keeping everything below his waist covered. "Close your eyes. Think of your favorite place. Pretend you're there and relax."

"Got it. I'm on a beach. Go figure."

She gulped. Could that beach be the same one on the Florida Keys where they'd spent two weeks falling more in love? She hoped. The memory still warmed her. Maybe it would do the same for him.

Gently, Judy applied her skill as a masseuse to the knotted muscles of her battle-scarred patient. Over his shoulder blades and down his spine she kneaded until some of his stress let go. When he rolled his shoulder, she applied another round of tender massage to the scalene muscles of his neck. He might not remember her, but she knew him. Harley carried his worries in the taut muscles melting beneath her fingertips. When he groaned, she knew she'd achieved her goal.

"How does that feel? Any better?"

He didn't answer. Judy peered over his shoulder. She'd accomplished her goal all right. Harley was fast asleep, his face scrunched into the pillow like a little boy. She covered him with a heated blanket and dimmed the lights. Remember or not, he was hers. For now.

Eighteen

Harley had no more than fallen asleep when Raj returned, a scowl on his face.

"Thanks for sending Mark and Libby," Judy said before he could spill the bad news she could read in his eyes. "Mark was exactly who Harley needed."

Raj shrugged. "No big deal. I figured he'd relate better to another military guy."

"They're back again, aren't they? The FBI, I mean."

"They never left." Raj looked over his shoulder at the porthole window in the door. "You need to know. Mr. Johnston's involved now."

Judy cringed. Mr. Johnston, the hospital administrator, was all about following correct protocol, something she hadn't adhered to since she'd shown up last night. It was early Sunday morning. Careers were now at risk.

"I can't let the FBI take him, Raj. They'll treat him like a criminal. I won't be able to get near him. What can I do?"

Raj deliberated for all of one second. "Where's that gentleman you came in with last night?"

"Good idea. See if Alex is still in the hospital. Hurry. Tell him I need him." Her heart thudded. She never thought she'd live to see the day she'd need Alex Stewart again.

But she was too late. As Raj opened the door to leave, there stood an unhappy hospital administrator with FBI Agent

Holman at his heels. "Miss O'Brien," Mr. Johnston said sternly. "Is what I'm hearing true? Is your friend the sniper who's been terrorizing D.C.? And you've been hiding him in my hospital?"

"No. They're wrong. It's a lie."

Agent Holman huffed as he angled through the doorway to stand one step ahead of Mr. Johnston. "Not according to the warrant a federal judge signed in the middle of the night. He's ours. Take a step back and think about what you're doing, Miss O'Brien."

She blinked at that thinly veiled threat. What exactly was she doing besides protecting a defenseless victim from a bully? Judy moved between Harley's bed and Agent Holman. "He's not going anywhere."

"Now Nurse O'Brien." Mr. Johnston's normally strong voice turned thin and appeasing. He meant to give Harley up. She could hear it in his voice.

"No," she barked. "He's sick. He stays."

Agent Holman's right cheek hooked into a patronizing smirk. His eyes narrowed. "You think you and your friends are big enough to take on the FBI, do you?"

Judy turned to Mr. Johnston. "Sir. Please. You know Harley and me. I've called his neurologist and VA counselor. I'd recommend we wait until—"

"Not going to happen." Agent Holman already had a pair of handcuffs opened in his hand. "You might have friends in high places, Miss O'Brien, but this cold-blooded murderer does not. No one can help him now."

"Mr. Mortimer does require a specific regimen," Mr. Johnston offered.

"And I care about that why?" Holman stepped around Judy and snapped the cuffs onto one of Harley's wrists, the other end onto the bedrail. "Plenty of boys like him come back from the war whining and crying. Bunch of cowards if you ask me. We know how to take care of him."

"Sir, you really cannot cuff a patient like that," Mr. Johnston advised with absolutely no conviction in his voice. "It's against the law."

Agent Holman stared the man down. "I'm a federal agent. This man is a terrorist. I'll do whatever I need to protect my country."

Judy's knees about buckled. Holman was taking Harley. She gulped. Mr. Johnston would not defend her position. More than ever, she needed Alex.

"We'll see about that." She gathered what was left of her ragged courage. Now was not the time to make a scene, but she knew someone strong enough to do just that. With her heart pounding, she left Harley in the hands of the same monster who had berated her less than twelve hours earlier.

Panic clawed up her throat. It was all she could do to not fall against the wall outside the recovery room door. A scuffle sounded from inside. A tray fell. Mr. Johnston's was quickly lost in Harley's angry roar of, "Where's my men? Damn you! Get this thing off my damned—"

Silence. She trembled. Her nightmare had started all over again.

"Judy!"

She jerked around to see Alex running toward her. Two other men followed closely behind. Of all things, Alex was dressed in exercise pants and a sweatshirt. "Are we too late?"

She burst into tears. "They've got him, Alex. He's cuffed. They won't let me—"

"Like hell they won't." His hand gripped her elbow and he spun her around.

Glancing over her shoulder, Judy caught the tender smile of Jed McCormack. "Didn't I tell you to call me the next time you needed something, young lady?"

She nodded mutely as the man in the business suit with Jed stepped forward. He offered her one quick nod before he put his palm to the door. "This won't take long."

Alex pulled her into his side. "Calm down. They aren't taking Harley anywhere. You'll see."

"But, Alex..." She bit her lip, wanting to believe, but her heart couldn't take much more. She'd seen the cuffs. Holman didn't care one iota about rules or the law.

The hospital administrator exited the recovery room. A sheepish Mr. Johnston looked at Judy and then her benefactor in surprise. "Jed. Why are you here?" His gaze darted to the door he'd just closed. "Is it for—?"

"Just helping out a good friend of the family," Jed replied as calmly as if arriving in the nick of time was no big deal. "Judy and Harley are two of the best. He's a hero like my boy, but I'm sure you already know that."

Mr. Johnston seemed at a loss for words. When he walked away, Judy leaned into Alex, thankful for the man she'd once considered an interference in her life. His hand tightened around her waist. A sob crept up from her chest. She tried to control it, but a tremor escaped anyway.

"Wait for it," Alex whispered in her ear. "It isn't everyday the National Director of the Federal Bureau of Investigation pays a house call."

"The National Director?"

"Andrew Strong in person." Jed winked at her. "It seems two enterprising private contractors filed their first official report in the wee small hours this morning. I don't think he was even out of bed before they gave him their intelligence brief."

"Roy and Connor?"

Jed nodded. "Once he'd seen their evidence, Andy called me to arrange this meeting. Seems Alex's agents could prove your young man's whereabouts from the minute he left home yesterday morning until he was found last night."

"I told them it couldn't be him." Judy wiped her face, finally feeling a measure of relief. She turned to Alex with a lump in her throat again. "You knew this might happen, didn't you?"

"Actually," he said somberly, "I was out looking for my wife when Jed called. Roy and Connor acted without my knowledge."

Judy lost it. Here he was helping her again. He'd devoted men, his dogs, and all his resources to locate Harley, but there was nothing she could do to help him. Sorry did not cover the hurt in her heart for this suffering man. "Thank you," she whispered.

It took less than a minute before a very subdued Agent Holman accompanied his boss out of the recovery room. He did not look at Judy when he walked past, at least not that she could tell through his dark glasses and with his head down.

The Director took over. "On behalf of the Bureau, I personally apologize for the way this affair has been handled. No charges will be filed against Mr. Mortimer. You will see a formal retraction in the press."

"Thank you," Alex replied calmly. "May I ask what instigated this course of action to begin with?"

Director Strong sighed. "As you know, Mr. Stewart, we in the Bureau are trained to lean forward, to be ever vigilant and ready to intercept our nation's enemies at all times. Let's just say someone leaned a little too far forward, shall we?"

He nodded toward Judy. "Miss O'Brien, I owe you an apology, as well. You should not have been detained or questioned without probable cause yesterday. Your belongings will be delivered back to your custody as soon as it's convenient for you and Mr. Mortimer. Good day."

Without another word, he turned and strode down the hall where Agent Holman stood cooling his heels.

"Boss is sure pleased with us." Roy hung up his cell phone after speaking with Alex.

Sunday morning found him and Connor parked in their van east of the Mall on Independence Avenue, their focus spread between the Capitol and the Senate office buildings. Security footage and traffic cameras had yielded more shots of the mystery food truck, most recently outside the Dirksen/Hart Senate building; an odd happenstance for what most people and especially Congressmen, considered a day of rest.

The way Roy had it figured, the sniper was prowling, maybe scoping out his next target. Or maybe, the target was already marked and just didn't know it. They'd checked the last reported sighting, but came up with nothing. For now, it was a game of wait and see.

Most private contractors in the covert surveillance business would have been challenged and rousted by FBI or Metro PD. Since 9-11, federal law had drawn a strict zero tolerance line in the sand. Any infraction in the vicinity of federal property could and would bring repercussions from any number of federal bad boys, including the Secret Service's very capable and accurate sharpshooters. Three assassinations had only made the Feds more intense. But for the grace of the FBI contract, Roy and Connor would have been targets too.

"He should be pleased," Connor answered, his nose planted in the bank of monitors.

"Director Strong didn't look none too happy though. Guess he's not a morning person."

"Nope," Connor answered automatically, his mind not on the conversation like Roy would have preferred.

He had to admit, not only was the young man a good operator, but he'd made Alex and The TEAM look good. The kid should have been a politician. He'd compiled a Situation Report, a sitrep, for the FBI Director that hit all the high notes, including a detailed description of the fast food truck, precise ballistics, and the standing theory on how the sniper might have been able to take those three fatal shots.

He'd then supported every argument with surveillance photos and offered Roy's expert opinion as to the sniper's profile: most likely an older man, ex-military, and trained by the very government he'd now declared war on. If that wasn't enough, Connor had craftily inserted rock solid evidence of Harley's whereabouts during each assassination, again with enough pictures to reject Agent Holman's claim of Harley as sniper and Judy as accomplice.

"Still can't figure what evidence the FBI thought they had on Harley though."

"Ah huh." Connor supplied another half-interested response, only this one made no sense.

Roy jumped off his chair to double-check the monitors. "What are you looking at?"

Connor's focus never strayed from the monitor he had his nose against, but his tapping foot betrayed his nervous energy. "I'm working."

"A girl? I should have known."

Their rooftop scope had caught live action crossing the street. Connor's target was the sweet young thing dressed in extra long legs and strappy red heels that matched her short skirt and revealing sweater top. Long black hair swung cheerfully behind as she bounced along the crosswalk, her movement full of grace, vitality, and good old-fashioned sex appeal.

"You, junior agent, are a horn dog. She's a cutie, but a mite young for my taste."

Connor spun around on his chair to face Roy. "You want me to grab us some coffee?"

"Hell no." Roy grinned. "All you want is an excuse to get into that little gal's trajectory. I know how you young guys think, and it ain't with your brains. 'Sides, you'd probably forget the coffee once you caught up with her and I'd still be thirsty."

"Seriously? You think I'd forget an old man's coffee?" Connor's eyes were teasing, mischievous, and their normal lady-killer blue this morning. A look shifted across his face that made Roy think the kid might beg. Roy swiveled the scope back to the work at hand. "Focus."

"Just because you're way past your prime, doesn't mean I am" Connor let out a low whistle. "Damn. I see you, oh yes, honey, I do see you." His foot tapped like an old coonhound with an itch.

"You're incorrigible." Roy didn't ask again. By the time he'd checked several other feeds, Connor was back on task, more or less, and another long day of covert surveillance had begun.

But Roy lived to tease. "I'll make the coffee run. You want anything?" he asked as he stepped to van door.

It worked. "Oh sure, I see how it works. I'm stuck in here with a... with a..."

"Stop feeling sorry for yourself. You want coffee or not?" Roy couldn't help but grin. The girl-hungry kid was an easy mark.

"Ah, Roy."

"Come on. I'll get her number if I run into her. You want a muffin too?"

"I'm serious. You've got to see this. I think our mystery truck just parked down the street." Connor scooted out of his chair so Roy could verify.

"Who drove it in?"

"That's the thing. I don't see anyone. Looks like the truck drove itself. The front seat is vacant and the windows are darkened. I don't see anyone, do you?"

Roy checked another angle of the same shot. "Sure not. Looks like an open cab. There's a curtain behind the driver's seat. I can see that much."

"You think someone drove it here by remote control? Never thought of that. Crap. Our sniper friend could be running his entire operation by robotics."

"This ain't Hollywood. There's a flesh and blood man in the rig. We're just not seeing him yet."

"You do know robotics are not science fiction, don't you?" Connor insisted. "Look at the drones coming out of McCormack Industries. In ten years they'll replace boots on the ground."

"Not going to happen. Keep an eye on the truck. Anybody takes a step out of it, and they're ours. I'll advise our friends at the Bureau."

Nineteen

Harley woke to the cheerless face of a strange man sitting in the corner of his room. He looked familiar, but Harley couldn't be sure. His brain had told him wrong too many times lately. Between body parts and shopping carts, he wasn't sure what was real and what was illusion. Minutes ticked by.

Harley ventured a guess. "You in the wrong room?"

The man looked up, startled and kind of sad. "How you doing, son?"

Great. This guy's my father? The man had tired blue eyes, but he didn't seem old enough. *No way. He can't be my old man.*

Dressed in running pants and a gray sweatshirt with bright gold USMC screaming across his chest, he looked kinda like he might be a friend. Maybe. Harley would have known for sure if that sweatshirt was olive drab and screamed ARMY like a truly decent shirt should.

"I'm good," Harley answered because that's what soldiers tell each other. They could be half-dead, shot to hell, missing limbs and an eyeball, but still insist they were good.

"Thought I'd see how you're doing now that you're no longer FBI property," the man said quietly. "I told Judy I'd sit with you while she ran home to get her massage table. We've been worried."

"Judy?" Harley asked as he pulled himself into a better sitting position. "Oh yeah. The nurse."

The guy sounded familiar. Maybe he knew him. Heck, maybe this guy could explain how he'd gotten the welts around his wrists. He held up one hand intending to ask, but the man beat him to it. "The FBI cuffed you. I guess you didn't much appreciate it."

FBI? Cuffed? The memory eluded him like so many others.

"They were out of line. They should have never done that."

"Am I a prisoner or something?"

"No. They're just jackasses."

"I know you?" he asked as politely as possible. No sense in offending the first person he ran into in, umm, wherever he was.

The man rose to his feet. Harley jumped, startled at the man's sudden movement. Anxiety roared to a fever pitch. In one split second, fight or flight stomped the living crap out of him all over again. Harley reached for the rifle even though he knew it was not alongside his leg anymore. His lungs clamped shut. He couldn't breathe.

"It's okay," the man soothed like he needed to calm a skittish dog. Oddly, it worked. The tone in his voice melted a lot of Harley's unfounded nervousness. The guy pulled his chair next to the bed where he sat again. "Take it easy. Just thought we could talk until Judy gets back. That's all. Do you remember me?"

"Nope." That was one thing Harley was sure of. He didn't know shit.

"Did Mark stop by last night?"

Harley started to shake his head, but he did recall a dark-haired guy with a little blond sticking close to his side. They were both extra kind, and…. Oh yeah. Mark and Libby. They had a new baby. JayJay. They were his friends. Good to know.

"He was here. Why'd you want to know? You looking for him?"

The man with blue eyes relaxed. "No, but I hoped you'd remember me too. I'm Alex."

Harley stared, his mental fingertips whirling over the damaged Rolodex in his head. *Alex. Alex. Nope. Not coming up with anyone named Alex.* His feet started tapping a fast beat against the sheets as anxiety ramped up again. This guy was making him nervous.

"You remember Whisper and Smoke?"

Again with the frantic mind search. No guys named Whisper or Smoke bubbled up. Tension slithered over the back of his skull. His hair prickled. *Do I know anything?*

"No problem. Whisper is my black Shepherd." Alex kept talking softly. "Thought you might remember him. He thinks you and Kelsey walk on water."

Kelsey? Harley blinked. Okay, that name sounded familiar. *Kelsey, huh?* A lightning storm flashed in his broken brain. *Not Kelsey, but Kelsey Girl. Yeah. That was her name and she… And she…*

"I think I might know her. Sexy brunette? Long legs? Small boobs?"

A soft smile crinkled the corners of Alex's eyes. "She's my wife."

Shit! Harley coughed because he wanted to die. *Mortimer, you dumb ass. First time you open your mouth, you stick your whole damned leg in.*

"S-s-sorry." Embarrassment flamed up his neck and the walls closed in. "Didn't mean to—"

"Forget it. She wouldn't mind."

Smart or not, Harley caught the drift in the sad words. Something had happened to Kelsey.

"She okay?"

"I hope so," Alex whispered.

His lack of detailed information created another wave of nerves. The man needed to leave. Harley feared the answer to his next question because he knew so little. What had he done? What hadn't he done? He asked it anyway. "Did I... hurt her?"

"You'd never hurt Kelsey, son." Alex shook his head and there was that word again. *Son.* It spoke of a link, but it soothed as much as it aggravated.

"You love Kelsey, and she loves you."

That didn't help. *I love his wife? She loves me? He doesn't have a problem with that?* Somehow, Harley could not believe he was that kind of dumb. The weight of the world sat square in his chest, and he could not catch enough air. Nothing made sense. This Alex dude didn't look like the kind of guy who'd allow another dude cheating with his wife.

"You saved her life a couple years back. You rescued her." Alex kept making it worse.

Harley squeezed his eyes shut, wishing it were easier to think. Still.... Rescuing a man's wife seemed like a good thing, a lot better than cheating. *Kelsey Girl. Help me out here. Send me a sign.*

The image of a black German Shepherd filtered up through the spinning Rolodex. The goofy dog growled like he thought he could talk. Droopy ear. Shiny, black licorice lips.

He'd found something. Someone. Another flash hit Harley's memory board, lighting it up with information.

Harley gasped. Suffocation escalated into hyperventilation. An image of a gentle woman tied to a tree, her hair chopped off and her face bloody. Kelsey. Whisper kept licking her; she kept crying. He climbed onto her lap, whining like he was telling Harley, *I found her. Stay back. She's mine.*

Another man's face, a man with greasy blond hair and a rifle, penetrated the fog. He fell to his knees with Harley's bullet in his skull. Anxiety fled.

"I killed her ex," he declared firmly. Proudly too. Air filled his lungs. *Now I remember. Hell, yeah, I'd send Nick Durrant to hell every chance I got.*

A spark of relief lit Alex's tired eyes. "Yes, and I'm grateful every day you did."

Harley straightened in his bed and sucked in a deep breath. *Okay. Alex can stay. We're solid. We're good.* "I get the feeling you're my boss?"

"I'd like to think I'm more than that."

Harley found himself pulled into a bear hug. Alex was right. The embrace felt bigger, like Harley had hit shore, like Alex was anchor and compass all rolled into one. Maybe more.

"You run yourself down all the time, but you are no idiot, Harley. You're a damned sharp man and a professional sniper. You've made this world a better place. Give yourself some credit. I'm lucky you work for me and not some other security company. Hell. We all are."

Whoa. That came out of the blue, but it helped.

"So tell me about Rick Cross, Snakes Flynn, and Kent Roosevelt."

Shit! The universe shifted in a hard about-face turn. Harley choked. One minute hero, the next—what? Bastard? Coward? Shame crept up the back of his throat. Alex leaned away, but the lightning rod of his arm and hand remained solidly connected. "It's time to remember, son. Trust me. I've been through it too. I'm right here."

Thousands of memories downloaded spontaneously.

BLAM! Playing poker at Camp Wolfe in Kuwait with the guys. Hot stretches of desert. The most ungodly dust storms that swallowed the whole sky. Brown-eyed children. Unbearable tension. Every-damn-where.

OOMPH! Direct hit. Mongrel dogs he wasn't supposed to touch much less sneak food to. Relentless Scud attacks. Night skies full of the wrong kinds of light and thunder. Ancient men with leathery faces and deep-set eyes. The smell of sewer and death. Always death....

INCOMING! Humvees. MRAPs. IEDs. IEDs. The download seemed stuck in a loop. IED. IED. One particular IED.... That IED. That one particular sonofabitchin IED.

He gulped, his fingers automatically searching the back of his head for a handful of blood. Sure enough, only the one he'd expected to find was different. Bigger. Bloodier.

"Where's my men? You know don't you?"

"You tell me." It wasn't what Alex said or how he said it, but something about those words felt like a winding circular staircase that morphed into an endless chute with a killer drop-off at the end of the ride. Terror ratcheted up Harley's throat, stealing breath with every tightening crank until it hurt to inhale.

"Rick." He was barely able to spit the name of his buddy out of his dry mouth. He tried again, his heart ready to explode. "Rick Cross. Where is he?"

Darkness pushed the peace away. Harley wanted Alex to leave and never come back, but he couldn't let go of the man's arm. He was drowning in desert sand, and Alex was the only life vest in sight. He gripped his boss's shoulder. "Don't lose me."

"Never." Alex pulled Harley into a solid wall of brotherhood that knew the cost of a man's heart in war.

Harley sucked in a deep breath through his nostrils, snuffing back the wave of terror building up in his head. The words fell out of his mouth, the sorriest words he'd ever known, like bells tolling. Funeral bells. "My men! My men! My men!"

The curtain of smoke parted, and Harley saw them clearly. Corporal Rick Cross, best damned liar in the 4th Infantry. Man, the guy could spin a yarn that would make the truth look bad. A guy never knew when Rick was being straight or lying through his teeth, but the stories he could tell. The jokes. The concussion from the IED threw him off the side of the Humvee where shrapnel laid him low. So much blood. Shoulda never gone to war. Shoulda been a stand-up comedian. Shoulda lived....

Harley gripped Alex harder, his breath coming in short, tight huffs, and Alex hanging on with a death grip. Sergeant Kent Roosevelt's grinning face showed next, truly a brother from another mother. Black as the deepest south, Kent was deeply Baptist and profoundly religious. Said that's why he'd joined the Army, to be all he could be cuz his mama would whup his butt if he didn't make something more out of himself than a fry cook at the local barbecue hut.

Of course she cried her eyes out the day he enlisted, but he was the closest thing to a brother Harley'd ever known. An only child straight out of New York couldn't ask for better family than the 4th. Or a better brother than Kent.

The flood of memories continued. Captain Percy Flynn who insisted everyone call him Snakes or risk a verbal slap down. His baby brother had recently joined up. About time. Snakes was proud. Got all misty-eyed and everything.

Carlton Jenner, proud new daddy who'd show anyone who would listen, and even some who wouldn't, the latest picture from home of his brand new baby girl. She had pink pajamas with little gray tabby kittens. And she'd never remember her Daddy cuz she never got the chance to meet him, not even once.

Harley choked. He wanted to meet that baby girl, to hold her and tell her what kind of man her daddy was. He wanted to smell her hair and hug her little baby-powdered body, maybe pour some of her father's love for his country into her.

By the time the show ended, Harley was limp and convinced. Death alongside them would've been noble. Living without them sure wasn't. "I killed 'em."

"No, you didn't. War killed them. You were just there when it happened." Alex clamped onto Harley's hand, one of those extra strong and mean clamps that would still be holding a two-by-four joist together long after the tornado blew the house away.

"But I left them."

"So? You damned near got your head blown off. What else could you have done?"

"They're gone, and I'm... Not." He cringed at the pathetic sound of those words in his ears.

"No." Alex bumped the right side of Harley's chest very gently. "They're not gone. They're right. Everyday. Don't ever forget them. Honor them. Let them be the heroes they are. They gave you a gift. Not a curse."

Goosebumps swept over and through Harley. He could breathe. Sucking in a deep lungful of air, he blew it out slowly. And then another. The knot in the back of his neck diminished. The black feeling faded. *Okay. Alex can stay.*

"Besides." Alex leaned in so close Harley wasn't sure if he was going to kiss him or bite him. "You needed to survive that day so you could keep Durrant from killing my Kelsey. That's another mission you ran head first into. No one could have done it but you. Only you."

Harley nodded. That helped. He lifted his head high again. He wasn't a waste of skin. "Thanks," he croaked, his throat nearly too dry to speak.

Alex released him. "No. Thank you."

"It's getting dark again."

The afternoon sun began its lazy descent toward the western horizon. Of course, Raymond noticed. He resembled a grumpy child who needed a long nap and maybe a time-out. Spending the night with a twenty-five-year old afraid of the dark wasn't her idea of fun either.

"It gets dark every day, doesn't it?"

"But I don't want to be out here in the dark again cuz there might be a skunk with some poisonous gas, and he might spray me, and that wouldn't make me very happy cuz then I wouldn't be very happy, and then I wouldn't smell so good neither, and everyone might call me stinky Fred." He sucked in a deep breath.

Kelsey had to smile. If nothing else, he could get a lot of words into one Raymond-sized sentence. "What would you like to do?"

"I wanna get out of these stupid trees. They is bugging me." To prove his point, he picked up his pace. His effort didn't last long. In minutes, Raymond was on the ground again.

Kelsey knelt beside him, holding his hand while he struggled for air. "Calm down. Take slow breaths. You'll be fine."

This breathing attack was the worst. It seemed harder for him to draw in sufficient air, as if his lungs were compromised along with his heart. Or maybe they weren't as big as the rest of him. Maybe they didn't develop enough at birth to support the giant he'd become. Whatever. She was more worried for him than spending another night in the woods.

She breathed slow and steady so he'd follow her example. He leaned back, drumming his fingers anxiously on his chest.

"Don't get excited." Kelsey peered into his face. His eyelids fluttered before they closed again. She panicked. This was not how his story was going to end, not after all they'd been through.

"Wake up." She patted his cheek harder when he gave no response. Her hand snaked out in fear. She struck him once, twice, and a third time. His head barely moved from the impact. Terror seized command. With one knee in his chest, Kelsey hit him again, tears blurring her vision. "Don't you die. We made a deal."

One big hand clutched her wrist before she could make contact again. "Stop it. Why is you hitting me?"

She flung her arms around his neck and burst into tears. The stress of the last two days sneaked up on her. "I'm so sorry. You stopped breathing. You scared me. Don't you ever do that again."

When she pulled back, he put one big finger under her eye and wiped the tears away. "You didn't hit me very hard, cuz you is not big enough to hurt me cuz I'm a big guy. It didn't even hurt. Please don't cry."

Wiping her face with the heel of her hand, she blew out a deep sigh to steady her frazzled nerves. "Stay here and rest. I'll collect firewood."

"But I don't wanna sleep in the woods again."

"Me either." What she wouldn't give for a hot bath. Their food and water were nearly gone. The prospect of surviving seemed awful darned bleak. Kelsey leaned to her back on the ground alongside her sad friend. The firewood could wait.

"I wanna hamburger," he wailed. "And I want fries. A extra big bag. And hot. And lots of 'em."

It was easier not to argue. He was hungry, and the whole world knew hungry boys were grumpy boys. Now was not the time to argue with a five-year-old having a temper tantrum. Raymond would have to come to his own decision about all those big demands he had.

"The first thing I'm going to do when I get home is take a hot bath," she offered quietly. "Then I'll fix you the biggest hamburger you've ever seen, and maybe a chocolate cake. Alex will make you a platter of fries so big you can swim in them."

When no response came from her camping buddy, she risked a sideways glance. Big tears streaked down the side of his head. His bottom lip stuck out so far an eagle could have perched on it. Her heart fell. Poor Raymond. The innocence radiating from him overwhelmed her. He rubbed the tears away with one swipe of his hand, still staring overhead and blinking.

"I'd be lost without you," she added quietly.

She felt it then, the tear-dampened hand searching across the grassy earth between them. When he found what he was looking for, he plopped his palm over the back of hers and there they lay. His attack was over.

"The sky is blue," he stated simply, patting her hand and snuffling. "The trees are big, and you is my bestest friend in the whole world."

Another thump of his hand on hers and Kelsey blinked a tear away. Some people might view him as an idiot, but Raymond had just summarized what was essential in life, and he'd done it very well. Poor Raymond. How many times had this extra big little boy cried himself to sleep because no one cared if he lived or died?

"Only very strong men are brave when they're scared," she said. "That's what makes them heroes. They do what's right no matter how scared they are. You are my hero, Raymond."

"I is?"

Kelsey sighed. Her head hurt and she was tired, but her heart swelled with gratitude for the simple man at her side. "All we can do is stick together. I'll take care of you, and you take care of me."

"I is gonna take good care of you."

"I know," she whispered, no doubt in her mind.

It took a little longer, but eventually she settled him down for the night and built another campfire. They ate a meager dinner and drank the last of their water. High in the dark branches overhead, an owl hooted. Feathered wings whispered as the predator floated on its nightly hunt. Something made a short squeak, probably a meal for owlets in some far off hollowed-out tree. Kelsey shivered in the evening chill. Mother Nature had a mean streak.

"You got sparks in your eyes," Raymond said quietly.

She turned to look at him, unaware he'd been watching. "Sparks?"

He scooted into a more upright position. "Ah huh, kinda like the fire is in 'em, and the air smells really good. I like it a lot."

"Are you cold?" She moved closer to his side, her palms testing the temperature of the sleeping bag. One shooting spark could spoil everything.

"Nope. I not cold. I Raymond," he said slyly.

She had to look twice. He'd just cracked a joke.

"What you'd really like is a cheeseburger though, huh?" she teased back.

"Yeah."

A sound caught her attention, footsteps along the path between her and the paved road. Her heart kicked in. The forest hushed. She pushed to her feet, her fingers around the spear. A fist-sized stone filled her other hand. The bolo dangled from that same wrist. It wasn't much, but who knew? Luck might be on her side tonight.

She cocked her arm and swallowed hard, her body trembling with what was to come. Raymond looked up at her, but there was no time to offer solace.

God, help me kill her. Kelsey cringed, ashamed she had prayed for another's death, even one so wicked as Ethel Durrant.

Two men stepped out of the dark.

"Whoa. Hold on. Put that thing down." One of them had his palms forward in submission. "You wouldn't happen to be Kelsey Stewart, would you?"

Twenty

"Roy. Connor. Do you copy?" Murphy's voice sounded clear as a bell in their earpieces.

"What's up?" Roy answered.

Night was falling. Shadows stretched across Capital Hill. He and Connor were out walking, mostly to squelch Connor's agitation with the Bureau. In true bureaucratic fashion, they'd officially taken over surveillance of the fast food truck. To prove their superiority over their hired help, they'd gone directly to Murphy to make sure Roy and Connor heard it through their chain of command. Hands off.

Connor was ticked to the bone, but Roy shrugged it off as the usual, petty nonsense. He didn't care who took down the sniper as long as someone did. They'd still fulfill the terms of their contract though, watching the crowd of tourists for anything suspicious, and taking pictures as they walked. For now, Connor stood on Pennsylvania Avenue, east of the Peace Monument, while Roy stood at the opposite end at Maryland Avenue, east of the James Garfield Monument.

"Looks like we got another local hero," Murphy said. "Senator Hyde will address the nation at five o'clock this afternoon from the Senate Building. He's another one against funding DoD. Thought you should know since you're closest to his location."

"Don't these guys get it?" Roy exclaimed in disgust. "They need to keep their big mouths shut until we catch the guy."

"Know what you mean. The FBI tried to shut the press conference down but Hyde is one determined guy. You want to talk with Alex? He might be in shortly."

"Sure don't." Roy couldn't resist the opportunity to torment Connor. "Not if he's still singing the praises of some new junior agent. The kid's already got a fathead, can barely squeeze through the van door as it is."

"I heard that." Connor's cool, calm voice replied.

"Where's Alex?" Roy asked.

"Back at the hospital," Murphy answered. "I think he was out looking for Kelsey earlier."

"Any more news?"

"Not since the photos yesterday."

"We need to finish this op," Connor said. "We should be helping our boss, not the FBI."

"I'm all for it," Murphy said.

"How's the facial rec program going?" Connor asked. "Any solid leads?"

Roy smiled. The kid had proved his worth in aces, no doubt about it. He'd come up with the idea to run all their surveillance photos through Ember's program. As fast as Ember downloaded the images they'd acquired, her program bumped every face in them against federal, state, and local records. Plenty of interesting data on people with a multitude of misdemeanors and petty charges popped to the surface, but none who fit the sniper profile close enough for a second look. Not yet anyway.

"Why? You got more pictures?"

"In fact I do," Connor answered. "Tell her I'm emailing another batch right now. It's a big file. Hope my phone can handle sending it."

Roy listened as Murphy relayed the message. What kids could do with their cell phones these days. "Hey, Murph. You guys work all night again?"

"Until we find Kelsey," Murphy replied. "David staked out Alex's home last night, but whoever brought the pictures did not show again."

"So aside from yesterday's three photos, we've got nothing," Connor stated the obvious.

That finished the conversation.

"Talk to you guys later."

"Copy that," Roy replied.

"Senator Hyde should be safe if he stays in his office, shouldn't he?" Connor asked.

"One would think so." Roy scanned the multitude of tourists west of the Capitol. Sniper or not, Americans seemed willing to take their chances. "But I doubt that's where he'll hold a press conference. He'll be in the rotunda. It's all about face time. The more reporters, the merrier."

"You want to know what the words on this monument say?" Connor asked quietly.

"Sure. What's it say?"

"Well, first of all, it's the Peace Monument. It commemorates the men who were lost at sea during the Civil War. You knew that, didn't you?"

"I didn't, but that's cool." Roy faced north, watching his junior agent gaze up at the stone monument nearly the length of the Capitol building away. That alone was quite a picture, a blond-haired young man with his face tilted upward in reverence.

"It's two women. One symbolizes Grief; the other's History. Anyway, Grief is crying on History's shoulder. It's really something."

"So what's it say?" Roy had seen a lot of monuments the last two days. They all said something great.

"It reminds me of two mothers who just got notification their boys were killed in action." Connor coughed, his fist lifted to his lips. "It says, *They died that their country might live.*"

Roy knew all about those seven eloquent words. This particular monument must remind Connor of his mother, Bridgette, a widow who'd raised seven sons and now faced the reality of them all following in Connor's footsteps. The Corps was a noble profession, but a heartbreaker for most moms. Out of those seven sons, four were already jarheads. She'd lose the others as soon as they graduated from high school. Bridgette should be proud, but the patriotism she'd instilled in her young men came at a high price. That was another reason Roy liked this junior agent. Connor loved his mom.

"This op getting to you, kid?" he asked softly.

Connor cleared his throat and shook his head, but Roy caught the quick swipe across his eyes. "Nah. It's just a cool statue. Made me think. So many good men and women have died so people like Hyde can practice free speech and shoot their mouths off."

"Stop thinking. It's getting late. Let's get back to the van."

Roy waited for his partner to cross the distance. The kid might be girl crazy, but he was one of the few and the proud. Men didn't come much better.

"Let's grab a sandwich," he suggested when their van came into view. "No sense everyone staring at the truck. It isn't going anywhere."

"Oh no?" Connor pointed at the vehicle in question. "Look. Is it… smoking?"

Roy followed Connor's direction. Sure enough, a misty vapor wafted out of the cab window. "Was the front window opened before?"

Conner unholstered his pistol. "Don't know, but something ain't right. You coming?"

Roy contacted Mother to advise they were both moving to investigate. A black FBI sedan rolled by as Connor stepped off the curb.

"What's up?" Roy asked the agents, nodding toward the target.

"Not sure," the agent in the passenger seat said. "Stand back though. No sense all of us sticking our necks out."

"It's not smoke," Connor advised. "Looks different. Be careful."

"You've got that right." The agent chuckled. "We'll let you know how it goes."

"Might be a job for hazmat," Roy warned. "Maybe you guys ought to hang back. Let's call for backup."

"The Bureau isn't afraid." Their car rolled forward.

"Can't say you didn't warn them." Connor crossed the street following the sedan.

"They think they're so smart, let them handle it," Roy said. "Do not approach."

"Don't plan to," Connor assured him, speaking through his earpiece now. "But I can see the customer window better from this side. No canvas tarp today."

"Copy that."

"Are we sure it's the same truck?" Connor asked as the FBI agents parked their sedan in front of the vehicle in question as if they intended to block its getaway.

Roy grimaced. If the fumes coming from the truck window were toxic, the FBI was about to lose two men. "Dumb asses."

"You talking to me?" Connor stood a safe distance from the scene while both FBI agents approached the vehicle, their guns drawn, their intent obvious.

"Only if you're dumb as they are. Hang back. If they want to be first on the scene, let 'em." Roy was halfway across the street when he stopped to watch. Both FBI agents were on Connor's side of the truck, their weapons drawn. One rapped against the closed window. The other assumed firing position, his left foot forward, his weapon cupped and pointed at the cab.

"You ought to see this," Connor said quietly. "The truck is parked directly over a—"

WHOOSH!

A tremendous shockwave knocked Roy to his knees. Smoke poured from the vehicle, now a white-hot carcass with burning truck parts plummeting back to earth. He brushed the stinging smoke out of his eyes.

"Connor?" Roy scrambled to his feet. The steady ringing in his ears made his earpiece useless. Another fireball belched out of the gaping hole that used to be the cab. Burning wreckage turned into spinning shrapnel. He ran across the street and into the frag zone. This was no ordinary fire. "Connor!"

He hit the curb, brushing ash out of his eyes. When the billowing smoke lifted, Roy saw him standing with his hands over his face and wreckage at his feet.

"Don't look at it!" Roy ran to his junior agent. The odor of burned flesh struck his nose. He knew without looking. The FBI agents were dead.

Connor faced him, his jaw working but no sound coming out, and Roy saw why. The kid's face was blistered and burned. Bloody tears tracked down both cheeks. He sank to his knees. "I'm hurt. I'm… I'm really hurt this time."

The surprise in his voice ripped Roy's heart. He grabbed the young man's elbow, forcing him to his feet and back to their van. Soldiers always sounded shocked when they got hit, like they thought it could never happen to them. Like they were invincible. Untouchable. They weren't. "That's a magnesium fire, kid. A big one. Keep your head down. Don't open your eyes."

Connor stopped dead in the street, the panic in his voice raw. "My eyes."

"I got that. They hurt like hell. Tried it once. I know what to do. Hang on." Roy circled Connor's shoulders with one arm, directing him to their van. Sirens screeched in transit. The heavy thunder of emergency vehicles vibrated underfoot, but Roy had one mission in mind. *Save this kid.*

"Sit," he commanded once inside.

Connor collapsing onto the nearest seat, shaking like a leaf.

Roy popped several bottles of water open and drenched Connor's face while he attempted to slow the burn. "Open your eyes, son." Roy poured another soothing stream over the young man's face. Facial burns were not the problem. Skin could be grafted. Eyeballs were a different story.

Connor's whole body went rigid with the effort. Blisters bubbled over the backs of his hands and neck. "Sweet Mary and Joseph. You're killing me."

"Got to. Sorry. I know it hurts." Roy glanced over his shoulder, hoping an available EMT would notice. The dead agents had no need of emergency aid, but Connor sure did.

"Stop helping me."

"No way. You're going to the hospital." Roy poured more water slowly over Connor's face and eyes. The poor kid was deep in the throes of an adrenaline rush, his body's flight or fight impulse rattling him off the chair. "Magnesium burns hot and fast, but I got to you in time. You'll be fine. Now lean back and let me work."

"I am. Honest, I'm trying to listen. Only I can't see and… Damn! Feels like red-hot sand in my eyeballs." He blinked through tears and water, shaking his head and struggling to obey. "I saw 'em, Roy. I saw 'em both. Those two guys. God, they burned alive."

Roy cast another desperate glance into the street. Everyone seemed occupied with the smoking corpses. "Hey! Get me some help over here!"

Mission accomplished. In minutes, Connor was on a gurney and inside an ambulance. Roy waited outside while the EMTs treated his eyes, face, and hands. He knew the second that pain relief hit Connor's system. Roy let out the breath he'd been holding. His kid was safe. Connor was going to make it.

"Are you hurt too, sir?" One of the EMTs clutched Roy's elbow, concern written on his face.

"No. I'm fine, just take good care of my boy."

The medic, another black man, shot Roy a tender look. "What'd you do? Adopt this pasty white kid?"

"Damn straight." Roy was proud enough to do just that. "He's all I've got." Connor wasn't all Roy had. Not really, but no father could stand to lose any kid under his command. Ever.

He climbed into the ambulance alongside his just adopted son, his composure plenty shaken. Connor had been stripped to his waist and an IV inserted into his forearm, but his boots kept bouncing. He gripped the rail of the gurney with gel-slathered hands.

"It will be a couple days before you're chasing short skirts again. You're lucky, son. Damned lucky."

"Those FBI guys weren't."

Roy looked back at the flaming debris that only minutes before had been their first viable lead. The explosion had thrown both FBI agents back twenty or so feet. They hadn't suffered; that much was good. He wiped his eyes. The damned smoke kept making him tear up.

"You saved my life."

"Shut up." Roy dropped to the street. "Enjoy the ride. I'll come visit as soon as I'm done here. Maybe you can go home tonight."

"Wait. I saw something." Connor's hand groped empty air as he reached toward Roy's voice.

"What?" Roy grabbed the younger man's ankle so Connor would know where he was.

"The truck's parked over a storm drain. That's how he's doing it. I was wrong. He's not shooting from the truck. It's a decoy. He used it to access the tunnels under the street. He could be anywhere in this whole city."

"There's going to be no living with you once Alex gets wind of this, is there?"

"Thanks for—"

"Forget it. Get out of here." Roy stepped away and let the medic shut the rear gate of the ambulance.

The ambulance had barely pulled away when he heard the 10-32 police code for a man with a gun issued over a nearby radio. "Shots fired," the dispatcher advised. "All units respond to Dirksen/ Hart Senate building. At last report, sniper is south of the complex. Be advised FBI is on scene."

His blood ran cold. Connor was right. The sniper had killed again.

Roy called Mother. "Connor's on his way to the ER. Send me another agent or two."

"Oh, no. What happened?"

Roy relayed how the explosion had killed two FBI agents and injured Connor. "I need you to cross-check the EOD sniper list against your facial rec program. You shouldn't get many matches, but you might get a few. Step on it. I'll be waiting."

"Will do. Sending Junior Agents Eric Reynolds and Morgan Humphries to you."

"Thanks." Roy ended the call, his sharp eyes sweeping the scene behind him. If Connor was correct, the sniper had utilized the tunnels D.C. was known for. Most were secure since 9-11, but obviously, some were not. The sniper had not taken his kill shots from the tunnels, but they were how he'd become invisible so quickly after the assassinations. Roy headed across the street to chat with the closest police office. Law enforcement needed a team underground right damned now.

That single thirty-aught-six shell nagged at the back of his mind. He wasn't the only one who had gotten a new hunting rifle all those years ago.

Twenty-One

"Yes, I'm Kelsey Stewart." Kelsey lowered her embarrassing excuse for a weapon. The rock in her hand fell to her feet along with the bolo, but she did not release the spear. Embarrassing or not, it was her best weapon.

"Glad to meet you, Mrs. Stewart." The older man extended a hand, a big smile on his face. "Jeff Watson, ma'am, and this here's my neighbor, Newton Bridges. We've been looking for you. Heck, every Search and Rescue team on the east coast is looking for you."

"I'm so happy to meet you. You just don't know." She shook their hands, resisting the urge to hug the stuffing out of these strangers. "Do you have a cell phone?" Excited relief wiggled up her spine. She'd be home tonight.

"Sorry, ma'am. Cell phone service doesn't reach this far, but I've got a CB back at the ATV. Come on. Let's get you out of here."

"Wait!" Jeff spread his arm wide as he positioned Kelsey behind him. The beam of his flashlight skated over poor Raymond's bewildered face. "There's something under that tree. Holy cow. What is it?"

"It's Raymond." She brushed past her rescuers to kneel at his side. "See these kind men? They're going to take us home."

"Is they nice?" he whispered, his eyes barely making direct contact with the men.

Kelsey didn't know who looked more frightened, them or him. "Yes, these are very good men, Raymond, and they are going to help us. Aren't you?" she asked pointedly since neither of them had spoken the right words yet to lessen Raymond's fear.

Newton nodded, but his eyes were as wide as Raymond's. "Sure, but what's wrong with him?"

"His name is Raymond." She repeated, needing to be sure these guys understood he was not dangerous. "You ought to be worried about Ethel Durrant, not him. She's the one who kidnapped me."

"Who?" Newton asked.

Kelsey spelled it out. "Ethel Durrant. She's tried to kill me once before."

"She mean," Raymond muttered. "She really mean."

"News reports didn't say anything about a killer on the loose." Newton aimed his thumb back to Jeff. "Don't you worry none. We aren't armed, but we'll keep you safe."

An icy tendril of unease skated down Kelsey's back. Unarmed? Keep you safe? How did those opposing concepts work? "Excuse me, but where we are?"

"Northeastern Shenandoah, ma'am." Jeff's gaze was still fastened on Raymond. "He sick or something?"

"I'm not sure," Kelsey admitted, not willing to leave Raymond's side despite the rescuers in their midst. "I'm afraid something might be wrong with his heart or lungs."

"I is a big guy," Raymond whispered timidly. "I needs to rest cuz I is a big guy, and I needs to breathe a lot more 'n you too."

"You're scaring him." She ran a hand over his matted hair still trying her hardest to reassure Jeff and Newton this Frankenstein look-alike was safe.

"I not a scared," Raymond mumbled, the first lie Kelsey'd heard him say. All ten of his fingers kept running nervous loops over and under each other on his chest. He'd started rocking again.

"Don't worry. They're here to help us," she soothed. "I promise. They won't hurt you."

When Newton peered closer, she laid her spear alongside Raymond.

"Who are you, son?"

"I is Raymond."

"You're a big guy, aren't you?"

"Uh huh. I is." Raymond reached for her hand. "And Kelsey is my bestest friend, and she calls me Red Rover, and… and… I is a really big guy, but I is Red Rover too."

Newton smiled, glancing back at Jeff. "Come on down. Raymond isn't smart enough to hurt a fly. He's just a big kid."

Kelsey winced at the bluntly spoken truth. Newton didn't seem to mean anything cruel by it, but it hurt her feelings. "He's in my care. We had a secret word when I went looking for the road. That's what he meant about Red Rover. That's all."

Newton looked around their meager camp, a smile tugging at his mouth. "Looks like you folks were bedded down for the night. How about I go back for the ATV, and we get you home instead?"

"I'd really appreciate that, but please contact my husband first. Tell him I'm okay. You can reach him at his office. His team will know where he is." She gave him the numbers, including the one to Alex's cell phone, which might work if he hadn't used it for fastball practice during the last two stress-filled days. The love of her life did have a hellacious temper.

"You bet. Jeff, stay here with Kelsey and her boy." Newton winked at Kelsey. "Not sure the ATV will be large enough, but leastways, I can let everyone know we found you. I'll notify the sheriff too. I'm sure he'd like to talk to you about that Durrant woman."

"You folks hungry?" Jeff asked as Newton tramped into the dark.

Kelsey noticed his small backpack. Her stomach gurgled an embarrassingly loud answer. "Yes, please. We haven't eaten much the last two days."

Raymond straightened. "You gots hamburgers in there?"

Jeff's eyes lit up with humor. "It's a little hard to pack a good burger, son, but I've got a bag of trail mix and some bottled water I'd be glad to share." He dropped to his knees beside Raymond and unzipped his backpack.

Kelsey's heart lurched at the way Raymond peered into the bag. He was so hungry. When Jeff pulled a good-sized bag of trail mix into view, a toothy grin split Raymond's face. His tongue raced a couple laps over his bottom lip, ending with a resounding smack.

"Look at this." Jeff opened the bag. "You want some?"

"Kelsey," Raymond yelped, rocking faster. "He gots food, and it's for you and me."

"I see that." She sat cross-legged beside her best friend in the whole world. "Thank you, Jeff."

He shared everything and Kelsey wanted to cry. The nightmare was over. Raymond would finally get the medical care he needed, and he'd never be hungry again if she could help it. And Alex. Her throat constricted every time she thought of him. She had to look away as a tear got the best of her.

Within the hour, the trail mix was gone and Newton rolled his ATV to a halt on the trail. He was right. There was no way the two-man vehicle could transport Raymond.

"Don't worry, ma'am," he reassured her. "I called your husband. He's on his way. He's bringing a helicopter. We oughta hear him within the hour, maybe sooner by the way he sounded. There's a good-sized meadow not too far from here. It will make a good landing zone. Let's get you folks situated over there."

"What'd he say?" The lump in her throat kept making her eyes tear up.

"Just that you need to stay put," Newton answered with a twinkle in his eye.

Kelsey turned away. Alex was on his way. No better words in the whole world.

Jeff heard it first. Another engine revved up the path the ATV had just travelled, its headlights jostling through the brush as it bounced over the hard ground. "Aw, for Pete's sake," he groused. "What knucklehead's four-wheeling this time of night?"

The vehicle roared alongside the ATV, its high beams blinding everyone. When a door slammed, Jeff stood, his hands shielding his eyes to see beyond the glare. "Where the heck do you think you're—?"

BLAM! BLAM!

Two thunderous gunshots roared. Kelsey threw herself across Raymond. Jeff dropped to his knees, his hands clasped over his stomach. He gurgled incoherently until he collapsed to his side. Newton made no sound. He just leaned backward to the forest floor. Only then did a frumpy shadow step into the headlights' piercing beam.

The witch was back.

"Where is she?" Alex asked.

"Shenandoah," Mother answered. "Two local men found her. They were assisting Search and Rescue. Said she's safe, but she's travelling with some guy named Raymond."

"They say if he's a big man?" He pressed one palm to the wall for support. He hadn't eaten in days. Of all things, good news was about to drop him to his knees.

"Sounds like the fellow in the pictures. They'd be on their way home, but he's too big for their ATV."

Relief coursed over him. Finally!

"Go get her, Boss." Mother's voice quavered. "I called Mr. McCormack. He's got one of his choppers standing by. The pilot's waiting."

"Thanks. Tell Zack to meet me there. Tell Jed I'm on my way."

"Already did."

She hung up on him, and for once he was glad. His feelings were too tender. He ran for the elevator, his heart literally in his throat, and his head making plans for a new security system at home, inside and out. If Kelsey wouldn't budge out of that cracker box house, he'd turn it into a fortress. This would never happen again.

New rule—the dogs could sleep indoors from now on. Hell, they could sleep in bed with her if they wanted. He hit the elevator call button. It was past time to book a cruise to Alaska. If that's where she wanted to visit, then by damn, that's where they'd go.

The door slid open, and he resisted the urge to push the nurse with the wheelchair-bound patient out of his way. His brain caught up with his heart the minute his thumb rested on the ground floor call button. Harley's face came to mind. Another plan materialized, one Alex would be hard pressed to achieve without a certain nurse's assist. He hit the fourth floor button, glancing at his watch and his head spinning. When he pushed Harley's door open, Judy glanced up from the wooden table next to the window.

"Hi Alex. I was just going to give Harley a massage. You're next if you'd like."

"No thanks." He didn't have time for chitchat, and he'd never had a massage in his life. Wasn't going to start now. "You feel like going for a ride?" he asked Harley, his mind mentally counting down the minutes he was willing to allow for implementation of this insane idea.

"Sure." Harley's eyes lit up, but he glanced at Judy with a glimmer of concern.

"No." Judy shook her head. "He is not going anywhere. For Pete's sake, Alex, the man's just had surgery."

"No. I'm good," Harley argued, his blanket tossed to the side and his bare feet on the floor.

"You are not." The massage table was forgotten and her dander was up.

"Yeah. I am." He pushed off the bed and glared at his bossy nurse, she in her scrubs and he in an open back hospital gown with his butt cheeks showing.

"They found Kelsey." Alex would have laughed at the comical scene before him if Kelsey's lovely face had not been imprinted on his burning heart. "I need you to come with me, Harley. You've got two minutes to dress."

"They found Kelsey?" Judy asked. "Where?"

"Shenandoah. Come on. Let's go."

"No, Alex." Judy defied him, her hands on her hips, and her chin stuck out. "I'm happy you've found Kelsey, but he isn't going anywhere except back to bed. It's against hospital rules. It's illegal. It's... It's wrong!"

Harley rolled his eyes. "Yes, Nurse O'Brien, I am too going. It ain't wrong. It's what I do. Now I want my clothes and my boots. Where are they?"

Alex ran a hand through his hair. He hadn't thought of a change of clothes, and he didn't have time to fight with Judy. She was right. He tried another tack. "Judy, listen. It may help him remember."

Her emerald greens sparked. She did not look convinced.

"He rescued Kelsey once before. Don't you see? This may help him get his head back in the game."

"What I want is my pants," Harley grumbled, still looking confused.

"What he needs is..." Judy's lower lip quivered, and Alex felt like an ass. Here he was dragging Harley away when she'd barely gotten him back, before Harley even knew who she was. Maybe this wasn't such a smart idea. She didn't need to take the risk of losing her job either, but what choice did he have?

Her hand clenched Harley's shoulder like she meant to push him back to bed. "You think you can come in here and just like that, Harley is well enough to go gallivanting to the Shenandoah after your wife? Tonight? In the dark?"

"Yes." He stood his ground. "I need you too. Grab a medical bag."

That got through to her. "Me? Why? Is Kelsey injured?"

"I don't know, but I have to go now." He jerked a thumb to the door, time running out and his patience with it.

Judy walked around the bed to her massage table. Without a word, she lifted a small travel case off the floor and ripped the zipper open, upending the bag onto the bed. Bottles of massage oil, candles, and hand towels fell out. Something else landed on top of everything else—a faded pair of men's jeans, an olive drab T-shirt, underwear and socks.

Alex could've kissed her. Judy was a woman after his heart. Always prepared.

Harley stood blinking at the pile on the bed, a puzzled expression crinkling his face. "You like boxers?"

"Tidy whities are old school." She didn't miss a beat as she picked up the clothing items in question and tossed them into his face. "Don't ask. Don't tell. Just put 'em on, and let's go get Kelsey. And you." She stuck a pointed finger dead center in Alex's chest. "I'm putting my job on the line for this crazy idea of yours. You'd better damned well be right."

He smiled for the first time in days. Yeah. Harley would remember Judy in no time at all. She was too formidable to forget.

Twenty-Two

"Who the hell are you?" Jeff asked, his hand fisted into his stomach. Poor Newton lay curled to his side, his knees pulled up to his chest.

Ethel stopped directly over him, the revolver pointed at his head.

"No!" Kelsey let her spear fly, but instead of impaling Ethel, it glanced off her shoulder and bounced away. She'd dropped the gun though. Jeff was safe. For now.

Kelsey wasted no time barreling into her. The impact sent both women tumbling over backward, and clear of the weapon. Before Ethel could recover, Kelsey grabbed her by the throat and pushed her to her back. Ethel grunted and dragged her fingernails over Kelsey's forehead, nose and eyes.

It hurt. Kelsey released her and Ethel pushed her off. Now Kelsey was back to the ground and fighting to breathe, but Ethel had chosen poorly. With her hands in Kelsey's hair, she pulled, tearing a handful out by the roots. Kelsey thrust her knee upward and into the old woman's unprotected gut. Then she head-butted Ethel hard enough to hear the crunch.

Blood spewed out of Ethel's nose. She rolled to her side, groaning and her hands to her face. Kelsey wasted no time. She flung herself across Ethel's shoulder, reaching for the weapon. Just that fast, Ethel rammed her elbow into Kelsey's solar plexus, knocking the wind out of her. She crawled on hands and knees, her hand outstretched and her fingers nearly on the business end of the barrel.

Terror gripped Kelsey. She'd never fought with anyone like this before, never even raised her hand in anger, but Alex's words echoed loud. *Never lay down to a bully. Never! He might get a meal, but make sure you get a sandwich.*

With her fingernails full of dirt, she pushed off the ground and launched another attack. Her eyes watered. Her scalp and stomach hurt, but pain she could live with. Ethel Durrant—never again.

Kelsey dropped, digging her knee square into the middle of Ethel's back. The old hag whimpered, but the time for tricks and sympathy was past. Somewhere in the background, Raymond whined, but rage ruled the schoolhouse tonight. Kelsey was in a take-no-quarter mood. Linking her hands together into one mighty fist, she slammed the side of that ugly face with the best powerhouse sandwich she could muster. "Stay. Down."

"Stop it." Ethel whined, spit and bled, her hands flailing to block the blows coming at her from behind.

Shaking with strength she'd never realized, Kelsey hit the other side of Ethel's head.

"I said stop it. You're hurting me."

Well, too bad. Her jowls bounced, but Kelsey recognized a lying snake when she saw one. She had the psycho pinned. Her head pounded with adrenaline she could not and did not want to control. Not now. This was what self-defense training was about, sending the other guy bloodied and beaten to the corner. Better yet, scoring the ultimate KO and kicking her ass!

She hit her again.

"I give. You win. You win," Ethel complained, face down in the dirt and all ten fingers twitching like little flags of surrender at the side of her head.

Kelsey wanted to hit her one more time, but her decent streak prevailed, darn it. Alex had better be on his way because he'd never explained how to deal with a prisoner. She didn't have a pair of handcuffs or a piece of rope, but there was no way she'd let Ethel get away this time. Maybe Jeff or Newton had something?

She looked up to see how they were doing, but it was too dark to see that far and her head was full of noise. Righteous revenge bellowed to finish the job. *Kill the witch.*

God, she wanted to. Instead, she leaned over Ethel and grabbed the weapon, instantly checking its chamber. Three rounds left. She slapped the six-round cylinder shut and wished she were cruel enough to use it.

The sweet side of her soul waged war with the devil she'd never realized lay within. She didn't want to be like Nick. Never like Ethel. Yet here she was, wearing another person's blood on her hands and proud of it. The ugliest, most gloriously fierce beast roared to life within the heart that had once sought God. Revenge swelled to the uppermost heights of her being.

Even justice demanded its due. *Do it. Kill the damned witch. Now!*

She could do it too. The old woman squirmed beneath her, and Kelsey felt powerful. She'd won. Ethel Durrant would either die by lethal injection or spend the rest of her worthless life in prison. She could have been a grandmother, singing lullabies to two little boys who would have loved her despite herself, but no. Ethel had chosen bitterness over joy. She'd lost everything and everyone. And she'd done it to herself.

Experience whispered. *Don't trust her.*

"Stop moving." She dug her knee into Ethel's meaty back, content to torture her until Alex showed.

"But I can't hardly catch my breath. You're hurting me, girl."

"Good." For once in her timid, good-little-girl life, Kelsey wanted to walk the streets knowing Ethel Durrant lay six feet under. Most of all, she wanted Tommy and Joey to know their mother thought of them every single day; that the woman responsible for their murders would never hurt anyone again.

"Kelsey?" Raymond's gentle voice stilled the storm in her head.

She looked across the clearing amazed he was flat on his back after the ruckus. His hand stretched out to her, his fingers curled and beckoning. The frightened look in his eyes stabbed her. Kelsey knew in an instant.

Raymond needed her now.

Roy knew where he was headed. A short cab drive across the Potomac to Arlington would get him there. If his gut was right, he'd have a tough decision to make before the night was through. If he was wrong? Well, maybe he'd have a beer with an old friend and call it good. He hoped to hell he was wrong. A cold beer would be the better way to end the day.

Wouldn't Emmet be surprised to see him? They could laugh about the odd coincidence of that thirty-aught-six shell. Hell, they could laugh about a lot of things. Then Roy could go home and get a good night's sleep. But if he was right....

Mother's voice sounded in his earpiece. "Hey, Roy. You copy?"

"Yes. What do you have for me?"

"Ran the facial identification program you requested. Sorry it took so long. There were a lot of faces on all the photos you and Connor been taking. It took a while to cross-reference."

"Tell me what I don't know." The lights of D.C. flew by. Down the Potomac, the Jefferson Memorial glowed across the tidal basin. A string of headlights spanned the Fourteenth Street Bridge while the ugly job that lay ahead rankled deep in his gut.

"There is one face that doesn't add up. An African American male, about your age, dressed as a Metro police officer in one shot, but he's wearing an FBI badge on his belt in another. He was in the last batch you sent too. In a SWAT uniform."

"You got a name?" *God, not Emmet.*

"Yep, sure do," she rattled cheerily on, "I ran it through—"

"Just give me the name." He didn't have time for Mother's never-ending explanation of how much she knew, or every step she employed in the course of doing her job.

"Emmet Grant."

Roy hung up, angry with her for being annoying and himself for losing his temper, but damn it anyway, his gut was right. He faced his reflection in the cab's window and cursed heaven for bringing this duty to him. There was no time to contact Alex, and Roy chose not to engage the FBI. No bureaucratic know-it-all should make the decision that need making. Not tonight.

He stilled the relentless banging in his heart. All roads led to Emmet.

At his destination at last, he paid his fare and sent the cabbie on his way. Giant oaks sheltered the street, their roots buckling the sidewalks in some places and cracking it in others. The older neighborhood of Arlington spoke of simpler times where hard working mothers and fathers had once raised good boys and better girls; where grace was offered at every meal and television sets didn't get turned on until homework was done, dishes washed and put away. Chores were a fact of life for kids back then. That's how life was in the fifties, least ways in his parents' home. Simple. Honest. Fun.

He stuck his hands into his pockets, very aware of the pistol holstered against his ribs. The damned P238 Scorpion should not feel like the friend he'd always considered it to be, not tonight and not for the work that lay ahead. How many times had it saved his life? He couldn't count that high. Didn't want to any more than he wanted to rely on it again.

He shuffled onward, kicking against the relentless prick of honor bound duty. Gradually, his parents' old home came into view. They were both gone now, but the sentimentality of the moment warmed him like it always did. Here he was the good son, the war hero, and his father's pride and joy. Home. His nose twitched remembering when his family moved north to Virginia from Georgia. Everything had smelled so different. Of all things, he'd missed the dust of Alabama and hated the change in his life until he met the next-door neighbor who would become his best friend. Emmet.

Roy took twenty more steps to the house next door and ducked behind a tall ornamental shrub where he could wait without being spotted. He'd been here before and not too long ago either. The cigarette butt can behind him stood next to two folding lawn chairs where a couple old soldiers had told stories and lies 'til all hours. Those were good times.

But this was now.

Emmet still lived in his parents' home. An older building of bricks and the standard white trim of past decades, it said nothing about the lonely African American man who lived inside other than Emmet Grant was tidy, kept his lawn mowed and the weeds out of the cracks in his driveway. There was no hint of the bitter widower, or the angry father who'd lost his only son in a far off desert conflict.

Roy did not have to wait long. Within minutes, his friend walked up the same sidewalk with the purposeful strides of someone who meant business, someone who still had a job to do. Did he know he'd missed and Senator Hyde was still alive? He had to. It was a sniper's job to know.

Roy stepped out of the shadows. "Emmet."

His friend stopped cold, his hand automatically reaching for the bag at his side. The telling expression on Emmet's face flickered from surprised to concerned and ended at guarded. He answered with words as cold as his sniper's rounds. "What do you want?"

Roy stepped between Emmet and his front door, his hands spread wide to reveal his intention of paying nothing more than a late evening call. "Can't an old friend stop by for a cold beer and a little conversation?"

Emmet eyed the six-foot-three friend blocking his path. He still wore the black uniform of an FBI SWAT officer, minus the bold lettering on his jacket and the badge. But Roy saw the angular shapes hidden within Emmet's bag, no doubt a short stock breakdown rifle and scope. The thirty-aught-six shell was a misdirect.

"Let me by. I got no use for company tonight. Go home."

Roy took a step toward him. "You been out for a walk or something? That don't sound like you. What happened? You turning into an exercise freak in your old age?"

"What's it to you? You ain't been by since Ben's funeral."

"You're right about that, and I'm sorry," Roy admitted. "It's been a while since I've stopped by for a visit. Work's been busy. We've all got hectic lives, but hey, I'm here now. How about we throw back a few beers? You've got time for that, don't you?"

"Not tonight. Come back tomorrow if you're so interested in talking."

Roy crossed his arms, fingering the weapon at his side. "I can't do that."

Emmet glowered in the weak glare of his front porch light. "You been a good friend up to now. Don't make this any of your business. Don't get in my way."

Roy took another step toward his friend. "What's in your pack?"

"It ain't what's in my pack you ought to be worrying about, now is it?" Emmet dropped the bag to the sidewalk behind him and squared off against Roy. As quickly as he snapped his revolver up and targeted his old friend, Roy did the same. The two highly trained and decorated soldiers faced each other, comrades in arms devolved into opposing sides of the law.

Roy's aim was every bit as deadly. Both ex-Marine scout snipers, they'd hooked up in the jungles of Vietnam when luck brought them together under the same commander. That was back in the day when their hero, the legendary USMC Gunnery Sergeant Carlos Hathcock, held the record long shot of two thousand, two hundred and eighty-six yards. Neither Roy nor Emmet came close, but their combat experience forged a bond like no other.

"You didn't use a thirty-aught-six to kill Covington," Roy stated the obvious.

"You found the shell? Figures. Damned cops ain't worth a lick these days."

"Was it just another decoy? Like the truck?"

"What do you think?"

"I think you're as good a shooter as you ever were."

Emmet sneered. "You weren't supposed to be there."

"What you use, Emmet? Winchester?"

"You're so smart, why don't you tell me?"

"I figure a Winchester Magnum. Maybe .338 Lapua." Roy hoped to tie down the details of the murders before things got out of hand.

"A lot of weapons use those rounds. Specs don't really matter, do they?"

"Try telling that to the two FBI agents you murdered tonight, or my junior agent with second degree burns. Don't you worry about collateral damage anymore? We never targeted innocent civilians in Vietnam."

"Why don't you jump on off your high horse and grovel in the mud with those of us who ain't had it so easy 'fore you start judging. Some civilians ain't innocent. You know that as well as I do."

"I'm sorry you had to deal with Ben's death." Roy brought the conversation back to what was really eating at Emmet. "Especially so soon after Lois passed away. That had to be a lot of grief for one man to bear."

"Shut up. Stop being the concerned friend who just happened to be walking by. You don't care. We both know why you're here. It ain't cuz you're my friend."

"But I can get you help. It doesn't have to go down like this." Roy pleaded for common sense to rule the night.

"And then what? What happens when another idiot in Congress decides to pass a bill, you know, maybe make it illegal to fund the boys they voted to put in harm's way in the first place? My boy didn't want to go to war, Roy, anymore than you and I did."

"You're right. We were a couple kids doing the best we could to stay alive, but it wasn't all bad. Remember China Beach? Bangkok? We had some good times even in the middle of a stinking war, didn't we?"

"Knock it off." Emmet's eyes glittered. "I don't need a trip down memory lane. Leave me alone."

"Is that what this is all about, the funding cuts? Some stupid men in Congress? Hell, Emmet. That's life in America. It's always been like this."

"It ain't about the funding cuts," Emmet ground out. "It's about good boys who lost their lives doing what their country asked 'em to do. It's about honoring them instead of treating 'em like they's nothing. Ben did his duty to his country. He died, Roy. My boy died so jerks like Hyde and Winston, Conway and Covington can shoot their mouths off to get a few votes. My son died so bastards back home can be media darlings and look like heroes when..." He choked. "When the real heroes are coming home missing legs and arms or not coming home at all."

Roy saw the hesitation. Emmet lowered his gun a fraction, lost in the anguish of his only son's death.

"It's about my boy," he bellowed. "My boy died, Roy! You wanna know how that feels? He's gone. Do you think Hyde, Winston, or Conway even know? Do you think anyone cares?"

"I care, Emmet. I know your boy died. I came to his funeral. I helped you carry him down the chapel steps." Roy swallowed hard. If not for the weapons between them, he would've gone to his grieving friend and crushed him in his arms. He tried another tactic. "And my son's in Afghanistan right now. Stephen's a Marine. I'm damned proud of him. You should see him in his dress blues. You'd be proud too."

"Is he?" Emmet's gaze wandered heavenward. For a moment, it seemed the long lost memories intruding into his plan were working every bit as hard as Roy to change the outcome of the night. "Stevie's a good boy. He ever get married?"

"He did." Roy breathed a sigh of relief. Maybe there was a chance. "He met a real nice gal, and they got a little boy now. Jacob Roy. Named him after his ornery old grandpa and me. You want to see a picture?" He reached into his back pants pocket for his wallet.

Emmet's eyes glazed over. "You had a good father, Roy," he said quietly.

"I did. A mean bugger when I crossed him, but like you say, he was a damned good father." Roy offered the photo, anything to distract Emmet from the path he was on.

"Stevie's a good boy. So was Ben." With that calm statement, Emmet's gun moved back to target. "Put your pictures away. I ain't got time for reminiscing. Too many good boys ain't coming home. It ain't right."

"You don't want to shoot me." Roy returned his wallet to its place, hoping the truth still mattered. "Come on. You and me should be pulling through this together, not fighting each other. Look at us. We've done good. Ben and Stevie are sons to be proud of."

"Was, Roy. *Was.* Ben *was* a son to be proud of." The finality in his voice rang sad and cold on the warm spring night. He stuck a sharp finger eastward toward the National Cemetery. "You know where I go to chat with my boy? At a chunk of marble over the hill. I ain't going easy."

"You don't have to go at all. I can help. We can get through this thing together."

"Walk away. That's all I'm asking."

"You know better."

The two men stared each other down. Emmet lowered the gun and stepped into the barrel of Roy's, his chest pressed hard against the end of the weapon and his other hand in his pocket.

"Put one in me," he pleaded. "If you were ever my friend, Roy. Put one in me."

Roy stared into the soul of his buddy, his pistol still tight against Emmet's chest.

"Give me some peace. Please. Kill me so the pain will finally let me be."

"I won't do that," Roy replied sadly.

In that instant of heartfelt compassion, Emmet lunged around him. Now he stood between his front door and Roy.

"Don't do this." Roy reached for his friend, but Emmet used Roy's outstretched arm as leverage, and shoved him backward onto the walk. Roy stumbled off balance and fell. Emmet withdrew a detonator from his pocket.

"I'm done with killing." Tears trickled down his face. "I'm done with everything. I wanna see Ben again. I want Lois to ask me how my day was and if I want gravy on my hash and beans. I just wanna go home." He took a step back. "Save yourself, Roy. I'm going. Now."

Roy rolled facedown to the ground, raising his arms to shield his face as the explosion roared over him and sucked the breath from his lungs. A roaring cloud of orange flames belched from Emmet's home, surrounding him with fire and brimstone. He never flinched, just stood there sad and empty. Roy let the darkness of the bleak night envelope him.

Emmet Grant was finally home.

Twenty-Three

"Move," Kelsey ordered, the revolver in Ethel's back.

The old woman grunted to her knees, and whined all the way to her feet. "You're hurting me, Kelsey."

"Meant to." She noticed how all of a sudden Ethel used her real name instead of anything derogatory. The witch. Always working an angle.

"You wouldn't hurt an old woman, would you?"

"Damn right I would. Get your hands on top of your head. Now walk. When we get to Raymond, kneel. Make one wrong move and I'll shoot you like you did Jeff and Newton."

Ethel wiped her bloody hands on her baggy pants. "Whatever you say."

Kelsey hated to put her so close to Raymond, but she had to keep them both within view. "Give me a reason. Just one."

"I've got cuffs at home," Newton muttered weakly from beyond the headlights' glare. "Didn't think I'd need them on a rescue."

"And you don't carry a gun when you're out on S&Rs?" Kelsey could barely make out his face where he lay.

"No, ma'am. Never have. Never will. I don't believe in killing."

She bit back her opinion on that stupid belief. Did he believe in being murdered instead of defending himself? "How bad are you hurt?"

"She got my thigh. Bone's broke. Bleeding pretty bad."

"Who is she?" Jeff asked, his voice tight with pain.

"Ethel Durrant."

"How do you know her?"

"Married her son." The reality of her situation overwhelmed her. Three injured men and a deranged prisoner? Alex better hurry it up and get there.

"I can't kneel without using my hands to get on the ground," Ethel complained. "I'm just an old woman. You don't want me to fall, do ya?"

"Then do it." Kelsey's eyes flitted from Raymond to Ethel. He sounded just as bad as Jeff, not breathing as much as wheezing. All the drama he'd just witnessed didn't help. Another shooting wouldn't either.

The second Ethel crouched to her knees she reached for him. "My poor boy. What's she done—?"

"Don't you dare touch him," Kelsey ordered. She wished she'd thought of it sooner, but the last of the pillowcase might be enough to restrain Ethel.

"Kelsey," Raymond rasped.

"Shhhhh," she soothed, working the strips of cloth out of the backpack with one hand, while keeping the revolver on Ethel with the other. "Breathe easy. Help is almost here."

"Ain't none coming," Ethel crowed, her hands to the top of her head again and her lying tongue hard at work. "She's gonna kill you dead, Ray—"

Kelsey dug the gun into Ethel's back. "One more word and we're going for a walk. I'll show you dead."

Ethel sniffed. "Whatever you say, Kelsey Durrant."

"Kelsey Stewart!" Why did she ever think she should let this vicious woman live?

"Is you gonna kill her?" Raymond asked, his voice trembling.

Kelsey bit her lip, hating her name on Ethel's tongue, but needing to respond to the poor man. "No, Raymond. Decent people do not kill. It's up to the law and the Lord what happens next. Not me."

She crouched, needing both of her hands to properly secure her prisoner. This would be tricky. "Put your hands behind your back where I can see them."

Newton clawed one hand into the dirt, struggling to drag himself toward her. "I can help."

"No. Stay put. You're hurt."

"At least let me hold the gun on her." He rolled onto his side. "'Sides, you're the only one left. Us guys need you to stay alive. Let me help."

Kelsey was tempted. Any help would be better than none, but from a pacifist? Did he even know how to hold a gun much less shoot one? She hesitated. Not too long ago she'd been just like him.

She took the chance, keeping Ethel covered with the gun as she hurried to his side. The second he accepted the revolver she raced back to bind Ethel's wrists. With every loop, Kelsey breathed easier. Alex would be on the ground soon. He'd know what to do.

"Not so tight, girl," Ethel complained as Kelsey tied another knot for good measure. No way could she get away now. Alex would be proud. The ordeal was over. Almost.

Raymond groaned. She bolted away from Ethel, but instead of going straight to him, she went to Newton first. He was shaking so hard she feared the gun might accidentally go off. Taking it gently and resting it on the ground beside him, she asked, "Do you have a first-aid kit in your ATV?"

"I do. Not sure it's gonna have what you need though."

She ran to the ATV and hauled the heavy backpack to where Newton lay.

Raymond complained, "I is... a scared."

"I know. I'll be right there." She was plenty scared herself. Her fingers were shaking so hard, she could barely open the neatly organized kit. The plastic container marked 'Severe Bleeding' offered gloves, scissors, maxi-pads and rolls of self-adhering wrap. Hurriedly, she wrapped Newton's leg with one pad and a couple layers of the wrap. After making sure she hadn't completely cut off his circulation, she asked, "Can I get you a drink?"

He offered a crooked smile. "Who do you think you are, Wonder Woman? Go. Take care of your Jeff or your boy. I'm feeling better already."

Kelsey choked at that very kind description of Raymond, but he wasn't the one bleeding. Jeff needed help first. She secured the gun and hauled her meager supplies to where he lay with his eyes closed and both hands splayed over his abdomen.

"Jeff." She lifted his hands to hold several pads in place. They soaked wet and dark with blood the moment they met the hole in his abdomen. "Can you hear me?"

"Yes, ma'am," he murmured faintly.

She brushed her fingers over his brow. He had curly gray hair, something she hadn't noticed until now. A wedding band glistened on his bloody fingers. "Do you have children? A wife?"

"And grandchildren," he whispered.

"Think of them. Make up your mind you are going to live for them." Kelsey quelled the panic rising in her voice. "Don't let this witch win, Jeff. Please hang on. Do it for—"

"Watch out!" Newton yelled.

Kelsey looked up to see Ethel coming at her with a demented scream. She ran over Raymond, her boots on his chest and a switchknife suddenly in her hand. Raising one arm to shield her face, Kelsey fell backward to keep Ethel away from poor Jeff.

Just that fast Ethel was on her. She stabbed out with the long thin blade, but Kelsey was quicker. Cocking her knee to intercept Ethel's full weight, she grabbed the old woman's wrist and forced it away from her face. The long thin razor's stokes still dipped too close.

Newton muttered something, but Kelsey was too busy fighting for her life to decipher his meaning. Ethel clutched Kelsey's neck in a chokehold with her other hand. Her fingernails dug into Kelsey's neck. She struggled for air, but focused on the blade. The tip of it flicked dangerously near to her face. Ethel grunted, spit dripping off her bottom lip. Darkness shifted at the corner of Kelsey's vision. Only her knee prevented full on body contact.

God, no! No. Not like this. Not at her hand.

Ethel was stronger than Kelsey expected. Heavier too. The old woman pressed all of her weight forward, her forearms mashing Kelsey's chest. She turned her head to avoid the blade, but it nicked her cheek. Warmth washed down her neck.

"Don't worry, Kelsey Durrant," Ethel whispered. "You ain't going to die right away. Oh, no. I need you alive to watch while I gut Raymond. He'll cry like a stuck baby pig, but there won't be nothing you can do to help him."

Already facing Raymond, the gentlest blue eyes reached across the distance to Kelsey. Ethel was scaring him but she was right. He'd be easy to kill, Jeff and Newton too. Kelsey clenched her jaw at the cold hard truth. There was no one coming to her rescue this time. Everyone would die.

She pushed as hard as she could to create a pocket of space between her body and Ethel's, but Kelsey was afraid. She needed room to breathe. To move. Maybe she couldn't win this fight after all. *No, God. No! No! No!*

"And then," Ethel taunted, "I'm going to Alexandria for that thing you shacked up with. He ain't your husband. I know better. You're already married. You'll always be Kelsey Durrant. You belong to Nicky."

"Never!"

"Oh yes. You're Nicky's, and Stewart's gonna pay for what he's done. Bastard's gonna squeal louder than Raymond by the time I'm done with him. Got me a special knife. Fact, I got two. Nicky's and Buck's. You remember Buck, don't you?"

A shudder ripped through Kelsey. How could she forget the men who nearly killed her?

"Been honing them knives for months. They're finally sharp enough to strip the meat off a man's bones just to hear him scream." Kelsey could smell the dead teeth in Ethel's mean mouth. "It's time, Mrs. Nicky Durrant, time to cut that lying tongue out of your ugly face."

The fight was nearly over. Ethel knew it. Kelsey knew it. She could not hold the murderer off. The switchblade dipped closer. It kissed the underside of her jaw. She took a final breath. One more cut like the last and her throat would be cut. Kelsey sent a fervent prayer heavenward. Ethel's face wrinkled into a mask of demented joy. The Lord had his chance. So did the law. A fist-sized pocket of space opened between her and the witch and—

BLAM!

Ethel's pig like eyes widened with sudden enlightenment.

"You bitch!" Ethel had forgotten the revolver Kelsey had made sure not to drop in the scuffle. The one pointed into the blackest heart on earth. "That's for your grandson. Remember him? His name was Tommy."

BOOM!

Ethel's eyes opened wider. "B-b-but—"

"For Jackie!" The glorious beast was once again unleashed and seeing red. Two shells down. One to go.

The revolver roared in awful triumph with her. "For Raymond! You wanna tell me what you're gonna do to him now, you child-murdering pig?"

Ethel was past hearing. One leg kicked involuntarily out to the side. A strand of bloody drool slipped between her lips. The evil light faded from her eyes while the knife dropped to the ground.

Kelsey pushed the woman off and jumped to her feet. One more round would have been perfect. One for Alex. Maybe two more for Jeff and Newton. She bounced from the adrenaline surging through her. She'd won this round. Champ. Winner. Mother. The witch was finally dead.

"And my name is Mrs. Kelsey Stewart!" she informed the blank-eyed sociopath at her feet.

"Good girl," Newton groaned from the dark.

Angry she'd been hurt again, she wiped the back of her hand over her bleeding cheek. Sucking in the first breath in a world that would never again know the likes of Ethel Durrant felt good. She jerked her head toward the sound of boots hitting the ground behind her. Alex led the charge with Harley, Judy, and Zack on his six, bright lights in their hands. No friends ever looked better. Or more shocked.

"Kelsey?" Alex stopped in his tracks, his eyes darting over the grisly scene. "Are you hurt?"

She jerked her head in quick denial. The scratches and cuts were nothing. "No. Why?"

"Honey." He approached warily and reached for the revolver in her trembling fingers. "You're covered in blood."

She looked down at her clothes and her arms, drenched red and wet. "Yeah, well, it's been kind of a bad day. My men. They're hurt. They need help."

Zack, Harley and Judy rushed by her, but tenderness tugged at Alex's mouth. "Your men?" They stood face to face, the invisible force field between them warning him off.

"Yes. My men."

Kelsey was not the same quiet little mouse he'd married. Not anymore. The deed was done, but she could not release the gun that had just saved her life even though his hand encompassed hers. If only her heart would give her a break and stop racing. If only she could think again.

"It's finished," he said softly, pointing the barrel of her weapon down.

But it wasn't. She could not catch a big enough breath to quench the awful excitement flooding her. Every bone in her body shook. The truth hit righteously, frighteningly hard. She understood why Alex did what he did. Logically, it made sense that he and his men chose to walk into danger despite the very real possibility they'd be killed. It all came down to the survival of good in the world. Evil could not win. But still....

She, Kelsey Stewart, the mother of sons had killed tonight. The paradox of who she'd become in the last two days did not fit the paradigm of who she used to be. Her heart felt locked in battle with her head. What had she just committed? Self-defense? Murder? Bile climbed up the back of her throat. She sought Ethel's eyes for the answers, but Alex cupped her cheek, turning her to him.

"No," he said firmly, one hand skimming over the bloody bump on the side of her face and the other still holding fast to her shooting hand.

"No." Just as firmly, she refused to release the revolver. It was all that had saved her and her men. "She might... She might...."

"She won't. It's over, sweetheart. Give me your weapon. Do it now."

"Yeah, Kelsey Girl. I'm pretty sure you got her," Harley muttered somewhere in the background.

"I killed her," she confessed and the fight went out of her. The forest spun, and suddenly, she was off her feet and in Alex's arms. He dropped to one knee, his hand gently unlatching her fingers from the revolver while he folded her against him. Burrowing into him, she needed that cool assurance he always brought with him, that certainty she had not committed a grievous sin. Needing forgiveness.

"Kelsey," he breathed her name a prayer against her forehead. "You had no choice. She would have killed you." His strength absolved her instantly.

"I love you." Her fingers dug into the sides of his head, forcing his mouth to hers. Alex complied with fury, his hand at the back of her head, holding her in a vice to his lips. His need matched hers, the growl rumbling up from his heart feral, filled with pain and anger, desperate with needing her. She cried, finally where she belonged, but so very much a different person.

He stilled, pressing her beneath his chin to the thunder in his chest. Alex secured both his and her weapons somewhere on his body. She didn't know where. All she felt was the band of his arms holding her together. She breathed him in, not wanting the reunion to end but knowing more work lay ahead. "I need your help. Please. Everyone's hurt."

"I'm here. Tell me what you need."

Her hands flew to his face. Their roles were reversed. Tears moistened her hero's cheeks.

She eased out of his gentle grasp. "Please help me help them."

"Your cheek. Your head. Sweetheart, you're bleeding." He set her feet to the ground, his hands still smoothing over her.

"I'm fine. It's Raymond." She held his wrist, pulling him forward. "Jeff and Newton, too."

The scene had already changed to medical triage with Zack securing another tourniquet on Newton's leg. Judy knelt over Jeff, her medical bag opened while Harley assisted.

Alex caught sight of the carnage. "Durrant did this?"

"Yes. Raymond and me were next."

"Medical chopper is on its way," Zack reported grimly. "Sheriff should be here soon. This guy's lost a lot of blood, but I've slowed the bleeding for now."

"Thanks." Newton's hand reached for Zack. "Name's Newton Bridges. Damned glad to make your acquaintance."

"Zack Lennox. Rest easy. We'll get you out of here in no time at all."

"My patient is gut shot," Judy announced grimly. "Harley, give me more packing."

"Yes, ma'am. There's another first-aid kit in the chopper. I can run back and get it."

"Then do it," she snapped.

Harley pushed slowly off the ground, nodding toward Kelsey as he hurried by. "Looks like you've been in a dammed war, darlin'."

She had to agree. It had been a war, but winning did not feel as good as she'd expected. Too many casualties lay in mortal danger. Even Harley did not look well.

She went to Raymond's side. Alex knelt with her.

"Who have we here?" He clenched Raymond's hefty shoulder.

"Kel... sey," Raymond whined, leaning away from Alex. "He's touching me."

Kelsey took his hand to comfort him. "This is Alex. Harley, Judy, and Zack too. They are going to save us."

"Where's—she?"

"You mean Ethel? She's dead." She didn't have the heart to explain anymore.

Alex interrupted. "It looks like Kelsey's been taking good care of you. How about we get you home now? Are you ready to go?"

Kelsey could have cried. Leave it to Alex to be just what she needed. Calm. Sure. And absolutely right.

Twenty-Four

"Call Life Flight again. Tell them we've got a cardiac emergency. Code blue. I need them here yesterday."

Zack nodded and stepped away.

Judy knelt at Raymond's side. Jeff was stabilized for now. Newton too, but both were in bad shape. But Raymond was worse.

She turned to Kelsey. "Talk to me. What are his symptoms?"

"He's been having trouble breathing, more so tonight. He tires easily. Can't walk far. He falls down a lot. The last couple times, his pulse was racing. He blacked out earlier." Like every other panicky mother, Kelsey rattled off the highlights in typical civilian terms.

"Calm down. Think. How often has he blacked out?"

"Once. I thought he'd died."

Judy looked across to Alex. "I expect you know CPR?"

"Yes, ma'am."

"Me, too." Harley crouched alongside Alex. "Count me in. I'm here to help."

"Not you. You'll tear your stitches out." She looked to Alex instead. "Stand by. If things turn bad, keep your compressions steady. One hundred per minute. Go deep. He's a big man. You're going to get a work out."

Zack stepped up. "I'm next."

When she tried to undo Raymond's shirt, he shoved her hand away. "Kelsey, She… scary."

Kelsey clutched his massive hand in both of hers. "It's okay. She's here to help."

Judy slipped her stethoscope beneath Raymond's shirt. Anxiety she could not disguise radiated through her. This was not what she'd expected on a joy ride with Alex, damn it. Two men critically injured, one in obvious cardiac distress and a dead body? How was any of this supposed to help Harley?

"Judy is like the doctor I told you about." Kelsey caressed his cheek while Judy finished unbuttoning his shirt. "She'll take good care of you."

"She is kinda pretty," he whispered out of the corner of his mouth.

"She is, isn't she?" Kelsey's sad eyes met Judy's.

Judy wished she could offer encouragement. There was none.

"No." Kelsey shook her head, clenching his hand and denying Judy's unspoken message. "You're here just in time. You can save him. I know you can."

"He needs a cardio-surgeon and a crash cart, not a nurse. Talk to him. Keep him calm."

Raymond arched his back, angling his shoulders in pain. "Kel… sey…" He squeezed her fingers. "I is… a scared."

"I know," she crooned. "Red Rover. Red Rover. Let Raymond come over."

A smile worked one corner of his mouth. "You… is… singing to me."

She nodded, tears welling up and spilling over. Judy had to admit. Kelsey was one hundred percent mother, even to this child in an ungodly-sized body. Here in the middle of nowhere, she meant for him to know the peace he'd probably never known in life.

"Red Rover," she murmured against his ear, tears glistening off her eyelashes in the stark glare of the high-powered LED lights.

A gentle baritone joined hers. Of course it was Harley, never ashamed to step up even if it made him look goofy. Judy sniffed back her tender emotions when he knelt alongside Kelsey and took Raymond's hand while his other hand snaked around Kelsey's waist.

"I'm here, darlin'," he murmured into the side of her head

Judy blinked her jealousy away. He should have been kneeling alongside her, but of course he'd gravitate toward Kelsey. She was the nice one.

Zack added another level of baritone to the childhood ditty while he applied butterfly bandages to Kelsey's cheek and chin. Her eyes were bright with appreciation, and Judy was ashamed. Judging by the light in Zack's eye, everyone loved her simply because she loved them first. Who could resist a woman like that?

"Keep singing, Kels," Zack urged, winking. "We're with you all the way."

"Thanks." She sniffed and wiped her face with the back of her bloody hand.

"Red Rover, Red Rover." Another voice joined in. That surprised Judy. She'd never heard Alex sing before, a first and possibly the last performance, but there he was, looking a little sheepish maybe, but deeply in love with his lady.

Peeling the sterile wrap off a long hypodermic needle, Judy got back to the business of saving Raymond's life. "This is atropine," she explained to Kelsey. "In case."

"In case what?"

"In case his heart stops," Judy whispered. She turned on Zack. "How long before the chopper? You did tell them we have a cardiac emergency, didn't you?"

"They're on their way, and yes, ma'am, I did."

Kelsey offered the only lullaby she could, her unlikely choir of war-hardened soldiers blending in with the mellowest accompaniment Judy had ever heard. She blinked the tears away.

Soon the hack-hack-hack of a far off helicopter filtered through the dark night sky. Zack stepped away to greet it, but Alex stayed fast, his arm stretched over Raymond's broad chest to clasp Kelsey's hand. When Raymond groaned, Judy's heart pinched. It was happening.

"Kel—sey." He stiffened, crunching her fingers in his mighty grip. Drawing in a deep breath, he squinted as if he couldn't see anymore. Judy held her breath wishing miracles were real, that good people did not have to die before their time. But most of all, she wished she were smarter and more skilled. More capable. Just more, damn it!

"I'm here," Kelsey answered faithfully. "I'm right here, Raymond.

"You... gots... tiny hands." The softest blue eyes searched for her in the darkening shadows.

She leaned into his cheek, sobbing. "I love you, Raymond. I will always love you. No matter what happens, you will always be my Red Rover."

He smiled, his eyes unfocused, the light in them fading. His head slumped to his shoulder, his wide square jaw slack against his thick neck, and, "My... bestest... friend," whispering out of him on a sigh.

Judy yanked his shirt open and plunged the hypo directly into his heart. Alex knelt forward and positioned the heel of his right hand in the center of Raymond's chest. Placing his left hand over the right, Alex interlocked fingers and began, his hands sinking into the big man's ribcage.

Judy bit her lip, her heart screaming what she would not let her tongue speak. Inserting a sanitary mouthpiece between Raymond's lips, she began resuscitation. Anything was possible.

Kelsey sat back, her gentle cries lost in the frantic race to save this man's life. The scene turned surreal when the EMTs arrived.

"Oxygen. Now!" Judy barked at them. "Defib!"

"Yes, ma'am," the blond-haired medic said as he knelt alongside Raymond. Thankfully, they'd brought oxygen and a portable defibrillator. Alex kept pumping. The EMTs spoke too seriously into their shoulder radios even as they obeyed her orders.

"Step back!" Judy ordered. God, she sounded like the Gestapo, and she did not care.

Alex enfolded Kelsey into his arms and moved out of the immediate shock zone. She buried her face in his chest, a slow sad whine crawling out of her mouth while she watched.

The medic applied the paddles. "One. Two. Three. Clear!"

Raymond's body arched off the ground, and Alex pulled Kelsey farther away.

Judy pressed her stethoscope to Raymond's chest, hoping her eyes did not betray her fear. *Please breathe, Raymond. For Kelsey. Come on. You can do it.*

When no pulse answered her prayer, she leaned back, and the medics leaned forward. Another order of, "Clear," and the second shock entered Raymond's poor body. Judy could not bear to look at Kelsey. The terror-filled expression on her face matched her brother Joshie's from years ago. He'd been so close to dying that day, and now here Judy was again—unskilled for the job at hand and desperately fighting the unforgiving laws of nature.

Further communication was not necessary. Judy pressed the stethoscope to the emptiness in Raymond's chest, and Zack stepped up to continue compressions. He never looked her in the eye, just dug in to the relentless chore of pump, count, pump.

Moving Raymond to the gurney proved arduous. The medics rolled him to his side just enough to get a backboard beneath him. Lifting him strained every vertebra between Alex, Judy and the medics. The gurney squeaked in metallic protest. Zack never missed a beat.

"Climb aboard," a medic instructed, so Zack straddled the unconscious body on the gurney, his hands locked together and working relentlessly, a light sheen already on his forehead and down the middle of his back. Determination chiseled his face.

Moving the over-laden gurney to the waiting chopper proved tough despite its rugged, balloon tires. Alex helped. Judy too, but when Harley stepped forward, she came unglued. "I'm not telling you one more time. Back off."

"But I—"

"But nothing. Stay with Kelsey." Judy nodded curtly at the poor woman left standing alone.

"Damn. I was just going to help." He sloughed off his jacket to cover Kelsey's bare shoulders as they followed. "You're cold," he whispered, pulling her under his arm.

Judy looked away. There it was again, his overwhelming kindness for another woman. She hated and loved him for it.

At last, Raymond's gurney was onboard with Zack still firmly planted on top and working steadily. The medics couldn't risk losing precious heart muscle in the time it would take to swap him out. Judy covered him with a light absorbent sheet to absorb the sweat pouring off his shoulders as much as to keep him semi-warm. Helicopter rides were fast, drafty, and cold.

"Sorry, ma'am." The paramedic stopped Kelsey and Alex at the door. "I know you're hurt, but this guy's in bad shape. We don't have the room. We're going to Georgetown—"

"No, you're not," Judy shouted over the rotors. "You're going to Washington Central."

He shrugged his compliance. "Like the lady says. We're going to W.C."

Alex pulled Kelsey against him. "It's okay. Meet you there."

"But I need to be with him." Kelsey sagged into Alex, biting her lip and crying.

Judy dashed her own tear away. This ride was going to be crowded. She stripped off her soiled gloves and tossed them aside, donning another pair quickly as she turned to do what she could for Jeff Watson. Soon Newton Bridges was safely aboard. Zack kept pumping compressions. Alex debarked to stand with Kelsey. The life flight helicopter lifted vertically from the meadow.

Judy latched onto a handgrip dangling from the ceiling to steady herself. Harley and Alex stood with Kelsey between them looking upward. Judy was not even able to wave goodbye. This was no mercy flight. She just could not bear to break Kelsey's heart by telling her the truth.

Raymond was already gone.

Twenty-Five

Harley stared out the chopper window. He, Alex, and Kelsey ended up staying long enough to answer a few questions with the sheriff. For the most part Harley was spare baggage, just along for the ride. All he seemed to do was irritate his grumpy nurse.

Things did not add up. Alex was the boss, but Miss O'Brien sure bossed him plenty. And he'd snapped to and obeyed every time. Well, almost every time. The oddest sensation lingered. She looked so familiar.

Rain hit the windshield when the lights of D.C. glittered ahead. Kelsey still wore his coat, and he shivered, only he wasn't cold. Scared more like it. He just did not know why. Maybe he should have stayed in bed. Maybe coming with Alex wasn't so smart after all. Harley scrubbed a hand over his face, tired down to his bones. The ache in his chest had grown more noticeable. A bed would be nice. That bossy nurse might have been right.

Efficient. Expert. Enticing.

All kinds of E words kept showing up in his head.

She'd sure been kind to Kelsey. He'd watched her hands while she worked on Raymond. A ring sparkled on her right hand. So—she wasn't married. Not like he cared, but something about the ring rang a bell.

Another E word showed up. *Engaged.*

Well, that solved it. Nurse O'Brien was probably engaged or maybe promised.

Exactly.

A blanket hit him in the face.

"You look cold." Alex had Kelsey on his lap and snuggled into another blanket, his arms protectively around her.

"Thanks, Boss." Harley pulled the blanket around his shoulders like a shawl. Warmth settled in and the nervous feeling disappeared. The Potomac glistened like a dark shiny snake below. Lighted bridges spanned the river, and of course, the monuments always impressed. The pilot's voice crackled to life in his headset, requesting permission to land at Washington Central. Even the name of the hospital sounded familiar.

"Mr. Stewart," the pilot said. "I've got a woman on another frequency requesting permission to be patched through to you."

"Let me guess. Her name Mother?"

"Yes, sir. She said you'd want to talk to her."

"I guess. Patch her through."

It didn't take Mother long. "Roy got him, Boss. Roy got the sniper."

Harley raised his brows. *What sniper?*

"Where? How?" Alex asked.

"Caught up with him over in Arlington. Name's Emmet Grant. Guess he worked with Roy in Vietnam. They grew up together too."

"How'd it go down?"

"According to the fire marshal—"

"What fire marshal?"

"The one at the fire, Boss."

"What fire?"

"The one from the explosion."

Alex straightened in his seat and rolled his shoulder. "What explosion, damn it?"

Harley leaned back and listened. The picture of a trim, white-haired woman with blue eyes came to mind. Mother. She thought she ruled the world and the boss along with it. The more Alex questioned, the more she led him by the nose. Finally, he had enough.

"Has the FBI been informed?" he asked curtly.

"Well, of course, Boss. I took—"

"Is Roy alive?"

"Well, sure. I'd have told you right away if he'd died. Fire didn't touch him. Mostly, he's just got a minor concussion. Nothing to worry about with his hard head and—"

"Where is he?"

"Washington Central."

Alex clicked his headset off, tossed it aside and hugged his wife. The chopper felt kinda like home in a really weird way

"Hey. You in there?" Connor leaned over Roy's face as he nudged his sleeping senior agent's shoulder one more time. "You ready to go home yet?"

"Huh?" Roy looked up groggily at the young man peering down from somewhere high above. One more nudge and Connor would be sporting more than dark glasses.

"Come on. Wake up and start moving, old man. I'm tired of waiting for you to get your beauty sleep." Connor poked his shoulder again.

Roy closed one eye and then the other as he decided which viewpoint improved Connor's looks. The dark glasses perched on the kid's nose did not help. Neither did the burn ointment glistening on his cheeks, forehead and nose. To make matters worse, he smelled like bad hospital coffee and his hands were bandaged. Plus, he was hyper, the product of too much time spent in the hospital waiting room compounded with caffeine.

Roy pushed himself into a better sitting position. "What are you still doing here?"

"Well, let's see. As I recall, you said you'd come visit me after they hauled me off to the emergency room. And, oh yeah, you were also supposed to give me a ride home." When Connor adjusted his dark glasses, Roy could see the gauze-covered eyes beneath the rims. "On account of I kind of got a little flash burn on my retinas, and I'm *bblliinnddddd*. Any of this sound familiar?"

"You've been waiting all this time? How long I been in here?"

"A couple hours. You scared the hell out of me when they first brought you in. Why'd you take that guy on all by yourself? You should have called for backup."

"My backup was in the hospital." The last thing Roy recalled was the sad look on Emmet's face. His friend hadn't faltered once, just stood there while the flames took what was left of his heart and soul. "Besides, he was my friend. I didn't want just anyone out there with me."

"He's dead," Connor said quietly. "Not sure why you aren't. The explosion blew out the entire front of the house, but it mostly just knocked you down. You've got a concussion is all, of course I can't see to be sure. You might have less hair."

"Doubt that." Roy rolled his shoulders to ease the ache of lying still too long. A man who shaved his head every day couldn't lose much of it to fire. He'd learned that early as an EOD guy, back when he had hair.

"How'd you know he was the sniper? How'd you know where to go?"

"I didn't. Just had a bad feeling. The magnesium fire made me think maybe we were looking in the wrong direction. We were focused on malcontents not heroes."

"Emmet Grant was a hero?"

"You bet. One of the best."

"Good call," Connor murmured. "Damned tough way to go though, blowing yourself up."

Roy shook his head. "Not when a man believes he's already living in hell."

"How far back did you two go?"

"We grew up together in that same Arlington neighborhood. Played Little League baseball together. I've known him almost my whole life."

"I'm sure sorry for your loss."

The picture of two little boys playing soldier together filled Roy's mind. Like best friends and blood brothers, they spent every summer day at the local public swimming pool. When they weren't there, they were Mickey Mantle and Joe

DiMaggio on the neighborhood baseball diamond. Superman and Batman on bikes with playing cards stuck in the spokes with clothespins and pillowcases for capes. Best friends and wannabe brothers.

"How you doing, boy?" Roy changed the subject. Looking back never made a man feel any better, but this spunky kid always did.

"Good, now they put that anesthetic goop in my eyes. I gotta ask you something though. There's a really cute sounding nurse coming in to check on you in a couple minutes. I was wondering...."

Roy smiled even wider. "I'll tell you if she's hot. Or not. You never know. She might have a sexy voice, but look like—"

"Oh, good. You're awake." Nurse Jan peeked around the door. She did have a sexy voice.

"Ah, yeah." Roy couldn't help himself anymore than Connor could. He sat up straighter when Nurse Jan came to his bedside. Connor was right. She had a way cute body to go along with her voice, definitely model material—blond, blue-eyed, about six feet tall and Connor's type. At least she was Connor's height. The girl should have played basketball she was that kind of athletically tall. And tan. And drop-dead good looking.

"First of all the good news." She checked his monitor and scooted the sliding table aside to remove the blood pressure cuff. "We're not going to keep you any longer, not even for observation. You only suffered superficial burns from the explosion and a minor concussion, so you get to go home tonight. It sounds like you were a very lucky man."

Roy blew out a deep breath. "What's the bad news?"

Nurse Jan gently pulled the IV needle from his arm. She covered the tiny blood spot with a bandage. His spirits improved immensely just watching her holding onto his arm like she was. If he were a younger man, he'd give Connor some good stiff competition where Nurse Jan was concerned.

"The bad news is you'll need to come back tomorrow for a couple more tests. Doctor Remington wants to make sure you're not having any headaches or double vision. You did take quite a bump to the back of your head."

"I guess I can live with that. And what about my friend over there? Can he go home or do you need him to stay in the hospital awhile?"

"Mr. Maher?" Nurse Jan's voice turned a tad sweeter. "He can go if someone drives him and stays with him. He might need help."

"Don't worry. He'll be staying with me."

"But you can't drive, Mr. Hudson," she said. "Is there someone you can call?"

"Murphy and Mark are already downstairs," Connor added. "But I'll have to come back tomorrow too, won't I?"

"Not really. If you keep your eye patches on for the next forty-eight hours, you'll be fine."

"But, ah, don't you think maybe you ought to check my sight tomorrow just in case? You probably don't want to be leaving something as important as eyeballs to a guy like me."

Roy grunted. What a lousy line.

"Well, you could come back with Mr. Hudson when he comes tomorrow. If I'm on shift—"

"And your shift would be?"

Roy watched the dialog fly back and forth between the conniving blind man and Nurse Jan. It wasn't too many years ago that he'd have been the one making a fool of himself.

She stood at Connor's elbow tucking a piece of paper with her phone number into his jacket pocket. "If you have any questions, call me," she said sweetly.

His nose twitched, and Roy smirked. The hound dog.

"Yes, ma'am. We will. Ah, I mean I'll be calling you, that's for sure." Connor tipped his hand to his dark glasses as she left the room. He might be temporarily blind, but the kid was not stupid.

"I thought you needed help? Looks to me like you're doing okay," Roy exclaimed.

"But what does she look like? With that voice, she's gotta be a babe. I'm right, aren't I?"

"If you like women with five o'clock shadows."

Connor's jaw dropped. "She WHAT?"

"Yeah. That sexy voice is coming out between two big old buck teeth." Roy placed both feet on the floor as he prepared to stand and get back into his clothes. "She's got a harelip too."

A broad smile lit up Connor's face. "You're lying. She's a babe. I knew it." He punched the air with one fist. "Yes!"

"Call her what you want. Fido. Spot."

Connor threw an empty paper coffee cup in the direction of Roy's voice.

"Fluffy. Spike."

"Come on, old man." He felt his way across the room until he reached Roy's offered arm. "Let's get going."

"Tiger. Max. You do know Babe was a pig, don't you?"

"I'm never going to hear the end of this, am I?" Connor rested his hand on Roy's shoulder. "Keep moving. Once they see us in motion, someone's bound to get us a wheelchair."

"Bucky. Fang. Lassie?"

Twenty-Six

No one spoke. Murphy and Mark had just been ushered into the hospital family counseling room. Zack sat in the adjoining chair, his head down and his fingers interlocked between his knees. He never looked up. Harley caught the drift. Bad news travelled fast.

Alex sat with Kelsey securely inside his arm. Miss O'Brien had whisked her away the moment the helicopter landed, and now Kelsey was dressed in a clean pair of hospital scrubs. Her hair was wet and tied back. Nurse Judy must've taken her someplace to clean up. That was thoughtful.

As usual, Miss O'Brien seemed to think she was in charge. She'd shot Harley a dirty look the moment their eyes locked. He was first to break the hold. A man didn't have to be a genius to recognize a woman's wrath. Harley just did not know what he'd done to set her off to begin with. Sheesh! Was she still ticked because he'd gone with his boss to the Shenandoah? What was her deal? He didn't want to stay in the hospital. He was Army. Didn't she get it?

Enticing.

He sneaked another peek at her. Yeah. She was enticing all right. Sad too.

She focused on Kelsey who seemed to be staring at the wall, not making eye contact with anyone. Poor Kelsey.

Never in a million years did he believe she could have killed anyone, not even Ethel Durrant. As hard as it must have been, his chest swelled with pride. That old hag deserved to die.

"You see, Kelsey, besides being mentally impaired, Raymond suffered from a very rare disorder known as acromegaly."

Harley lifted his gaze. Grumpy or not, Miss O'Brien was attractive. Easy on the eyes. Tall and strong. Kinda mean, but kinda gentle too. He liked how she focused on Kelsey even though Kelsey wasn't looking at her. Miss O'Brien's hands on his back and neck had done wonders. She did know how to make a man feel good. His eyes drifted to her bosom, not much to look at in scrubs. But perky.

He groaned, pushed the stupid thought away, and focused. She did have the faintest sprinkle of freckles on her nose and just the uppermost part of her cheeks though. He always liked freckles. They were evidence of times spent in the great outdoors, and any woman who enjoyed being outside like he did—

Damn. He could not stop thinking about her.

"Acromegaly is a dysfunction of the anterior pituitary gland, usually caused by a tumor. It causes the gland to produce excess growth hormones," Miss O'Brien continued. "Normal hormone levels range somewhere between fifty and two-hundred-fifty. For people with this disorder, their levels may go as high as four thousand. That little gland has no off switch. It's been overloading Raymond's system with growth hormones throughout his life. It's crucial that you understand, Kelsey. By the time you met him he was already dying. There was nothing anyone could have done to change the outcome."

Kelsey lowered her head, and Harley wiped his face. He didn't have to see the tears to know she was crying. From the first second he'd seen her in that Washington forest years ago, Kelsey always got to him, no matter how tough he tried to be.

"There are many different treatments available today," the nurse continued. "Some are quite effective. They might have made a difference if Raymond had been diagnosed as a child. But for a man with no healthcare, it was just a matter of time. The disorder took a tremendous toll on his body. Your poor friend had to be in a lot of pain every day, and not just from his heart condition. Advanced acromegaly affected his musculature, his skeletal system, all of his organs, and, well, pretty much his entire body. Once he coded, there was nothing we could do."

Green eyes drifted to Harley, but he wasn't ready for another visual slap down. He jerked his gaze from Miss O'Brien's stern face and focused on Kelsey. No one else spoke. If they were like him, they'd probably put their boot in their mouth and spoil everything. He kept his lip zipped.

"I know this isn't what you wanted to hear. I'm so sorry."

Alex rubbed Kelsey's arm, and Harley wondered where his jacket and the blanket had gone. She looked cold. Gray scrubs were not her best color. It made her look washed out. Sad. Her brown eyes filled to the brim. "Can I see him?"

"Of course." Miss O'Brien pulled Kelsey into her arms for a tender hug, and Harley was a goner. He looked away, blinking hard and not understanding how other men maintained control at times like this. He sure couldn't.

With his eyes on the floor, Zack still looked like a loaded spring. Alex was doing his share of blinking. Harley succumbed to the moment and wiped his face with his sleeve.

There was no sense denying what everyone else already knew. He was a sap.

Kelsey pulled away from Miss O'Brien with a deep breath. "I want to see him."

Nurse Judy opened the door to the adjoining trauma room where Raymond lay beneath a sheet. Harley took the seat opposite Kelsey and Alex. Murphy and Mark took their post at Raymond's enormous feet. Zack brought up the rear, closing the door behind him.

The room stilled, the heavy hand of gloom a weight Harley could feel. The damned place felt like a morgue. He shifted his feet. The familiar palpitation in his heart started again. He wanted to stay for Kelsey's sake, but he didn't want to fall apart in front of everyone either, especially not Miss O'Brien. Something had to give soon.

Judy's hands shook when she lifted the sheet off Raymond's face and folded it over his massive chest. It was like looking at Frankenstein without the green tint and bolts in his neck. The guy's face had been washed and his hair was combed with a neat part on the right. He looked like he was dreaming with the corners of his lips turned up like they were.

The sheer size of Raymond amazed Harley all over again. He had to be around four hundred pounds, maybe more, and at least seven and a half feet tall. The table he'd been laid on was actually two tables with another butted up sideways at the bottom to accommodate his feet.

"Do you want us to leave you alone, Kelsey Girl?" Harley asked quietly.

"No. Please stay. I'm glad you're all here with me. I didn't get to see my sons before...."

Harley bowed his head. The poor thing deserved a break. She lifted one of Raymond's hands, and rubbed a spot on the pad of his thumb. "She made him dig a grave. He couldn't get out of it once it was done, so he had to use a ladder. He pinched his finger. He got a blood blister." Her voice sounded far away. "I couldn't just walk away and leave him."

Harley closed his eyes. They'd all been through two days of hell. God, it had to end.

Her voice cracked. "We had a secret code. He was my Red Rover. My poor little boy. I'm sorry I couldn't protect you. You never had a chance, did you?"

"You're amazing." Alex pulled her into his chest. "Everything started Friday night when your friend here kidnapped you. It's two days later, and you've been taking care of him the whole time. Figures."

"He was afraid of the dark, only he said he was *a scared,* the way little boys say it."

"He was sure a *big* little boy—seven feet three inches and close to four hundred pounds. It's no wonder his heart gave out."

"I knew it was serious. He had a headache all the time, and he couldn't catch his breath. But we couldn't stay where we were. We thought Ethel would...." She leaned against Alex.

"I know, honey, I know." He wrapped his arms around her. "Nothing she did made sense, did it?"

"None of my boys ever hurt her," Kelsey whispered.

Zack stepped forward, blinking hard and his jaw clenched. "Boss. I need your wife a minute." When Alex released her, Zack wrapped her in a bear hug, his face in her shoulder.

Harley couldn't bear to watch. His entire body had turned into heartache along with Zack's. Lowering his forehead to his clenched fists, he blocked the view, but he could not block the words.

"I tried, Kels. God knows I tried. I didn't let up once, but I couldn't do it. I'm sorry."

"It's all right. Thank you for helping him. For helping... me."

How did women do it? How'd they reach out to others when they were broken too? Harley didn't have a clue. He wiped his face and wished he were stronger.

"It's not okay." Zack's anguish poured out of him for all to hear. "It will never be okay. I should have saved him."

Harley winced, blinking furiously. Zack had just voiced every good soldier's worst nightmares. They all began with *I should have....*

"I thought you might want this." Once again, Nurse Judy interrupted a tender moment. "I asked one of my nurses to make it for you."

She handed Kelsey a plaster cast of one of Raymond's handprints. The thing was the size of a turkey platter. Multicolored crayon printing rounded the edge, but Harley couldn't make out the inscription. Murphy passed the box of tissues. Zack stepped to Kelsey's side as she accepted the gift.

A funny expression shifted across her face. She handed it back to Judy, her voice ratcheting higher with every word. "I'm sorry, but... I don't want this. I don't. Not another memory. Not another handprint of someone's hand I can't hold anymore. No more. That's all I've got, and I'm sick of it. I'm tired of everyone I love dying!"

Everyone stilled. Alex's eyes widened at the sudden outburst from his usually tranquil, predictable wife.

"This is what I want. This!" She grabbed Raymond's giant mitt in hers, glaring at her friends while tears drenched her pretty face. Harley could not look away.

"I want Raymond to live in a real house with Snow White and the Seven Dwarfs instead of a cardboard box on the street. I want to grill him a cheeseburger the size of the whole damned ocean! I want to make him a chocolate cake. I want to watch him eat every last piece of it. Don't you get it? I want another secret word. I want... I want...." She choked. "I want my boys back! I want all of them back!"

And Harley lost the battle. Not everything she'd said made sense, but he got the drift. He bowed his head again. *Me too, Kelsey Girl. I want Rick to tell me another bad joke. I want Kent to tell me what his mama fixed for dinner last night. And Carlton. I want to meet his baby girl. Maybe she looks like him. Maybe....*

Whoosh. Pop. Fizzle...

A gentle breeze poured down from the ceiling. Harley lifted his face as fuzzy shapes descended and materialized into—men? His men? Rick. Snakes. Carlton. Robbie. Kent. Garth. They all appeared. Only they were not dead. In somber formation, they took their place around Raymond's bed, all dressed in tactical gear, rifles slung over their shoulders and dusty boots still on their feet. Snakes gave him a silent nod. Rick winked, that sly old devil.

Harley shook his head, seeing things for sure. His throat went dry. *No freaking way!*

Kent's dark face lit up with his usual bright, toothy grin. "Why ain't you called my Mama yet? You lost her number or something?"

Harley gulped, his heart pounding fast and furious. Did no one else see these guys?

Kent kept grinning as he placed his palm in the center of Raymond's chest. "'S okay, brother. We just come to take this soldier home. You ready, Raymond? It's time to go."

Of all damned things, Raymond grabbed Kent's hand and lifted off the bed. Only he didn't, but he did. His body stayed there, but a shimmering white shadow that looked like him sat straight up. He smiled, the most radiant smile Harley had ever seen, crooked teeth, unibrow, and all.

"Hi, Harley." His fingers splayed in a goofy wave. "Is you good now too?"

No way! He didn't just say that, did he?

Kent clutched the big guy's hand in an assist off the table. "Time to go, buddy. Your battle's done. You're going home."

Harley scrubbed his face to make the apparition vanish. *None of this is real. It's not happening. Is it?*

"You was supposed to call Mama, Corporal Mortimer." Kent's grin was gone. "Tell her she was right. I should've listened. Army food ain't no good at all."

"Tell Kelsey I love her." Raymond waved one last time. "She's my Mama for ever and ever."

Harley nodded, stark raving crazy for sure.

"You good now?" Kent asked as he and Raymond turned into pixilated vapor that merged with the other men's already fading shapes. *Ah, ghosts. Umm, soldiers. Oh, what the hell!*

"Harley. I asked you something. You hear me? Are you good now?" A voice drifted down from the ceiling. "Don't forget. Call Mama."

No faces. No vapor. Just ceiling tiles. Harley answered anyway. "Yeah. I'm good. You bet. I'll call your mama."

"You promise?"

"Yeah, buddy. I promise."

The vision, or whatever it was, ended. When Harley lowered his head, everyone in the room was looking at him like he'd lost his mind. Well, that was one big 'Duh!'

Judy held a clenched fist to her lips, but it was Alex who spoke. "Are you okay, son?"

Define okay?

Harley wiped his eyes, convinced he'd seen his men. Between E words and apparitions, he couldn't win. *Hell no, I'm not okay. I'm insane!*

The silence stretched, broken only by Kelsey's soft whimper. She even cried like a lady, full of grace in everything she did. How did Alex ever get so lucky? Better question, how did Harley get so screwed up? Seeing ghosts? And they took Raymond? And they called him a soldier? Didn't make one lick of sense.

I need a pain pill.

He contemplated telling Kelsey what Raymond had just said, but held back. There was no way his friends would believe him right now.

"I'm still here," Alex whispered as he pulled Kelsey back into his arms.

She turned and hid her face in his shirt, her shoulders trembling with sobs. Harley watched the tenderness. His earlier panic slipped away along with the saltwater fountain leaking out of his eyes. It washed the hurt away. Some of the guilt too. He could breathe again.

Best of all, he could lift his head. The buddies who'd died in that IED didn't hate him like he thought. They'd just paid a visit to prove it. It almost made it easier to live with himself. Maybe he wasn't insane. Maybe they'd really been here. Yeah. He was good with that scenario. Damned good.

"Do you know what I see when I'm looking around this room?"

Of course, Miss O'Brien would be the one to ruin the reverent moment. Harley shot her a disparaging look. Couldn't she see this was private? She needed to butt out. This was TEAM business.

Kelsey was more gracious. She sniffed and asked politely, "What, Judy?"

"I see Raymond's sweetest and maybe his only friend in the whole world," Nurse Judy said softly, "and she's surrounded by a fierce group of guardian angels who would do anything for her. Look at these guys, Kelsey. They're all twice your size. They're all gentle giants, especially the one with his arms wrapped around you. And they all love you. Even I can see it now."

Harley blinked. He hadn't expected Judy to sum them up like she did, but she was right. Alex always did have the warrior angel thing going for him, toughest dog in the fight and for sure, the one guy every man wanted in his corner when it came time to brawl. Zack and Mark too. And of course they all loved Kelsey. Judy got it. She got them.

Kelsey looked around her circle of friends, sniffing as she settled down. "But Ethel still killed him."

"No, she didn't," Judy said sternly. "Listen to me, Kelsey. Ethel didn't kill Raymond any more than Harley killed his men. Acromegaly killed Raymond, and an IED killed Kent, Rick, and everyone else that day in Iraq. Understand that right here and now. Do not live with guilt for something you did not do."

Ouch. Damn. Low blow. She could not have hit Harley harder if she'd physically knocked him down and stomped his butt into the linoleum. He watched for another sneak attack. Damned if she wasn't—right again.

"Besides," Alex declared, "Raymond got to meet you. He was a lucky kid. Just like me."

"And me." Murphy sniffed as he offered his sincerest.

"Libby loves you like a sister." Mark's eyes were red-rimmed and teary. "Me and JayJay too."

"I'll always have your six, Kels," Zack said. "Anytime. Anywhere."

Harley offered a wink. "You're my Kelsey Girl. You know that."

Kelsey took a deep breath and wiped her cheeks, her voice squeaky as she held Raymond's big hand against her cheek one last time. "I'm going to miss you, my sweet lost boy."

Twenty-Seven

Alex was wrong. Trotting Harley out to the Shenandoah hadn't helped him remember anything. Judy couldn't take anymore, and she was tired of the way his face lit up every time he looked at Kelsey. Yes, the two of them had a history. Romantic or not, it was more than Judy could bear.

Murphy and Mark lingered, filling Alex in on the conclusion of the sniper operation and Roy's resulting injuries. Apparently Roy and Connor were in the emergency room here in the same hospital. Zack and Kelsey chatted quietly. Harley stayed seated where he was, so Judy slipped out of the door.

The reflection of an aggravated woman in the plate glass window at the end of the hall caught her eye. She tilted her chin up, ready to get back to work and put the day behind her. The reflection tilted its chin too, and Judy went to her.

"I'm just tired," she whispered to herself in the cold glass.

A door opened and closed behind her. Judy rolled her shoulders, ready to be Nurse O'Brien again. Great. It had to be him. Harley. She watched his reflection as he approached. Tall and slender, the man had long legs that never failed to make her think of a cowboy. Slender hips, a little bow-legged, and sexy as all get out, the drawl fit him to a T. He was her kind of man through and through. A cowboy. A lost cowboy.

"Ah, ma'am?"

"What do you want?"

He took the hit, blinking in surprise, and she felt bad. He didn't deserve her attitude and she knew it. She just couldn't stop.

"Why'd you, umm, leave?" He seemed so timid, a sure sign he was not the man he used to be.

"I have a job to do. I don't belong in there."

"Seemed to me like you belonged."

"No." She'd read his body language. He didn't want her there. Not really. "You should be back in bed."

The big oaf spotted his reflection. Like the kid at heart he was, Harley ran a hand over his unruly hair from one side to the other, swiping it down like he always did. Only his hair had a mind of its own. Harley didn't need fancy products to get that trendy spiked look. He was born with it, just never appreciated it. Once he looked semi-presentable, he reached for her shoulder, but froze before he made contact. No kidding. Why would he want to touch a bitchy woman?

"Go back to your friends." She slanted away from his long fingers.

"I can't."

"Since when?" He'd never had a problem leaving her before. "Go see what Alex wants. Go hug Kelsey Girl. Just... go." Again the snarky tone rang in her ears. Why was she taking it out on him? None of this day was his fault. Sudden moisture in her eyes turned the bright lights of the city below into a blurry blob.

He lowered his arm. "I might not be the sharpest knife in the drawer, but I know when a woman says, 'Go,' she really means, 'Don't you dare leave.'"

Judy rolled her eyes at his sincerity. Harley always was perceptive like that. There was a time he could read her like a book. Two days ago.

He tried again. "Can I help?"

"I don't know. Can you?"

Again his hand reached for her but didn't connect. If he'd just grab hold and spin her around like he usually did, maybe it would solve everything. Why didn't he? Oh yeah. He was probably thinking of Kelsey Girl.

"Elephant," he blurted, lowering his hand to his side, a bewildered look on his face. He shook his head as if he didn't know why he'd just said that incredibly stupid word. "Elegant," he said more firmly.

She looked closer, not sure if he was playing a game or displaying a symptom. Attention Deficit Disorder revealed itself through blurting, but so did other brain-related dysfunctions, including his mild case of TBI. Usually, those words reflected a patient's inner feelings. So what was he trying to tell her? Or Kelsey?

He licked his lips, his brows crinkled with concern. "Exquisite."

"What are you doing?" She didn't turn around, just kept track of his reflection.

"I, umm, don't know." The bewildered look on his face warmed her soul. At least, he was honest. "It's gonna sound like I'm losing my mind, but every time I look at you, an E word lights up in my head like a big old neon sign."

Okay, that helped. He was thinking about her. Rack one point for Harley.

"Exciting. Entangled." He was on a roll now.

The sight of him standing so close tempted her to turn and fall into his arms. Would it make any difference? Would she still be Nurse Judy, or would he suddenly recall they had a more intimate history? It seemed a simple solution, but what if he pushed her away? The risk of rejection loomed too possible and too painful.

"Go," she whispered. *Please.*

"Energy. Extravagant. E—"

"I have one for you." She pulled the ring off her right hand and turned around. Face to face, his hazel eyes lit up. An E word popped into her head too. Endearing. That was Harley down to his toes, the most gentle, endearing man she'd ever known—a lover of children, old folks, any animal on Nat Geo, and, until recently, her. He was the only man she'd ever loved. How did he not know that? Her heart stuttered. Would this next impulsive act hurt or hinder? Another word popped into her mind, superimposing itself on the other.

"How about enough?" She held out the ring on the palm of her hand. "That's an E word."

He backed away, his eyes on the stone. "Chocolate diamond," he whispered.

"Yes." Rack two for Harley. At least he'd recognized the ring.

The day he'd given it to her came back crystal clear. Right in the middle of a Wisconsin airport concourse, he'd dropped to one knee and asked her to be his. It was not a marriage proposal, but it came close. He wanted her to move to the East Coast to live with him. She'd been dying for some kind of sign he was interested. The ring was definitely it. Only now....

"Take it," she pleaded. *Touch it. Remember us. Remember me.*

"No, ma'am." He shook his head, his palms forward to ward it off. "I can't. It's yours, isn't it?"

"Take it," she ordered. The tear spilled over.

"I gave it to you, didn't I?"

She wiped her face, the ring still extended.

"Exceptional."

Terrific. Another E word. The worry etched on his face stabbed her heart. What was she doing? He needed medical care, not torture by some demented ex-girlfriend. It was time she backed off and let a professional counselor take over. Remembering would have to wait for another day. She stuck the jewel into her pocket.

"Did I love you?"

Rip! Her heart shattered. *Did? Not do? Way to go, Mortimer.*

"Never mind." Judy steeled her rising flood of emotions. "I should never have allowed you to leave the hospital. It wore you out. You're sick."

"No, I'm not." He took a step into her comfort zone. "Answer me. I need to know. Did you love me?"

"Forget it," she snapped to get him to back off. How could she answer? He didn't know who she was.

"Tell me." He made contact, his hands gentle but firm on her biceps. "My brain's not working so good right now, but I didn't forget you, did I?"

What a dumb question. His fingers trembled on her arm, his intentions so sincere she wanted to scream. He wouldn't have to ask if he remembered, but that was her Harley, solid as a rock with a brain that fell down on the job every once in awhile. And that's why she loved him. She could see past the handicap he had to deal with every day. She saw the tender side of the stone cold sniper who never should have enlisted in the first place.

Shoving her emotions into the pocket along with the ring, she became efficient Nurse O'Brien again. With a twist of her hands, she regained control. "You, sir, are sick. Let's get you settled into your room. Your VA counselor will stop by in the morning. You can chat with him."

"I am kinda tired," he admitted. His hair had sprung back into a few spikes. Black circled his eyes. "But you'll talk to me for awhile, won't you?"

"We'll see." She led him to the elevator. Patients didn't usually get to come and go as they pleased. Thankfully, his room was exactly as he'd left it no doubt because of her status on the staff. The bed was made. It didn't take long to get him back into pajamas, an IV ordered, and the monitor reattached. The massage table she'd brought to the hospital earlier stood unused beneath the window. No problem. She folded it, planning to take it home the next day. A full-blown get-reacquainted massage was out of the question now. She wasn't up for it, and nobody else had better touch him.

"Why did I give you that ring? It must have meant something. Come on. Tell me about it. Was it at dinner? Some place romantic?"

"No big deal," she lied. "Just friends at college."

His face crinkled into one of his funny faces. "I went to college?"

Typical. He would zero in on the wrong lie. Harley scratched the top of his hard head, but his eyes were heavy. "It's a mighty big stone. Looks expensive."

"Good night, Mr. Mortimer." She kept it business. The ring was expensive all right, a spur of the moment impulse from that sweet, banged up brain. It wouldn't take long now. Once he was prone, he was either asleep or... She brushed the other possibility away. So not happening. Not tonight.

"You're leaving?"

"Yes." She turned at the door, another white lie ready on her lips. "I have rounds to make. Other patients. You need to rest."

Longing filled the hazel gaze riveted on her. "You sure you don't want to maybe sit on the edge of my bed and talk with me? I won't try anything. Honest. I'll keep my hands to myself."

And that was the problem. "I'm sure. Goodnight."

"Maybe when I'm better? We could go out for a drink or–"

"You don't drink," she barked. What was wrong with this man? Didn't he know he was a recovering alcoholic either?

"'Kay," he said softly. "But if you change your mind, I'll be here."

"I won't." She shut the door and walked away, her heart stuck in her throat so tight she couldn't even cry. Maybe tomorrow would be a better day. This one sure sucked.

He slept like a rock. Some guy named Raj checked on him in the middle of the night. Woke him up to give him a pill to put him back to sleep. At the crack of dawn, a different guy showed up to check his knife wound. The nametag stitched on his jacket pocket declared Doctor Statler. He performed his examination quickly, taking a listen with a cold stethoscope when he was nearly through.

"Deep breaths," he ordered.

Harley took deep breaths.

"Again."

Harley breathed again.

"Must be love." The doctor draped the stethoscope around his neck.

"Excuse me?" Harley caught the busy man's wrist. "What'd you say?"

Dr. Statler grinned. "I said it must be love. The only reason you're not dead is by the grace of God and Judy. What day is it?"

What a dumb question. Harley took a stab in the dark. "Wednesday?"

"It's Monday." Again with the smug expression. "Do you remember who brought you to the hospital?"

If this wasn't Wednesday, what difference did anything else make?

"Umm, Mark Houston?"

Dr. Statler wiped the look off his face. "The paramedics brought you in through the emergency room Saturday night. Your friend, Mark Houston, came in at the same time, but he was in another ambulance."

"You sure?" Harley studied the doctor. Statler didn't seem to be lying, but Harley was pretty sure he'd seen Mark in the ambulance with him.

"You have a mild TBI, a traumatic brain injury caused by a blow to the back of your head, Mr. Mortimer, which you sustained in an automobile crash. You also have a seven-inch laceration on your calf, and a puncture wound directly below your sternum. For some reason, the knife missed every vital organ in your abdomen. You should be dead."

"I get that a lot," Harley muttered. "So when can I leave?"

"Tomorrow." The doctor's hand remained on Harley's shoulder while he examined the stitches on the back of his head. "I hear you went for a chopper ride yesterday. Not a smart move for a man in your condition. At least, you had the sense to take Judy with you. Any other aches or pains I should know about?"

"No." Pains or not, Harley wanted to see Judy again. They had to talk.

"Okay then." Statler stopped at the door. "Your neurologist should stop by soon, and I believe you're due for a visit from your VA counselor sometime today. Any of this sounding familiar?"

"Yeah," Harley admitted. Kinda. Sorta.

"Good." Statler looked satisfied. At least someone was. "One of the nurses will be in to re-bandage your leg. Do yourself a favor. Get some sleep while you're here and do not leave this room unattended. Understood?"

But it was not Nurse Judy who showed. It was Viki. Blond, perky Viki with big boobs and one of those crew cut women's hairdos that made her look like a guy. If it wasn't for her chest....

Harley watched her unwrap his leg, check it, and apply more dressing.

"Where's Judy?"

"Not on shift today, I guess. Why? You need something?" She batted clumpy black eyelashes from him to the folded massage table. "I give a mean back rub."

Hell, no. "Just wondering where she was. That's all."

"Call the kitchen if you're hungry." She moved his phone from the nightstand to his bed, her hand uncomfortably on his wrist while she explained, "Dial 3. If you want meals on time, you'll have to place your order early. The kitchen only serves sandwiches and soup after 5p.m., but you can have all the fluids you want any time. Anything else?"

"Nope." He rearranged his pillow to get her to move her hand. "On second thought, where's my clothes?"

She pointed to the closet door. "Bet they're in there. You want me to check?"

"No." He remembered now. Judy had hung everything up for him before she left last night. It had seemed natural how she'd straightened his shirt on the hanger. She hadn't even asked, just took care of him like it was no big deal.

"I'll be in later to give you a sponge bath." Viki kept batting those clumpy eyelashes and offering what else, he did not care to find out.

Enough said. Harley was out of there and on the street before Nurse Viki had the chance to make good on her threat. It took him awhile to wrangle a cab, but then he had no money. Worse, he could not remember his home address, only where he worked. Good enough. The cabbie took him to his office. Harley had to ask the cabbie to call Mother to come down and please pay the fare so he'd stop swearing and leave. By the time Harley limped into the elevator and was seated at her desk, he needed a place to hunker down and hide.

"Where's the boss?"

"Alex didn't come in today," she replied. "He's taking a couple weeks off with Kelsey. You want some coffee?"

"No." Harley waved it off. He needed something a lot stronger than caffeine in his blood. "Where's Roy? Murphy?"

"Roy is at home recuperating. Murphy took a personal day."

"Mark?"

Mother grimaced. "Home."

"Who's here then?"

"Me." A heavy hand clasped Harley's tired shoulder. Zack. "What are you doing here? Why aren't you home?"

"I... don't know where I live," Harley said simply. *I don't know a damned thing.*

"Sure you're okay? You look three sheets to the wind." Zack hadn't moved his hand yet.

"Where's my desk?"

It only took sinking into his chair for Harley to realize what he should have known all along. The framed picture of gorgeous Nurse O'Brien on his desk explained everything. Only she looked happy then, her long hair blowing in the breeze against an aquamarine ocean backdrop. Better yet was the genuine relaxed smile on his face with her sitting on his lap and facing him the way she was. Her lips looked a little sunburned and swollen like she'd been kissed hard. It did not escape his notice that no bikini straps showed in the picture. No tan lines either. The notion enticed. And panicked.

"Am I married?" *God, I hope not. A wife will never forgive being forgotten.*

"You don't remember Judy yet," Zack stated, making himself comfortable on the edge of Harley's desk.

Pushed back in his chair and searching his mind, Harley studied the picture in his hands. "Evil eye," he blurted, his frustration growing with the incessant word game. "Hell, Zack, I remember you guys. I can even remember the guys in my squad now. Why can't I remember her?"

"What's your doctor say?"

Harley shrugged. "I don't know. He wanted me to stay another day. I opted out."

"You need to go back. Your neurologist can help."

"Haven't seen him yet. You know me. I don't do hospitals. Do I?" Harley had to think. Sometimes he actually sounded like he knew what he was talking about.

Zack folded his arms over his chest. "You can't stay here. You're not fit for work. What do you want to do?"

"I need a drink," Harley grumbled, searching the drawers of his desk for a bottle. "You got anything? I'm coming up dry."

"No," Zack answered sternly, shaking his head. "That's not like you, man. Booze screwed you up last time. You are not starting that crap again. You know that."

"But I got nothing, Zack." The walls seemed to close in. "No wallet. No phone. I can't remember where I parked my Jeep, much less where I live. And I got a really bad feeling," Harley stabbed his thumb into his tender chest, "that doesn't have anything to do with that old bag who knifed me. Damn. I can even remember Miriam. Why not Judy?"

"Scratch your Jeep off your to-do list. It burned to a crisp in the accident. And stop worrying about your memory. Give yourself a break. It's only been a couple days. Maybe seeing your apartment will jog something loose." Zack kept his voice real calm like he was handling a skittish horse. For good reason. There was not enough air in the room.

"Nurse O'Brien lives with me, doesn't she?"

Zack nodded.

How could the gorgeous redhead in the photo live with him, a loser? Made no sense. Neither did the anxiety creeping up his spine. "Don't think she wants to see me. Kinda felt like she was happy to get away from me last night. Good riddance. You know?"

"Come on." Zack offered an arm up. "Judy's not that way. It takes time. Trust me."

"You think?"

"I don't just think, I know," Zack replied. "Let me check first. She was staying at a hotel down the street. Judy might be closer than you think." He reached for the phone on Harley's desk and punched in a number. Wow. He sounded sure of himself.

"Mind if we stop for a drink along the way? You buy?" Harley tried again while Zack was on the phone. Sometimes a man needed to strategize with a few good buddies over a couple beers before he did something drastic like facing an angry woman.

Zack shook his head and ended his phone call with the hotel. "It's your lucky day. She'd already checked out, and no, we are not stopping at a bar. You don't do booze, you don't do drugs, and you're almost as good a shot as me. Now get your ass in my car. I'm taking you home."

"What if she's there?" Harley balked, a full-blown case of nerves rattling his last resolve.

"Good. You two need to talk. Give her a chance. Judy's the best thing that ever happened to you."

"But what if she won't let me in?"

"Shut it, Mortimer." Zack waved toward the elevator. "You're going home."

Twenty-Eight

Judy couldn't wait. The FBI had contacted her at her hotel to return the belongings they'd taken. Could she meet them? You bet she could. Judy was itching for another round with Agent Holman. Only it wasn't him standing at her apartment door with two other agents and three hand trucks stacked high with cardboard boxes and computer equipment when she arrived. It figured.

"Good morning, ma'am." The nearest agent nodded politely toward the boxes. "We're returning evidence from our investigation."

She bit her tongue. Lashing out at this guy was pointless. Wordlessly, she unlocked the apartment and entered her home. It took them five minutes to wheel their cargo inside, but Judy made them stand and wait while she opened and examined the contents of each box. Not until Harley's engagement ring was located did she look at them again. "Where do I sign?"

The same agent offered a pen and the property release form. He wasn't bad looking. Tall. Nicely combed blond hair. Tan. Neither was he rude. But he was FBI. He needed to leave. With the form signed and back in his hand, he nodded again. "Have a nice day."

She couldn't get them out of her home fast enough. Only when her apartment door was closed with the dead bolt engaged did she breathe a sigh of relief. One battle down. One to go.

Judy faced the mess that once was Harley's sanctuary. She pushed her sleeves back. Organization was one of her major talents—or sins, the way Harley saw it.

Digging in, she tackled the entertainment center first. Organizing his vinyl record, eight-track tape, cassette, and CD collection of country and cowboy music went quickly. Alphabetically. A nice touch. One he may never appreciate, but a nice touch nonetheless.

Next came the extra bedroom that doubled as an office, a filing nightmare all by itself. No problem. Her fingers flew while her mind worked the puzzle of Harley. The complexities of the damaged brain created a wide range of dysfunctions that impacted a patient's feelings, memories, knowledge, and abilities. Fortunately, he didn't suffer from impaired basic cognitive skills. He just seemed stuck in the greatest traumatic event of his life, the poor man.

The resilience and pain threshold of some of the ex-military she'd come across never ceased to amaze her. Alex's team was a prime example. All battle-hardened and tougher than most, they seemed able to compartmentalize their pain until they had time for it.

Harley was the same, ready to throw himself back into work even if it was just a walk in the woods with his boss. Last night should have gone differently. At the end, Judy had flown off and left her future husband with the woman he still dreamed about.

Yeah. She knew. He'd blurted Kelsey's name plenty during nightmares and dreams. Of course, he'd blurted other names too, and now they all made sense. His brain had been trying to tell him something for years.

Judy stood at the open gun safe with a bucket of hot, sudsy water. She pushed the irksome feeling aside that always surfaced at thoughts of Kelsey and Harley together. Roy's bit of gossip explained a lot. Of course, they'd bonded at that more than intimate moment when rescuer met victim. The way Harley was at that time in his life, he'd bonded like super glue to the gentle woman he'd saved. Who didn't like Kelsey?

"There," she said to herself when the safe was cleaned and his extra holsters and other paraphernalia in proper order. She almost felt like she'd accomplished something until she closed the door. Her fingers came away from the brass handle crusted with Harley's dried blood. Reality intruded. Her indomitable energy flagged. She could organize the heck out of his belongings. He still wasn't there.

The house phone rang from the kitchen wall. Her foolish heart skipped a beat. It could be him.

"Judy O'Brien," she answered hoping to hear a familiar voice on the other end of the line.

Heavy breathing responded instead. A man's deep voice groaned into her ear. Not Harley's. More heavy breathing. Great. A prank call. Wasn't that the perfect end to another dismal day?

Judy slammed the phone into its wall cradle. Prank calls did not scare her. One way or the other Harley would come home, and when he did, she was going to get that romantic encounter she'd passed up. Never again would she miss an opportunity to be with the man she loved.

She had a shower to clean.

"Extravagant," he blurted at Zack's black Porsche. The oddest words popped up at the strangest times. Maybe he was wrong. What if none of these words had to do with her?

"Say what?"

"Nothing. I keep coming up with E words." Harley sank into the passenger seat and pulled the door closed. "Starting to bug me."

"That's weird." Zack cranked up his CDR system, and Harley closed his eyes, content to let the reverberations of smooth jazz drown his discontent. Weird didn't begin to cover the way his brain was working right now.

Entertaining.

Right on cue. Another stupid E word! At least, he didn't blurt this one out. Harley sank lower into his seat. The Porsche wove through traffic but he ignored the view, just kept his eyes closed, wishing everything would return to normal the next time he opened them. When the car slowed, he gave it a shot, but the view failed in the 'Honey, I'm home' department.

"You ready?" Zack asked.

"Why not?" Harley pushed the car door open. Climbing slowly to his feet, he scanned the building. Nothing registered. Not the red brick. Not the elevator ride to the fourth floor. Not even the apartment door Zack assured him was his.

"I live here?" Harley stood at his door, not quite ready to knock.

Zack stuck a fist in front of his face and gave the door five sharp raps.

Instant panic hit. "I was going to do that."

Eventually.

Ugh. Not again!

Zack shrugged, his palms spread upward. "You snooze, you lose."

The suspense mounted. Harley's mouth dried. What could he possibly say to an angry, hurt woman? Maybe Zack shouldn't be here. It might get ugly. The knob turned. Nurse O'Brien opened the door. Her sleeves were rolled up like they'd interrupted her in the middle of something important. Surprise flashed over her features, and dead on its heels, irritation.

Ewww....

"You're supposed to be in bed." She opened the door just enough to talk.

"Yes, ma'am," Harley's mouth answered automatically. Out of the blue, his Texas accent showed up. "That wouldn't be an invitation, would it little lady?" He cringed before the words were out of his mouth, which was hard because his foot was in there too. No woman likes a smart-aleck come on when she's madder than a wet hen.

Sure enough. Emerald greens glared a mean shot in Zack's direction. "Was this your idea, Lennox?"

Harley winced. She tended to use last names when she got mad. Next, he'd be just dumb old Mortimer.

"Don't blame me," Zack explained. "I figured he'd better get home before he fell down in the street. We don't want to lose him again, do we?"

She opened the door, scowling like a gargoyle at the warning in Zack's tone. "Fine. Enter."

Harley gulped and stepped into her, umm, his apartment. Clean. Fresh smelling. A hint of detergent and jasmine in the air. He headed straight to the couch and sat. Zack was right. The stupidity of the day caught up with him. Sit or fall. Once down, he studied the carpet between his boots while Zack chatted at the door. Always a lady's man, he usually knew what to say. Didn't seem to be hitting it off with this woman though.

Another E word flashed loud and urgently clear. *E. X. I. T.*

Harley glanced at the open door. Maybe his brain was right this time.

"Why here, Zack?"

"Just bringing him home—"

"He belongs in the hospital. Take him back."

Ouch. She sure knew how to make a guy feel welcome.

"Nope. He's all yours." Zack left. Just like that. He didn't even come in to be sociable. The coward.

Judy stood silent, her eyes stabbing into the top of Harley's head. He could feel 'em. At last, he looked up. Sure enough. Still mad.

"Hi," he said quietly.

Expelled. Escape. Exposed.

Wow. His brain really knew how to offer— *Encouragement.* He cringed. Now, he was doing it.

A glimmer of tenderness shifted over her face. "Why didn't you stay in the hospital, Mortimer?"

Right on cue. He was Mortimer instead of Harley. The idea niggled that maybe he did know this woman better than he thought. How else would he have known her tactics?

"I... I...." He didn't have an answer. "I reckon I didn't want to."

When she didn't move or reply he tried again. "Nice place you got here."

Her lips twisted. Sarcasm poured out. "It ought to be. It's yours."

Blew it, Mortimer. Going down. Again.

Embolden.

Harley scrubbed a quick hand over his face. He was caught between an over-talkative brain and an angry woman, no man's land for a simple thinker like him. The whole day was wearing him out and it wasn't even noon yet.

Exhausted.

Shit, he cussed silently to himself. *I'm not exhausted. I'm stupid. This won't work.*

"Can we talk?" he asked. "I'm not good at playing games."

"And yet here you are." She folded her arms across her very full and lovely breasts.

Elegant. Elegant. Elegant.

Okay, that was weird, three of the same E word in rapid-fire sequence.

His one hundred percent male eyeballs scrolled up and down her figure. For a change, she was garbed in something besides scrubs. Tight fitting jeans and a green knit shirt with three tiny buttons at the open neckline did her justice. She had her sleeves pushed up like she meant business. Lips to hips, she was his kind of woman. Full of curves. Soft. Sassy as hell.

Her long hair played along, flouncing over her shoulders and teasing his tired eyes with its variegated shades of cedar.

One minute red, the next burnished bronze that glimmered into hints of blond and brown. Why hadn't he noticed it yesterday? Oh wait. He did, only it was pulled into a boring ponytail, not sexy like now. Everything about the woman was just plain—

Exciting.

He raked his fingers through his hair, his gaze drifting down her sultry body to her open-toed sandals. Shimmery brown polished toenails finished the summery effect she had going. Was the color of that bikini she wasn't wearing in the picture ob his desk orange? Blue? Déjà vue whispered green, but not green. Maybe one of those light colors women called pastels. Whatever. It had to have looked good on her. Off too.

Erotic.

Oh, yeah....

Tossing the bullshit, he went for broke and patted the couch beside him. "I can't talk to you when you look like you're gonna make a break for it. Why don't you come on over here?"

She huffed, but she did join him, sitting at the edge of the couch, all stiff, prim and untouchable. "So what now—"

Exigent.

"Just hush," he ordered, his hands on his knees so she'd settle down and he could stop shaking. The damn woman was making him nervous, like that was hard to do. And if his brain chimed in with one more E word, he'd scream. Hell, now it was tossing words Harley wasn't positive he'd heard before, much less knew what they meant. At least he wasn't blurting them out loud anymore.

Verging on hyperventilation, he gave her the chance to lie again. Friends in college? No way. "You and me live together. Right?"

Her brows shadowed an intense glare. "I told you this was your apartment."

Exhilarated.

"Listen, Miss O'Brien. I might have been born at night, but it wasn't last night. Even a dumb guy like me wouldn't have bought the stone on your finger for a casual friend. And if we live together, we're either married or pretty damned serious."

She pursed her lips. Okay, so this was going to be harder than he guessed. Judy was stubborn. He liked that. But those lips, full and soft, all scrunched together like she was too mad to talk were hard to resist. He wanted to kiss that angry pout right off her face. At least, she was still wearing the ring. That had to count for something.

Endurance.

God, I'm caught in the middle of virtual Scrabble!

"Trust me?"

"I used to," she said softly, her lips still tight. She combed her fingers through one side of her hair, pushing the silken mass over one shoulder, but leaving the other a dividing curtain between them.

"I told you last night I been bombarded with E words." Securing a handful of reddish silk, he lifted her protective barrier aside to see her face. "Maybe I got Tourette's syndrome, I don't know, but all these words have something to do with you. Would you help me out?"

Another huff and he had her right where he wanted her. Still mad. Still stubborn. Still—

Exasperated.

"I propose a test." He shifted his butt a teensy bit closer to hers.

Examination.

"No." She backed away.

Wow. She didn't waste much time thinking about that. He edged closer, the back of his fingers against her neck while he kept hold of her hair, careful not to pull it or scare her.

"Kiss me."

"No." Her nose tipped up just a titch. He had half a mind to tickle her. She just looked so danged cute. Maybe tickling had gotten him past that gruff exterior before. He decided against it.

"Come on. Just one kiss. What would it hurt? No tongue. Just lips. I promise. I won't even breathe hard."

"You don't remember me. Why would I kiss you?" She moved again. Inch by inch he was losing the battle, but he had a feeling he was winning the war. She hadn't run.

"I think I do." He bumped his hip into her. Thigh to thigh and against the arm of the couch, she had no retreat. "One kiss. That's all. If I'm wrong, I leave. But if I'm right, you get to tear my clothes off and make love with me right here on the couch."

Encounter.

Harley ignored his mind and focused on her. He couldn't resist tossing that dare into the mix. Anger wasn't the only vibe pouring off this lovely lady. His male instincts weren't confused. They'd zeroed in on her desire the moment she'd acquiesced and sat her pretty backside down. A woman with murder on her mind would not have done that.

Encouragement.

Judy ran the tip of her tongue over her bottom lip, her eyes on his. Baiting him like he was baiting her, another positive sign. When she didn't say no, he closed the distance. Tired as he as, he wasn't dead.

Exhume.

A statue could not have moved less. The closer he got, the more rigid she became until... Until... He leaned forward and grazed her lips with his. Her breath hitched, another definite plus. She closed her eyes, a good enough yes for him.

He closed his and pressed a chaste kiss onto the tender flesh that melted like the sweetest honey with a hint of jasmine He savored the sensation of her mouth to his, letting it fill his senses. Their breaths mingled and he wanted more. Tongue. Nipples. All.

The Mortimer train was on the track and rolling. E words or not, this was right and good. The Army calls it muscle training when a troop does something so many times he could do it in his sleep. His heart definitely knew its way around this woman. He trusted that muscle right now.

Smoothing one hand up her arm from her elbow to her shoulder, he aimed for the back of her neck with the other, not relinquishing the taste of her, just pushing her off balance enough to upset her marble countenance. The statue thing she had going relaxed with a soft sigh. Marble turned to warm flesh and blood. He cupped the back of her skull, holding her in place as he deepened the contact, asking for more and willing to take all she'd allow.

Please let me remember something. Anything. Don't let me lose this woman.

Ah, she smelled good. He inhaled deeply. All the stress he'd been carrying melted away.

"Judy." He poured the last of his heart and soul into her name. If she'd only reach for him, pull him closer, give him just one sign he wasn't the loser he felt like.

I love you. I know I do.

"Harley," she whispered between lips and tongues. A slender hand touched his chest, not pushing him away, just planted there like it might want to do more. Any minute now. Did he dare press forward? Was he that kind of brave? Hell, yeah.

The snaps to her bra went next. Muscle memory served him right again. Even through the fabric of her shirt, the three snaps succumbed easily. A moan thrummed up from deep inside of her, and he took that for permission to proceed.

Besides, any minute now it was all going to come back to him. He knew it, so he kept on going, his hand fumbling the hem of her shirt, pulling it up and out of his way. With those tantalizing breasts warm against his chest, the mission was clear.

Remember, damn it. Find a way. Love this woman. Today. Tonight. Always.

Her hand moved from his chest to his wrist, stopping his mission dead in its tracks. He pulled back, just enough to read her intentions, and, of course, to take in the extra soft jiggle beneath her shirt. Those luscious breasts were unleashed, and his heart did a triple somersault, banging so hard against his ribs she had to be able to hear it. Tender nipples waited to be teased to perfection if she'd let him. He could make her real happy. He knew it. With all his soul, he wanted to do nothing but please her.

"Who am I?" she asked, her eyes hazy and warm. Judy leaned in for another kiss, tugging his lower lip in a gentle nibble.

"Judy O'Brien, the woman of my dreams."

She smiled against his mouth, believing him. He hoped.

"You're wearing my ring," he told her the obvious, sure his brain would help him out any second now. Until that last news flash, it had grown oddly quiet in the E department.

"Where were we when you gave it to me?"

Oh, hell. A test. Her mouth was still fully engaged with his, savoring him as much as he was her. He kept kissing, deepening the contact and stalling for time. Where had he given her the ring? A big dead zone answered, offering absolutely nothing but empty space in his brain. A raft of really good lies bubbled up. Right here in their apartment? On that beach in the picture? Candlelight dinner? A groan escaped from his gut, but it was not a sound of passion. More like the agony of defeat.

Another tangle of tongues and the gentle hand on his wrist turned into a rigid stop sign. She pulled back. Pointy green microscopes scanned his eyes looking for someone to be home.

Sorry. The lights are on, but....

"You don't know, do you?" Her voice lingered all deep and breathy against his lips. Yeah, she was turned on. Good deal. But still sad.

"No." He could not lie. "I'm sorry. I'm trying, but I don't."

Sadness shadowed her face, but instead of being angry, she pulled him to his feet with her. After tucking her shirt in place, she headed to the hall still gripping his hand. Was she going to take him to bed with her in the middle of the day? Well alrighty then.

The less than honorable thought had barely flitted through his mind when other women's faces in other times and darker nights shuddered over him with a chill. Sleazy women. Skanky women. Not ladies. Surely not Judy.

He balked, suddenly not so sure of himself. A sickly sensation pitched in the bottom of his stomach. There was a time he'd sought women like them out. They were good enough for the mess of a man he was—then. The image of a guy lying against garbage cans in a dirty ally materialized next. It was raining. The man looked half-dead. Gray. Strung out.

Zack's words came back. 'You don't do drugs.'

But I did and—that guy is—me.

He shook the ugly images off. What the hell was he thinking?

Holding fast to Judy's hand, he gulped the nauseous realization down. He'd thought this game of cat and mouse would lead he and Judy to bed, but more, he'd hoped to find the place called home again. Everything in his soul told him it was with this elegant, sexy woman. It had to be her. They seemed to fit together. Only his brain seemed unconvinced, steadily tsk, tsk, tsking at every thought and hope, filling him with doubt.

The air in this apartment seemed suddenly stale and not enough. He squeezed her fingers half-afraid she'd evaporate like everything else good and decent in his life. One truth had finally fallen into place.

She's too good for me.

Twenty-Nine

Harley could be such a dumb ass. Did he really think she was taking him to bed when he didn't have a clue who she was? Oh no. Judy had other plans. The only way he was getting into their bedroom again was to remember. And he would.

With her hands on his shoulders, she stopped him dead in his tracks at the entry to the hall. For her plan to work, they had to take this trip back in time together. She meant to hold off until he was healthier, but since he'd shown up unannounced, why not?

Judy forced all the charm she could muster to her face, eyes and voice. "Are you Harley Mortimer?"

"Umm, well yeah, hi." His brows furrowed. Fatigue stalked his usually bright eyes, turning them dull. She nearly changed her mind. The flirting tease she'd seen for a moment in the living room looked more like the living dead right now. Something was happening inside that poor man's mind. Maybe this wasn't a good idea.

Determined to try, she reached into the entertainment center anyway, tapped a couple switches and let the quiet music fill the room. The lights dimmed in sync with the volume of the music. Placing one palm in his, she lifted it. Her other hand settled on his shoulder which put her breasts in proximity to his chest.

As predictably as the sun rising in the east, he looked down at her cleavage. She knew her man. Full breasts and long hair distracted Harley in a snap. Putting all of her feminine wiles into play, she counted on his inherent weakness as a red-blooded male to get him where she needed him to go. All he had to do was remember one tiny detail from their past, and everything else would fall into place. It had to.

"I hate to be forward, but would you care to dance?"

"Who? Me?" He chewed on the right side of his bottom lip. "Umm, I don't think I usually dance until I've had a few drinks, but, umm, Zack... He tells me I don't drink anymore, and...."

Half of her wanted to laugh, the rest wanted to cry. She knew the body language, the way he rolled his shoulder like his neck hurt. Because it did. Tension had to be tweaking his back and neck muscles all the way to the top of his scalp. When a hint of sadness shadowed his eyes, her hand tightened. He looked so damn handsome and still lost, as if he might pull away.

Judy gulped. Was she torturing or helping? She didn't know anymore. Searching her mind for all the words she'd said the day they'd first met at Mark and Libby's wedding, she whispered, "I promise I won't step on your feet."

"Please?" Judy's voice quavered and, oh, why not? It's not like she'd asked him to boogie or do the twist. One spin around the living room couldn't hurt.

"Sure." Harley's heart thudded in his chest. Everything he'd wanted to do with her before seemed shallow now.

The dance began slowly. For some reason, he expected she'd lead, but she didn't. He took a step to the side, and she followed. Then another. She moved in under his chin, resting her ear over his noisy heart like she wanted to be there. A wave of protectiveness filled him when her body melted into his. The fragrance of jasmine filled his nose. A sensation of floating lifted his feet. She was shaking now too.

"I think you've done this before."

"Me too," he admitted, his mind on the verge of… something. He reached for the small of her back and pressed her tight. Judy had a way of making him feel like he could do anything. Two steps backwards, one to the left, maybe with her in his arms, he could finally remember. He closed his eyes and wished with all his heart it were so.

A half step forward and—the room spun. For just a split second, rainbow shards of light from a disco ball he knew did not exist in her living room fell over a gorgeous redhead in a white sleeveless gown. Her green eyes shone with a light so rare. Glitters sprinkled over the tuxedo he did not realize he was wearing. Over Mark and Libby's wedding dance. Over....

"Eau Claire," his dumb mouth said.

"That's right." Her fingers tightened at the back of his neck. "Tell me more."

He swallowed hard. The illusion vanished. Eau Claire was all there was left. It wasn't even a proper E word, not pronounced O like it was. His brain had just pushed him into the line of fire without a gun in his hand, but it had to mean something. Memories were stirring.

"Maybe this will help." Taking a step into him, Judy pushed him gently against the wall, one leg between his and one hand on his chest. Her eyes filled with seduction even an idiot couldn't miss. Her hand slid up the back of his head, her fingers long and tender on his scalp, carefully not touching the goose egg and stitches. The softest breasts pressed against his chest, and damn, he could not think.

"Harley Mortimer," she whispered all breathy and low. "I want to come home with you. I'm tired of never seeing you."

He nodded, trying with all of his heart to make sense of what she was telling him with her mouth instead of her body. His hands sank to her hips again, his thumbs caressing the crease where her thighs joined with her body.

Don't let me disappoint her. Help me out. Please.

This was that word-on-the-tip-of-his-tongue moment, and it better not start with an E. Burgeoning memories pushed him toward... something. He was so close, standing with his toes over the edge and not able to take that final step. Not able to let go and fall.

But nothing, absolutely nothing came to him when he needed it most. Very tenderly, he eased Judy back a step. Unfulfilled expectations glimmered in her sad eyes. He saw it there, a promise and a trap he could no longer avoid.

"Don't do this," she groaned. "Don't go."

The futility of trying so hard felt a lot like deceit. She was doing it too. They were both lying to each other and hoping this game turned into reality. A gentleman did not treat a good woman like this.

"I'm sorry," he mumbled, his eyes to the carpet and his heart down there with it. Anxiety began its relentless shoulder tapping, reminding him he didn't belong. Not yet. Maybe never again. His throat went dry. Palpitations resumed their steady beat in a heart that had just seconds ago been trying so hard to fall back into love.

He looked toward the door. *Where the hell is Zack?* "I should go."

When she released his hand, he knew he was the world's biggest ass for leading her on.

"Harley." Her voice cracked. "We can work this out."

He pulled away. Nothing he did was right. Liquid courage might have helped loosen his tongue, but it could not restore his memory. Whatever was going on, he needed space and time to think. Staying would only hurt Judy, and he had a feeling he'd done enough of that already.

"Please," she whispered from the hall where he'd left her.

By then, his hand was on the door and his head pounding. "I'll be in touch," he said, relief seconds away, but he knew better. There was no reason to come back if he didn't belong.

He closed the door and stood there, the knob still in his hand. How does a fool begin to pick up the pieces of a life he cannot recall? How does he put a woman through that kind of hell? Just fumble along until one day his brain kicked in and gave him his life back? How fair was that to her? Of all the words for his damned brain to come up with, it sabotaged him now.

The. End.

Harley pressed his forehead to the wooden barrier between him and the woman he was pretty sure he loved. "Judy," he whispered. "I'm sorry."

Silence echoed in the empty apartment. Harley's apartment. Only he was gone, not willing to try anymore. The stark realization in his eyes crushed her. Judy sank to the floor, her hard head in the palms of her hands. Angry sobs wrenched out of her in painful hiccups. This was her fault. She'd pushed too hard. Too fast. And why? Did she think she was so smart now? Did she always have to be right?

Loss hollowed out the thing that used to be her heart. Like a melon-baller gone wild, it sliced and diced, peeled and carved everything inside of her until drawing a breath hurt. She choked, angry for not knowing the secret to unlocking his mind.

Logic screamed back at her. She should have driven him to the hospital. She should have left his recovery in the hands of professional counselors. She should have known better.

Her throat felt ready to vomit her heart out on the carpet if only it would stop the pain. A whine eked out of her. "He's gone..."

The kitchen phone rang. Hope flared. It was possible. It could be him. Maybe he was standing in the hall and ready to try again. Maybe he was as sad as she was. Maybe—

"Hello?" she asked timidly as she brushed the tears off her cheek.

"Judy. Judy. Judy." It was that same irritating prankster. "It's now or—"

"Leave. Me. Alone!" She slammed the phone into the wall, picked it up and slammed it three more times out of sheer frustration. "I just want Harley, Harley, Harley!"

Zack looked surprised when he found out he got to pay the cabbie. "Why are you here? You were supposed to spend a little time with Judy."

"Sorry," Harley mumbled apologetically at the curb. He seemed to be saying that a lot lately.

Extinguish.

The dictionary in his head just would not let up.

Zack didn't pry, the good thing about a man who knows when to mind his business. He and his wife had just settled down for an early dinner with their daughters. Mei bounced out of her chair the moment she laid eyes on Harley. Between her hug and the excited squeals of Zack's two little girls, LiLi and Song, Harley almost felt decent, but not hungry. Mei insisted he join them at the table, but the warm sensation of being in Judy's arms lingered. It had felt right. Why wasn't it—

Enough?

He cussed to himself. *Damned E words. Let me be.*

"Uncle Harley. Are you sad?" LiLi asked, vermicelli rice noodles dripping off her lip from the chopsticks in her hand.

"Nah, darlin'." Harley reassured her. "Just need some place to stay for awhile."

"You know you're always welcome here," Mei said as she placed a small portion of noodles in Baby Song's bowl. The little tyke was into feeding herself by hand. It made for a mess, but the adorable two-year old seemed to enjoy it. Song was all smiles and noodles.

"Don't talk with your mouth full, LiLi," Mei reminded her oldest daughter.

LiLi slurped until the soggy strings were tucked inside of her mouth. "You can sleep in my bed if you want. I'll sleep with Song."

"He'll be fine in the guest room," Zack interrupted. "Don't you have homework?"

"Already did it, Daddy," LiLi answered, another chopstick full of noodles headed to her lips. "It was easy. Just multiplication. I'm on my eights. Teacher says I'm ahead of all the other kids, so I get to go on a field trip to see George Washington's old house. Can you come with me?"

Harley played with his plate of Vietnamese food, half listening to the gentle family conversation floating around him. He'd been over to Zack's enough in the past to know Mei's good cooking. Funny. He remembered things as simple as rice noodles, pho, and marinated shrimp. Why not Judy?

After a hot morning shower, Judy wound her hair on the top of her head, stabbed it with a large comb and dressed for another day. Zack had called her to let her know where Harley was. He might not be where he belonged, but he would be. She just needed a little help from another alpha male. She dialed his number.

He answered, abrupt as ever. "Stewart."

"Hi, Alex."

Instantly, his voice softened. "Good morning, Judy. How is Harley?"

"That's why I'm calling." She gulped. "He's staying with Zack right now. He doesn't know me yet, and I... umm, need a favor."

"Sure. Glad to help. What can I do for you?"

Thankfully Alex hadn't pried into why Harley wasn't home. Surprised at her sudden nervousness, she wiped her sweaty palm on her jeans. "Well, I thought if I could tie up all the loose ends from that day the IED blew up, maybe he could move on. Maybe once he's put everything to rest and he understands exactly what happened, he'll, umm, remember."

"Sounds reasonable."

Alex sounded willing, so she pressed forward. "I'm trying to locate his men. I need to know what happened, maybe talk with his commanding officer or someone he was close to."

"No problem. I can get you a copy of the Army's after action report."

"Would it include that Knicks person Raj mentioned in the ER? Remember?"

"Who? Oh, you mean Sergeant Knicks."

"Yes. Do you know what happened to him?" Judy paced. "Was he killed that day too?"

"Her," Alex corrected. "Sergeant Knicks is female. I'd be glad to help you locate her. She might be the perfect one for you to spend time with. I've worked with a few Army Rangers over the years. If I can't track her down, Murphy can."

Judy bit her lip, unable to answer. In the hospital, Harley had asked her out for a drink – the last thing he needed. He might not have time.

"Why don't you come over for dinner tonight? Kelsey would love to see you."

"How is she doing?"

"It's been a tough day. She's working with the mortuary on the funeral service. We've decided to bury Raymond in our family plot."

"Like he was part of your family?"

"As far as Kelsey's concerned, he was. And Jed is setting up a shelter for homeless kids like Raymond in D.C. Kelsey will manage it. She'll be busy. Come for dinner," Alex offered again with what sounded more like an order than a request.

"Maybe." Judy left it at that. "Thank you, Alex. Bye."

Didn't it just figure? Another woman.

The one night turned into a week. Then two. Zack went to work most days, leaving Harley to help Mei around the house with Baby Song. Mostly he played with the little gal, they watched television together, and as regular as clockwork, they fell asleep on the couch or floor together. Baby Song needed her naps and apparently, so did Harley. The comfort of being in a loving family softened the hollow feeling in his heart. The blurting compulsion diminished until the only E words that came out of his mouth were the ones he thought of all by himself.

Zack had a couple of pit bulls: Fluffy, a brindle, and Moo Moo, named because he was black and white like a cow. LiLi named them. It made Harley smile to see Song pulling Moo Moo's floppy ears to peek inside his hard head.

He taught the girls some easy commands like *sit, stay*, and *drop it* for the occasional time-out when Fluffy decided to chew Barbie and Ken's heads off. Mostly he played with the dogs, gentling them into acceptable family members. Easiest job ever. Dogs were the best medicine. The time spent with the Lennox children and their pets worked its magic.

Alex stopped by for a visit. Mark and Libby too. The only one who never showed was Judy. Harley missed her. Nights were long and incredibly—empty.

Day fourteen was LiLi's field trip. He volunteered to take the bus ride to Mount Vernon with her so Zack wouldn't have to miss work. Neither Zack nor Mei wanted LiLi to go so far from home, but Harley argued she'd be fine. After all, he would be there; he'd keep track of her.

"So when did old George build this place?" He eyed the impressive twenty-one room mansion while he and LiLi lunched together. They'd seen every exhibit and watched every movie on George Washington and the Revolutionary War by then. He'd expected her to take off and want to be with her friends, but instead, she acted more like she was chaperoning him. Funny little girl. LiLi was her mother, Mei, in miniature. Pretty. Loving. And a little bit bossy.

"He didn't," LiLi informed him patiently. "His daddy built it. George Washington only made it bigger and nicer. He was a very smart man."

"He built all the other buildings though, didn't he?"

"Ah huh," she agreed. "It's a neat place only no one lives here anymore. Teacher says we should be sure to see the blacksmith's barn and the gristmill. Want to see the graves first?"

"He's buried here?" Harley so did not know his American history.

LiLi bounced off the bench. "Ah huh. Let's go. I'll show you."

After discarding their lunch debris, they walked the leafy trail to George and Martha Washington's tombs. Giant trees sheltered the brick structure while wrought-iron gates protected the site. Two of the mothers were already there with their groups of children, but it was the whitened sepulchers inside the tomb that caught Harley's eye.

"Stand over there. I'll take a picture of you." LiLi had her cell phone already poised to record the moment.

"No, darlin'," Harley said quietly, not wanting any photos of him taken near a grave.

The somberness of the moment resonated. Here lay the man history referred to as the Father of Our Country, but all Harley knew about George Washington was war related. Valley Forge. The Delaware River. Princeton. The man was known for his courage in battle. He'd risked his life for his men. He was another survivor. A hero.

LiLi's warm little hand found its way inside Harley's. The other groups had begun their trek uphill and back to the bus, but for now, silence filled the air. Even the birds in the trees stilled.

For a moment, he and George Washington were not so different. Warriors were the same throughout history. Soldiers too. Patriotic. Committed. Proud to serve. Harley could almost see himself following the man on that frigid winter morning so long ago to take on the mercenary Hessian Army.

The day after Christmas. Battle of Trenton. His mind conjured a whiff of gunpowder.

He envisioned the matchlock muskets the soldiers might have carried. The flintlock rifles. The British Army's reliable Brown Bess. Kentucky long rifles. He might have been one of those guys at the frontline on bended knee, reloading while soldiers behind him fired over his head.

And Martha never wavered. No doubt she'd waited faithfully for her gallant husband, devoted and true, keeping the home fires burning while he was away. And Judy would have waited forever too. Maybe she and Martha—

Judy. A lightning bolt struck out of the clear blue sky. The perfect image materialized. A stunningly beautiful woman with creamy skin and brownish-red hair. She called it auburn. He called it red. That Judy. His Judy. *My Judy.*

And he knew why his mind had doubted. How could he remember her when he didn't know who *he* was? Judy was future promise, not past regret; the difference between what he had allowed himself to disintegrate into, and the man he'd chosen to be. And he'd been backsliding since he'd awakened up in the hospital. Until now.

His shoulders straightened. Furthermore, his brain wasn't full of holes either. Hell no. That was a weak man's rationalization for sinking into drugs, booze, loose women and dangerous stupidity. That was the old him, the guy who blamed everyone and everything else, until....

Sonny. Another memory stepped smartly forward, the only counselor in a Texas rehab facility who'd finally gotten through to Harley. And he'd done it by using nasty old drill sergeant tricks with a touch of ex-Army know-how and good old-fashioned prayer. And from that moment on, Harley was a changed man.

His chin stuck out. That damned Zack was almost right. Harley didn't need booze or drugs, but he was hands-down Alex Stewart's best sniper. Not Zack. The liar. Harley took a deep breath and sucked in the fresh air of a damned good day. He needed to go home. He had a woman to love, and it was high time she knew it.

The expectation of her smile warmed him. Judy would be so happy to see him. He'd take her on that dance she'd wanted and they would end up in bed. So where was she? What was she doing?

"On second thought." He released LiLi's hand, his mind made up to finish the field trip in record time. "How about if I take a picture of you before we leave?"

She smiled her cheesiest, but then insisted he had to take a more serious picture, and man, the girl liked to pose. After the third goofy-face picture, he called it quits. "Miss LiLi. Enough of the ham. Let's get to the bus and go home."

She grinned and took his hand again, skipping beside him as they trekked up hill. "Are you and Judy gonna break up?"

"Not if I can help it." He searched his mind for Judy's schedule. She'd be working her usual graveyard shift. That meant she was home sleeping. In their bed. At this very moment. He had time. Extricating his cell phone from his front jeans pocket, Harley called the hospital to make sure. *No. He'd just missed her. Judy had taken time off. Indefinite time off.*

Harley hung up. He didn't like the sound of that. His throat went dry as he dialed Judy's cell. The call went straight to voicemail. Dialing again, he rang his apartment. No answer.

Damn. What did indefinite mean anyway? One week? Two? Had she gone back to Wisconsin for a visit? To stay? Each scenario went from bad to worse. Of course, she went home to her parents' place. Why shouldn't she? He'd given her no hope, just walked out on her like he was the only one with the problem. Worse, he'd done nothing to contact her in the meantime.

The oddest sensation shivered over his shoulders. He might not have time. He needed to get home. Now.

Thirty

Where are they?

How could one set of car keys vanish off the kitchen counter when Judy was the only one in the apartment? Afternoon traffic on the Jefferson Davis Highway would be crowded. Sergeant Knicks was scheduled to fly in. Her plane might already be on the ground. Judy needed to be gone already!

She had taken time off work just to show the sergeant around town and hopefully, get to know her better and what happened to Harley too. Woman or not, any friend of his was a friend of hers. Darn his handsome hide. He seemed to attract some beautiful women. Just once, she'd like one of them to be dog faced and homely for a change.

When her sunglasses slid down her nose again, she gave up the battle and stuck them topside into her hair. They'd be more helpful as a hair pick. Her house phone jangled, but because she'd broken it in a fit of temper, it went to voicemail. Just as well. The last thing she had time for today was a prankster. Sheesh! People these days! Don't they have better things to do?

Hurriedly, she made another sweep through the kitchen and down the hall, her mind going a mile a minute. Alex was no doubt toe-tapping his impatient foot at Reagan National, waiting for her to show. Any minute now, he'd be calling her cell phone, wondering where she was and why she was late.

He had been good for his word. Although full of acronyms she'd not understood, the Army's report provided greater detail on the fateful day that had taken Harley's men. Despite his own injury, he'd actually pulled two of his men from the burning Humvee. Corporal Carlton Jenner was already deceased, but nothing stopped Harley from trying to resuscitate him. And then he'd scrambled to collect body parts until he collapsed from hysterical exhaustion. No wonder he couldn't remember. It wasn't just his Hummer that blew up that day. More like his whole life.

Oddly, Sergeant Knicks' name did not show up in the report, but no matter. Judy would get to meet her soon enough. Pausing at the doorway to his office, she knew darn well her keys were not in there. On top of everything else, the house phone rang again, and right on top of it, the doorbell, cranking up her need to be gone.

Judy made one quick dash down the hall to her bedroom. How could she lose her keys so fast? She'd only been home long enough to make a quick change out of her scrubs. Scanning her's and Harley's bedroom revealed nothing more than her soiled scrubs beside the bed. She hadn't even wasted time tossing them in the hamper.

Pausing at the bathroom door, she shook her head. Nope. She'd been two places, the kitchen and the bedroom. The calm demeanor she'd hoped to present when she met Sergeant Knicks flew out the window. If one more thing went wrong—

Once again the doorbell nagged. She marched into the hall. Whoever was on the other side of that door was going to get a piece of her mind. She jerked it open. FBI Agent Holman's big foot landed inside her apartment before she could slam the door in his face. He looked different somehow. Who did this jerk think he was to show up like this?

"It's about time you opened up. I've been waiting."

"What do you want?" she barked.

"To talk."

The silk in his voice set off a whispering alarm in the back of her mind. *Run.*

"I'm sorry, but I don't have time right now." God, he bugged her. "I was just on my way out." *To catch a cab, darn it anyway.*

"I beg to differ." He leaned casually inside the doorframe, his palm spread flat against the door.

The hair on the back of her neck lifted. Instinct whispered a little louder. *Run.*

"Get out of my home or I'll—"

"You'll what?" He raised his other hand into view.

Judy froze. A set of keys dangled off his index finger. Her keys. He'd been in her home. Him. Holman. Within the last fifteen minutes. Since she'd dropped her keys on the counter. While she was in her bedroom. Changing clothes. Half-dressed. Her whole body jerked back a step.

RUN!

He pushed the door open wider. The man still wore his black suit, white shirt and black tie, but nothing about him declared federal service. Predator, maybe. Angry man, for sure. Killer....

She backed into the kitchen as he entered. Sliding the top cabinet drawer open behind her, she felt for the stainless steel knife set. Pulling one out of its place, she clenched its handle tightly.

He dropped her keys on the counter. "You think you're clever, don't you?"

Come one step closer, and I'll show you clever.

"Twenty-six years of federal service," he said as he snapped his fingers to his thumb. "Gone, just like that and all because of you."

"Get out of my home," she demanded again, her heart rate off the charts as she calculated her next move. The knife had to hit his jugular or his heart. But her fingers trembled. The knife slipped.

"You want to play whose is bigger?" He reached into his suit jacket and pulled out a stainless steel cleaver. Hers. "I think I'd win that game too Judy, Judy, Judy."

A cold chill slid down her back. All those prank calls were—him. Holman. He'd had been stalking her for days. Mind-numbing terror flooded her very logical brain. He'd been watching. He had her trapped in her own apartment! There was no back door, only a fire escape off her patio, the whole living room away.

Judy backed into the hall. Running might give her time, but he was right. A steak knife was nothing against a cleaver. He might loose a pint, but she'd lose an arm or worse.

"Do you know what I thought the moment I laid eyes on you?" His voice dropped lower as he took a step in her direction.

"I don't care." She stepped backward, her breath coming too fast and furious.

"Oh, but you do." His lip twisted into a sneer. "There you were sitting all high and mighty in my interrogation room like you thought you were somebody. You needed to be put in your place in the worst way."

"Please, just go. I don't want to hurt you."

"Hurt me? Oh, baby, I'm sure it will work the other way around."

Every muscle of hers from the ground up shivered with his sinister pronouncement.

"You surprised me when you pulled Jed McCormack out of your bag of magic tricks. He and Stewart are thick as thieves, aren't they? Of course, they'd come to your rescue."

Judy gulped. If she ran through the living room, she might have a chance. Carefully, she let the handle of the knife slip through her fingers until she held only the tip of the blade. That's how Harley threw his knife when he practiced throwing. If he could do it, so could she.

In one quick motion, she cocked her arm and threw the blade. Not waiting to see where it landed or if it even struck, she sprinted into the living room and headed for the open door.

"I knew you'd keep things interesting," he purred.

Her heels hit the linoleum floor in the hallway. The door wasn't open as she'd hoped, but she could make it. She had to. The knob was almost in reach when his body slammed into hers. He hit so hard, her cheekbone impacted. Stars exploded in her head. A dizzying wave of blackness welled up around her, but there was no way to fall. He had her pinned in a vertical position. With one hand to her shoulder, he jerked her around to face him. She offered her cheek to avoid his twisted gaze raking over her.

Gripping her throat in one fist, he commanded her, "Look at me."

Jerking her knee upward, she met the resistance of his thigh. Damn. He'd been prepared for that kick to his groin. Her options dwindled.

"I said look at me!"

Fear compelled her to obey. She almost didn't recognize the man who'd interrogated her. Whatever Holman had stuck in his veins or up his nose was now in control. Icy dark eyes glittered back at her, eyes so hollow no pigment showed, only cold, black evil. His upper lip twitched continually, and every bit of the man shook, including his head.

A long strand of gray hair had broken free of the thirty-weight oil he'd combed it back with. It hung in his eyes, adding to the demented twist to his features. Her inner nurse diagnosed even as he squeezed the breath out of her. Meth? Cocaine? Heroin? Designer drugs? All of them?

God, I don't care. He's going to kill me!

"I'll tell you what I thought. I thought what a rocking good time you and I could have before I cut you into little chunks and wash you down the drain, you arrogant bitch." He leaned in to her face. "Chunks so small Mortimer will wonder where you went while he's standing over the same drain taking a shower. Won't that be ironic as hell?"

A whine started low and desperate in her gut. Judy angled her face to the right to avoid him, but he jerked her back until she was nose to nose again.

"Chunks," he hissed, "so small that a man might think the roasted snacks on his kitchen counter were tasty before he realized what he had in his mouth. If he ever figured it out."

No, no, no! This nightmare cannot be happening. Not to me!

Growling, he slid her body up until her feet lifted off the floor. She reached her fingernails toward his eyeballs, but he clenched his fist tighter around her neck the second she lifted her hands. Judy gasped. The room spun in a lazy circle. She'd lost. He'd won. And now she was going to die. She clenched his forearms and pushed with all her might.

"Let me assure you, Judy O'Brien," he whispered. "Size really does matter."

She sagged, not an ounce of strength left. Harley's sweet handsome smile drifted through her mind. The kitchen phone rang in the distance. Holman turned toward it.

Suddenly, the door shuddered behind her. Her head banged against the wood. It burst open with force, pushing her nearly deadweight into Holman. He couldn't get a good grip fast enough before her face hit his shoulder and then the floor.

"Judy!" Harley roared from somewhere very far away. "Who? Why you sonofa—!"

BLAM!

A cannon's roar filled the entryway. She curled her body into the smallest possible size. The floor shook, but there was nowhere to hide.

BLAM! BLAM! BLAM!

Someone screamed and cried. Panic crawled up her spine. Holman was coming for her. He had a cleaver. Deafened, she ducked her head into her shoulders and covered her ears. The most horrible smell of blood and body fluids filled her nose. A strong hand pulled her off the floor. With her eyes squeezed tightly shut, she struggled to get away.

"Damn it, Judy. Stop screaming. I've got you now."

She drew in a deep breath, fighting out of control hysteria. Harley wrapped his arms around her. "It's me. I'm here. I'm home."

"He... He..." The world stopped spinning, but words would not come. She clung to him as all out panic stormed through her.

"Shhhhh. You're safe. It's okay, Judy. I'm here now." Lifting her in his arms, he carried her into the hall and shut the door behind them.

Terror would not let her go. Her heart pounded through every vein and artery. The images. The thoughts. She pressed her face into Harley's shirt to block the nightmare.

"Settle down. You're safe. God, you're safe." Warm moist lips brushed across her forehead even as he barked at her. "Damn it to hell, woman. Answer your damned phone next time I call, will you?"

"I, I, I b-broke it."

They sank to the floor together. Nothing felt better than his arms and legs around her when he settled her into his lap. Nothing smelled better than his shirt. His sweat. She took a deep breath and let it fill her; so thankful he was there. Adrenaline burned through her in shuddering waves she couldn't control.

"Good hell. That guy just would not drop. He kept coming at me with that cleaver. Did you see it? Who was he?"

She nodded, needing to explain, but not wanting to talk about that guy. Whatever Holman had ingested, he'd seemed to have had the strength of a dozen men. She knew the scenario from drug addicts she'd treated in the ER. The crap people chose to put into their bodies could turn them into the most lethal killing machines.

Harley was scared too. He trembled, but he compensated quickly by holding her tighter, and she needed him to do just that. His heart thudded as loudly as hers. Maybe louder. Certainly stronger. Judy calmed to the rhythmic beat of her man. Her world.

She lifted her eyes to look at him as her trembling fingertips skimmed the clean-shaven jaw she loved so well. "Harley?"

"Yes, darlin'," he answered without a hint of hesitation.

"You know me?"

He rolled his eyes. "Hell yes. In every sense of the word, I know you, Judy O'Brien soon to be Judy Mortimer. Good gosh damn, woman, I've been trying to reach you all afternoon. You want to explain to me why you took time off? I got news for you. You are not moving back to Wisconsin."

"But you know me." She cupped his face between her hands. Her heart swelled with love. Her man had finally come home.

He smiled, his hand to the back of her head as he pulled her forehead to his. "Damned right I know you. I gave you that chocolate diamond in the middle of the airport in Eau Claire, Wisconsin. I didn't even have a change of clothes that day, just showed up. The only thing I had was that stone in my hand. Hell, I didn't even know if you liked chocolate. All I wanted was you." His lips caressed the center spot of her forehead with warmth and tenderness. "Do you remember that crazy day?"

"I do," she said quietly, soaking in the love radiating from his entire body.

"I'll tell you what else I know. You are the best damned RN in the Washington Central emergency room, maybe the whole world. Your father runs the hardware store in your hometown, and you have an older brother named Josh, only you call him Joshie. The day he got tore up by a chain saw was the day you decided to become Wonder Woman. You wish I'd drive something besides a Jeep, because... because...." He choked. "Because you love me, Judy. I know you do. You want me to stop driving fast so we can live to be one hundred together. And you weren't wearing a stitch the morning I took that selfie of us off the Florida Keys. And another thing, you are totally smitten by my good looks. Always have been. Always will be. Now do you believe me?"

Tears got in the way. Harley's mouth enveloped her lips in the sweetest crush of longing. It stole her breath and her heart all over again. How could a man pour so much love into one fervent kiss? He literally melted the last of her fear away.

Still holding her tight, he reached into his pants pocket and pulled out his cell. "Hang on a sec. I've got to call the police, and let 'em know what I've done before someone else does." He quickly dialed 911. "I made enough noise to wake the dead."

Judy listened while he gave the dispatcher his address and explained the circumstances. Just hearing his address roll confidently off his tongue instilled a greater calm. He also placed a quick call to Alex. There was a day that would have irked her, but no more. Alex was big brother, and that made Kelsey sister. Judy understood. She got it now.

"You're what?" Harley asked his boss. "Where? Oh yeah? Why?"

Despite her harrowing experience, a small smile tugged at the corner of Judy's lips. Alex was no doubt telling Harley where he was and why. Well good. She was ready to meet Sergeant Knicks now. The sooner the better.

When he finished the call, Harley pulled her to her feet and ushered her to the elevator. "Come on. We'll wait in the lobby. Alex is on his way. So are the cops."

Judy let Harley lead, but in leading, she remained in the crook of his arm with his long lean body ramrod straight beside hers. Snuggled against his ribs, she basked in the knowledge that of all the women in Harley Mortimer's world, she was the most loved and the most rare.

A woman couldn't ask for more.

Thirty-One

Damn, God was good. Zack wasn't so bad either.

The sheer dumb luck of the afternoon amazed Harley. Thank God Zack hadn't driven his Porsche to work. And an extra high-five to the man upstairs that Zack kept his .357 Magnum right where Harley would have, in a specially designed holster built into the driver's door.

They'd already given their statements when the coroner's van pulled to the curb, Alex right behind it. That big old black GMC nightmare he insisted on driving never looked so good.

"Did she make it okay?" Judy asked Alex the moment he stepped inside the apartment building lobby.

"Kelsey took her over to our place. Come over when you're done here."

"That might take awhile," Harley said. He didn't know what they were talking about. He had enough on his mind.

"Understood." Alex nodded at the police officers. "Call if you need a lawyer."

"No need." One of the newly arrived detectives motioned to Harley. "You need to see this Mr. Mortimer." But then he turned to Judy. "Please stay here with Mr. Stewart and the officers, ma'am. Your boyfriend will be right back."

Harley accompanied the detective back up to his apartment where he was instructed to don paper booties before he entered. The smell of blood and gore struck his nostrils the moment the door swung open. Crime scene tags littered the kitchen counter and floor. Hell, they pretty much littered the whole place.

"Back this way." The detective directed Harley down the hall and into his bathroom. Wordlessly, he nodded to the gray-tiled shower stall. Larger than the traditional glassed-in version, the stall was surrounded on three sides by solid walls to support a tiled-bench and the plumbing of several showerheads. The fourth wall was glass and chrome. Judy and Harley had spent plenty of quality time there. Never again.

"Holy shit." Harley was instantly mad enough to put a couple more shots into Holman's dead carcass.

Standing in the middle of the shower over the drain was a heavy-duty metal tripod. Judging by the hook and pulley system in place, Holman had meant every word of his threat. An array of ceramic butcher knives lay on the tiled-bench along with a roll of black plastic sheeting and a silver duct tape. Beneath the bench stood a jug of household bleach. A black rubber apron hung off one of the shower nozzles.

Harley's heart thudded with what could have happened. "Holy shit," he repeated.

"We've seen this MO before with mob killings," the detective said somberly. "Maybe Agent Holman thought he was above the law. Maybe it was the drugs in his system. Who knows? His prints are all over the bathroom, the cleaver, too. Based on what you and Miss O'Brien told us, the chief's called this case closed. You two are free to go."

"We're not coming back here. We're moving." Harley declared, not sure why he felt the need to share that instant decision with the detective.

"I would," he replied, extending his hand. "You have my number. Call if you have any questions. We're here to help."

Returning the handshake, Harley nodded. "Understood."

Shaken to his core, he strode out of his apartment with a new future taking shape in his mind. Judy would never re-enter this place, not even to pack. No way. His friends would help him move. Back downstairs, he pulled her into his arms as soon as he could. "From now on, the dead-bolt stays latched no matter what time of day it is."

Her eyes widened at the no-nonsense tone to his voice.

"And we're moving. You are not to re-enter that apartment to get anything, not even your toothbrush. Do you hear me?"

"You're shaking."

Hell yes, he was shaken to the core. He'd nearly lost his reason for living the same day he remembered it. All he could do was hang onto her for dear life. Finally, the thunder in his chest stilled. He drew her close and kissed her lips with an intensity he could not control. She was everything that made his pitiful life worth living. He shuddered as he broke the kiss, crushing her to his chest with the need to squeeze her back into his soul again.

"God, Judy," he muttered into her neck. "I would die for you."

She melted against him. "No, Harley. Live for me. Please. Let's live for each other."

He couldn't speak. Judy did have a way with words.

"Let's go you guys," Alex said.

Harley looked up to piercing blue eyes. He'd forgotten all about his boss.

The ride to Alexandria was fast in Zack's powerhouse of a car, but Harley was glad to leave it at the curb and get his hands on Judy again. She still wouldn't tell him what Alex was talking about or why he'd been at the airport. Whatever surprise Alex and she had planned, the events of the afternoon had stolen their thunder.

With her fingers tucked into the waist of his pants, she leaned into him every step up the Stewarts' front walk. He did not waste time knocking, just opened their door and ushered her into his home away from home.

"Judy!" Kelsey shrieked the moment she saw Judy. In two seconds flat, the women were hugging and crying all over each other, and Harley had to look out the window or lose his grip. Women. God, he loved 'em and especially these two. They'd both been through hell and still needed to comfort each other. What was not to love?

"Are you gals going to cry all day?" Alex teased from the kitchen doorway. "Come on. Let's get this show on the road."

Judy wiped her eyes. "I don't know if I'm ready for this. I'm a mess."

"You look fine." Kelsey smoothed a hand over her tangled tresses and gave her a final squeeze. "You're a survivor, sweetheart. Just like the rest of us."

And that's all it took to send the women into another crying, hugging spree. Harley caught the tender look in Alex's eye at the feminine goings on. His love for Kelsey seemed to reach out and enfold her even though he stood feet away. The stuff of legends....

"Coming?" Harley asked, his hand outstretched to take Judy's.

She pulled away from Kelsey with a tearful smile, and just like that, he couldn't breathe. There she was, the woman of his heart. His goddess. His universe. The urge to take her by storm rolled over him. This visit had better be short. He had a woman to make mad passionate love with and no place to do it. Yet.

Alex beckoned everyone into the backyard. Judy grumbled to him in passing, "You still haven't told me her first name."

"You'll see," Alex replied with a funny smirk and a nod to get out. He walked to the gate when they were finally assembled on the patio. "I'll be right back."

The Stewarts' backyard was as tidy as ever. Whisper and Smoke sat alert in their kennel as if they knew something was up. Kelsey had taken her place on a nearby lawn chair while Harley gathered Judy onto the porch swing to sit with him. "When you gonna tell me what's going on?"

Just then, the back gate opened and—

It couldn't be. No way. Harley choked.

"What's going on?" Judy asked in alarm. "Are you okay?"

He dropped to his knees. Tears filled his sorry eyes. "My girl. My baby girl...." He couldn't finish, his throat closed tight with emotion. "Nyx."

"Knicks?" Judy asked, now totally bewildered. "Sergeant Knicks? Where? I don't see—. Do you mean to tell me—? Alex!"

Harley patted his thighs, his heart literally stuck in his throat as he coaxed the wary animal toward him. "Come here, girl. Don't you remember me?"

The black Labrador with a crooked white lightning bolt on her chest slunk to her belly and crept toward him inch by inch. Once her nose made contact with the tips of his fingers, she broke loose with a strangled whine and climbed onto his lap, licking his face and wiggling to get closer. Burying his nose in the wiry fur at her neck, he wrapped his arms around her and breathed in the second best smell in the world—his dog.

"Nyx," he cried. "You're here."

The frantic beast lifted her muzzle and let forth a long happy howl mixed with excited barks that would not quit. Whisper and Smoke joined in until the Stewarts' backyard sounded like a pack of wolves lived there—happy, howling wolves.

Harley coughed as bittersweet joy roared over of him. Holding Judy in his arms was nothing short of perfect, but now Nyx too? The best damned EOD dog in the entire US Army, and she was alive? He could not believe his blurry eyes. For a man who had nothing just this morning, it sure felt like he owned the world now.

"Sergeant Knicks is a dog?" Judy's hands were on her hips and her very direct question aimed at Alex. "You let me believe I was meeting a female soldier these last two weeks? And she's a dog?"

Alex shrugged, his face lit with mischief.

"You lied to me."

"No, I didn't. Unofficially, she's an Army K-9 Sergeant."

She smacked Alex full force on his bicep. "I dressed up for a dog. You're an ass. Damn you."

"Ouch." He chuckled as he staggered back a step in mock pain.

Kelsey hooked her arm through Alex's. "He's been just like a little boy at Christmas, dying for this day to get here."

Harley knew he was witnessing a rare event. Alex was playing. He looked relaxed, and Judy, for all her pretended anger and the disaster she'd just survived, looked amazing. The woman seemed to glow from the inside out with an inner strength and peace. Yes, Kelsey was happy too, dabbing her teary brown eyes and smiling at the crazy antics, but Judy?

She was nothing short of breathtaking. The universe ceased breathing right along with Harley. There she stood with Alex pulling her into a hug, and Harley couldn't love her more. She'd never given up on him even though he'd left her. She'd never stopped loving—him.

Tears filled his eyes. When a pink washcloth kind of a tongue swiped his cheek again, he wrangled his dog's head into the crook of his arm and pointed at the only woman in the world. "You see that pretty lady up there, Nyx?"

Judy smiled from the one-armed hug of the man she'd just belted.

"That's who we get to spend the rest of our lives with, girl. She's our sun, Nyx. You and me are just dark little planets orbiting the most beautiful star in the universe."

Pushing away from Alex, Judy knelt with Harley, her hand on his knee and the other making friends with Nyx.

"You found my dog."

"Alex helped." Judy cast another sharp look of irritation toward the underhanded and still grinning man in question. "She wasn't there that day, Harley. You left her behind."

"I remember now." The day stormed over him again. Shit. Did it never stop hurting? But now he had a solid grip with one hand on Judy, the other on Nyx. Kent's smiling face came back to him. Garth's. Carlton's. Even Raymond showed up for head count.

Nyx got rambunctious and pushed Harley flat to his back. She climbed onto his belly, her big paws on his chest and slathering him with puppy kisses.

"Excuse me," he grumbled. "I got two females in my arms at the same time and I...."

A sob broke loose. He raised his arm to cover his eyes. Here he was sputtering and bawling in front of the woman he adored, and the dog that adored him would not let him be. For the life of him, he could not let either of them go.

So many fragments of memories floated detached and homeless inside his head, but another had just settled into place. He'd left Nyx behind in her crate that eventful day. She'd suffered a touch of heat stroke, a fairly common occurrence among four-legged troops in the scorching desert clime. The dream of her getting shot and killed by those Iraqi Guard soldiers was just a trick of his banged-up head. There'd be more memories to deal with, but he was ready now. Bring 'em on.

Harley pulled Judy to her feet along with him. "Sit," he whispered hoarsely to his dog.

Nyx complied promptly, her tail wagging and her two bright black eyes glued to him like she'd never lost track of him. Like he'd never left her behind. Like she still lived to obey every word that came out of his mouth. Man's best friend, and he so undeserving.

He brushed the tears off his cheeks, ashamed and happy at the same time. Judy wrapped her arms around him, her eyes plenty misty too. Nyx growled, so he egged her on. Each time he growled, she slapped her big feet to the ground and growled back at him like she used to do.

When Nyx set to howling her happy puppy song again, Harley recalled the day his parents threw him out. Yes, he went against their wishes when he'd joined the Army straight out of high school. They had a right to be mad with their only child, but the truth was he'd been looking for home ever since. Fort Hood in Texas came close. Even Camp Wolfe in Kuwait felt a little like it sometimes. Alex and Kelsey had taken him into theirs, but he was always third-wheel to their happily-ever-after and jealous of what they had.

But standing there with his dog at his knee and his woman in his arms, he'd come full circle. His war was done. His men didn't hate him for living, and Nyx, his faithful companion on all those dark nights when America's Patriot missiles battled Iraq's low-tech Scuds, was alive and home. But best of all, the lady of his heart loved him.

Harley looked his boss in the eye. "Thanks for taking care of my girls."

Alex winked at him, his arm draped comfortably over Kelsey's shoulder. "No, son. Thank you for taking care of mine."

EPILOGUE

Roy strolled the hallowed grounds of Arlington National Cemetery. Would there be room enough for him when the call came? He hoped so. Visitors and tourists rode tour buses, but Roy preferred the quiet honor of walking among the noble dead. Arlington's reverent stillness always soothed the ragged edge of grief simply by a man putting one foot ahead of the other.

Nature was peacefully at work among the endless rows of snow white markers. Birds sang overhead or flitted among the trees. The breeze shifted silently up hill and dale. The reminder that man was just another child of Nature resonated across the orderly landscape.

He knew the whole story now. With the precision planning of any good sniper, Emmet Grant had kept a log that spanned his USMC service years. Part of a family website that Roy suspected Ben had set up for his father, it listed what every good sniper record should: targets, schedules, as well as observations taken during preliminary planning. The man had thoroughly noted minute details like light conditions, wind direction and velocity, plus anticipated kill sites for all his missions in Vietnam.

But that's where it got interesting. The last entries were less than a week old. Locations like Arlington Memorial Bridge, the Lincoln and Jefferson Memorials, the Tidal Basin, and World War II stood out in bold font. To further incriminate himself, Emmet included types and numbers of rounds used as well as a tick mark if the shot was successful.

Four tick marks. Four cartridges spent. Four targets acquired. Three times the appraisal column was annotated with, *'Terminated with extreme prejudice.'* The fourth annotation was more telling. *Non-lethal hit. Do over.* Emmet had made a mistake.

In a sad, twisted way, the blog opened to the dress blues portrait of his only son, USMC Lance Corporal Benjamin Franklin Grant, the victim of a Taliban suicide bomber in Kabul, Afghanistan. A bright, smiling young man, he'd written across the lower right corner of the scanned portrait: *To the greatest hero in the world—My Dad, All my love, Ben.*

Roy sighed as he walked. The truth was clear. Whether Emmet realized what he was doing or not, he'd sent a direct call for help to his friend from a different era.

In the end, Roy was the only one to step forward to take care of his friend's remains. The sniper who'd terrorized D.C. was old news, the nation back to business, and Emmet Grant already forgotten. Just like Ben. That's why Roy walked the hallowed grounds today. He owed his lifelong friend a debt he could never repay.

At last he came to his destination. A robin stood watching nearby as Roy settled down on his knees to face the simple white stone marker of Marine Corps Lance Corporal Benjamin Franklin Grant.

"Hey, Ben." Roy's soft southern drawl whispered like a lullaby amongst the reverent silence. "Your dad can't join you like he wanted, at least not here on this side of eternity. He's at rest now, son. Just wanted you to know."

The robin pulled a worm out of the soft warm earth and cocked its head as if listening to the quiet eulogy.

"I don't know if you and your old man will be together in the hereafter. I don't know how eternity works. People say a lot of stuff because they want everyone else to believe the way they do, but nobody really knows. 'Cept you cuz, well, you're over there. And your dad cuz he's there too. If you run into him, look him in the eye and tell him you love him. You be proud as hell of your old man. He was a hero, you hear me, boy?"

Roy wiped the tear off his cheek. Damn it, he didn't mean to get emotional, but his heart hurt for the friend he hadn't been able to save.

"They aren't gonna call him a hero, but you and I know better. He wasn't himself there at the end. No, he missed you and your mom something awful. He loved you, Ben. That's a powerful lot of hurt to shoulder when everyone you love has been taken away. He was hurting, but at the very end, he was still man enough to save my life."

That nosy little bird hopped closer as Roy sucked in a breath of the fresh spring air and wiped his face. "Sorry I haven't been by much to visit. I'll do better from now on. Brought you something."

With a final nod to the silent soldier, Roy took a small plastic bag from his jacket pocket and emptied the contents around the base of the white marker. The forgiving Arlington lawn accepted the ash without judgment or opinion, just took it in the same as sunshine and rain. "Rest easy, Emmet. You're home with your boy now. Give Ben my love. Tell Lois I still think she's the prettiest gal this side of heaven, will you?"

Roy rolled onto his butt and sat a moment longer, his arms on his knees. Wrong or right, some of Emmet's heart was in that handful of ash. He was finally with the son he'd grieved so deeply for. It didn't matter in the whole scheme of the universe anyway. God would take care of the details.

Two soldiers. Two sacrifices. Two heroes. Together at last.

Kelsey stood inside the wrought iron fence of the Stewart's family plot. She'd been here three times too many. Once, to reinter her sons when Alex had their caskets moved from the Pacific Northwest; again to position the bronze memorials. Now for Raymond.

Leave it to Alex to surprise her. He had a bronze created of a special needs child with Raymond's rare disease. Soft blue eyes smiled from beneath the gentle protuberance of a unibrow that itself rimmed the stocking hat trailing in the breeze. Alex made it worse when he placed Raymond a step behind Abby. With her right hand flung back the way it was, she seemed to be reaching for his hand. Kelsey cried when she saw it. Raymond would have loved a sister and brothers.

She leaned back into the solid wall of the man who held her tightly, his chin buried in the crook of her neck. Alex. Only he could know how to make this new sorrow bearable. That little girl in the ground beside her three brothers was his. Kelsey gulped at the enormity of all they'd lost and endured together. God, she needed him. She gathered what was left of her heart and prepared to get on with the business of living without. Again.

Alex placed a warm kiss on the edge of her ear, his palms gently interlocked over her stomach. "I think we should visit your doctor."

Shivering, she drew him closer. "Because I'm depressed?" Depression did not begin to cover the way she felt.

His lips moved to her neck. "I know it's tough right now, but you're one of the strongest people I know. Look at Jeff Watson and Newton Bridges. They're alive today because of you. And you single-handedly brought down one of the most cold-blooded women in the country. Police in three states were looking for Durrant."

"Why?"

"Because she didn't just desert Nick's father the night you told me about. She killed him." Alex hesitated, and Kelsey knew something just as sad would come out of his mouth next. "The police found another body at the Durrant's rental in Idaho. A little girl. Five years old. That's why she took off for the Northwest."

Kelsey turned in his arms to face him. She'd never understand the likes of Ethel if she lived to be a million. "She killed a daughter? Why not Nick?"

"Who knows what goes on in a murderer's mind? Think about it, Sweetheart. The world's safer because of you. Besides, I was thinking more along the lines of Dr. Sweeney, your fertility doctor."

"You want a baby?" she asked, not sure this was the best time or place for the topic.

They'd had it before. Alex wanted children. He'd wondered why they hadn't gotten pregnant despite no attempts at birth control. The fault seemed to reside within her mind, not her body. The doctors said keep trying, but she'd finally put the dream aside when the stress of that monthly, unfulfilled expectation became an all too consuming burden she was not willing to inflict on Alex. If a child was meant to be, it would have to come in its own sweet time. Not hers. Certainly not according to some fertility doctor's demented schedule that turned the sweet act of lovemaking with Alex into a chore.

"Our baby," he said, his forehead pressed to hers and his breath in her face.

"I've put you through so much already."

"You haven't put me through anything," he insisted as his palms smoothed down her shoulder blades to her backside, his favorite resting place. Most men hugged their wives' shoulders or waists. He had a particular craving for her bottom. "Besides, we need the practice."

Kelsey tipped her chin to absorb the light in his eyes.

"I know us. If we've proved anything at all, it's that our love will find a way. Besides, I'm taking you to Alaska next week. I hear it's still cold up there. We might need to make our own body heat."

Tears filled her eyes. The tender depths to this rugged, powerful, fearsome man drew her like a moth to a flame. Her empty cup did not feel so chipped and cracked when he held her.

"And then we're going to New Orleans. Think of it. Bourbon Street. Jazz. Hot steamy nights." With one soft pat on her ass, he clenched her tightly against him right there in the middle of the cemetery—as if life could go on after so much loss. As if one more tiny life might possibly want to chance coming to earth to join them. This man had unquenchable faith. He knew the wreck she was, and he offered what she needed most. Hope.

"Then we're going to Peru. I've always wanted to see Machu Picchu, don't you?"

His incessant love for adventure made her smile. "Will it be dangerous?"

"Did you forget who you're married to?" He kept dreaming and helping her look forward. "'Course, I've always wanted to see you on the Eiffel Tower at sunset too."

"We're taking a world tour?"

"Who? Us?" His palm cupped her chin while he wiped her tears away with two swipes of his thumbs. "Sweetheart, just wait. You and me are taking the world by storm."

And that was why she loved him. The hurricane called Alex Stewart was her world.

Who am I looking for?

Harley raced in his dream. Always a few elusive steps ahead, he could never catch up with her—whoever she was. With each dainty step, the lovely woman disappeared into a misty green curtain of spring air and the refreshing fragrance of newly mown grass. Her hair streamed behind her in silky ribbons that teased the tips of his fingers, but never gave him enough substance to grab onto; never enough he could reel her gently back where she belonged.

Who is she?

One minute the ribbons seemed red; the next brown. The lovely spring scene transformed into horror. Thunder crashed overhead and he was running. Time ran with him, urging him to fly. Unseen danger lurked everywhere. The need to find her filled his gut with acid and that awful feeling he'd missed his one and only chance.

Am I too late? Can I save her—just in time—again?

Feet pounded alongside.

"Who are we looking for, Bro?" Kent asked, his face shiny with sweat although he'd just appeared out of nowhere.

"My woman." Harley's throat closed with the panic of his nightmare. *I think.*

A pitch-black wraith flitted just ahead. Nick Durrant. He wore a black business suit with a cleaver dangling out of its sleeve. And duct tape. The knowledge of all he stood to lose suffocated Harley. She'd scream and cry, but tape over her mouth would not allow him to hear her or to find her. To save her.

Run faster!

He did. A shiny metal tripod blocked the way. Intent on crushing it with his bare hands, he reached for it, but in the way of dreams, it moved. He stretched, desperate for just one finger hold. It floated, always beyond reach.

Another monster appeared. A man with two holes in his head. Holman. His lip curled back in a demented smile. And Harley could not run fast enough.

"What's her name?" Carlton asked.

Harley glanced to his other side. Another buddy had joined him. A little girl waved happily from Carlton's back where she was getting a piggyback ride. She was wearing pink pajamas with gray tabby kittens. The pink pajamas transformed into a white flowing veil. It wasn't Carlton running beside him anymore. It was—her. The woman he'd been running after. After all he'd done to find her she'd found him.

"Do you know me?" she asked, her hand stretched out to welcome him. The moment her fingertip touched his cheek, the dream let go. He tumbled, head-over-heels in a dizzying spiral that ended with—

"Harley? Wake up, honey. You're dreaming."

Blinking his eyes open, the dream lost its grip and faded fast. Only the sensation of having arrived just in time persisted.

Judy's fingers were cool on his cheek. "You were dreaming again, weren't you?"

Breathing hard, he turned with a big grin. "Of you."

She had the good grace to blush. "Do you want to talk about it?"

"No." He rolled over and crawled onto her until she had no choice but to lay back and get comfy. The drab green *Go Army* T-shirt draping off her shoulder enhanced all of her very delectable bumps and curves. He pushed it out of his way. The nightmare had left him with a definite need.

She combed her fingers into the sides of his head as he worked his mouth over her collarbone and up her neck. When she wiggled, he eased back an inch and blew into her ear. Mission accomplished. His woman shivered, a definite sign the Mortimer train might need to build up a little more steam.

"Are you sure you don't want to talk about it?"

"Drop it."

Ah, this nosy nurse needed to let it go. He could barely remember the nightmare as it was. Good riddance. The only thing that mattered was the lady in his arms. Harley gave her earlobe a gentle nip, eliciting another wiggle and a catch of her breath. Goosebumps lifted on her skin beneath his fingertips. She had no choice but to kiss him if she wanted to breathe. He let his fingers do the goosebump-walking while his mouth did the, umm, talking. Judy wrapped herself around him, her hands peeling away the clothes they no longer needed.

When his shirt hit the floor, he was done talking and dreaming. Judy might come off all prim and proper in nurse's scrubs, but once he took them off, prim and proper flew out the window.

His hand slid down her belly to parts below. Her fingers walked up his chest and over his shoulders. Within minutes, they were under the covers, tangled up like the lovers they really were. He roved over every inch and crevice of her body, thrumming tender nipples to attention until they begged for attention. She arched her back, offering a mouthful. Ah, she knew what he liked.

There was no way to get enough. It should work the other way considering how their bodies interlocked so perfectly together, with his definitely on a mission inside of hers. But not once had they made love when she did not fill him more than he could ever fill her. It had nothing to do with their physical connection, and yet—it did.

As much as he gave, she always seemed to give more. He craved. She satisfied. Each heated kiss, every gentle stroke and touch until the consummation of their love burned the life out of him. Or into him. That's how he felt by the time they lay satisfied in each other's arms. Filled with life. And love.

Her fingernails dug into the cheeks of his ass. With one last groan of pleasure and shuddering intensity, they strove for every last bit of the other they could reach. She whimpered, a sweet surrender of all she had to give. And she was his. He surrendered back to her. All. Everything. Right down to his true confessions. Somehow, he knew. Two alls had just made the perfect one.

Opening his eyes, he could not help but smile at the good job he'd done on this particular mission. Their wrestling had taken them all the way to the edge until one of them was arched half-off the bed. And it was not him.

"Nice view," he said between heavy breaths, his fingers running down over her stomach as she leaned backward in an awkward position. "Are you okay down there?"

She was breathing as hard as he was, her body still clenched in aftershocks. "I'm standing on my head, thank you very much. Here. Pull me up."

He brushed her hand aside and traced the centerline of her body from her navel upward with his index finger. "You're perfectly symmetrical. I like that in a woman."

"Wow. You used a big word," she teased. "Come on. Pull me up."

He tickled her again, inciting another round of wiggles. "I know all kinds of big words. Sym-met-ri-cal. It means you got two boobs, one on each side of yer body." He poured on the Texas twang as he reached for his nightstand drawer behind him. The drawl always worked before. He counted on it for distraction now.

"Stop it." Judy tried to sound stern, but giggles came up from the carpet. She reached for him again, the silly woman, like he'd give up so easily.

"Ooooo. Do that again." He enjoyed the way she'd just tightened in all the best places. A man didn't get to feel the upside-down version of his woman often enough. Why rush?

"Harley!"

"Yeah. Right there. Do it again, darlin'." He rocked into her a few times as he extracted the ring from its box. "Okay. Give me your hand. Come on. Stretch. You can do it."

"It's about time." She reached for him.

"Nope. Just need this one." He latched onto her left hand and slipped the ring onto the finger next to her pinkie. The chocolate diamond he'd given her still sparkled on her right hand, but this pure white stone meant something entirely different. His breath caught. Their world was about to change.

"What's this?"

"Do I have to explain everything?"

She didn't answer.

He stopped thinking he was charming. "You still okay down there?"

"No. I'm not playing anymore. Help me up."

He obeyed. With his nose in her hair and his heart thumping, all he needed was one word to make his life complete. Judy breathed hard against him, her face in his shoulder. She hadn't spoken yet, but she was holding on tight. That helped.

He started slowly. "I know we just signed a thirty-year mortgage on this old farm together, but the truth is that surprised me. Guess I couldn't believe you'd stay this long, not with a guy like me."

She looked up, her eyes brimming with tears.

"It's kind of strange how the people you least expect to turn their backs on you, do; while the ones who have every right to kick your ass to the curb—don't."

"But I love you. Surely you know that."

"I know, darlin', I know. But you've allowed me to treat you less than a lady, and for that, I am sorry. I've been taking you for granted. You deserve better than me. You always will."

The truest love glistened in her eyes.

He kept on keeping on. "People have been known to fall out of love."

"I'm not like your parents, Harley."

He hadn't meant them, but then again, maybe he did. "The thing is I'm not the handsomest guy around, but I have a good job and," his throat constricted with his heart stuck in it like it was, "I'm sure not the smartest. You are. The god's honest truth is all I've got to offer is—I love you, Judy. I can't imagine waking up and not having you by my side. It's high time I do the honorable thing. Would you grant me the pleasure of living with you and for you the rest of my life? Would you marry me?"

Harley gulped, the question asked and his heart on the line. Despite the fact she'd moved across country to live with him, this was a long shot. She'd never say yes, not to a lifetime with a guy like him. Living together was one thing, but marriage? No way. Judy O'Brien was a smart lady.

"You have a lot of nerve asking that after you let me stand on my head," she said quietly.

Okay, that was not exactly the answer he wanted, but it was the one he deserved. The game was on. If he could dish it out, he could take it.

She pulled away. Judy could not have looked prettier, her entire body flushed to match the cascade of silken fire spilling over her shoulders. Everything about this woman glowed, from the trim but nicely rounded backside she was almost showing him to her pleasingly full breasts. He enjoyed the view more when she stretched to reach her nightstand and removed something so small from the drawer that he couldn't tell what it was.

When she straightened that luscious body against his again, Judy intercepted his left hand. Raising it to her lips, she placed a kiss on his ring finger along with a silver ring. "I've been waiting to ask you the same question. Would you, Harley Mortimer, be my soul mate for all eternity?"

Her eyelashes glistened. So did his. Harley had no defenses against this lady. None whatsoever. With a groan, he pressed her to his heart. She didn't need to see him cry. Not again.

"I already am," he breathed into her hair. "I love you. You mean everything to me. I will honor you every second for the rest of my life, darlin'. I promise. I swear. God, yes."

Her sigh warmed the hollow of his neck. "I have no doubts about you, Harley. I never did. My answer was yes the moment I asked you to dance."

He anointed the top of her pretty head with a few more tears.

Eternity. Best E word ever.

THE END

Sneak Preview of Connor

Book 5
In the Company of Snipers

Eighteen months earlier....

"Damn it."

USMC Sergeant Isabella Ramos cursed as her ammo clip hit the dirt on the other side of the wall. The farther she reached for it, the more newly promoted Sergeant Connor Maher could not help but notice. He didn't write the rules of nature. A man's always gonna look, and this particular gal's derrière, albeit camouflaged in the uniform of the day and plenty of dust, made for an excellent view. What red-blooded, all American male would miss a free show?

One minute Ramos was seated all nice and comfortable on that three-foot wall. The next, she was bent over it, damn near ass over teakettles with her boots, legs and butt on display. He glanced away, not wanting to be caught looking, at least not by her.

He and his buddy Jamie were part of the United States' military response to the increasingly violent Iraqi insurgency in Fallujah. Ramos got the short end of the stick when their commanding officer decided someone needed to show the two newly arrived non-commissioned officers the lay of the land, and just like that, they got a snappy tour of U.S. Camp Baharia and along with it, a floorshow that couldn't be beat.

The good thing about predominantly USMC Camp Baharia was the large clear water lake in the center of it. The bad thing was it was still in Iraq. The once-upon-a-time desert-resort was now filled with hard-core military men and women who sometimes forgot how to behave. Like Lance Corporal Jamie Ramos, who by sheer coincidence shared the sergeant's last name, but obviously not her dedication to the Corps.

Already passed over once for promotion, Jamie was headed for trouble with his CO. He didn't seem to have a problem with his rifle qualification or combat fitness, but his true talents lay in another direction. Jamie was a tease to the mathematical power of a gazillion, and that was going to land him in the brig one of these days.

"You know you want to." He elbowed Connor again, urging him to do the unthinkable. "Just one little smack. It's easy. I've done it a million times. No one else will see you. Just walk over, lay one on her ass, and run like hell. She's short. Go on. Do it."

"Shut up," Connor muttered out of the corner of his mouth, glancing again at the ass in question and doubting the 'I've done it a million times' line. "You know better than to treat women like that. Knock it off."

"What's she gonna do? You're both the same rank." Jamie persisted. "She can't catch you. It'll be fun."

"Cut the crap. She's a lady."

"No, she ain't. She's a jarhead. Loosen up. Walk on the wild side for once in your geeky life."

Connor glanced at Ramos again. Damn. That ass was spank-a-licious and hard to keep his eyes off of. This dark-haired and olive-skinned beauty had potential in his book. Lots of potential. He didn't want Jamie's crazy antics to blow his chances before he knew if he had any.

Raised in a house filled with six younger brothers and no sisters, women still perplexed Connor. Sometimes they loved a guy who only two seconds earlier they'd hated. He couldn't keep up. Besides, his mother had taught him early what Jamie's education must have missed. A real man does not disrespect any woman. They were to be treated like ladies even if they cussed like sailors. He'd grown to appreciate Bridgette Maher's wise sayings more now that he was out of her house. *Treat a woman like a lady and she'll never turn into a nag.*

With a twinkle in his eye, Jamie edged closer to the irritated sergeant's backside, a big cheesy smirk on his trouble-making face. She tipped farther over the wall, the toes of her boots nearly off the ground and still cussing a blue streak. No way was Connor getting close to that action. He shook his head and mouthed a definite, *No. Do not do it.*

Jamie's eyes brightened with, *Are you daring me, man?*

Connor didn't know whether to nod or shake his head. Either way spelled trouble.

Jamie's left eyebrow spiked into an incredibly wicked, *'Here goes.'* His arm lifted higher.

Connor shook his head, disgusted at himself for letting Jamie take a prank this far. He stepped forward to halt the wise guy before things got anymore out of hand. Retrieving the clip in question would solve the Sergeant's problem and torpedo Jamie's stand-up comedy once and for all.

"Excuse me, ma'am—"

Jamie's perfectly white teeth flashed to a big shitty grin. His flattened hand lifted over the rump in question. Apparently, Ramos hadn't heard Connor leaning over the wall like she was. He was nearly behind her. "Ma'am, let me get that for—"

The Sergeant tipped one booted foot to the sky and exclaimed, "Finally. Got the damned thing."

SMACK! Jamie did it.

Sergeant Ramos came off that wall so fast she landed in Connor's arms. The deadly scopes of a sniper skewered her one man viewing audience. Connor gulped. He caught a peripheral of his trouble-making buddy. Jamie was on his knees. At the end of wall. Out of sight. Clear out of sight.

Ramos could only see—

Oh, sweet Mother Mary and Joseph.

Those sizzling brown windows to a she-devil's soul were pointed at—him.

Equal rank or not, something about this diminutive spitfire stomped the hell out of his ego from the first moment he'd seen her. She was a cherry bomb with a short fuse and right now, he was cannon fodder. With the meanest reputation in the squad, she could teach the drill sergeant's *How to Be an SOB* class all by herself.

Crap. I'll be busted back to private first class.

"You want to die right here and now, Boston?" she hissed, her shoulders rolling along with her swagger. How could a gal with such sexy brown eyes be so mean and sound so tough? His eyes refused to move off of her, even though her top lip was curled over a wicked Devil Dog bite. *Hot damn. If I'm dying, it's gonna hurt, but I'm going to heaven.*

"Ahh, no, sir – I mean—no, ma'am—I mean—" He took a full step back to get her out of her personal space, stuttering like an idiot until he noticed the pistol in her open holster. Crap turned to shit. Jamie still crouched with his hand clamped over his big fat mouth he was laughing so hard. Right then and there, Connor was tempted to hand his buddy over. But real men don't do that either.

"You think hitting another soldier's ass is funny?" She came to a stop under Connor's chin, her eyes dark and deadly, full of the promise of nothing but pain. Maybe death.

"No, ma'am, I do not."

God, she was so damned gorgeous. Yeah, she radiated a certain amount of radioactive hostility, and he was pretty sure he glowed already, but damn. What a package. He couldn't catch his breath with her standing this close. His nose filled with the lovely whiff of roses and incense. How fitting. The sweetness of a flower mingled with the unmistakable hint of burning ash. He'd been an alter boy. He ought to know.

That drab green T-shirt peeking up from her uniform did not conceal the rounded landscape beneath from a man of his height either. Six-foot-three should be the one doing the intimidating instead of peering down a woman's shirt like he was. The thought of peeling her out of those desert cammies tweaked his common sense. He wanted to touch. Hell, he wanted to fondle, pet, and a whole lot more.

Should I pour on the Maher charm?

Sizzling death glowered up at him, not even blinking once and full on daring him to keep breathing.

Ah, maybe not.

The verbal assault commenced. "I'm gonna make you wish you died during boot camp, you pig-faced, camel-lipped, piece of..."

He took it like a man - almost. His jaw kept moving, but sound had ceased coming out. Article 128 of the United States Code of Military Justice flashed through his oxygen-deprived brain. *Question: Is a slap on the butt considered sexual battery?*

Answer: Damn straight. Don't touch. Don't tell. And all that stuff.

Jamie howled, at last overcome by his own hysterics.

Ramos shot a scorching look over her shoulder. "You!"

The instant she looked way, the magic faded. Connor was half-inclined to cup her chin and direct her gaze back to him. Angry or not, at least she'd seen him. Just him. Not Jamie.

"Why don't you grow up?" Kicking a boot scrape of sand in Jamie's face, she stalked off, which only made him laugh harder. The dumb ass looked like he was having a heart attack the way his face was all screwed up.

Oddly, Connor felt a chill when she left. A chill in Iraq? How did that work? He watched her walk away, her dark brown ponytail twitching side to side in time with her butt, both sassy as hell. He took one step forward to follow and apologize before he came to his senses.

Not now. Let her cool off. Mad women were unpredictable.

"You shoulda... You shoulda...." Still laughing his guts out, Jamie had tears streaming over his cheeks. "I mean it. You shoulda seen the look on your face!"

"You could get me court-martialed," Connor ground out, his gaze back on the command tent Ramos had disappeared into. He wasn't so much scared as interested. Maybe it was all those blond brothers he'd grown up with, but dark-eyed girls always caught his attention. Hers seemed darker than most, full of sparks, promise, and a whopping dose of cayenne. The moment he'd seen her, he knew. They would spend time together.

"Oh, hell." Jamie pulled himself onto the wall. "Don't worry. She won't do anything. You're safe."

"Yeah, right. You ever heard of friendly fire? She was an MP sniper. Now I gotta watch my back the rest of my rotation."

Jamie guffawed through another laughing attack. Connor had half a mind to kick his friend's ass if it would douse the hysterics. Jamie was a fun-loving, risk taking Hispanic who could charm the socks off most ladies. Didn't seem to have had any effect on the sergeant though.

Finally, he turned semi-serious. "Don't worry. I've got your six. You know that, Bro."

"Bullshit, you do."

"No, really. I've seen how you look at her." Jamie almost sounded sincere. "Remember how I told you I'd never seen her before, how lots of us Hispanics got the same last names only it don't mean we're related? You know, like Martinez, Gonzales, Sanchez, Moreno, Garcia?"

"So what?" He could feel it coming. The joke wasn't over yet.

Jamie winked. "I lied. That's Izza. My sister."

Thank you for reading Harley!

Be sure to check out the rest of the guys and gals of Irish Winters' series: *In the Company of Snipers*

Other Irish Winters' books:

King of Hearts, Deuces Wild Series, *#1*
Joker Joker, Deuces Wild Series, *#2*
Smoke, Hearts and Ashes Series, *#1*
Ash, Hearts and Ashes Series, *#2*

Coming soon!

Seth, In the Company of Snipers, #17
One-Eyed Jack, Deuces Wild Series, #3

YOU are the key to this book's success!

Please tell other readers why you liked Harley and Judy's story by leaving an honest review at the retail site where you purchased it. Recommend it to your friends. Lend it. Most of all, enjoy it!

The best way to keep up with my new releases, giveaways, and actionable intel is to sign up for my spam-free newsletter at IrishWinters.com.

About the Author

Irish Winters

...is an award winning, Amazon best-selling author who, when she isn't writing, dabbles in poetry, grandchildren, and rarely (as in extremely rarely) the kitchen. More prone to be outdoors than in, she grew up the quintessential tomboy on a dairy farm in rural Wisconsin, spent her teenage years in the Pacific Northwest, but calls the Wasatch Mountains of Northern Utah home. For now. She believes in making every day count for something, and follows the wise admonition of her mother to, "Look out the window and see something!"

Connect with Irish!
On Facebook: https://www.facebook.com/author.irishwinters
On Twitter: https://twitter.com/irishwinters1
Or at www. IrishWinters.com

www.ingramcontent.com/pod-product-compliance
Lightning Source LLC
Chambersburg PA
CBHW061043190726

48286CB00006B/1592